THE MEDICI HERESY

VATICAN SECRET ARCHIVE THRILLERS
BOOK TWELVE

GARY MCAVOY

LITERATI
EDITIONS

BOOKS BY GARY MCAVOY

The Pompeian Betrayal

The Medici Heresy

The Voynich Codex

The Devil's Symphony

The Hildegard Seeds

Covenant of the Iron Cross

The Apostle Conspiracy

The Celestial Guardian

The Confessions of Pope Joan

The Galileo Gambit

The Jerusalem Scrolls

The Avignon Affair

The Petrus Prophecy

The Opus Dictum

The Vivaldi Cipher

The Magdalene Veil

The Magdalene Reliquary

The Magdalene Deception

PROLOGUE

ROME, SPRING 1533

Twilight spilled gold upon the dome of St. Peter's Basilica, a glimmering illusion against the charred memories Clement VII carried in his bones. High above the weeping stones of the Eternal City, the Pontiff sat alone in the Apostolic Palace, surrounded by the deep hush of his private study. Outside, the Vatican stirred with the low murmur of evening bells and the scent of oleander, but within, the silence bore the weight of a world unraveling.

Giulio di Giuliano de' Medici had never asked to be pope. Nephew to Lorenzo the Magnificent, bastard son of a murdered knight, and thrust by family ambition into the Church, his was a life always claimed by others. He had been forged not from piety but survival—shaped in the crucible of Florence, where intrigue hung heavier than incense. It was Leo X, his cousin and a predecessor, who had fattened Rome on Renaissance indulgence. On assuming the tiara in 1523, Clement also inherited the sins of that golden excess.

But gold was fleeting. In May 1527, retribution came not in whispers or heresies but in boots and blood.

He could still see it: the mercenary German *Landsknechts* crossing the Tiber like wolves into the fold, blood-mad and swollen with hunger. Holy Roman Emperor Charles V's troops, nominally Catholic, had become a demonic parody of the Reformation's rage, looting churches, defiling nuns, stringing cardinals from balconies by their silken sashes. Rome—*caput mundi*—was pillaged like a pagan village.

And Clement had watched it all unfold from the high battlements of Castel Sant'Angelo, a prisoner in his own fortress. For weeks, he had eaten salted horsemeat and rationed sacramental wine, his white robes yellowed by dust and fear. The papal treasury had been emptied to buy lives. The Swiss Guard, loyal to the last, had died on the steps of St. Peter's—147 of them cut down in crimson silence so that he could escape.

Clement had lived. But something inside him had not.

Now, six years later, that memory still clawed at him, even as he carried the mantle of Vicar of Christ. Trust had become a frail ghost. The very foundations of the Church trembled—not just from Luther's defiance, but from within. The Council he had long promised never convened. Florence simmered with republican revolution. The Medici name, once lauded in marble and oil, had become a political liability.

And then had come *her* gospel.

It had been found beneath the cracked foundation of a ruined church outside Fiesole, a Tuscan commune near Florence, brought to him in secret by a Dominican friar who died days later—whether of plague, poison, or penance, Clement never knew. Bound in vellum, inked in Greek and Coptic, its pages spoke with the voice not of a penitent prostitute, but of the Beloved—the intimate companion and spiritual twin of Jesus. It was a gospel of tenderness and spiritual parity, of a kingdom not ruled by hierarchy but by love, undermining not only the Apostolic Succession but the very concept of masculine primacy.

Clement had read it once. Then again. And again.

Each reading tore through him like a lance. The implications were seismic. Were this to reach the world—amid the already growing Protestant storm—it would fracture what remained of the Church's moral authority. Peter's keys would slip from trembling hands. The authority of bishops, the exclusivity of the priesthood, the divine right of the papacy—none could survive the revelation of such a gospel.

Yet neither could he destroy it.

To burn it would be to silence what he believed—what he feared—might be the truest voice of Christ's ministry. And so, tormented by conscience, the scholar in him sought a compromise: the gospel would be concealed, preserved within the Vatican's deepest sanctum, its whereabouts known only to his handpicked successors. He would compose eight letters—*guide letters*, he called them—each one a meditative reckoning of its power, its dangers, and its moral invitation. Each would be hidden apart from the others, guarded by symbols and riddles drawn from the very architecture and history of the Church.

The letters weren't simply warnings. They were maps for a time not yet ready. Perhaps no time would be.

He dipped his pen again.

To my successor, in whose soul doubt may rise like smoke from Sinai—

Clement paused. The words trembled on the page. He had just returned from Marseille, where he had presided over the ill-fated wedding between his niece Catherine and the French prince Henri, a marriage designed to restore Medici power through bloodlines. Yet all he had felt was hollowness. The political world, like the theological one, was slipping from his grasp. The emperor watched him with a hawk's eyes. The Reformers called him the Antichrist. Even the Romans, his own flock, cursed the papacy in the streets.

If you are reading this, the tide of silence has receded. The world has changed—or will. This manuscript is not false. But neither is it safe. You must decide what to do with it, as I have decided only to protect it...

Clement laid the pen down and closed his eyes. Outside, the stars bloomed over St. Peter's like candles in a cathedral vault. Beneath them, a secret gospel waited in the dark, pulsing like a buried ember.

And he, the last Medici pope, would entrust it not to history, but to faith.

CHAPTER

ONE

VATICAN CITY, PRESENT DAY

Father Michael Dominic cherished mornings the way a monastic scribe once revered a well-cut quill: not as luxury, but as necessity. In the hushed corridors beneath the Apostolic Palace, where the sunlight filtered weakly through narrow glass slits and history exhaled dust from every shelf, he found peace in routine.

Each morning began before the bells. Rising at five, he slipped into the worn cassock that had traveled with him from his Jesuit seminary days, now threadbare at the cuffs but softened with memory.

But for his pre-dawn run, the cassock stayed hanging on its hook. Michael preferred the quiet streets before sunrise—the echo of his footsteps on cobblestone, the scent of baking bread drifting from Trastevere, the soft hum of Rome preparing to wake. When he circled back toward the Borgo, sweat cooling on his skin, he made his customary stop at Pergamino Caffè just outside the colonnade.

Signora Palazzolo, who had run the tiny shop since her husband's passing, spotted him through the window before he reached the door. She bustled out from behind the counter with a small bundle wrapped in brown paper. "Padre Dominic," she said, wagging a finger at the sight of his running clothes, "the Holy Father may tolerate many things, but not a priest entering the Vatican dressed like a marathoner."

Michael smiled. "You spoil me, Signora. You know that, don't you?"

"I preserve your dignity," she corrected, pressing the parcel into his hands. Inside was a freshly laundered cassock—one of two she kept for him, neatly sewn and ironed, refusing payment beyond a whispered blessing. "The restroom is free. Go, go. Before the guard at Sant'Anna thinks you've lost your vocation."

He thanked her, ducked into the small restroom at the back, and splashed cool water on his face until the last traces of sweat faded. He unwrapped the cassock, slipping into the familiar black fabric and fastening the collar with practiced ease. The transformation was always the same: from runner to priest, from solitude to service.

When he stepped back into the café, Signora Palazzolo handed him a steaming paper cup. "For the road," she said. "And tell the Swiss Guard I said *buongiorno*."

Michael grinned, lifted the coffee in a small salute, and stepped into the crisp morning air. The Porta Sant'Anna gate waited a short walk away, its stone arch flanked by the bright uniforms of the Swiss Guard—his threshold to a world of parchment, secrets, and the quiet weight of history waiting to be unsealed.

Father Michael Dominic didn't resemble the image most

people carried of a Vatican archivist. Tall and athletically toned, with long, black hair often tied back and deep brown eyes that missed little, he moved with the quiet confidence of someone accustomed to slipping between worlds—faith and doubt, past and present, obedience and inquiry. Raised in Queens by his devout mother, the housekeeper of the parish rectory, Michael had spent his childhood in the company of priests, altar candles, and shelves of worn theological books. It was Father Enrico Petrini, the parish's pastor and the closest thing Michael had ever known to a father, who nurtured his restless curiosity and encouraged him toward the priesthood long before Michael understood what such a calling would demand.

He went on to study paleography at the Pontifical Institute at the University of Toronto and theology at the Gregorian University, credentials that earned him a coveted post in the Vatican Apostolic Archives. But what truly distinguished him was not his scholarship; it was his temperament. Michael approached hidden truths with the humility of a believer and the relentlessness of an investigator, guided by a conscience that refused to ignore what others preferred to bury. He possessed an almost unsettling ability to sense when history had been bent or softened for convenience, and he had learned that the Church's oldest secrets rarely slept quietly. In Rome, that made him invaluable—and, at times, dangerous to those who feared what he might uncover next.

His key—a heavy, iron-forged piece given only to him as prefect and to two deputies—turned with a low click in the Archives' bronze door. The great subterranean labyrinth beyond stirred only with the hum of climate controls and the occasional scurry of mice that had somehow defied Swiss Guard extermination efforts for generations.

He always entered alone.

Descending the spiral stone staircase into the belly of the Vatican, Michael would pause briefly before the marble sculpture of St. Lawrence, patron saint of archivists. The statue stood solemn watch in the vestibule, his martyr's gridiron beside him, eyes uplifted as if still seeking light in the depths. Michael touched the cool marble of its base, murmuring a quiet invocation in Latin: "*Custos silentii, ora pro nobis*"—Guardian of silence, pray for us.

Then began the work.

Today started out like any other. He had donned his archivist gloves, retrieved his logbook, and walked the long central corridor toward the restricted manuscript chamber. The hum of dehumidifiers formed a familiar backdrop to his thoughts. A new cataloging project awaited—three fifteenth-century codices donated by the Archdiocese of Seville, each wrapped in cloth and tagged in Vatican gray. He had been preparing a report for the Cardinal Librarian on the authenticity of their bindings. Nothing about the day suggested interruption.

But at precisely 9:43 a.m., as the daily delivery from the Vatican Post Office arrived via pneumatic tube—a sleek, hissing canister that thudded gently into the brass receptacle near his desk—his day unraveled.

The canister clunked against the metal lip with more force than usual.

Michael turned with mild curiosity. Inside was the usual: interdepartmental memos, two periodicals, and a sealed envelope marked *Bibliotheca Apostolica Vaticana*. But below them was something he didn't recognize: a flat parcel wrapped in vellum, the edges tied neatly with deep burgundy ribbon. It bore no address, only his name—*P. Michael Dominic*—written in looping script that instantly evoked another age.

He stared at it for a long moment before touching it.

The handwriting was unlike any he had seen in modern routine Vatican correspondence. Ornate, yet disciplined. The capital "P" had a serpentine curl; the "M" was double-looped in the style of Renaissance scribes. Someone had gone to great lengths to mimic or preserve an earlier penmanship, complete with sepia-toned ink. There was no seal, no watermark, no sender's mark on the reverse. Just a small, embossed Medici crest faintly pressed into the parchment—a shield bearing six spheres and a lily crown.

His pulse stirred.

He turned the envelope in gloved hands. The sender had access to the Vatican's internal postal network. That narrowed the list considerably—and dangerously. Only a handful of people were authorized to send mail directly to the Secret Archives via internal courier, which meant one of two things: either a trusted insider had left him a relic or someone had breached the Vatican's most secure internal system with cunning precision.

Either way, it would require discretion.

Michael slipped the package into his document satchel and continued his day as if nothing had happened. But the weight of the thing, though barely a few ounces, gnawed at the back of his thoughts like a thread working loose in a tapestry.

Later, after lunch in the Sala Clementina with two fellow scholars, he retreated to his personal workroom. It was a modest chamber tucked off the northeast passage, just large enough for a desk, three chairs, and a carved wood icon of St. Jerome, patron saint of librarians and biblical scholars, in his study—a fitting presence in a place where symbology saturated every hallway, painting, and page, speaking in codes as ancient as the Church itself. The room smelled of old oak, wax polish, and aging paper.

He shut the door, drew the curtains, and sat.

With deliberate calm, Michael untied the ribbon.

Inside was a folded letter on parchment that had yellowed with age but remained pliant, as if it had been lovingly preserved. No brittle edges, no flaking. The ink had faded in parts, but the script remained legible—calligraphic Latin in a bold humanist hand. The opening line read:

Ad futurum pontificem, qui veritatem non timebit... *"To the future pontiff, who shall not fear the truth..."*

Michael leaned forward, his breath shallow.

The salutation alone stirred unease. Not merely because of its boldness—but because of the signature. Faint, in the lower corner, faded but unmistakable:

Clemens VII, Pontifex Maximus

For several long moments, he stared at the name.

Clement VII—Giulio de' Medici—was one of the most politically embattled popes in Church history. His papacy had spanned the brutal Sack of Rome, the rise of the Protestant Reformation, and desperate diplomatic dances with Francis I and Charles V. The idea that Clement had left behind a secret letter—undocumented, unarchived—was staggering.

But then he read on.

Rome, the Feast of St. Mark the Evangelist, Anno Domini 1533

To my successor, in whose soul doubt may rise like smoke from Sinai—

If you are reading this, the tide of silence has receded. The world has changed—or will. This manuscript is not false. But neither is it safe. You must decide what to do with it, as I have decided only to protect it...

I write not as Sovereign Pontiff, but as one burdened by knowledge too fragile to bear the papal seal. There are truths which the Tiara cannot touch without unraveling, and it is such a truth that now coils around my soul like incense refusing to dissipate.

In my final years, the Lord permitted that a document should reach my hands—unbidden and unblessed. It was not borne by nuncio or legate, but by a friar whose hands trembled with reverence and whose lips bled from silence. He died three days after its delivery, whether from fever or fear, I cannot say. What he brought was not a heresy, nor an apocryphon in the usual mold. It bore no mark of Gnosticism or madness. It was, in its way, painfully lucid.

It claimed to be a testimony. Not from a prophet, nor from one of the Twelve—but from her who stood beside Him in death and rose to proclaim Him living. From the one whom Rome later draped in penitence and shame.

I will not name her here. You know of whom I speak.

The words within that document are carved in the flesh of theology. They do not merely challenge our structures—they undo them. They proclaim a communion without hierarchy, a grace without ordination, a love that refuses the architecture we have so diligently erected over centuries.

In reading it, I felt both awe and vertigo. It was as though a familiar cathedral were shown to me upside down: beautiful still, but terrifying in its reordering of heaven and earth.

And so I ask: What if the first church was not built upon a rock, but upon tears?

I have not destroyed this document. Nor have I revealed it. I have preserved it—sealed it—until such time as Providence should declare a soul ready not merely to possess it, but to be possessed by it.

If this letter has reached you, that time may be at hand.

But beware: the key does not turn for the ambitious, nor the curious. It opens only to the one who approaches with fear and truth in equal measure.

You must not seek clarity from this letter alone. There are others—seven more—written in silence, placed like stepping stones for the heart to follow. Some will lead you backward in history. Others, inward into conscience. All will ask more than they answer.

I could not entrust the full weight of this truth to any single hand, lest it be crushed under the pressures of cowardice or ambition. Let these eight letters, scattered across the bones of Christendom, call forth only the one willing to walk the full Via Veritatis—*the road of truth.*

To begin, I offer this:

Follow the ink that weeps gold.

It stains only those prepared to be marked.

Seek not the treasure first, but the wound that precedes it.

With trembling hand,

✠ **Clemens PP. VII**

Pontifex Maximus

Michael stared at the final lines, reading them again and again, as if repetition might clarify what Clement had deliberately veiled. *Follow the ink that weeps gold...* The phrase lingered like incense after Mass—haunting, poetic, elusive.

The script was genuine, the watermark faint but distinct. The Medici crest, a subtle impression on the lower corner, sealed the letter's pedigree like a fingerprint from history. But it wasn't the external clues that disturbed him. It was the voice.

This wasn't some elaborate forgery or theological curiosity. It read like a confession. A burdened man on the edge of death writing to posterity—not with pride, but with trembling hope. And if Clement's words were true, he had held something that defied not only doctrine, but the very foundations of the Church's authority.

A gospel. Written not by one of the Twelve, but by *her*. The first witness. The Beloved.

Michael sat motionless for nearly ten minutes. He didn't take notes, nor reach for his cataloging software. Instead, he simply absorbed the implications, each one heavier than the last.

Who had brought this to him? Who had waited nearly five centuries to let it breathe? And why now?

At last, he reached for his secure tablet and composed a brief text message to the one person whose instincts he trusted as much as his own:

Meet me by the Cortile della Pigna at sunset. We have a ghost from the Renaissance who wants to speak to us.

THEY MET beneath the towering bronze pinecone of the Cortile della Pigna, a relic of pagan Rome now perched like a fossilized thought in the Vatican's Renaissance courtyard. The hour was shifting, twilight dissolving into dusk, and the last of the sun lay like a fading brushstroke across the travertine walls.

Hana Sinclair was already there, seated near the fountain. She wore a slate-gray linen jacket over her blouse, the soft glow of the courtyard lamps catching in her hair. A reporter's notepad rested loosely in her lap, more instinct than necessity, like a catechism waiting to be opened. When she saw him approach, she rose and tucked the notebook into her jacket.

Hana had the air of someone who carried her own weather with her, a quiet intensity softened by a quick, discerning intelligence. She carried the poise of someone who had learned to listen before she spoke—a trait that had made her one of *Le Monde*'s most respected investigative correspondents. Paris had shaped her manner, but Rome had sharpened her instincts, and nothing in the Vatican surprised her anymore. Except, perhaps, the way Michael looked at her now, with the quiet certainty of a man whose life had shifted after a single sealed parchment.

The reforms enacted by the late Pope Ignatius, allowing priests to marry under specific conditions, had changed both their futures. After years of shared danger, whispered trust, and unspoken affection, Michael and Hana were now engaged—a truth they held gently between them, as private and steady as breath. The Church was still adjusting. So were they.

"You sounded… urgent," she said.

Michael Dominic glanced around, quietly noting the

open archways and shadowed windows above. No guards lingered. The clatter of tourists had long since faded. A nun passed quietly to the west, rosary in hand. They were, for the moment, alone.

Only then did he draw the archival sleeve from his satchel and hand it to her.

She took it without a word, her fingertips brushing his for a moment before she stepped aside to read. As the last of the sun poured over the courtyard, she opened the parchment and let her eyes drift down its lines.

Her lips moved silently. Her breath grew shallow. By the time she reached the final passage—"*Seek not the treasure first, but the wound that precedes it*"—her expression had darkened with something between awe and apprehension.

She looked up slowly.

"Michael… this isn't just a letter. This is a riddle. A lament." Her voice was barely above a whisper. "It doesn't name the gospel, doesn't describe it… but the implications are—"

"Devastating," he finished. "If they're true."

"Clement read something he couldn't burn. And couldn't share." She shook her head. "He wasn't protecting the Church. He was protecting its image. Its structure."

Michael nodded. "It shook his confidence in the very thing he was meant to uphold."

Hana reread a line, eyes narrowing. "'*The one whom Rome later draped in penitence and shame…*' That's Mary Magdalene. It has to be. He's all but saying it."

"And he calls her the first to proclaim the Resurrection."

She folded the parchment and exhaled slowly. "So, the

gospel Clement received… if it exists… rewrites apostolic authority. It places *her* at the center, not Peter. Not the hierarchy. Not the priesthood."

Michael said nothing.

"And this line here—*'follow the ink that weeps gold'*—is he sending the reader to another letter?"

"I think so. There's a path he's designed. Breadcrumbs across time."

Hana frowned. "Why? If he wanted to suppress it, why leave clues at all?"

"Because he didn't want it lost forever. Only buried until someone was ready." Michael's tone was quiet. "And he thought that person might be a future pope."

"But instead, it landed in your hands." She tilted her head. "Do you think this was meant for you?"

He hesitated. "I think… someone inside the Curia wanted it to be."

Hana looked sharply at him. "An insider?"

"It came through internal channels. Quietly. Discreetly. That takes access."

"Then this wasn't a leak. It was an *invitation*." Her brow furrowed. "Or a trap."

Michael nodded grimly. "That's what I don't know. If they wanted to reveal the gospel, they'd go to the media. Or scholars. Not to me. Not like this."

"You think someone's testing you."

"Or baiting me. Either way, it's calculated."

She stared at him, her voice now edged with urgency. "If what Clement saw was real… it would shake every theological pillar on which the Vatican rests. Not just women's roles, but the idea of hierarchical grace, apostolic succession… even priestly absolution."

"It would democratize the divine."

"And the moment that idea gains traction…" Hana didn't finish the sentence. She didn't have to.

They sat in silence for a long moment. As the sun dipped behind Rome's ocher rooftops, a low peal of bells rolled across the city, solemn and resonant. From the dome of St. Peter's to the shadowed courtyards of Trastevere, the call to Vespers drifted through alleys and over piazzas like a blessing carried on evening air. The sounds were peaceful, but the feeling between them was not. It was the stillness before a fracture.

Finally, Michael rose.

"I'll scan the letter tonight," he said. "Privately. No logging. I'll cross-check Clement's handwriting and reach out to Florence for ink comparison. Quiet channels only."

"And I'll begin pulling every known piece of Clement's private correspondence from his final year," Hana said, rising beside him. "Any marginal notes, off-ledger entries, even librarian rosters. If there are more letters, they may already be hidden in plain sight."

He nodded. "And if this is only the first of eight…"

"Then we've barely scratched the surface."

They strolled from the courtyard, side by side, shadows stretching long behind them.

Above, the dome of St. Peter's loomed in silhouette, serene and immovable. But somewhere beneath its weight, truth had begun to stir. And this time, it wouldn't return to silence easily.

CHAPTER

TWO

VATICAN CITY

Father Michael Dominic stood alone on the fourth sublevel of the Vatican Secret Archives, surrounded by the ancient breath of memory: the smell of ink, mold-softened leather, and the faint ozone hum of climate regulation systems. The air here was always just cool enough to raise the skin, and today it traced a line up his neck like a warning.

All around him, sealed folios, iron-clasped codices, and unindexed *registri* loomed in stacks of metal shelving, centuries deep. This was the Church's memory palace. A place not for forgetting, but for *hiding*. Diplomatic betrayals, unratified bulls, letters of excommunication never sent, and correspondence from popes who had seen too much—these were not myths. They were shelf marks.

Now, Michael was searching not for confirmation, but for contradiction.

Follow the ink that weeps gold... Clement's phrase had

gnawed at him all night. The letter said almost nothing outright—no names, no places, no timeline—but its tone was unmistakable. It was the voice of a man who had touched something sacred and terrifying and had chosen to seal it away. Yet he left the door cracked, as if inviting a future soul to peer through.

Michael had risen before dawn, unsettled, and gone straight to the Archives. He knew where to start—not with theology or philosophy, but with accountancy. Doctrine could be hidden in sermons. But secrets left fingerprints in ledgers. And ledgers would capture the reckoning of gold.

He now stood before a vault containing the *Registra Vaticana 1533*, the papal expense ledgers from Clement VII's final year. Painstakingly written by hand in red-ruled columns, they chronicled the Church's daily transactions: indulgences granted, reliquaries commissioned, bribes disguised as "gifts," and crypt renovations quietly assigned under ambiguous headings.

Here, if anywhere, the gold-stained ink might show itself.

He retrieved the folio for April–June 1533—Clement's final spring. Turning pages slowly, he traced line after line with gloved fingers.

Entries passed in familiar succession:

"Payment to the Florentine silk guild for Corpus Christi banners."

"Repairs to the Lateran baptismal font."

"A stipend to a monk in Arezzo for illuminated Psalters."

Then one entry stopped him.

9 May 1533 – 600 florins to the Chaplaincy of San Giovanni Decollato

"For preservation of reliquary materials and cryptic reconfiguration."

Michael stared at the line. It wasn't that the payment itself was impossible—chapel maintenance was common. But this chapel? *That* amount?

San Giovanni Decollato had never been prominent in Church hierarchy. It was a brotherhood chapel used for last rites to the condemned, not a reliquary site. Even in the sixteenth century, its role had been peripheral. Yet here was an entry noting a substantial disbursement—600 florins, more than some bishops earned in a year.

The handwriting shifted, too. Most of the entries in this folio bore the tidy, compact penmanship of Clement's notary, Cardinal Innocenzo Cibo. But this line had been added in a different hand—slightly angled, with distinctive, exaggerated loops on capital "R"s and "P"s.

The signature at the margin read simply: **Giulianus Florentius**.

Michael blinked. He'd never encountered the name. A cleric? A monk? Or a pseudonym?

Florentius—"of Florence." It was too neat, too conveniently Medicean. Possibly even a cipher.

Clement had given no specifics in his letter. But this… this was something. It wasn't proof of a hidden gospel. It wasn't even proof of concealment. But it was an echo. A resonance. The ink, if not gold, was glinting.

He photographed it and quietly returned the folio to its slot. Before leaving, he checked the corridor through the oval security mirror.

The Archives were silent. But Michael had worked here

long enough to know that silence could be a curtain. And this letter—this trail—was something someone might want to stay hidden.

Not just forgotten. *Erased.*

By early afternoon, he stood in the polished interior of the Swiss Guard barracks, an austere warren of stone corridors, weapons lockers, and the low murmur of men trained to speak in half-tones. The scent of oiled leather, steel polish, and clean sweat gave the place a martial dignity.

Karl Dengler and Lukas Bischoff were in the armory, cleaning their halberds with the ceremonial precision of men who knew their role was far more than symbolic. When Michael entered, both looked up.

Karl straightened, smiling. "Either you're here for our weekly confessional, or you've sinned spectacularly and need a two-man penance team."

Michael raised a brow. "If I needed penance, Karl, I'd bring wine. This is worse."

Lukas set his weapon aside and wiped his hands on a cloth. "You look like you've seen a ghost."

Michael closed the door behind him. "Not seen. Read."

Karl exchanged a glance with Lukas, the sort that carried a whole chapter of memories from prior misadventures.

"There he goes again," Lukas muttered. "Always the scenic route to danger."

Michael drew the letter from his satchel. The parchment crackled faintly in the archival sleeve. The weight of the past made itself felt in the room.

"You both speak Latin, don't you?"

"Of course," Karl said. "Since it's the official language of the Vatican, both Lukas and I took advanced courses during our training."

"I need your discretion reading this. Completely. It doesn't leave this room."

Both men stiffened. The mirth in their expressions faded into professional attentiveness. These weren't simply guards. They were veterans of secrets.

Michael handed the letter over. Karl opened it first, then passed it to Lukas. They read in silence, the words sinking in like water through old stone.

When they were done, Lukas placed it on the table between them. "This... this doesn't name anything. But it *implies* everything."

Karl nodded. "He never says what the document is. But he's afraid of it."

"And the reference to the 'one who stood beside Him in death'..." Lukas shook his head. "That's Magdalene."

Michael leaned on the edge of the table. "He doesn't name her. He doesn't name the gospel. But he confesses its weight. He *hints* that it undermines hierarchy. That it reimagines communion itself."

Lukas narrowed his eyes. "So... if this is the first of eight..."

"It's a breadcrumb trail," Michael said, "which means someone wants it followed."

Karl was already nodding. "And someone delivered it —to you."

"Through internal channels," Michael confirmed. "Quietly. Which means they didn't want it intercepted, but they *did* want it discovered."

Lukas crossed his arms. "Then either you're being trusted... or you're being watched."

Michael looked between them. "I need help. Quiet surveillance. Eyes on who accesses the Archives. Who asks questions about me. And I'll need access to San Giovanni Decollato. Discreetly."

Karl grinned. "The church of St. John the Beheaded? After hours?"

Michael nodded. "There's a payment from Clement's ledger—a large one—to that chapel. No details. Odd phrasing. It may be where he began hiding... whatever he was hiding."

"Then we'll find a way in," Karl said. "We'll sweep the place before you go."

Lukas tilted his head. "Have you trusted anyone else with this?"

"Only Hana," Michael said. "No one else."

Karl nodded once. "She's family," he said, and Lukas saw the faint, familiar smile tug at his mouth. "My cousin may be a journalist, but she has instincts sharper than half the Curia."

Michael returned the smile. "And she's earned her place at my side more times than I can count."

The three of them exchanged a look laden with unspoken history. They had stood together before—catacombs in Avignon, a vault in Budapest, the ruins below the Vatican—each time walking away with just enough luck to make them believe they might survive the next adventure.

"Then we proceed," Karl said. "Quietly. Whoever left this trail for you—whether friend or enemy—they've already made their move."

Michael gave a quiet nod and turned for the door. But as his hand reached the handle, Karl spoke again.

"If Clement feared this truth... feared it enough to bury

it—what will you do if you uncover it?"

Michael paused, looking back over his shoulder. "I'll weigh it the way he couldn't."

He stepped into the corridor and pulled the door closed behind him. The click echoed faintly down the stone passage, as though somewhere behind the walls, centuries were shifting their weight, waiting for someone brave enough to lift them.

CHAPTER

THREE

VATICAN CITY

The Vatican's secrets rarely shouted. They whispered—in margins, in omissions, in silences wrapped around a single word. This was a place where truth was often more dangerous than heresy, and both left trails for those who knew how to read them.

Michael Dominic began his search not in the Archives, but in the corridors above them—in the human machinery that made the Vatican breathe. Somewhere, a living soul had made the decision to put Pope Clement VII's secret letter into his hands. Someone who had access, discretion, and a motive. The question was: *why him?*

His first stop was the Office of the Postulator General— not to speak to anyone, but to study the staff logs. The daily rotation of internal couriers was tightly scheduled, every delivery signed and logged with obsessive precision. Michael had long been granted limited access to administrative logs as part of his role as Prefect of the

Secret Archives—an authority that rarely needed to be exercised. Today, it did.

The morning delivery that brought Clement's letter had been routed through Postulant Route B, a restricted corridor used primarily for transporting confidential material between the Apostolic Palace, the Congregation for the Doctrine of the Faith, and the Biblioteca Secreta. Only six couriers were authorized on that route, and of those, only two had clearance to deliver to the Archives.

He scanned the manifest again:

Courier: P. Scolari, 9:57 A.M.

No deviation. No anomalies. The pneumatic capsule had been logged at the tube entrance and signed for by Padre Dominic at 9:43, as expected.

But Courier Scolari swore—unprompted and perhaps too readily—that he had not handled the letter itself. "I only placed the material in the canister, Father. The item itself was prepared by Monsignor Terenzio in the Mail Office. I never touched it."

Monsignor Terenzio. A quiet, fussy man with dry hands who had a habit of underlining his notes in red. A career bureaucrat. Devout, methodical, and never known for initiative. Yet when Michael visited his desk, Terenzio was absent. A family emergency, the secretary said. No further details.

Michael didn't believe in coincidences. Not here. Not now.

Returning to his office above the Archives, he sat quietly for several minutes, hands folded, eyes distant.

Terenzio was too careful to make mistakes. That meant

he was either a pawn—or a believer. If the latter, Michael had an unlikely but powerful ally.

He made a note in his private ledger: *Watch Terenzio's return. Interview under pretense of courier review. Check handwriting in personnel files.*

Whoever had sent the letter had done so through official channels, and that was the boldest clue of all.

MEANWHILE, across the courtyard, Hana Sinclair had requested access to the Archivio Storico di Stato Vaticano, the Historical Archives branch that stored documents not classified as Secretum but still sensitive enough to require vetted clearance. As an investigative correspondent for *Le Monde* with a decade of experience covering Church politics and European cultural institutions, she was no stranger to bureaucratic gates or guarded collections. Her reporting on Vatican diplomacy and her co-authored features with academic scholars had earned her a reputation for rigor rather than sensationalism.

Years of collaboration with the Vatican's internal scholarship board—along with Michael's quiet influence and a long record of responsible handling of archival material—had secured her the rare journalist's credential that allowed supervised research within the Historical Archives. By midmorning, she had been granted a modest corner desk, a small stack of catalog indexes, and a pair of white cotton gloves, the unspoken badge of trust that archivists extended only to those they believed would treat history as carefully as they did.

In this matter, she was searching for patterns, not answers.

Her approach was that of a journalist trained to see

distortion. She knew how history could be weaponized, softened, or made to disappear. In Clement's case, the official narrative was heavily redacted: the Sack of Rome, the French alliance, the Medici power plays, and the failure to call a general council. But what interested her were the *gaps*—places where the records became inconsistent or overly curated.

One such area emerged by midafternoon: a clerical void from March to June 1533, Clement's final spring.

During this period, letters from the papal chancellery dropped in volume. The number of papal bulls issued fell sharply. The registers grew sparse, while unrelated entries —expenditures for non-liturgical renovations, courier trips to peripheral monasteries, unexplained visits from Dominican inquisitors—spiked.

It was as though Clement's hand had faltered—not physically, but politically. Something had shifted. Or was being hidden.

One item stood out.

A diary fragment from a Florentine envoy named Matteo Corsini, preserved in Latin translation, noted an audience with the pope on April 19, 1533, in which Clement seemed "troubled by a storm he could not command." Corsini wrote:

> *"He spoke of fire beneath the altar, and of truths that would outlive stone. He said he feared not Luther, but something older. Something more tender. I did not understand."*

Hana circled the passage and typed it into her working file.

That line—*something more tender*—echoed Clement's own phrasing in the guide letter. A tenderness that terrified him. A truth he couldn't condemn but dared not release.

By the time evening bells rang, Hana had compiled a list of peripheral convents visited by unassigned clerics in 1533—possible places where the gospel may have been copied, concealed, or contested. One such location was the Oratory of Santa Chiara fuori le Mura, which appeared in three separate delivery logs without explanation. She prepared notes to send to Michael.

A peripheral chapel. A string of anonymous entries. And a pope surrounded by silence.

BACK IN THE SECRET ARCHIVES, Michael was still combing the papal ledgers.

He had already scrutinized one folio from Clement's final year, but this time he went backward, into the first half of 1533, cross-referencing treasury notations with the diary Hana had just sent him.

There, buried between a commission for new chalice moldings and a routine maintenance fee for the Sistine sacristy, he found it:

22 April 1533 – Transfer of 600 florins to the Chaplaincy of San Giovanni Decollato

For "cryptic preservation works and silent confessional renovations."

There it was again. San Giovanni Decollato. Different phrasing, same pattern.

This time the signature wasn't *Florentius*—but the handwriting was identical. Same hand. Same style. Same ink.

Michael leaned back in his chair.

Two separate disbursements. Two different months. Both involving unusually high payments to a marginal chapel known primarily for ministering to the condemned. Both in the shadow of Clement's death. Both signed in what now appeared to be a code.

And Clement's letter had said: *Seek not the treasure first, but the wound that precedes it.*

Michael now believed the wound lay in these ledgers. A treasure paid in florins, but that derived from the pain of a wound of doctrinal conscience.

He reached for his phone and typed a secure message to Hana:

I have another ledger entry. Same amount. Same chapel. Same false hand. Something happened at San Giovanni in April—and again in May.

Her reply came quickly:

Then that's where the trail begins.

FOUR

ROME

There were places in Rome where time lay thick upon the stones, not as memory but as sediment —a silence built over centuries. San Giovanni Decollato was one such place.

The chapel crouched at the end of a narrow side street, invisible to most who passed. Wedged between faceless plastered buildings and the crumbling footprint of the Forum Boarium, it had no tourist signage, no posted hours. Its façade, a sallow smear of weather-beaten stone, bore only a faint carving: the severed head of John the Baptist resting on a salver. Rain had worn the detail to a faint suggestion of eyes and beard, as if time itself were trying to forget the face.

Michael Dominic stood before the door, gloved hand resting on the rusted iron latch. Mist crept along the uneven cobblestones behind him, curling around the ankles of Swiss Guards Karl Dengler and Lukas Bischoff, who flanked him like living shadows. All three wore dark civilian clothing: field jackets and utility trousers in shades of charcoal and slate, faces half-obscured by the night.

"This is a bad place," Karl murmured, gazing up at the chapel's empty bell tower.

Michael nodded. "It always was. This is where condemned prisoners came to confess before execution. No choirs. No last rites. Just silence."

Lukas checked the alley behind them, then gave a curt nod. "We're clear. Let's move."

Michael inserted the Vatican-forged key into the heavy wooden door and turned the lock. The mechanism protested—iron scraping against stone—but soon relented.

They stepped inside.

Darkness enfolded them like a burial shroud. The interior was steeped in cold air and old dust. Their flashlights flared to life one by one, casting narrow cones of pale gold through the gloom. The nave was long and narrow, choked with decay: pews half-collapsed, candle stands warped by rust, plaster saints leaning from niches like they, too, were ready to fall.

Above the altar loomed a fresco so faded it resembled the aftermath of fire—blotches of ocher and blue, perhaps once depicting the beheading of the Baptist, now little more than bruises on the wall.

Michael stepped forward, boots echoing against flagstones. "Two ledgers, two payments," he said softly. "Both for work in the crypt. But the descriptions were deliberately vague—'preservation of reliquary materials' and 'silent confessional renovations.'"

Karl swept the side aisles with his beam. "Nothing ceremonial down here anymore. No trace of clergy for years."

"Good," Lukas muttered, scanning the floor near the altar. "Makes it easier to find what someone tried to hide."

They began their search methodically.

Michael knelt behind the altar and pulled back rotted sections of carpeting, revealing a floor of worn travertine tiles. He traced the seams with gloved fingers, looking for any irregularities.

Lukas took the north transept and Karl the south, each moving with practiced care, flashlights angling low across the stone to catch shadows where joints didn't line up or mortar had shifted.

Minutes passed in silence, broken only by the soft scrape of soles on stone and the occasional creak of timber far above them.

Lukas crouched by the choir stall. "Got something."

Michael and Karl joined him.

Half-concealed beneath a broken wooden kneeler was a narrow rectangle of stone with a small iron ring set into its surface—rusted nearly shut.

"Trapdoor?" Karl asked.

Michael studied it. "Too small for full crypt access. Probably a service hatch. Maybe it leads to stairs."

Lukas pried at the ring with a flat tool until the rust gave way. The hatch opened with a sound like a slow exhale. A puff of dry air emerged—cold and stale, edged with the faint scent of mildew and lime.

A steep stair descended into the dark.

Karl went first, sidearm ready, flashlight up.

The stairs turned once, then again, before opening into a crypt far more expansive than the chapel's modest frame suggested. They emerged into a low-vaulted chamber supported by squat columns, their surfaces flaking with lime efflorescence. The walls were stone and mortar, punctuated with alcoves—some empty, others containing crumbling reliquaries or what remained of ossuary niches.

"It's a maze," Lukas said under his breath. "Bigger than I expected."

"This whole undercroft predates the chapel above," Michael said, voice hushed. "The confraternity just built atop it. Clement could've used any part of this."

They spread out.

The air grew colder the deeper they went. The walls here were clammy, slick in places where groundwater seeped through ancient mortar. The light revealed details only slowly: a fresco of the Baptist's execution rendered in ghostly tones; a disused confessional booth, its grill torn and sagging; Latin inscriptions etched into the stone, most eroded to illegibility.

But one stood out: ***Et in ore silentium, in corde lux.***

"'*And in the mouth, silence; in the heart, light,*'" Michael read aloud.

He paused. "This was over the altar too. Clement may have reused symbols to mark the way."

"Breadcrumbs," Karl said. "Or misdirection."

Another ten minutes passed before Lukas called out softly. "Over here."

He stood in a narrow corridor off the crypt's eastern wall. A half-collapsed arch led into a niche that had once housed a sarcophagus. Now it was empty, except for a panel of stone set into the back wall.

Faintly visible in their combined light was a symbol—worn but still legible.

The Medici crest.

Michael knelt. "No reason this should be here. Not in this part of the city."

Below the crest, chiseled with roughness but precision, was a name:

Urbanus · PP · IIII

His heart quickened, recognizing the more harmonious and visually balanced form of the Roman numeral four used in that era.

Lukas was already kneeling beside the panel, fingers running along the edge. "The mortar's different."

Karl checked the corridor behind them, flashlight scanning the gloom. "I don't like this spot. Too exposed. We've got one exit, and no idea how much deeper this goes."

Michael reached into his satchel and withdrew a brush and probe. "Let's open it. Quickly."

It took nearly ten minutes of careful prying and brushing. The stone panel resisted—sealed as much by time as by intention—but finally gave way with a muffled thud as Lukas and Karl eased it free and set it aside.

Behind the panel lay a hollow recess—just large enough for a reliquary.

The box inside was simple: cedar darkened by centuries, silver bands oxidized to a greenish patina. On the lid, a sunburst medallion—the insignia of Pope Urban IV—tarnished but unmistakable.

Michael leaned forward, feeling as if the air itself had changed. "This is it."

Lukas checked the reliquary's sides. "No locks. Just a clasp."

Michael unfastened it and slowly raised the lid.

Inside was no sacred bone, no vial of saintly blood.

Just a single parchment envelope.

A thin thread of gold ribbon held it shut, and the seal—Clement VII's papal insignia—remained intact.

They had found the second guide letter.

Michael exhaled and reached for the envelope.

As his fingers closed around it, a sound cracked above them.

Not stone. Not water.

A sharp, deliberate *clack*—as if a heel had shifted on wood or iron somewhere near the crypt stairwell.

Karl's flashlight was up in a heartbeat, hand on his weapon.

Another sound, fainter this time. Something shifting. Then stillness.

Michael carefully closed the reliquary, tucking the letter into a secure sleeve in his coat.

"Let's go."

Lukas reseated the stone panel.

Karl scanned the corridor again and whispered, "We need to vanish. Now."

They moved quickly, retracing their steps through the crypt. No words were spoken. The air felt tighter now, and every footstep seemed louder than it should. As they reached the stairwell and began climbing, Michael paused and turned.

Somewhere in the dark beneath them, a faint echo stirred.

He couldn't tell if it was footsteps or the sound of something else.

Something watching.

Back in the chapel, they sealed the hatch behind them. Michael pressed the rug and broken wood back into place as Lukas double-checked the door. The mist had thickened outside. No sound. No footsteps. No one visible.

Still, the feeling lingered.

They exited quickly, the heavy door groaning shut behind them.

As they climbed into the waiting van, Michael placed a hand over the breast pocket of his coat, where Clement's second letter now lay.

He hadn't read it. Not yet.

Not until they were safe.

As the van rolled forward into the night, he glanced once more at the chapel's silhouette receding behind them.

For five centuries, the letter had waited in silence.

Now, someone else knew they had found it.

FIVE

VILLA AURELIA MEDICI, OUTSIDE ROME

The hills west of Rome had once been the playground of emperors, where marble villas sprawled across sun-drenched slopes and cypress-lined avenues whispered with intrigue. From the Janiculum to the Alban ridge, these heights bore the remnants of opulence—faded frescoes tucked behind ivy-choked walls, fragments of mosaic glinting beneath centuries of dust. In the days of the Caesars, senators and patricians had retreated here to escape the clamor of the Forum, sipping spiced wine in terraced gardens that overlooked the Tiber's lazy descent toward the sea. Time had softened the grandeur, folding it into the landscape like a half-forgotten hymn, but the air still carried the scent of laurel and ruin, and the stones beneath one's feet murmured of power once absolute. Now, the palatial estates were shadows but their bones remained, layered with imperial ambition, ecclesiastical secrets, and the slow erosion of empire.

Olive groves and stone-pine forests blanketed the rolling terrain beyond the Vatican walls, rising gently toward Lake Bracciano. Scattered among the ancient pathways and aqueduct ruins were villas that bore no address, no visible signage, and no real history—at least not the kind you could find in public records.

One such estate, nestled amid a grove of cypress and black laurel, was the Villa Aurelia Medici.

To the public, it was a heritage site in the loosest sense —"private residence, limited access, under restoration." The Italian Ministry of Culture had long since been paid to keep its records vague. At the owner's request, no satellite photo captured more than a glimpse of its vine-covered outer walls. And even those few in the region who remembered its name did so with a kind of detached reverence, like villagers recalling an ancient curse that had been quiet too long.

But inside, the villa was very much alive.

From the air, the estate resembled a small fortress: arched balconies, stone loggias draped in ivy, terraced gardens arranged in Renaissance geometries. An Etruscan cistern had been converted into a wine cellar. The old cloister had become an art gallery—private, of course, though its contents rivaled any Florentine museum. And beneath the main residence lay three additional levels of stone chambers: archives, security monitoring rooms, and one soundproofed room with a single leather chair and no windows.

Alessandro de' Medici preferred to work where he couldn't be watched.

He stood now on the east terrace overlooking the

manicured grounds, a lowball glass of amber-hued brandy in one hand. The air was warm with late spring, tinged with the scent of lemon blossom and the high, peppery trace of scorched rosemary from the garden's stone fire pit.

He wore a dark linen suit, unbuttoned, and a charcoal shirt with no tie. His hair was black and glossy, combed back from a high, angular brow. His face—refined, aquiline—bore the unmistakable stamp of old Florentine blood: sharp cheekbones and thoughtful eyes the color of ash and iron. He was in his mid-forties but seemed suspended somewhere between generations, as if history had decided to preserve him out of curiosity.

Behind him, the glass doors to the study slid open on well-oiled tracks.

A man in clerical black stepped into the light.

"*Signore*," the visitor said, bowing his head slightly. "We've confirmed it. One of the letters has reached the prefect."

Alessandro didn't turn at first.

He sipped the brandy, watching a kestrel circle above the treetops before vanishing into the twilight.

"Which letter?"

The priest hesitated. "We don't know. Only that it bore Clement's seal. Recovered through an internal courier network. Not from the Biblioteca—from deep archives. Something outside the registries."

Alessandro turned.

His voice, though soft, had an unmistakable gravity.

"Who authorized the release?"

"We suspect it wasn't officially sanctioned at all."

"Then someone is digging."

The priest nodded, lowering his eyes. "Father Michael Dominic. He has a reputation."

"Yes," Alessandro murmured. "I've read the dossiers." He turned back to the terrace rail and tapped one finger lightly against the base of the glass.

The priest waited in silence.

Alessandro's network was both deep and very old. It extended into every strata of Italian power—the state police, the Vatican Curia and press corps, half of the episcopacy, several Jesuit colleges, a major pharmaceutical consortium, and two media conglomerates. His formal title was nothing—just a surname with gravitas, a position on a few shadowy cultural boards, and a seat at no fewer than five offshore foundations. But his influence was considerable. He rarely had to ask twice.

The Medici name still opened doors.

But it could also close them, if history turned against it.

Alessandro set his glass down and folded his hands behind his back.

"I want to know everything Dominic has touched in the last thirty days. Travel, visitors, inquiries—particularly anything related to the Medici or to Clement VII's final year. If he's found the first letter, then he may already be tracking others."

"Understood."

"I also want eyes on the Secret Archives. Noninvasive. Passive monitoring only."

"*Signore*, the Archives are—"

"—sacrosanct," Alessandro finished. "Yes, I know. But sanctity is a matter of perspective. Use our contact in the Apostolic Library's restoration division. Quietly."

The priest inclined his head. "And if Dominic finds more?"

Alessandro's gaze sharpened.

"That depends on what he plans to do with them."

He walked back into the study, the floor cool underfoot, brandy glass trailing a faint scent of oak and spice. The room was long and high-ceilinged, with a carved walnut desk and a massive oil painting of Lorenzo il Magnifico looming behind it. A bronze bust of Pope Leo X—the first Medici pope—glared from a pedestal in the corner. Books filled the shelves: theology, Renaissance law, early printing history, forensic linguistics. A few had slips of paper protruding with Alessandro's own notes in Latin.

He stepped to the desk and tapped the console embedded in its center.

A monitor rose silently from the leather inlay.

An encrypted document opened, line by line:

Opzione Piuma

— Medici Archive Restoration Initiative, Internal Dossier #26

— Potential destabilizing elements in Clement VII's final communications

— Suspected reference to uncanonical gospel, likely feminist in nature

— Vatican suppression indicated between 1533–1535

— Threat level: Medium–High

— Primary Risk: Damage to Medici legacy as defenders of orthodoxy

— Secondary Risk: Historical reevaluation of ecclesiastical authority and gender roles

Alessandro's eyes narrowed slightly as he scrolled. At the bottom, a line had been added just that morning:

Intercepted confirmation from Curial intermediary.

**First letter recovered by Dominic. Nature unclear.
Further movement probable.**

He sat in the high-backed leather chair, fingers steepled.

The threat was still abstract. Clement VII had many writings. But these letters—if they truly spoke of a suppressed gospel, and if they linked the Medici name to its concealment—could undo what generations had curated. The Medici mythos had always balanced power with providence. Patron saints of the Renaissance. Stewards of the Church. To be seen as manipulators of spiritual truth… as silencing *her* voice?

That would reframe everything.

He rose and walked to the bronze bust of Leo X, staring into the pope's sardonic eyes.

"Your Holiness," he murmured, "we may have a problem."

Leo stared back in eternal bemusement.

Michael Dominic, he thought.

The prefect was too careful to leak anything. Too pious to publish outright. But curiosity had its own inertia. Once one thread was pulled, the rest followed.

The first letter would lead to a second. The second to a third. And somewhere along that path, a historian would start asking the wrong questions. A bishop would raise an eyebrow. A journalist—perhaps that Sinclair woman who hovered too closely to Dominic's affairs—would catch wind of something… dangerous.

And if the contents of the gospel ever came to light?

No. That was unacceptable.

Alessandro returned to his desk and tapped the console again.

"Prepare a secondary file," he told the voice recognition system. "Subject: Dominic, Michael. Contingency Protocol: *Cinerea.*"

A chime acknowledged the command.

He sat in silence a moment longer, then poured himself a second drink.

He wasn't yet prepared to eliminate Dominic. But interference was now necessary. Disruption. Doubt. A few delays in the Archives. A few redirected inquiries. Let the weight of the institution slow the man down. If that failed… well, there were older solutions.

The kind his ancestors had practiced with quiet perfection.

As the brandy warmed his throat, Alessandro de' Medici gazed out once more across the lamplit gardens of his ancestral villa.

The future is written by those who control the past, he thought.

And he wouldn't allow Father Michael Dominic to rewrite it.

CHAPTER
SIX

ROME

The trattoria sat tucked behind a wedge-shaped piazza two blocks from the Vatican walls, nestled beneath a canopy of potted lemon trees and wrought iron lanterns. It was the kind of place the guidebooks always missed—half-hidden by vine-covered shutters, its name hand-painted on a wooden board: Trattoria della Luce.

No menu posted outside. No uniformed waiters hawking for business. The only advertisement was the warm, garlic-laced air that drifted from the kitchen and curled through the alleyways like an invocation.

Michael arrived first, slipping into a shaded corner table beneath a trellis wound with bougainvillea. He shed his jacket and laid the leather-bound archival pouch gently on the bench beside him, resting one hand protectively atop it. A waiter appeared without prompt and offered a nod of recognition—Michael was something of a fixture here, his presence tied not to routine, but to moments of private reflection.

"*Padre, buona giornata,*" the man said. "Today you'll want the house ravioli. Fresh ricotta, lemon zest, mint. And the tomatoes this morning…" He kissed his fingertips and looked toward heaven.

"*Perfetto,*" Michael said, smiling. "And a bottle of Vino Nobile di Montepulciano."

The waiter nodded. "And Signora Sinclair?"

Michael glanced at his watch. "She'll want something earthy. Maybe the tagliatelle with wild boar?"

"*Cinghiale,* yes. It is excellent today."

Five minutes later, Hana arrived, brushing a strand of hair from her face as she slid into the seat opposite him. She wore a cream blouse rolled at the sleeves and a soft linen scarf looped loosely at her neck, eyes shaded behind tortoiseshell sunglasses.

"You ordered for me?" she said, smiling.

"You'll thank me."

She leaned in slightly, lowering her voice. "Do we read it here?"

Michael tapped the leather pouch with one finger. "In a moment. Let's eat first. The letter waited five centuries; it can wait twenty more minutes."

The waiter approached with practiced elegance, presenting the bottle before pouring their glasses without comment. Michael sipped his wine, savoring the deep, dark cherry tones as they settled on his tongue. Hana took a quicker sip, then met his gaze. Their eyes held for a quiet moment before their glasses clinked gently between them, a silent toast to the path that still lay ahead.

Their plates arrived soon after: Michael's ravioli glistening in olive oil, scattered with crushed pistachio and lemon zest, Hana's tagliatelle crowned with tender shreds of boar simmered in red wine and cloves. The pasta curled in silky ribbons, steam rising like incense from the plate.

"Oh my God," Hana whispered, fork poised. "If Clement had eaten like this, he might've been more optimistic."

Michael chuckled. "The Medici dined well. He probably did too."

They ate in near silence for several minutes, the kind of silence that companions earn over time—not uncomfortable but settled, like soil ready to be turned. Hana broke bread from the warm rosemary focaccia and dipped it lightly in the green-gold pool of Toscano olive oil between them, known for its grassy, peppery, artichoke-like bite. The boar was tender and perfumed with lemon and thyme, and the red wine, deep and smoky, wrapped the meal in slow contentment.

By the time they reached the last of the wine, the clatter of plates around them had softened to the muted murmur of a restaurant easing toward evening. Hana sat back, savoring the warmth that followed a perfect meal.

Her eyes drifted to the leather pouch resting beside Michael's chair. "So," she said softly, "that's Clement's second letter?"

He dabbed his mouth with his napkin and smiled. "It is."

"And you haven't opened it yet?"

"I wanted to," he admitted, "but not while we were eating. Even I have a sense of occasion."

She raised an eyebrow. "A priest with restraint—I'm impressed."

Michael chuckled and reached for the pouch, setting it gently on the linen between them. The candles on the table flickered, their light gilding the wineglasses and the quiet between them.

"Now," he said, his voice lowering, "seems right. I think this is Clement's second letter in a planned sequence. The first was a confession. This one might be a theology."

Hana stared at the letter a moment, then drew the sleeve toward her and unzipped it. She slid the parchment free, careful not to disturb its fibers, then placed it on the cloth between them, a clean teaspoon anchoring it to the table. The sunlight filtered through the trellis above, casting leaf-dappled light across the surface.

Michael translated as he read aloud, his voice steady but low, pitched only for her.

To the One Who Still Seeks—

You who have followed the first whisper—do not seek glory. Seek only trembling.

The one whose voice this is—she who wrote with the tenderness of the Nazarene's breath—does not call you to doctrine, but to undoing.

The text I received speaks not of priesthood or apostolic thrones, but of companionship. Of witness. Of the touch of a soul unbound by law. It declares that the Spirit is poured not through ranks, but through love—and that any who love with truth are already sanctified.

This terrified me more than any excommunication. Not because it was false… but because it felt truer than everything I had sworn to protect.

The gospel bears no rebuke, no fire. Only intimacy. A voice beside His, not beneath Him.

What would become of the Church if women were shown to have stood not in silence, but in equal light? What of the sacraments? What of the priesthood?

My brothers would say: It is heresy. I say: It is agony.

And so I buried it. Not out of fear of man, but out of fear for the faithful. I placed it beneath this sanctuary, amid the stones that once held the condemned. For what is more condemned than a truth which cannot yet be borne?

If you are reading this, then either time has ripened, or the earth has cracked.

"There is more. The third key rests not in stone halls, but in the place where parchments were taken to burn, and one was spared."

✠ *Clemens PP. VII*

Pontifex Maximus

For a long moment, neither of them spoke.

The letter lay between them, parchment faded but vivid in meaning, like a wound reopened across time. Not a historical curiosity. Not a scholarly relic. But a whisper from a dying pope who had weighed truth and found it too heavy to lift.

Hana reached out and touched the edge of the parchment with her fingertip. "He's not just confessing anymore. He's explaining what terrified him."

Michael nodded, eyes lowered. "That this gospel—this voice—doesn't reject Christ. It re-centers him. With her not beneath him, but beside."

"A Church built on communion, not authority," Hana said. "On experience instead of hierarchy. A shared table, not a guarded throne."

"And if Mary Magdalene was the first voice of the Resurrection," Michael added, "then the entire chain of apostolic succession has a fracture at its root."

She leaned back, hands loose on her lap, the weight of the idea sinking into her. "This isn't just gender. It's structure. Theology. Everything. If grace is already present in love… if it flows directly from God without mediation…"

"…Then what becomes of priesthood? Of sacrament? Of obedience to an office?"

Michael folded the letter slowly and returned it to the protective pouch, then sealed it with deliberate care. The late Roman sun was slanting now across the canopy of the trattoria, dappling their tablecloth with shifting shadows from the bougainvillea vines above. For all of the beauty, there was an ache in the air—like the hush before a thunderstorm.

Hana paused as she spoke again. "And now this line: *'The third key rests not in stone halls, but in the place where parchments were taken to burn, and one was spared.'*"

Michael drew a slow breath. "That's not metaphor. That's location. He's pointing us somewhere very specific."

"A place where books were destroyed. It could literally be a place where something like bonfires of banned manuscripts were burned. Or it could be more symbolic," Hana said softly. "Anywhere knowledge was considered too dangerous to live. And yet—somehow—one survived."

Michael nodded. "That means there's a record. Or a relic. A document thought lost but preserved in secret."

"A monastery, maybe? Or a tribunal archive?" She looked up at him. "Could he be referring to the Inquisition?"

"It fits," Michael murmured. "In Clement's time, inquisitorial suppression was deeply active. Rome. Avignon. Seville. Wherever something threatened doctrinal clarity, the scribes were there with fire. And not just literal fire. Redacted registries. Disappeared names."

Hana's voice dropped. "But one parchment was spared."

Michael sat very still, gaze fixed past her shoulder toward the horizon. "Which means someone disobeyed."

Hana blinked. "You mean Clement?"

"Possibly. Or someone under him. A scribe. A monk. Someone who read the gospel, or part of it, and couldn't bear to let it vanish completely."

They fell silent again as a breeze stirred through the patio, carrying with it the scent of fresh basil and faint smoke from a kitchen grill. Their waiter returned quietly, offered dessert—fig tarts, panna cotta, a digestif—and they both declined with the same absent wave.

Michael's hand rested on the pouch at his side.

"We need to look into every site in Italy tied to ecclesiastical censorship," he said. "Start with known burnings. Look for gaps in the records—instances where documents were supposedly destroyed but footnoted later."

"And we focus on the sixteenth century," Hana said, eyes already narrowed in thought. "From Clement's pontificate forward. Cross-reference with inquisitorial activity, suppression of mystical texts, anything tied to Mary Magdalene."

Michael nodded. "We'll also need Sister Teri to check digital records for any scanned indices marked as corrupted or redacted without explanation."

Hana gave a tight smile. "She'll love that."

Sister Teri Drinkwater had been the Vatican's unofficial queen of wires and whispering circuits for years, a former Silicon Valley engineer who traded stock options for a nun's habit and a life of quiet service. As the Holy See's telecommunications director—and one of Michael's closest confidantes—she knew every server, subnetwork, and forgotten basement router Vatican City had ever installed. If a document had been scanned, altered, or mysteriously erased, Teri would find its ghost.

Michael and Hana sat quietly for another few minutes. The sky was turning a deeper shade of Roman blue, the shadows now longer, the hush around them more pronounced.

Finally, Hana spoke again, her voice softer.

"Do you think Clement was wrong to hide it?"

Michael's eyes flicked to hers. "I think he was afraid. And not for himself. For the faithful."

"But don't the faithful deserve the truth?"

"Yes," he said. "But truth can wound before it heals. Clement knew that. He wasn't preserving ignorance. He was buying time. Consider the era, the culture and its political climate then. Not that today isn't fraught with strife as well, but society has made many strides in equality and spiritual insights over these centuries."

Hana tilted her head. "And now?"

Michael looked down at his hands, then slowly back at her.

"Now, time is running out. And someone—whoever sent that letter—has decided we're the ones meant to face it."

She reached across the table and laid her fingers on his.

"So we follow it."

He nodded once.

She smiled faintly. "And hope it doesn't consume us."

Michael exhaled, not quite a laugh, not quite a sigh. "We're not just holding a document anymore. We're holding the ember that escaped the fire."

CHAPTER

SEVEN

VATICAN CITY

The marble corridors of the Apostolic Palace were built for solemnity—cold, echoing spaces designed to mute the self and amplify the institution. But beneath their grandeur, behind the high frescoed vaults and Latin mottos carved in gold, bureaucracy still ruled.

And like all bureaucracies, it had cracks.

Father Michael Dominic strode through the north corridor of the Archives' administrative wing, passing a marble bust of Pius XI and a long shelf of orphaned incunabula awaiting cataloging. At his side walked his assistant, Ian Duffy, his long-legged gait giving the impression of perpetual motion, even when standing still.

"So, you're saying the courier's name wasn't on the manifest?" Ian asked, his voice still touched with his inherited Irish brogue from County Galway, even after years spent inside the Vatican walls.

"It was," Michael said. "But only nominally. His name appears in the log, but he quickly insisted he never handled the delivery directly."

"Quickly? Too clean," Ian muttered. "Nobody in this place volunteers with that kind of clarity unless they've something to hide."

"Exactly."

They turned into Michael's private office. It was a warm space, lined with maps, diagrams of medieval indexing systems, and a Roman oil lamp on the windowsill that Ian had once repaired for him with museum-grade epoxy and half a pint of Guinness.

Michael gestured toward a folder on his desk. "That's everything I could pull without triggering a trace request."

Ian opened the file. Courier logs. Transfer slips. Internal notes—some official, others handwritten and hastily filed. One name appeared repeatedly.

B. Altieri – Restoration Liaison, Biblioteca Apostolica Vaticana

Ian frowned. "Altieri?"

Michael nodded. "Assigned to the restoration division six months ago. On paper, he's tasked with coordinating between damaged text triage and transfer scheduling. But two weeks ago, he began shadowing the tube system—the pneumatic delivery corridors that run through the west quadrant."

"Archives and Library are separate divisions," Ian said, brow creasing. "We don't answer to the Biblioteca. Why would a restoration liaison be sniffing around the courier system at all?"

"That's what I want to know."

Ian rubbed his chin. "You think he's our leak?"

"I think he's someone's errand boy. And I think

whoever's pulling the string has enough influence to plant a watcher in the Vatican's deepest basement without raising suspicion."

A long silence passed between them.

Then Ian said, "Want me to make his life a little harder?"

Michael gave a small smile. "Subtly."

BENEDETTO ALTIERI MOVED through the undercroft corridors with the polished precision of a man used to institutional power.

He was in his early forties, immaculately groomed, with sandy hair combed back in a modest wave and tortoiseshell glasses perched low on his nose. His shoes were spotless. His passcard bore a special red diagonal slash—authorization for rare book contact. The other librarians referred to him with a mixture of amusement and wariness, as *"il benedetto—ma troppo."* Too blessed. Too smooth.

That morning, he had presented himself at the Secret Archives' reception alcove with a linen folder and a calm voice.

"Restoration transfer request," he told the junior cleric at the desk. "A retrieval of minor bindings and seals from the Sforza ledger codices—thirteenth-century vellum, flagged for examination. I've scheduled a pickup window."

The cleric blinked. "I wasn't informed of any—"

"I filed through the Biblioteca's digital requisition channel. You'll see it's been co-signed by Monsignor Radelli."

The name was enough.

A call was placed. Authorization was confirmed. And Altieri was waved inside—politely, if not warmly.

Ian was already waiting.

He stood beside the loading alcove in his usual uniform: dark turtleneck, sleeves pushed up, and a lanyard that bore three security stamps more than necessary. He smiled as Altieri entered.

"Ah, Signor Altieri. Heard we'd be graced with your presence today."

Altieri raised an eyebrow. "Mr. Duffy. A pleasure."

"Bit out of your way, isn't it? I thought the Biblioteca lads didn't like the air down here—too thick with secrets."

"Secrets should breathe too," Altieri said, lips curving.

Ian smiled, stepping in beside him. "Right this way."

As they walked, Ian kept the pace deliberately slow, forcing Altieri to match his stride through a long corridor of sealed vaults and iron-grated casings. Most were labeled only with codes: *AVS 1494, CLEM X INQ-3, URBANUS-BULLA.*

"So," Ian said, his voice casual, "what got your team so interested in thirteenth-century bindings all of a sudden?"

"Medieval adhesives," Altieri said smoothly. "There's a workshop in Milan attempting to reconstruct pre-Avignon glues for papal seal conservation. Our notes on the Sforza ledgers were incomplete, so I volunteered."

"Ah…" Ian let the word hang like smoke.

They reached the retrieval chamber. Ian waved his ID over the sensor, then typed a code with one hand while maintaining an unbroken gaze with Altieri.

Inside, the requested materials were waiting—three folios of minor significance. All real. All innocuous.

Ian handed them over.

As Altieri tucked them into his folio, Ian said, lightly,

"Funny, you've walked past the C-section corridor a few times. Easy to get turned around down here."

Altieri paused. "Is that where the Clementine documents are housed?"

"Depends which Clement," Ian said, smile sharpening. "Some of them are rather… sensitive."

"Of course," Altieri said evenly. "Best to let old dust lie undisturbed."

With a courteous nod, he turned and left.

Ian waited until the echo of his shoes had faded.

Then he locked the chamber and made a call.

THEY MET that evening in the Vatican Canteen—after hours, when the kitchens had closed and the staff had gone. It wasn't glamorous: Formica tables, fluorescent lighting, and vending machines that dispensed bad espresso and better gossip.

Michael sat at the corner table with Ian and Sister Teri, who was sipping chamomile tea from a mug that read *CTRL + ALT + PRAY*.

"You should've seen the lad," Ian was saying. "Smooth as silk. Too smooth. Like he expected to be challenged and had rehearsed the deflections."

"He's being fed," Teri said flatly. "Nobody that polished is operating alone. Restoration division doesn't authorize physical retrievals at that level without a go-between."

Michael nodded. "He's the go-between. Someone— probably from the outside—is using him to get eyes on the Archives. Possibly to intercept what we're uncovering. Possibly to monitor me."

Teri frowned. "You're not thinking of that Medici

descendant, are you? The one you flagged last year over that dispute about the Palazzo Rosso documents?"

"Alessandro de' Medici?" Michael confirmed. "Yes, it's possible. He's connected, privately wealthy, and very quiet—until you threaten the Medici mythos."

Ian tapped the table. "So, we're not just being watched—we're being anticipated."

Michael leaned forward. "The question is, how much does he know?"

Teri gave a grim smile. "If he's Medici, probably more than he admits and less than he fears."

They sat in silence for a moment.

Then Michael said, "I want to keep Altieri inside the perimeter. For now."

Ian raised an eyebrow. "Why?"

"Because he's a link. If we push too hard, they'll replace him with someone smarter. Or sneakier. Someone we have to ferret out. But if he thinks we're not watching…"

"…he'll get lazy," Teri finished. "And we'll see who's pulling his strings."

Michael nodded. "Exactly."

Ian sat back. "So what do you want me to do?"

"Watch him. Shadow his access requests. Delay what you can. Re-route him when necessary. Make it look like incompetence or bad scheduling. And if he pokes too close to Clement again—"

"I'll box his ears," Ian said, grinning.

Teri sipped her tea. "What about the tech side? You want me to ghost his digital trail?"

"Can you?"

She gave him a look. "Father, *please*."

Michael smiled. "Then yes. Just enough to make him

doubt his own recall. Swap timestamps. Buffer logs. But don't erase him completely."

Ian stood. "So we're building a net."

"No," Michael said. "We're building a mirror. I want him to see his reflection."

As the room fell quiet again, the fluorescent lights above them flickered once, then steadied.

The Vatican had always been a place of shadows. But now, the shadows were watching each other.

CHAPTER

EIGHT

PALAZZO DEL SANT'UFFIZIO, ROME

The Sant'Uffizio loomed like a shadow cast by the Vatican itself.

The Palazzo della Congregazione per la Dottrina della Fede—also known as Palazzo del Sant'Uffizio or the Holy Office—stood just outside St. Peter's Square, an angular mass of travertine and iron that brooded at the edge of the colonnade's elegance. To tourists, it appeared to be just another anonymous building, perhaps some secondary administration office. But behind its unmarked door and patrolled façade lay centuries of fear, secrets, and silence.

This was once the headquarters of the Roman Inquisition.

Now known as the Dicastery for the Doctrine of the Faith, it remained the Church's official watchdog over orthodoxy, canon law, and theological "deviations." Even

60

its digital footprint was sparse. Few Vatican staff spoke of what went on inside. Fewer still were allowed access to its archives.

But Michael Dominic had been there before.

"This is the place," he said quietly as he and Hana approached on foot from Via delle Fornaci, "where the second letter leads. I'm sure of it."

Hana stopped and looked up at the building, its windows darkened with ancient dust. "The place where parchment was taken to burn…"

"… and one was spared," Michael finished. "If Clement wanted to bury something beneath a fire meant to destroy it, this would be the site. The locus of the Inquisition."

"And no one would question its disappearance," Hana murmured. "The Inquisition never needed footnotes."

A pair of plainclothes guards stood near the entrance, conversing quietly. Neither wore insignia, but their posture was unmistakable—Vatican Gendarmerie, the Holy See's police force. They weren't stationed there for show.

Michael gestured to the side street. "Let's go around the back."

They circled through a narrow alley, where vines climbed the high courtyard wall and traffic noise dulled to a hush. The rear of the Sant'Uffizio revealed a smaller service entrance—barred by a heavy wooden door with a rusted iron bolt.

Michael produced a slim Vatican keycard and slid it into the auxiliary access reader. It had been issued to him years ago, tied to his role as Prefect of the Archives.

A green light blinked.

The lock clicked.

Inside, the air was cool and dry, faintly scented with old leather and something sharper—preservative oils, or maybe the residue of disinfectant long since absorbed by the walls. They found themselves in a side hallway of the basement level: brick vaults above, worn stone tiles beneath, and rows of sealed wooden doors lining either side.

Michael flicked on a flashlight and whispered, "The modern archives are upstairs. But the Inquisition's records were kept below ground, under guard and cipher."

"And fire," Hana added, running her hand along the wall. "You can feel it. The suppression. Like the stones remember being complicit."

They moved carefully past sealed reading rooms and unlit stairwells. The flashlight cast long shadows on carved doorframes marked with obscure Latin acronyms: *ARVIA, DECRET VETUS, PENALIS 1570.*

Michael stopped in front of one: *IND.EX. PROHIB. – 1543–1590*

"The Index of Prohibited Books," he said quietly.

Hana's eyes widened. "This is the list of texts the Church forbade?"

"Many of which were burned. Some here. Others were ordered destroyed abroad. But not all were lost. Some were studied—and others debated—before being condemned."

"And maybe... one was spared."

Michael nodded.

He crouched and studied the door's lock—an old keyhole beneath a modern keypad. The keypad blinked orange. Standard Vatican archival codes wouldn't apply here.

Then he reached into his coat and retrieved an old brass key on a tarnished chain. It had been given to him by Pope Ignatius before his death—no explanation, just a quiet nod and the words *"for when the doors won't open."*

Michael inserted the key and turned.

The lock gave with a dusty clunk.

Inside, the room was narrow, walled in shelving, and entirely unlit. No digital terminals. No climate control. Just cold stone and paper.

They stepped inside.

Dust motes spun in their flashlight beams. The smell was overwhelming—like walking into a room sealed since the Council of Trent. The shelves groaned under the weight of ancient bindings. Many were scorched along the edges, some stamped with red wax seals bearing the sigils of long-dead inquisitors.

Hana moved slowly between the stacks, whispering titles as she passed.

"*Dialogus de aequalitate divina*, anonymous… *Epistulae Clarae de Spoleto*… this one's in Provençal."

Michael froze halfway down the second aisle.

On a lower shelf, amid the singed remnants of condemned manuscripts, lay a slender folio bound in red leather, untitled.

What struck him was the seal.

Not papal. Not Inquisitorial.

It bore the Medici insignia of Clement VII.

He knelt, carefully lifted the volume, and opened the cover.

Inside was a slip of parchment, pressed flat between pages of vellum with charred edges.

He read the inscription aloud.

To the one still seeking:
This was spared. By hands not mine, but faithful still. What survives is not full—but it is flame-kissed and true. Seek it in Avignon, below the chamber where silence was imposed on

*prophets, and where one letter escaped the fire. The cell marked
'Numéro Trois.'*

Michael looked up.

Hana was already leaning in.

"He's pointing us to France."

"To Avignon," Michael said. "The Antipope's seat
during the schism. Another city of exile. Another seat of
fear."

"But someone hid this piece here," she said, "within the
Index."

Michael nodded. "Whoever spared the gospel—or part
of it—must've also preserved Clement's guidance to find
it. The third letter wasn't here. But this clue… this is the
bridge."

They photographed the inscription and carefully
resealed the folio, then returned it to the shelf.

As they turned to go, Hana whispered, "The Vatican
thought it had burned everything that could hurt the
Church."

Michael glanced back at the dark shelves.

"They were wrong."

CHAPTER

NINE

VILLA AURELIA MEDICI, OUTSIDE ROME

Evening cloaked the estate in shadows, drawing long silhouettes across the loggia where Alessandro de' Medici stood with a tumbler of brandy balanced lightly in one hand. Beyond the terrace, the cypress trees murmured in the breeze, whispering to one another like conspirators.

The villa behind him glowed with ambient light—strategic and discreet. No room burned bright enough to reveal his position from a satellite. Every window had been treated with mirrored security laminate. The interior surveillance system fed directly into a private network housed three levels below ground. If there was a safer place to control the destinies of others, Alessandro had yet to find it.

But tonight, he wasn't at ease.

He stared out into the darkness while a soft footfall

echoed on the flagstones behind him. A voice followed, low and unobtrusive.

"He went inside."

Alessandro turned slowly.

The speaker was slender, clean-shaven, dressed in a cleric's cassock with no insignia. His face bore the forgettable symmetry that made Vatican watchers so difficult to trace. He was known to the surveillance logs only as Father Augustin, though Alessandro doubted even that was his real name.

"Inside where?" Alessandro asked, voice cool.

"The old tribunal. The Dicastery. Through the south entrance, with the Sinclair woman. They were in the building for over an hour."

Alessandro's jaw tensed, almost imperceptibly. "Unusual. The Doctrine of the Faith doesn't permit unscheduled civilian visits."

"No, *Signore*. They used back-channel access. Dominic used a legacy code, confirmed against older clearance authority."

"Which means someone inside still favors him."

"Or," the priest added, "they don't know what he's really looking for."

Alessandro turned back to the view. Somewhere beyond the trees and rooftops, the Vatican shimmered like a sacred reliquary in the distance. But even from here, even across the dark hills and burnished domes, he could sense the shift. Clement's letters were no longer rumors. They were active.

"And what did they access?" Alessandro asked.

The priest pulled a folded page from the inside of his cassock. "I had one of our restoration couriers tail the courier logs. They entered an unsealed archive connected to the *Index Librorum Prohibitorum*. Inquisition-era material. They retrieved a folio bearing Clement VII's seal. Inside was a slip of parchment, which Father Dominic photographed. After they left, I did the same thing." He handed over the folded page.

Alessandro took the paper and read.

His mouth went still as his eyes scanned the reproduced inscription:

To the one still seeking:

This was spared. By hands not mine, but faithful still. What survives is not full, but it is flame-kissed and true. Seek it in Avignon, below the chamber where silence was imposed on prophets, and where one letter escaped the fire. The cell marked 'Numéro Trois.'

He exhaled, fingers tightening on the page.

"So. The trail leads to France."

"Yes," said the priest. "Avignon. The Palais des Papes."

"Where Clement's authority might still have had a shadow," Alessandro murmured. "An echo of Rome, but one removed enough to bury something irreparable."

He crossed the terrace slowly, setting his brandy on a marble pedestal beside a bronze statue of St. Michael. The archangel's sword gleamed faintly in the ambient light.

"They're getting too close," Alessandro said. "I thought they might be chasing legends. But if the letter references Avignon specifically, then there's more than nostalgia involved. There's fact."

"They'll leave Rome."

"Of course," Alessandro said. "Which means they believe they're on the right path."

The priest waited, saying nothing.

Alessandro turned back to him. "I need to know how this trail came into Dominic's hands. Have you traced which Vatican restoration teams have handled the Clement folios in the last ten years?" Alessandro knew that, with the vast number of unrestored documents held in its Archives, the Vatican often hired outside teams simply to restore them and keep them in a preserved state until formal categorization by Michael's assistants. Clement's folios had been one of those sets of documents needing preservation.

"Only one—assigned three years ago. A temporary contract hire, overseen by Radelli. But the hire vanished after six months. We believe he may have taken a copy of the original inventory register with him."

"Name?"

"Carlo Zanetti. Graduate of Sapienza. Marginal background. Former Jesuit novice."

"Find him," Alessandro said. "Quietly. If he sold what he learned, I want to know to whom. If he still has it, he may need reminding that the Medici do not appreciate theft."

The priest gave a slight bow. "And Dominic?"

Alessandro considered the question for a moment.

Then he walked back into the villa, the priest following soundlessly, the doors hissing shut behind them.

Low amber light bathed the study inside. A wall of books stood behind his desk—volumes arranged by color, not title. Behind one shelf was a biometric safe. He pressed his palm against the hidden panel, and the door clicked open.

Inside lay a slim folder marked *Speculum*. "To watch."

He removed it and opened to the second page: a dossier on Father Michael Dominic, compiled over the years—his movements, his publications, his associates. There were pictures of Dominic's fiancée, Hana Sinclair. Of his trusted assistant, Ian Duffy. A still from an Archive security camera. A lunch receipt from a trattoria not far from the Archives.

He closed the folder and set it gently on the desk.

"Dominic," he murmured, "doesn't need to be eliminated. Not yet."

The priest tilted his head. "Then what shall I do?"

"Keep watching. Let them reach Avignon. Let them find the third letter."

He walked to the window and stared out once more toward the Vatican skyline, the cupola of St. Peter's dim against the night.

"If the third letter confirms the gospel," he murmured, "then I'll know what must be done."

"And if it doesn't?"

Alessandro turned, a faint smile touching the corners of his mouth.

"Then we let them keep going. Let them exhaust themselves chasing ashes. And when they finally come up empty-handed—"

He reached for the dossier, tapped the cover with two fingers.

"—we remind the world that not all Medici buried their mistakes."

TEN

AVIGNON, FRANCE

The Dassault Falcon 900 touched down on the tarmac at Aéroport d'Avignon-Provence just after dawn, its landing gear hissing softly as the private jet taxied toward a discreet VIP hangar at the far end of the airfield. The rising Provençal light spilled across the surrounding vineyards, their green rows glowing gold at the edges, while the Rhône River shimmered beyond the distant horizon.

Inside the sleek, leather-trimmed cabin, Father Michael Dominic pulled back the window shade and exhaled slowly. He looked over at Hana across from him and smiled.

Hana met his gaze with the relaxed ease of someone accustomed to early flights and unfamiliar runways. The jet—one of several assets she had inherited from her late grandfather's Franco-Swiss media holdings—was the kind of luxury she rarely mentioned and never flaunted. It simply allowed her to move freely in a profession that often demanded speed, discretion, and oceans crossed at a moment's notice. Michael had learned long ago to accept it with quiet gratitude; her resources had saved their lives more than once.

Yet as he watched her now, hair caught by the first rays of the Provençal sunrise, he felt again what he had felt from the beginning. None of this—the polished cabin, the private hangar, the comfort she had been born into—was what bound him to her. He had loved her long before jets and headlines, through years of shared danger and whispered trust, through nights spent chasing truths that might have broken lesser bonds.

And as the jet slowed to a halt, Michael found himself thinking of next spring, of the vows they would make under whatever sky God allowed, and of the life waiting for them beyond missions and manuscripts—a life he looked toward with a steadiness deeper than any luxury the world could offer.

In the rear of the cabin, Swiss Guards Karl and Lukas secured the equipment cases—subtle, lightweight black containers housing compact scanning tools, micro drones, encrypted comms, and more analog tools of the trade: miniature chisels, latex gloves, and carbon analysis kits. They moved with quiet efficiency, the calm of men who had rehearsed contingencies few would believe.

"Security looks light at this airport," Karl muttered, glancing through the small porthole.

"That's the point," Lukas replied. "No Customs presence. No tail."

Michael stood and reached for his coat. "Let's keep it that way."

The door unfolded, and the aircraft steps descended

onto the sunlit tarmac. A waiting black Mercedes van stood ready at the hangar entrance. Within fifteen minutes, they were on the road, curving through the narrow lanes of Avignon, its medieval walls still intact, casting long shadows across the cobbled streets.

Soon, the Palais des Papes—the ancient Palace of the Popes—emerged ahead, massive and brooding.

The fortress-palace loomed above the Place du Palais like an outcropping of stone judgment, all harsh angles and towering ramparts. Constructed in the fourteenth century as a seat of the Avignon Papacy, it had once served as a rival to Rome, an alternate throne for Peter's successors. During the Great Schism, it held seven popes and countless intrigues. Its walls had watched trials, tortures, and decrees burn their way into history.

Today, tourists strolled the open courtyard with guidebooks in hand, unaware that beneath the grand halls and painted chapels lay a tribunal chamber long since sealed—and a secret the Church had hoped would never surface.

THEY ENTERED under the guise of a private academic delegation from the Vatican, armed with letters bearing the seal of a supportive French cardinal. Their cover: a comparative study of fourteenth-century tribunal records in relation to Avignon's unique legal architecture.

The palace interior was dim and hushed, its arched ceilings whispering echoes of centuries past. Gold-framed maps, portraits of popes in exile, and painted vaults lined the upper floors. But they didn't linger above ground.

Guided by a discreet palace historian named Émile Sarrau, a man who had spent his career tracing the contours of Avignon's medieval subterranea, they were granted access to the lesser-known regions of the southern foundation—rarely opened to the public.

"This chamber," Sarrau explained as he guided them down the electric torch-lit stone stairwell, "was once used for proceedings not documented in the official registries. Ecclesiastical judgments, often based on accusations that came from within the court itself. The chamber lies beneath what used to be the Hall of Justice."

He paused beside an ancient wooden door reinforced with iron ribs, its hinges pitted with rust.

"I'll let you proceed from here. But be careful. The passage narrows, and there are still voids—subsidence points that have never been fully mapped."

Michael offered a nod of gratitude. "We'll be careful."

Sarrau inclined his head and departed, his footsteps fading.

Michael turned to Hana. "He knows more than he says."

"He also knows when not to ask questions," she replied.

They passed through the door and the stone staircase narrowed, curving sharply before descending into a low, vaulted space that smelled of lime dust and ancient dampness. The walls here were untouched—raw stone and mortar bearing scorch marks that could only be the remnants of long-extinguished torches or, more ominously, fires not meant for light.

At the bottom, the chamber opened into a rectangular hall. It was windowless and eerily still, a space entombed by centuries. The ceiling pressed low, its vaults supported by thick, square columns of ashlar stone that seemed to lean inward under the weight of time. The air was colder here and acrid with mildew, yet faintly tinged with something metallic.

The center of the room was bare, but dark stains marked the flagstones—remnants of soot, Michael suspected, or something older and more troubling. Inquisitors once convened here. Judgments passed. Flames lit.

At the far end stood a raised stone dais, roughly hewn and bluntly symbolic. On it, the old papal judges would have sat, cloaked in silence, to pronounce sentence on heretics and dissenters.

Karl slowly panned the room with a compact thermal device, its screen casting a bluish glow across his face. "Cool air shift at the back wall," he murmured, adjusting the gain. "Something's pulling temperature—possibly a cavity, or just airflow."

Michael moved toward the dais while Lukas swept a beam of light along the perimeter.

"Not seeing any clear seams," Lukas muttered. "If there's an access panel, it's masked."

Hana joined them, her brows furrowed. She unpacked her compact multispectral imager and began a methodical sweep across the surface of the stone wall. "There's thermal disparity here," she said after a few moments. "But the stone's been tampered with in more than one spot. There might be multiple voids—or false ones."

"Decoys," Michael said. "That would be clever. Clement wouldn't have made it easy."

Karl tapped the side wall. "Hollow resonance here— but same on the opposite end. That's deliberate symmetry."

Lukas ran his gloved fingers along the edge of the platform. "Mortar's uneven on the far left side. Sealed more recently, and not consistent with the rest of the masonry."

"Let's check it," Michael said.

He crouched beside Lukas, eyes narrowing as he traced the join. "There—a reset joint, but thinner than usual. Could be a façade."

Hana repositioned the imager and toggled to density scan. The screen flickered, then stabilized.

"There's definitely a pocket behind it," she confirmed, then frowned. "But—wait. There's a secondary void about a meter deeper. That one's larger."

Karl straightened. "Could be a trap vault. First one might've held decoy relics to mislead intruders. Classic misdirection."

"Clement was playing a long game," Michael muttered. "He knew the inquisitors' paranoia. They built concealment into concealment."

Lukas withdrew a micro pry bar and gently inserted it at the joint. He paused. "Stone's thin here. Could fracture."

Michael nodded. "Try to lift it clean. Let's not destroy anything—yet."

With careful pressure and no small amount of patience, Lukas edged the stone outward. It gave with a groan of protest, releasing a stale breath of air tinged with old ash. Behind it lay a narrow cavity, a shallow recess with nothing inside but soot and fragments of charred wood.

"Empty," Hana whispered. "Deliberately burned."

Michael frowned. "He left a decoy. That wooden tube was destroyed—on purpose, maybe as a decoy."

Lukas ran his light into the deeper recess behind it. "There's something back there."

He reached in, arm fully extended, and his fingers brushed something rigid.

"I've got it," he said—and withdrew slowly, revealing a sealed tube carved from darkened olivewood, bound in brass bands blackened by fire. It was scorched at one end, but intact. The surface was cracked with age but still carried the elegant simplicity of deliberate craftsmanship.

Michael took it gently. The wood was cool to the touch, but not brittle. On its base, barely visible beneath a smear of soot, was a carved insignia: **C VII**—*Clemens Septimus.*

His breath caught.

"No label," he said. "No title. But this is his mark."

He broke the wax seal with reverence and slid the cap free.

Inside the tube was a scroll of parchment, tightly rolled and astonishingly preserved. Michael unspooled it gradually on a clean pad, the crackle of aged vellum the only sound in the room.

No one spoke.

Clement's third letter had been found—but not without some resistance. Even after death, the pope had hidden his truth with cunning and perhaps a trace of fear.

The familiar seal—**C VII**—glimmered faintly in the lamplight.

The parchment felt heavier than the others—not in weight, but in the density of what it might reveal.

Michael cleared his throat, and the others leaned in.

Then he began to read aloud.

To the one who still seeks—

You now tread a path that I, in my own time, dared not complete. What was placed in my hands was not a scroll, but a fire—and though I could not bear its light, neither did I extinguish it. I buried it. But I did not forget.

By the hour this letter finds your eyes, know that mine were already dimmed with the weight of obedience—not to God, but to blood. I wore the ring of Peter, yet it scorched my flesh with every blessing I gave, for I knew the ring was forged not only in Rome, but in Florence. The crown was set upon my brow not by the Spirit, but by hands I once called kin.

The Medici name—my own name—demanded not revelation, but restraint. They feared not error in doctrine, but disorder in empire. It was not heresy that shook them, but the specter of spiritual equality. The gospel entrusted to me— whether by Providence or punishment—threatened to undo centuries of authority built not on holiness, but hierarchy.

This gospel did not attack the Creed. It whispered something more devastating: that Christ had walked not in isolation, but in companionship; that He did not reign above, but sat among. And at His side, it named her—Maria Magdalēnē—not as penitent, not as ornament, but as Beloved. First witness. Equal herald. Apostle without title.

The courts of Europe murmured of such things. Francis of France sent humanists posing as poets, men who carried diplomacy in their ink; Charles of the Empire asked questions whose answers he did not want. They circled me like dancers at a fire, never stepping in, never stepping back. One told me, "It is a dangerous time to find new truth." Another warned, "Doctrine is what survives war, but truth is what survives Christ."

I was cornered in every chamber. My throne bore lions, but I ruled among jackals. Not by swords was I threatened, but by ancestry—the velvet bonds of dynasty and papal pageantry.

And yet, I did not face this burden alone.

I summoned a council—not sanctioned, not recorded— composed of minds I trusted above titles. One of them was not invited. She had no official voice, no seat at the table. But she heard every word. She transcribed what the others dared only speak in private. Her quill ran with the ink of sorrow and conviction.

Her name was Apollonia, a Benedictine sister of Santa Marta al Prato. She was not present as a theologian, nor as a delegate, but as a listener in shadows. She believed the gospel's voice—her voice—must not be extinguished again. And when we, the council, chose silence… she chose remembrance.

She paid dearly for that choice.

It was not Rome that exiled her. It was Florence. It was family. Mine.

They called her disobedient. They called her corrupted. But what she was—what she remains—is witness.

I became, in the end, a pope in chains—a crown entombed in velvet bonds.

The fourth letter I placed where velvet becomes veil, and lineage becomes mask. Seek the convent once tied to the Medici line—not closed by decree but collapsed in disgrace. There, where Apollonia last raised her voice, the red thread begins to fray. There, the truth waits—not in flame, but in ruin.

✚ ***Clemens PP. VII***

Pontifex Maximus

Michael lowered the letter, his eyes still fixed on the final lines.

Hana's voice was low and taut. "He wasn't just afraid of losing control. He was afraid of *being controlled.*"

"By his own bloodline," Michael said. "The Medici had installed popes before Clement. They knew how to twist papacy to preserve dynasty."

"And other rulers knew," she added. "Francis I. Charles V. They didn't demand the gospel be burned. They just made sure it would never be read."

"Heretical silence," Karl muttered from the corner, eyes still on the chamber's dark walls.

Hana read the last line again aloud. *"'Seek the convent once tied to the Medici line—not closed by decree, but collapsed in disgrace.'*

"There were Medici-funded convents across Italy," she added. "But most of them were absorbed, not closed in disgrace. Except—"

Michael met her gaze. "You're thinking of Santa Marta al Prato?"

Hana nodded. "Near Florence. The convent that lost its charter after a scandal—unverified accounts of one of its nuns writing inflammatory spiritual texts. The documents were said to be destroyed… but no one ever confirmed who ordered it."

"And some say she was a Medici cousin," Michael added. "A scandal too close to the bloodline."

Lukas crossed his arms. "Then that's our next destination."

Michael carefully re-rolled the parchment and sealed it back in its tube.

"Pack everything. Let's move. The deeper we go, the closer we are to someone else's red line."

Hana looked toward the chamber door, the torchlight flickering in her eyes.

"And now we're pulling at the red thread."

CHAPTER

ELEVEN

FLORENCE, ITALY

The Falcon 900 banked low over the Tuscan hills, its sleek wings slicing through the golden light of late afternoon. Below, the Arno River shimmered as it curved through the ancient heart of Florence, where terracotta roofs blazed under the sun like coals in a hearth. Hana sat near the window, her fingers tapping absently against her espresso cup.

"This is the city where the Medici perfected their masquerade," she murmured. "Here, power always wore a different face in public than it did behind closed doors. Half of their brilliance was art, the other half deception, and Florence learned to applaud both."

Michael glanced across the aisle. "And the Medici became experts at hiding the cost of it."

Lukas and Karl, seated in the rear cabin, had begun prepping the gear again—only this time, there was an edge

80

in their movements. They had felt it too. Ever since Avignon, something had shifted. The quiet opposition they had sensed in Rome now bore sharper teeth.

Their destination wasn't marked on any modern tourist map.

The ruins of Santa Marta al Prato, a fifteenth-century Medici-sponsored convent, sat crumbling in the northwestern quarter of Florence, just beyond the shadow of the ancient city walls. Officially, it was designated "ecclesiastical property under restricted reclamation." In truth, it was abandoned. Half of the outer wall had collapsed decades ago. The chapel roof was gone. The cloister was little more than weeds and bones of stone.

But it was here, according to Clement VII's third letter, that the Medici had buried more than scandal. They had buried a woman—Apollonia, the nun who once dared to "last raise her voice," with a truth not meant to survive.

And possibly, her letter remained.

By dusk, they reached the site.

The rented van rumbled up a gravel path overgrown with wild sage and spindly cypress. A rusted chain-link fence encircled the perimeter, patched in places with barbed wire. Lukas cut it clean with bolt cutters and they passed inside, boots crunching over loose gravel and charred leaves.

The structure loomed ahead like a corpse still dressed for Mass—arched windows gaping, walls bowed inward from centuries of neglect. The last of the light caught on a worn fresco of the Virgin above the entrance, her face eroded into a smear of white and rust.

Inside the chapel, stone columns stretched toward nothing—no roof remained, only a skeletal framework and open sky. The floor was strewn with debris: shattered plaster, broken pews, and wind-scattered pages from forgotten breviaries.

Karl swept the left transept with a flashlight. "No movement. The place is dead."

"Not quite," Lukas said, pointing to a row of disturbed floor tiles near the apse. "Someone's been here recently."

Michael knelt beside the tiles. They were misaligned—shifted slightly, as if pried loose and hastily replaced. He lifted one with a gloved hand. Beneath it was a hollow void, dark and narrow.

"Possibly a hiding place," he said. "But it's been opened before."

"Could the letter have been taken?" Hana asked.

"Or moved," Michael said. "Hidden again. Possibly deeper."

They continued into the remains of the cloister—a low quadrangle lined with cracked stone arcades. Weeds choked the inner garden. A broken statue of St. Catherine leaned drunkenly against a wall.

It was there, just beyond the west arcade, that Lukas halted. He raised a clenched fist. The signal was unmistakable.

Michael and Hana froze behind him. Karl moved to flank.

"Movement," Lukas whispered. "Three shapes. Maybe four. Far cloister corridor. They're not tourists."

"Armed?" Karl asked, eyes scanning the deepening shadows.

Lukas gave a small nod. "Tacticals. Close formation."

Hana's voice was low and hard. "Someone followed us."

"Or they were waiting," Michael said.

Then the first flash came, a glint of steel in motion, followed by a muffled shout.

The attackers moved with professional precision—no words, no warnings. They wore dark clothing, partial masks, and communication headsets. Their weapons were compact: short-barreled batons, modified stun rifles, perhaps nonlethal—but that didn't matter. Not here.

Karl met the first one mid-sprint. His boot caught the man center mass, sending him back into a column with a sickening crunch.

Lukas ducked low, driving his shoulder into another, then twisted and disarmed him with a clean elbow strike.

Michael turned as one figure broke off and lunged at Hana.

She didn't hesitate, sidestepping and jabbing upward with a steel pen from her jacket, catching her assailant just beneath the chin. The man stumbled back, stunned, and Hana followed with a quick kick to the groin that sent him down hard.

Michael found himself grappling with a fourth figure who had circled behind. The man was fast—too fast for a street thug. Trained. Michael blocked a jab to the ribs, countered with a short strike to the collarbone, and grabbed for the man's mask.

Beneath it was a clean-shaven face—dark-eyed, Eastern European. No insignia.

A ghost.

Lukas delivered the final blow to the man now facing Michael—an open-palm strike to the throat that dropped the last of them. Silence returned, broken only by heavy breathing and the low rasp of wind through the chapel ruins. Those assailants who weren't now lying unconscious had run off.

Karl crouched beside one of the bodies and pulled a small device from his belt: a Vatican-made signal scanner.

"Encrypted radio. Local frequency. No affiliation tags."

Michael caught his breath. "They're trained. Not random. And they knew we were coming."

"They weren't trying to kill us," Hana said, checking her arm for abrasions. "They wanted something."

"Or to stop us from finding something," Michael replied.

Karl stood, gaze scanning the perimeter. "We need to secure the site. Fast."

Michael walked slowly back into the chapel, past the broken altar and the empty apse. He stopped beneath the open vault where moonlight now streamed across the floor like spilled silver.

He looked up at the stars. "Who else knew about this place?"

Hana joined him, still tense from the fight. "Besides Clement? Maybe Apollonia. And now us."

"No, I mean now," Michael said. "Someone else. Someone who sent those men."

He glanced back toward the dark garden, where Lukas and Karl were zip-tying wrists and confiscating gear. Gear whose intentions came clear to him.

"They were here to erase," he said. "Not search."

Hana turned toward the ruined sacristy. "Then we keep looking. We do it before they return. But we don't rush it."

Michael shook his head. "No. We don't disturb another stone tonight." Looking around at the fallen attackers, he added, "Once they wake up, these goons will beat feet back to where they came from."

He walked slowly to the center of the chapel and placed a gloved hand on the cracked marble floor.

"Tomorrow," he said quietly. "We come back at first light. And we find what they were trying to bury again."

The hotel was a quiet nineteenth-century villa just off the Arno, its ivy-covered façade aglow with golden sconces as the team entered past midnight. The clerk, drowsy but discreet, handed them keys without commentary.

Though engaged, Michael and Hana chose separate rooms on the second floor, more out of exhaustion than intention. Karl and Lukas took a twin suite at the end of the hall. The hallway soon quieted under the weight of bruises, fatigue, and adrenaline finally ebbing away.

Michael dropped his bag inside his room and stood for a moment in silence, listening to the city's hush. The soft lap of the river. A distant Vespa. The subtle hum of Florence dreaming.

Then he crossed the hallway and tapped lightly on Hana's door.

She opened it without surprise.

Her jacket was off, hair tied back, sleeves rolled. The room smelled of bergamot tea and old stone. She stepped aside to let him in and he entered, nodding once in thanks.

Neither of them spoke for a moment.

Then Hana said, "They were waiting for us, Michael."

"I know."

"They weren't amateurs."

"No."

She sat on the window ledge, pulling her legs up loosely. "It changes the rules."

Michael leaned against the desk. "It confirms what Clement feared: that even now, someone wants the gospel buried."

"Or protected," Hana added. "Depending on how they see the truth."

Michael smiled faintly. "Same thing, sometimes."

She studied him. "Do you think the gospel is real?"

"I think something is. Something Clement believed in deeply. Enough to risk history for it."

Hana picked at a thread on her blouse. "And if it says what we suspect? That Magdalene's voice was equal to his? Do you know what that would do to the Church?"

Michael met her gaze. "It would break it."

"Then why keep going?"

"Because it might also heal it."

Silence fell between them again, but it was the kind of silence that spoke of shared burdens, not retreat. Finally, Hana asked, "What about Sister Apollonia?"

"She tried to speak," Michael replied. "And they branded her for it."

"I wonder what she lost."

Michael gave a tired nod. "Likely everything."

"Then we owe her the rest of the story."

He stood, walking to the window and stopping beside Hana. "At dawn, we go back."

She didn't look at him, but her voice dropped a register. "I know you booked your own room. You always do. But... if you'd rather not sleep alone tonight, I wouldn't mind the company."

For a moment, the words hung between them, charged not with urgency but with something quieter, long delayed. Their engagement had changed everything and almost nothing at the same time. Between Michael's duties at the Archives and Hana's relentless chase for stories and management of her grandfather's estate, they'd had precious few moments to simply be together without danger or deadlines pressing in.

Michael said nothing. Then, quietly, "I wouldn't either."

But he didn't move closer yet, and neither did she. They simply stayed there for a while, side by side at the window, letting the silence settle around them. Below, Florence stretched out in amber light, and the distant tolling of bells drifted across the sleeping city like a benediction they both needed more than they could admit.

IN THE ROOM across the hall, Karl stood shirtless at the sink, running a damp towel across a long bruise forming on his ribs. Lukas sat cross-legged on one of the twin beds, cleaning the stun welts on his forearm with antiseptic wipes.

Neither spoke for several minutes.

Then Karl said, "You took that last one down pretty hard."

Lukas smirked. "He had it coming. Besides, you were busy impressing the columns with your footwork."

"I thought I cracked one," Karl said.

Lukas tossed a wipe into the waste bin. "We've had close calls before, but this wasn't random. That formation? Those tactics? Someone trained them."

Karl's jaw flexed. "I know."

A pause.

"Are you afraid?" Lukas asked.

Karl turned to look at him. "Not for myself."

Lukas gave a small nod.

Another silence passed, longer this time.

Then Lukas said shyly, "I wouldn't mind if you stayed in my bed tonight."

Karl met his eyes. "I wouldn't mind either."

And that was all. The lights went off a moment later.

Just two shadows in the dark, breathing the same quiet air, waiting for whatever came next.

CHAPTER

TWELVE

FLORENCE, ITALY

They returned at dawn.

The sky over Florence was a pale blue wash, and the bells of San Lorenzo tolled softly through the morning fog. A single ray of sunlight crept down the ruined bell tower of Santa Marta al Prato, spilling into the courtyard like a blessing across centuries of silence.

Michael, Hana, Karl, and Lukas moved with quiet purpose across the broken threshold, stepping over last night's damage: scattered stones, bruised columns, the faint imprint of boots in the dust.

The chapel stood as they had left it—solemn, half-destroyed, waiting.

But the air had changed.

"Listen," Hana whispered.

Michael paused. No birdsong. No wind.

Just breath and stone.

They moved through the side transept and into the

89

remnants of what had once been the sisters' library, a vaulted space half collapsed, its floor strewn with broken slate and charred beams. There, near the base of a crumbling wall, they found it: a marble plaque, knocked flat, partially buried under years of ruin.

Lukas brushed away the debris.

Carved into the surface, in Latin, they read:

"Apollonia of the Veil—sister, scribe, silenced."
"Faith is not given. It is remembered."

Michael traced the chiseled lines with his gloved fingers. "It's a memorial."

"Hidden here," Hana said, kneeling. "Away from the convent's formal crypt. Whoever made this wanted her remembered… but quietly."

"She was erased from the registry," Michael murmured. "But not forgotten."

They searched the surrounding area for nearly an hour, sweeping the walls, probing beneath the floor. Finally, crouching near the collapsed confessional alcove, Karl called out.

"Here…"

He knelt beside a hollow recess behind the altar, where a panel of bricks had been cemented with a crude mortar. The seams were obvious now, in the angled light of morning.

Lukas wedged a chisel into the seam and began carefully prying the bricks free. Within minutes, the panel crumbled inward, revealing a dry, narrow cavity less than a meter deep.

Inside, wrapped in a roll of red silk faded to rust, was a cylindrical bronze reliquary—the kind used to house sacred bones or papal decrees. On its lid was etched a stylized key overlaid with an open book.

Michael lifted it free and unscrewed the lid.

Inside was a single folded parchment.

He drew it out gently and unfolded the document across his lap. A wax seal, cracked with age but still recognizable, bore the keys of Peter—and the personal signet of Clemens PP VII.

Astonished, Michael looked at Hana. "This is it."

She nodded. "The fourth."

The others stepped close, their breath shallow.

Then Michael began to read.

To the one who still seeks—

What I received, I did not bear alone.

After the gospel was brought to me, I dared not decide its fate by my own hand. So I summoned a consilium—a secret council, unrecorded, unknown even to the Curia. I called them not by office, but by spirit. A scholar from Padua. A mystic from Bavaria. A French abbess with no tongue, only text. Eight in all, myself among them.

We met beneath the Apostolic Palace in the Hall of Clementine Shadow. We read the gospel aloud, line by line. We prayed. We wept. We disagreed.

Three feared it. Three embraced it. One could not decide.

We debated until the sun rose over Saint Peter's and the bells of Matins rang. Then we voted.

Three votes to destroy. One abstention. Three to preserve.

I voted for silence.

Not because I believed it false. But because I feared what it would do to the Church I had sworn to protect. We sealed the gospel. And we swore not to speak of the conclave.

But one voice did not remain silent.

She was not in the room. She was not invited. She was not allowed.

But she was listening. She had always been listening.

Apollonia.

A sister of Santa Marta. A scribe among shadows. She transcribed what we feared to write. She carried the truth we buried.

And for this, she was exiled. Silenced by the very house that bore my name—Medici.

I sent her here, with this letter, and with the memory of what we had done. She believes that time would come for the truth. I do not.

But you are still reading.

So now I place the burden on you.

The fifth letter lies where she will last kneel in prayer. Where she gives back to Christ the voice the Church has taken from her.

Look for her beneath the scarlet veil.

✠ Clemens PP. VII

Pontifex Maximus

The wind shifted, stirring the dust through the broken roof. A shaft of sunlight struck the parchment in Michael's hands, setting the faded ink aglow.

Hana stepped back. "He assembled a secret council. Unofficial. Unrecorded. He let others decide with him… and they chose to bury it."

"Out of fear," Michael said quietly. "Not of truth. But of collapse."

"And Apollonia was listening," she whispered. "Transcribing. Witnessing."

"She preserved the gospel in defiance of his silence."

Lukas looked down at the reliquary. "And the next letter?"

Michael re-read the final line: "'*Where she last knelt in prayer. Where she gave back to Christ the voice the Church had taken from her. Look for her beneath the scarlet veil.*'"

"She was buried," Hana said. "Somewhere in this convent."

"No," Michael said, eyes sharpening. "I think it means more than burial. It's a reference."

"To martyrdom?" Lukas asked.

"Or to relic veneration," Karl added. "The scarlet veil could be literal—part of her remains, or her habit, preserved in some way."

Michael sealed the letter and returned it to its reliquary, as though laying it into the hands of time itself.

Then he stood.

The gospel had not been silenced. Not by vote. Not by exile. Not by fear.

And now, with four of eight letters uncovered, the red thread drew tighter still.

CHAPTER

THIRTEEN

FLORENCE, ITALY

The first light of morning spread across the hills like a slow blessing, gilding the olive groves in soft gold and stirring long fingers of mist from the river valleys. The van cut a steady line through the winding roads outside Florence, tires humming low over cobblestones worn smooth by centuries of cartwheel and barefoot pilgrimage. A new day had broken, but the weight of their discoveries hung in the cabin like ancient incense—rich, pungent, and lingering in the folds of every thought.

Michael sat in the front passenger seat, his eyes fixed not on the scenery, but on the fragile scroll case resting in his lap—the bronze reliquary that had contained Clement VII's fourth letter. He hadn't reread it since sealing it again. He didn't need to. Its words remained etched in his mind with a kind of sacred violence.

Beside him, Hana drove with careful ease, the early sun

painting her cheek in light and shadow through the van's window. She hadn't spoken since they had left the ruined convent. Her silence wasn't withdrawal, but depth. She was parsing each detail, mentally triangulating Apollonia's trail across time.

In the back seat, Karl and Lukas reviewed the previous night's drone scans of the convent complex, searching for additional voids or cavities they might have missed, though Michael suspected the search was as much a ritual of calm as of necessity. After the previous night's ambush, every detail mattered. Every corner held risk.

"What do you make of it?" Hana asked at last, breaking the stillness.

Michael glanced sideways. "The veil?"

She nodded. "Clement's final line. *'Look for her beneath the scarlet veil.'* It's poetic, yes, but it's also directional."

Michael exhaled. "Veils in sacred language can mean many things: the curtain in the temple, the covering of the holy, even the metaphorical veil between flesh and spirit."

"But scarlet," Hana pressed, "that's specific. Not purple, not white. Scarlet."

Michael nodded. "The color of martyrdom. Of penance. Of a cardinal's robes. But also of—"

"Burial shrouds," Hana finished. "Red silk was sometimes used in high-status Florentine burials during the Medici era. Imported from Byzantium, dyed with kermes, priced like gold. It was reserved for women of noble blood… or those whose deaths came wrapped in a hint of spiritual scandal."

Michael's brow furrowed. "Florence always hid its sins in silk. Beauty was the camouflage."

Karl shook his head. "Nobility or scandal. One doesn't exclude the other in Florence."

Lukas added, "I did some digging this morning. There's a crypt beneath Santa Lucia al Magnoli. It's not on the main tourist route. The site was once under the jurisdiction of the Order of the Poor Clares, before being reabsorbed by the city."

Karl tapped his tablet. "The city registry shows that a donation of crimson funeral silk was recorded in 1534. Anonymously given. No recipient named."

Hana met Michael's eyes. "That's within a year of Clement's death."

"And just after Sister Apollonia's final disappearance," he murmured.

The van crested a hill, and the domes and towers of Florence unfolded before them in the golden haze—Brunelleschi's massive cupola rising like a beacon over the Renaissance skyline, the city laid out below like a painting too large for any one frame.

"Then we go to Santa Lucia," Michael said.

CHIESA DI SANTA LUCIA AL MAGNOLI, FLORENCE

The church stood discreetly along the southern bank of the Arno, its façade plain and weather-worn, its entrance hidden in the crook of two leaning streets. Pilgrims passed it by daily, rarely sparing more than a glance. But the air around it had a stillness that felt older than the city, like a breath held too long.

Inside, the nave was narrow and dim, and the frescoes faded to the color of tea-stained parchment. The floor tiles bore the patterns of forgotten centuries: fleurs-de-lis interwoven with vines punctuated by iron rings once used to anchor funeral biers. A modestly draped altar of rough marble stood at the front, with a silver icon of the Virgin resting beneath a canopy of carved wood.

A nun, elderly and silent, nodded as they entered but said nothing. She moved like a shadow between the pews, her rosary beads clicking faintly in rhythm with her steps.

Karl and Lukas took up loose positions near the main door, their eyes always scanning, always measuring. Lukas slipped a compact reconnaissance drone from his pack, its matte-black casing no larger than his palm. With a nod from Karl, he activated it, and the little device lifted soundlessly toward the rafters, settling into a slow survey arc above the nave.

"Drone is live," Lukas murmured. "No movement outside. Heat signatures stable."

Karl gave a quiet grunt of approval before returning his attention to the interior.

Hana and Michael moved forward together until Michael stopped beside the altar rail and turned slowly in place.

"Over there," he said gently.

To the right of the apse, behind an iron gate partially rusted shut, was a low corridor slanting downward, dimly lit by a small stained-glass window whose crimson panes filtered the sun into a blood-hued mist.

"The crypt," Hana whispered.

They moved carefully through the gate, ducking beneath the arch, their footfalls now echoing against colder stone. The corridor descended into a chamber no larger than a private chapel. Low niches lined the walls, some empty, others sealed with faded plaques. But one stood out.

Near the rear, beneath a half-collapsed fresco of St. Mary Magdalene holding a scroll in one hand and a spindle in the other, was a single sarcophagus, unadorned save for a carved veil flowing over its top like a scarlet wave of draped silk. The stone was worn smooth, but a faint sigil remained visible: **C VII.**

Michael stepped forward.

"Look for her beneath the scarlet veil," he quoted.

He ran his fingers along the veil-shaped carving, then reached carefully along the inner edge of the lid, where he found a minor groove.

With Hana's help, he slid the heavy slab aside, just far enough to peer inside.

There, resting atop a faded bolt of red silk, folded with reverence and age, was a small lacquered wooden reliquary, no longer than a shoebox, wrapped in a band of cloth bearing the seal of Pope Urban IV—his crossed tiara and the Latin inscription: *SIGILLUM VERITATIS.*

Michael swallowed. "This is it."

Hana leaned closer, her voice hushed. "The Seal of Urban."

They didn't open it. Not yet.

There, in the half-light of the crypt, surrounded by veiled bones and the silent weight of forgotten prayers, they simply stood.

It had taken four letters, two nations, and the near erasure of a woman's voice to reach this moment.

CHAPTER

FOURTEEN

FLORENCE, ITALY

The bronze bell of Santa Lucia tolled softly behind them as they emerged into the evening light, the crypt door shut once more behind stone and veil. Though no words had been spoken aloud, a shared gravity weighed upon them as they walked the narrow lane back toward the car, each of them inwardly changed by the relic now in their possession.

The reliquary was no larger than a prayer book, yet it radiated the hushed potency of something never meant to be uncovered. Even Karl, whose fingers had once held relics of saints without blinking, carried it as if it might fracture time itself. The wax seal of Urban IV was still intact, dulled to the color of old bone. Along its edge ran a golden inscription too faded to read fully, but unmistakably papal.

No one suggested opening it there. Even Lukas, who had little patience for academic ritual, kept his voice low as he drove them back through Florence's moonlit streets, past shuttered bakeries and cafés where the clink of wine glasses and low jazz still whispered from behind latticed doors.

Back at the Hotel Loggia degli Artisti, the air smelled of citrus and dusk. From the rooftop, one could just make out the red-tiled dome crowned with Verrocchio's golden sphere of the Duomo and the smudge of stars gathering above the Arno. It was a Florentine evening like any other —warm, deceptively gentle, bearing no clue that something buried for nearly five centuries was about to rise.

They gathered in Hana's suite, a corner room with tall windows that opened onto the garden courtyard below. The furniture was antique Tuscan—carved dark wood, wine-colored upholstery—and the lighting came from two sconces shaped like lilies.

The reliquary rested in the center of the writing desk, lit by the golden glow of a reading lamp.

Michael stood over it a long moment without touching it. His collar was loose, his cassock jacket folded on a nearby chair. The lines around his eyes looked deeper than usual.

Hana stood at his side. She wore the same travel-worn clothes from earlier, her sleeves pushed up, her hair drawn into a twist at the nape of her neck. Despite the fatigue in her posture, her eyes were sharpened by anticipation, alight with that strange fusion of journalistic hunger and reverent awe.

Karl and Lukas remained near the door, quiet, watchful —not as guards tonight, but as witnesses.

Michael took a breath and looked to Hana. She nodded once.

He broke the seal.

The sound was small, a dry crack, like old parchment folding in on itself. He opened the lid with care.

Inside, wrapped in a layer of red-dyed silk that shimmered like blood in the light, lay a single parchment scroll, tightly wound and bound with a ribbon of ivory. The script on the ribbon read in Latin:

"Non aboleatur quod Spiritus suscitavit."
Let not be destroyed what the Spirit has awakened.

Michael slowly unrolled the fifth letter. The parchment was stiff but supple, the ink remarkably preserved. The handwriting was unmistakable—the same humanist flourish as the previous letters, the same measured grief threading through each line.

He began to translate aloud:

To the one who still seeks—

This is among the last I shall write before I entrust my breath to the dust.

The others were confession. This is absolution.

For too long, I wore silence like a sacrament. I guarded what I should have grieved. I justified the suppression of something luminous, because I feared it would blind the faithful. I told myself that safety was sanctity. I was wrong.

Now, in the final days of my pilgrimage, I no longer fear what is true.

*The name of the gospel is **Evangelium Delecti—The Gospel of the Beloved**. I do not know who wrote it. I know only that it bears the breath of the Nazarene. It speaks in His voice, but not through His mouth. It is not dictated. It is shared.*

One passage remains with me, inscribed upon my conscience like flame on vellum:

"Blessed are those who bear the light without crown or collar, for the Kingdom knows no steward but Love."

This is what they feared. This is what we buried.

I placed the gospel where I believed it would remain untouched, but not unreachable. Not entombed, but waiting. I chose a place not gilded with triumph, but quieted by penance—the Oratory of the Good Men of Saint Martin, the house of the ashamed poor.

There, in a reliquary of cedar and silver, beneath the oratory's inner sanctuary, I sealed it with the sigillum of Urbanus Quartus—the sunburst crest of the pope who once sought to unify the fractured host.

You will know it by its mark: the radiant key inside the circle of thorns.

Do not trust the Curia. Do not trust the collectors. If you are to read it, it must be on your knees, not on a table.

The world was not ready in my time. Perhaps it never will be.

But if you have reached this page, then the Spirit has waited long enough.

Go now, and find what I could not protect.

✠ Clemens PP. VII

Pontifex Maximus

Hana sat down on the edge of the bed, her expression unreadable. "The Oratory of San Martino," she said aloud. "A place founded to tend to those who couldn't bear their shame publicly."

Michael nodded. "Exactly where Clement would hide a truth he believed the world wasn't ready for."

Karl looked puzzled. "But it's so small. A single nave, barely wider than a chapel."

"All the more reason," Hana said. "It would be overlooked."

"And it's still functioning," Lukas added, consulting his phone. "Open to the public. Maintained by a lay confraternity. No formal Vatican connection."

Michael's voice was quiet. "Which means no official records. No oversight. No interference."

Hana stood slowly. "Then we go tomorrow. And we find what Clement buried in silence."

CHAPTER

FIFTEEN

FLORENCE, ITALY

Beneath the spire of the Badia Fiorentina, bells tolled Prime as if reluctant to break the hush of the new day. The streets below gradually stirred—shopkeepers raising iron shutters, students sipping espresso at leaning counters, elderly women arranging flowers outside ancient shrines embedded into the stone. And through it all moved the quiet, the practiced, the professional.

They weren't all Florentine.

They wore their anonymity well—camera-laden tourists in linen hats, delivery men just off the piazza, a young priest with a limp and a map of Rome in his pocket. They didn't speak to one another. They had no reason to. But each carried the same instruction, passed from one encrypted message to the next: **Do not interfere. Observe. Report.**

From the rooftop terrace of the Hotel Loggia degli

Artisti, a man named Vittore Aulenti adjusted the focus of a small tripod-mounted monocular and watched the street below where the Mercedes van was parked. His fingers were adorned with a single ring, black onyx set in a gold band—no crest, no flourish. His coat bore the faint scent of musk and cedar, and his eyes never blinked more than necessary.

At precisely 08:47, he murmured into a concealed microphone beneath his collar.

"They're preparing to move."

INSIDE THE HOTEL SUITE, Michael stood at the window, arms crossed loosely over his chest, watching as a tram rumbled past, momentarily obscuring the van from sight. Hana sat at the desk behind him, scrolling through drone footage from their recent search of Santa Lucia. She paused the screen at a shadow that passed briefly across a stained-glass window.

"Again," she said, rewinding a few seconds. "See it?"

Michael leaned in. "Upper left. Someone's standing at the window."

"Not one of ours," she said, "and the nun never left the nave."

"Then someone followed us."

Michael moved to the wall and pulled out his encrypted tablet. A secure link flickered to life.

"Let's bring in Teri," he said.

VATICAN CITY – SUBTERRANEAN COMMS HUB

The screen lit with a soft blue glow as Sister Teri's face appeared, framed by the aura of server lights. Her dark-framed glasses reflected lines of code moving across her lenses. Behind her, the Vatican's core systems blinked silently—a modern heart beating beneath ancient skin.

"You're live," she said. "You're not going to like what I found."

"Talk," Michael said.

Teri leaned forward, her voice low. "Since you arrived in Florence, there's been an access spike on Vatican interdepartmental courier logs—but the requests are coming from an external IP traced to a private network in Frascati."

"Frascati," Hana echoed. "That's not far from Alessandro de' Medici's estate."

"Exactly. And the requesting party used credentials forged to look like they belonged to Monsignor Radelli's restoration division. Sloppy work—someone assumed no one would check."

Michael's face darkened. "So he knows."

"I'd say he's known for days," Teri said. "He's just getting bold now. You're not alone out there."

Michael exhaled slowly. "Can you watch our perimeter?"

"I'll lock Florence down tighter than a conclave," Teri said. "You just stay ahead of whatever's already coming."

BACK IN THE RENTAL VAN, Karl and Lukas finished prepping their gear. Karl slid a discreet sidearm into a thigh holster beneath his jacket. Lukas pulled out a collapsible baton and a comms earpiece shaped like a rosary bead.

"Visible tails?" Lukas asked.

"Two confirmed," Karl said. "Window washer with a tactical profile. Another reading *La Repubblica* too closely."

"Alessandro's tightening the noose."

"He's not ready to close it," Karl said. "Just wants us to know it's there."

Hana emerged from the hotel a moment later, a scarf draped around her neck and sunglasses helping to disguise her.

Michael left the hotel just behind Hana. He didn't look up at the rooftop across the street. But he knew someone was there.

VIA DANTE ALIGHIERI—THE ORATORY OF SAN MARTINO

The Oratorio dei Buonomini di San Martino—or Oratory of the Good Men of Saint Martin—was barely wider than the alley it nestled into, its stone façade humble, its door unmarked by any flourish. A simple carved niche above the entrance held a worn statue of St. Martin dividing his cloak with a beggar.

Inside, the oratory smelled of old paper and incense ground into the wood. The frescoes along the walls—works by anonymous fifteenth-century hands—depicted the silent work of mercy: a man feeding a child, a woman bandaging the arm of a prisoner. No glory. No triumph. Just compassion.

A small wooden altar stood at the front. Ten benches lined the nave.

The caretaker, an elderly man in a pale blue smock, greeted them.

"You are here for research?" he asked in accented English. "You sent inquiry last night."

Michael nodded. "Ecclesiastical history. Pope Urban IV's hidden patronage."

The caretaker smiled faintly. "Few ask for Urban. Most ask for Leo, or Medici. Come. I will show you the sanctuary vault."

They followed him through a narrow side door and down a tight spiral staircase.

The air grew colder. The walls closer.

Below the oratory was a vaulted chamber with a brick floor and a single iron candleholder. An ancient door stood at the rear—nailed shut with a wooden cross.

"This has not been opened since 1805," the caretaker said. "We believe it was once used to bury relics of those who died in quiet disgrace."

Michael's fingers brushed the worn wood. "Thank you. We'll take it from here."

The caretaker nodded once and left.

Michael waited until the footsteps faded, then turned. "Cover the door."

Karl and Lukas stepped back into position, weapons beneath their coats, eyes on the stairs.

Hana knelt beside the sealed chamber. "There's writing here," she said. "Faded Latin."

She read slowly:

"Lucerna abscondita sub mensa. In fovea misericordiae."
A hidden lamp beneath the table. In the hollow of mercy.

Michael felt along the floor, his fingers finding the faint

outline of a circle. He pressed. The tile gave slightly, then released with a muffled click.

A small section of the floor lifted upward.

Beneath it, wrapped in decaying linen, lay a small cedar box banded with silver, the lid sealed with wax imprinted with a blazing sunburst—the sigil of Urban IV.

They had found the reliquary.

But then Hana said, "Wait… Someone's here."

From above, faint but sharp, came the creak of a door. Then another. Then silence.

Karl's hand went to his weapon. Lukas pressed his back to the wall.

Michael looked to Hana. "Seal it. We'll read it later."

She slipped the reliquary into her pack, nodding.

Then the lights went out.

UPSTAIRS, two men stepped into the oratory.

They wore plain clothes. Tourist shoes. One held a folded city map. The other, a phone.

Both paused before the altar, glancing toward the side door.

One gestured toward the sacristy.

But before he could move, a shape dropped from behind the pulpit.

Karl. He moved fast—not to strike, but to block. Lukas came from the side, baton drawn. The confrontation was wordless. One of the men drew a taser. The other a blade.

But they weren't prepared for trained Swiss Guards. In less than thirty seconds, one was unconscious. The other stumbled backward into a bench, cracking his head on the wood. Blood pooled, slow and red.

Karl wiped his brow. "They were here to intercept. Not to observe."

Lukas knelt by the man's belt. No ID, but there was a crest sewn into the inside of his jacket. A Medici lily. Stylized. Modernized. But unmistakable.

Michael stepped into the light, his voice hard. "Get them out of here. Quietly. No police."

Hana's voice was calm, but resolute. "He knows we've found it."

Michael nodded. "But he doesn't know we haven't read it yet."

CHAPTER

SIXTEEN

VILLA AURELIA MEDICI, OUTSIDE ROME

The wine in Alessandro de' Medici's crystal glass remained untouched, the ruby swirl catching only the dim light of his study's sconces. Outside, the cypress trees on the far ridge stood like sentinels beneath the moonlight, unmoving and ancient. He stared past them, into the hills beyond Florence, imagining Michael Dominic and his companions standing amid the ruins of secrets that should have stayed buried.

The Seal of Urban. The cursed gospel. Clement's reckoning.

Everything Alessandro had worked to prevent was slipping beyond containment.

He turned from the window and crossed the room to his desk, where a dossier lay open like a fresh wound. Photographs—grainy but serviceable—captured the priest and the journalist outside Santa Marta al Prato. Others

111

showed the two Swiss Guards lingering near the Falcon jet. One image had been taken from across the square, showing Michael holding something narrow and ancient-looking, wrapped in cloth. That was enough.

He pressed the intercom on the wall. "Bring her in."

Moments later, the door opened and a woman entered —early thirties, composed, with a scholar's poise but the cold eyes of someone trained to lie without blinking. She wore a conservative charcoal suit and carried no bag, no phone. Her name was Valentina Ruspoli, and in the language of shadows, she was Alessandro's scalpel.

"You've read the movements," he said without preamble.

Valentina gave a faint nod. "They're moving faster than expected. Dominic found the fifth letter."

"Of course he did," Alessandro muttered, sinking into the leather chair behind his desk. "It's always him. The pope's pet archivist." His voice turned acidic. "Do we have anyone inside the Archives yet?"

"We have someone," she replied carefully. "The new restoration liaison in the Apostolic Library—Donato Scarella. He's Vatican-born, unambitious, and deeply under our thumb."

Alessandro's brow tightened. "Not the sort to take initiative."

"No. But perfect for inserting data into the Archivum system. If we give him access codes, he can track what files Dominic accesses. Redirect him, even."

Alessandro picked up one of the photographs and turned it over in his hand. "I want Dominic blind. I want his path altered subtly. Don't block him; mislead him. Send him to dead ends, phantom sources, rooms that don't exist."

Valentina's lips curled slightly. "Like the catacombs beneath San Sebastiano?"

Alessandro smiled. "Exactly. Let him chase phantoms while we move for the real prize."

She tilted her head. "The gospel?"

"No… not until we know precisely where it rests," he said, his voice lowering to a measured calm. "The letters are the map, and Dominic is obligingly reading them for us. Once the trail is complete—once he gets close—then we act."

He traced the edge of another photograph with his thumb. "If we reach the reliquary before they do…"

Valentina finished the thought for him. "You can destroy it before the truth becomes unmanageable."

Alessandro nodded slowly. "And with it, the last leverage those fools have over the Medici name."

"We've made further progress," Valentina said, placing a tablet on the desk. "Scarella installed the metadata patch I gave him months ago—he thinks it's a file-tracking enhancement for the Archives' cataloging system."

Alessandro leaned forward, curious. "And it works?"

"Flawlessly. Every time Father Dominic's team logs into the Archive terminals, the program pings our server. We know exactly which files they open and how long they spend on each."

Alessandro smiled faintly. "So the priest leaves his footprints in holy ground, and we follow. Ingenious."

"Just don't praise him for his piety," Valentina replied. "He'd never believe it's been digitized."

There was a pause. Then he added, "Make contact with the Carabinieri's antiquities division. Quietly. We may need them to seize something under the guise of national patrimony. The Vatican won't stop them if it's framed properly."

Valentina noted it without writing. "And the journalist?"

"Hana Sinclair is clever, but not invincible. She's due for a moment of misdirection. Give her something to chase —a false leak from within the Curia. I want her looking the wrong way."

Valentina nodded and stepped back toward the door.

"One more thing," Alessandro said. "When Dominic and his team return to Rome, I want eyes on them from the moment their plane touches down. Use the archivist's assistant if you have to—what's his name?"

"Ian Duffy."

"Yes. The Irishman. See if he's bendable. Everyone breaks for the right reason."

The door shut behind her, and Alessandro de' Medici sat alone, the shadows gathering again around him. He poured the untouched wine back into the bottle and looked once more toward the hills.

"Come home, Dominic," he murmured. "I'm ready for you."

CHAPTER

SEVENTEEN

ROME

Rome simmered under the afternoon sun, the ocher domes and travertine façades of the Eternal City washed in gold and shadow. Valentina Ruspoli stepped out of the black sedan near the Colonnade of St. Peter's, her heels clicking sharply against the worn stones of the Piazza. Around her, tourists ambled with gelato and cameras, oblivious to the centuries of secrets slumbering beneath their feet. She, however, moved with the practiced indifference of someone who walked among ghosts for a living.

She entered the Vatican through Porta di Santa Maria, the side gate reserved for authorized lay personnel, flashing a pass that bore a discreet emblem used only by members of the Apostolic Library's restoration division. The guards barely glanced at her credentials. That was the key: appearing so familiar as to become invisible.

Her destination was the *Archivum Secretum Apostolicum*

Vaticanum—the Secret Archives—though few used the full name anymore. Her real purpose, however, was not to examine fragile manuscripts or inspect climate-control systems. She had come to nudge a few variables out of place. To introduce noise into a symphony that was playing far too smoothly.

Down a corridor humming with low conversation and polished marble, she located Donato Scarella in one of the reading alcoves: small, balding, and fussing nervously over a parchment from the Council of Trent. His hands trembled ever so slightly; whether because of some inherent condition or nervousness, she couldn't tell.

"Signor Scarella," she said with a warm nod, "so sorry to interrupt."

He looked up with the startled guilt of a man caught doing something he hadn't yet decided was wrong. "Oh! Yes, of course, Dottoressa Ruspoli. You're from the restoration office?"

"In part. I've also been seconded to handle certain archival continuity issues related to the Curial transition." That wasn't a lie—at least, not entirely. Bureaucracy was the one thing in the Vatican no one questioned.

"Ah, yes," Scarella said, dabbing at his forehead with a handkerchief. "So many transitions lately. Too many, perhaps."

She sat across from him, smoothing the front of her slate-gray blouse. "It's my understanding that you've been granted limited metadata access to the Archive index?"

Scarella blinked. "Yes, yes, but only on the surface level —nothing under the codified tiers. I'm just an intermediary liaison. I catalog movements, flag anomalies in the request logs."

Valentina smiled. "Perfect. That's exactly what we need."

He looked as though she had just asked him to recite the Nicene Creed backward. "We?"

She leaned in slightly, lowering her voice. "There are those in the Secretariat of State—friends of Cardinal Giovanni Severino—who want to ensure that politically sensitive materials are not being… mishandled."

Scarella paled. "I assure you, I haven't—"

She raised a calming hand. "I know. That's why we're trusting you."

She reached into her portfolio and slid a folded slip of paper across the table. It contained a list of document trails —false ones. Fabricated cross-references that would lead Michael Dominic, if he accessed them, into a spiral of archival dead ends.

"Insert these into the cross-index." Her voice was velvet over steel. "Make them appear organic. Don't draw attention. Just… nudge. If Dominic searches anything connected to Clement VII's letters, these entries should surface."

Scarella stared at the list like it was a page torn from Revelation.

"This will confuse him," he said quietly.

Valentina's smile didn't reach her eyes. "That's the point."

LATER THAT DAY, Valentina slipped through the streets of Trastevere, where centuries of soot clung to medieval walls and the alleys narrowed into shadows. She entered a quiet *enoteca*, where a man waited at a back table beneath an oil painting of the Crucifixion. He wore a priest's collar, but not the bearing of one. His name was Father Manny Esposito, though no one called him that outside of Church payroll.

"You said this was urgent," he said, pouring her a glass of wine she didn't touch.

"We need you to speak with Hana Sinclair."

Esposito arched an eyebrow. "She doesn't exactly keep papal hours."

"Offer her a story. An anonymous source from the Curia. Leak that there was a suppressed council during Clement's papacy—not just a conclave, but a doctrinal trial. Something that leads her to Castel Gandolfo."

"There's nothing at Castel Gandolfo."

"You and I know that, yes. But she doesn't."

Esposito sipped his wine, eyes narrowing. "How far do we go?"

Valentina considered. "Far enough to buy us time—but not so far that she smells the trap. Give her just enough truth to keep her running."

By NIGHTFALL, Valentina was back in her apartment—technically leased under an alias, tucked within a quiet building near the Campo Santo Teutonico. She opened her laptop and activated an encrypted channel.

A moment later, Alessandro's face appeared in grainy silhouette. "Report."

"Scarella has the overlays in place. Dominic's next archive pull will be corrupted. I've also arranged a media decoy for Sinclair."

Alessandro's eyes sharpened. "And Duffy?"

"Not yet. He's cautious. Protective of Dominic. But I'm watching."

He nodded. "Make your next move subtle. I don't want brute force."

"Of course not," she said smoothly. "We're playing a long game."

"No," Alessandro said, his voice like a blade drawn slow from its sheath. "We're playing the endgame."

The screen went dark.

Valentina closed the laptop and stood at the window. The dome of St. Peter's loomed in the distance, gilded and unmoved, like a judgment silently waiting to fall. She folded her arms and stared out across the rooftops.

Let Dominic search. Let Sinclair chase ghosts.

By the time they realized the game had changed, it would already be over.

CHAPTER

EIGHTEEN

VATICAN CITY

The Vatican Gardens lay quiet beneath a canopy of late-morning sun, their hedges immaculately trimmed and fountains murmuring in polite harmony. Beyond the usual crowds of tourists who orbited St. Peter's Basilica like satellites, there remained pockets of peace still known only to the insiders of the Holy See. It was in one of these shaded corners, just behind the Casina Pio IV, that Ian Duffy and Sister Teri had claimed a modest stone bench for their weekly lunch.

Ian unwrapped a parcel of prosciutto and fig sandwiches while Teri pulled a container of roasted artichokes from her canvas tote.

"I still say your version of lunch is more civilized than anything you'd get in the Canteen," he said with a grin.

"Only because you eat like a seminarian with five minutes between Latin and Lamentations," Teri replied, passing him a bottle of San Pellegrino.

They ate in companionable silence for a while, watching two sparrows pecking at the base of a statue of St. Francis. The gentle hum of the gardens and the faint bells of a distant midday Mass gave the hour a suspended feel, as if the world outside Rome had taken a breath.

"You've been keeping an eye on Michael, haven't you?" Teri asked at last, her voice low but direct.

Ian nodded. "Ever since they left for Avignon. Now Florence. I get the sense something's dogging them."

Teri dabbed at her mouth with a napkin. "Same here. I intercepted a curious server ping last night from the Archive database—a search request routed through an approved credential, but… something about it felt spliced. Artificial."

Ian leaned forward. "You think someone's planting false records?"

She nodded. "Or redirecting queries. Not enough to be obvious, but enough to nudge a researcher off course."

Ian sighed, raking a hand through his ginger hair. "I wouldn't put it past Alessandro de' Medici."

Teri's eyes sharpened. "He's resurfaced, then?"

"Not openly. But someone with his kind of reach wouldn't need to do anything openly. Michael mentioned a woman shadowing them in Florence. Didn't get a name, just a look. Professional, detached, like a spy in business-casual."

Teri grimaced. "That's never good."

"Which brings us back to what you mentioned seeing," Ian said, pulling a folded sheet from his pocket—a printout of recent Archive metadata pulls. "Look here. Four requests tied to Clement VII, cross-referenced with known holdings. But these two"—he pointed—"lead to document entries that don't exist. At least, not in our system."

Teri scanned the lines. "They're bait. Someone's trying to lure Michael into a false trail."

"Exactly what I thought. And what you said confirms it."

She looked up at him. "Can you trace the source?"

Ian hesitated. "Maybe. The signature was tagged with an internal IP from the Apostolic Library's restoration division."

Teri raised an eyebrow. "Restoration? That's an odd place for digital mischief."

"Or the perfect place," Ian replied. "It gives them a reason to access fragile documents and justify metadata queries, all without drawing much attention."

They fell quiet again, the weight of their suspicions pressing down through the warmth of the day. Finally, Teri spoke.

"Remember what we said back in March, when that anonymous donor tried to fund the Archives expansion?"

"That nothing in this city comes without strings?"

She nodded. "Same tune, new verse."

Ian looked toward the dome of St. Peter's peeking above the treetops. "Michael trusts us. We can't let him walk into a trap."

"We won't," Teri said firmly. "But we need to be smarter than whoever's playing the board. And quieter."

Ian gave a dry chuckle. "Quiet I can do. Smart might take some coffee."

She smiled. "Then let's get to it."

As they gathered their lunch and left the gardens, neither noticed the man seated on a nearby bench, pretending to read a newspaper. He watched them go with careful eyes, then folded the paper and stood. In his pocket, a phone buzzed once. A text read simply: **DUFFY ACTIVE. NEED SURVEILLANCE.**

The game had widened. And the watchers were now being watched.

CHAPTER

NINETEEN

VATICAN CITY

The early evening light slanted across Rome in copper and rose, catching on the Tiber's surface in long, molten ribbons. The Falcon jet had landed an hour earlier at Ciampino, and now Father Michael Dominic sat in the back seat of the Vatican sedan as it passed the Ponte Sisto, the city's sacred skyline unfolding ahead like a manuscript being unrolled. It was a view he had seen hundreds of times, but tonight it felt darker, somehow layered with unseen ink.

Hana sat beside him, flipping through the transcribed contents of Letter V, her brow furrowed. Every few moments, she would murmur a line aloud—an ancient turn of phrase or a Latin inflection that had lodged in her mind like a splinter. Behind them, Karl and Lukas were unusually quiet—watchful, tense. No one spoke of it, but each of them felt it: the air in Rome was different now. Something unseen had returned with them, like an odorless smoke curling just beneath the surface of their senses.

They passed through the bronze gates of the Vatican compound just as the bells of Vespers began to toll, solemn and slow. The sound echoed through the courtyards and corridors like a benediction held too long. It should have been comforting. It wasn't.

The Archives were dark and quiet. Their footsteps echoed faintly as they made their way inside, the air cool with the scent of old parchments. Michael moved to the main terminal to log their return, but paused. The screen showed several metadata requests from earlier that day— most unremarkable, but two caught his eye. They referenced Clement VII by name, but used search parameters Michael didn't recognize. He tapped the screen to open them, frowning as the queries opened blank entries.

Hana leaned in. "That doesn't look right."

"It's not," Michael said. "I've never seen this string before."

Just then, Ian Duffy entered from the adjoining corridor, his red hair slightly tousled, eyes alert. Behind him came Sister Teri, her usual warmth muted under a thin veil of tension.

"Did you just see those queries?" Ian asked, gesturing toward the screen.

Michael nodded. "I was about to ask you the same."

"We need to talk," Ian's tone, clipped and serious, made Hana glance up sharply.

The group relocated to the staff kitchen just down the hall. The overhead fluorescent lights buzzed softly, and the whir of the old espresso machine filled the silence as Teri made a fresh pot. Ian spread a sheet of paper across the small table, weighted at the corners with sugar packets and a spoon.

"These," he said, tapping several lines, "show up as Clement-related metadata requests. But when you follow them, they route to records that don't exist. Or rather—records that should exist, but don't."

Teri added, "The access logs are real, but the document stubs are fabrications. Someone with restoration-level clearance is planting them."

Michael leaned forward. "That narrows it down considerably."

"I traced the IP signature to the restoration division," Ian said. "Specifically, someone using a subterminal that's only used for external transfers and cataloging.

"Found it," he continued, his fingers flying over the keyboard. "It's not a person—it's a patch. Someone buried a ghost script in the Archive database months ago. Every time you log into a terminal, it broadcasts the session data."

Teri leaned closer. "Who planted it?"

"Donato Scarella," Ian said grimly. "He's the new restoration liaison in the Apostolic Library. He said he was upgrading the catalog, but it's really a homing beacon."

"Can you kill it?"

"Already did. And I left a surprise—anyone trying to access our network now gets a Vatican firewall sermon in Latin."

Teri smiled faintly. "Make sure the translation's merciful."

Ian's grin was sharp. "Mercy's above my pay grade."

Karl, standing just inside the door, folded his arms. "So we're being led?"

Teri nodded. "Someone is trying to control what you find, and more importantly, what you don't."

Michael sat back in his chair, exhaling slowly. "This matches something else. While we were in Florence, Hana received an anonymous tip claiming a suppressed tribunal during Clement's papacy. The message pointed us toward Castel Gandolfo."

"Which we both know is highly unlikely," Hana added. "Clement rarely used the summer palace, and never for doctrinal matters."

Ian frowned. "You think it's connected?"

"I do," Michael said. "It's too convenient. A false archival trail here, a decoy destination there. They're not trying to stop us outright. They want us to keep moving— just in the wrong direction."

Lukas stepped forward, arms crossed. "Then we need to stop playing their game."

Michael nodded. "No. We need to *change* it."

He rose from the table and led the group to the Archives' central map—a floor-to-ceiling diagram of the stacks, vaults, and sub-chambers of the Secret Archives.

"If they're monitoring what we search, we give them something to monitor," he said. "We'll craft a series of controlled inquiries—harmless, but suggestive. Let them believe we're being diverted while we double back to something real."

Karl grunted approvingly. "A false scent."

Teri pulled out her tablet. "I can write a script to insert plausible decoy metadata entries—linked to fabricated subindexes. It'll look like Michael is building toward a revelation."

Ian nodded. "I'll reroute Michael's search credentials

through a separate token. That way, his actual queries won't leave a trace they can follow."

Hana crossed her arms, thoughtful. "And while they watch us dance through their trap, we dig under it."

Michael's expression darkened. "We know now that the letters Clement wrote weren't just confessionals. They were warnings. He knew something—something about this gospel that frightened even him. Whoever's trying to stop us has a vested interest in making sure that fear remains buried."

Teri looked up. "And what about the restoration liaison?"

Ian hesitated. "As before, it looks to be a reprise performance by one Donato Scarella. Low-level, unobtrusive. Perfect for subtle manipulation. But he wouldn't be doing this on his own."

"No," Michael agreed. "Someone's guiding his hand. Likely someone from outside the Vatican hierarchy. Someone like—"

"Alessandro de' Medici," Hana finished.

A silence fell over the room. The name hung like smoke.

Finally, Michael spoke. "Let's prepare the false trail. Tonight. Tomorrow, we act."

ACROSS TOWN, in a small hotel suite overlooking the Via dei Coronari, Valentina Ruspoli sat by the window with a pair of compact binoculars and a closed laptop resting on the table beside her.

Her attention was fixed on a nearby apartment building just opposite the Church of San Salvatore in Lauro. Through the lace curtains, she tracked a junior staffer from the Vatican's Secretariat of State—an overconfident man with a taste for late-night drinks and a loose tongue when pressed just right. Valentina had intercepted one of his routine messages to an internal tech contractor earlier that day. It confirmed what she suspected: someone inside the Archives had begun planting misdirection.

She smiled faintly, folding the binoculars and sliding her phone into a secure pouch.

If Dominic and his allies thought they were moving undetected, they were wrong.

The trap hadn't failed.

It had merely evolved

CHAPTER

TWENTY

ROME

Three days later, Michael stood quietly before the large central map in the Archives, feeling the weight of silence settle around him. The dim overhead lights cast soft shadows across the intricate layout, its vaults and hidden chambers like veins beneath the Vatican's skin. Hana stood close, her fingers gently tracing the edge of Clement's fifth letter, now carefully placed upon the table beside them.

"You think they bought our decoy queries?" she asked softly, her voice laced with a cautious optimism.

Ian glanced up from his laptop, nodding briefly. "The metadata traps Teri and I set are active. Scarella—or whoever's guiding him—should see exactly what we want them to."

Karl leaned against the nearby wall, his arms crossed, studying the map carefully. "Even if they do follow our trail, Alessandro won't be fooled for long. He's too cautious, too paranoid."

Michael nodded thoughtfully. "We don't need long. Just enough to retrace Clement's steps before Alessandro and his people realize they've been misled."

Hana's eyes drifted back down to the letter, its parchment curling slightly at the edges. "Clement was afraid," she murmured, almost to herself. "His warnings feel desperate, as though he were writing against the certainty that he would fail."

Michael moved beside her, feeling a similar dread that Clement must have felt centuries before. "He saw something coming—something he couldn't fully stop, only delay."

Ian's screen flashed briefly, drawing everyone's attention. He leaned forward, fingers flying across the keyboard. "Something's happening. A new metadata pull just registered—fast and automated, coming through restoration-level clearance."

Hovering near Ian's shoulder, Teri tensed. "Scarella's workstation?"

Ian shook his head. "No. Another terminal. Same division, different credentials."

Hana straightened sharply. "Verifying the decoys. Testing our trail."

Lukas finally stepped forward, his usually calm expression tense. "If that's the case, our window just got narrower. We need to act now, decisively."

Ian quickly accessed another document, nodding urgently. "San Sebastiano. We initially thought it was misdirection—but what if Alessandro tried to dismiss it precisely because it held truth?"

Hana's eyes widened in realization. "A double bluff. They'd expect us to ignore it as a phantom lead."

Michael exchanged a decisive glance with Karl. "Then that's precisely where we need to go. Now."

Within moments, the small team had moved swiftly through the darkened corridors of the Archives, emerging into the cool Roman evening. The streets beyond the Vatican's walls lay bathed in shadows, quiet yet charged with an unsettling tension.

Michael felt exposed as they quickly crossed the Piazza and descended toward the waiting Jeep. Karl drove, Lukas beside him, while Michael and Hana sat tensely in the rear, watching the streets slip past. Ian and Teri had remained behind to monitor any activity and provide a digital shield against further interference.

San Sebastiano's ancient façade soon loomed ahead, its classical portico softly illuminated by the glow of distant streetlights. The basilica stood dark and deserted at this late hour, a ghostly sentinel guarding its subterranean secrets.

Inside, the air felt cooler, tinged with the scent of ancient stone and distant incense. Michael moved swiftly toward the entrance to the catacombs, carefully descending the worn marble steps. Hana followed close behind, the soft beam of her flashlight cutting through the heavy darkness.

The tunnels beneath were labyrinthine, oppressive, whispering echoes bouncing gently off damp walls lined with tomb niches. Michael navigated cautiously, guided only by memory and intuition drawn from Clement's cryptic hints.

Karl paused, shining his beam toward a distant fresco, faded but visible in fragments. "Look," he said, illuminating an image of a woman cloaked entirely in red. "Mary Magdalene—the penitent beneath the scarlet veil. Another reference."

Michael stepped forward urgently, examining the fresco closely. Beneath it, a small niche, almost hidden by shadows, contained a narrow stone reliquary. His pulse quickened as he gently pried it open, revealing an intricately carved wooden tube—olivewood and brass, bearing Clement's unmistakable mark.

"Clement's sixth letter," he breathed, lifting it reverently.

Hana placed a steadying hand on his arm, both sharing the weight of history and urgency of their mission.

Above, in the world they had briefly left behind, Alessandro's spies moved in confusion, chasing ghosts conjured by Ian and Teri's digital sleight of hand.

But down here, deep beneath Rome, Michael and his team stood on the threshold of revelation—one that Clement had hidden away, knowing the chaos it would unleash, yet desperate to entrust it to those who might one day understand its true significance.

CHAPTER

TWENTY-ONE

VATICAN CITY

The journey back from San Sebastiano was undertaken in tense silence. Michael cradled Clement's sixth letter in his lap, fingers absently tracing the carved olivewood tube as if to reassure himself of its tangible reality. Beside him, Hana stared into the passing night, eyes lost in thought. Karl maneuvered his Jeep smoothly through Rome's ancient streets, with Lukas remaining alert, scanning the shadows for any sign of pursuit.

Returning to the Archives felt like surfacing after too long underwater, emerging into a space that, while not entirely safe, at least bore the familiarity of home ground. Michael took a moment, reassured by its quiet constancy. But the quiet held no comfort tonight—only a stark reminder of the danger encircling them.

Ian was waiting, pacing anxiously near the main workstation, Teri close by, her eyes fixed on her tablet.

"They've noticed," Ian said immediately, his voice tight with tension. "The metadata entries we planted are drawing attention. The forged credentials are actively tracking them now, checking our trail. It won't fool them for long."

Michael nodded, carefully setting the wooden tube down on the central table. "We don't need much longer. We have Clement's sixth letter, and this may change everything."

Hana reached forward, gently sliding the wax seal away from the tube's edge, her movements careful, reverent. Michael extracted the scroll within, spreading it carefully under the soft, protective glow of the reading lamp. The parchment crackled softly, the sound carrying centuries of whispers.

Clement's handwriting, flowing and precise despite his evident urgency, filled the page:

To the seeker who follows these lines:

Know that I write from a city shrouded in darkness and guarded by silence. Our fear of truth's upheaval binds tighter than chains of iron, hiding the light beneath the seventh star, where scripture and heaven meet.

You, bearer of light, must look beyond mere words. Beneath the great basilica, under the golden canopy that honors Peter's rest, lies the truth you seek. Yet, I caution you: unveiling it may fracture the foundations upon which all has been built. Act with wisdom, for the eyes of many, unseen and malevolent, watch from shadows older than the stones of Rome.

✠ Clemens PP. VII
Pontifex Maximus

Michael exhaled slowly, absorbing the gravity of

Clement's final warnings. "St. Peter's Basilica. Beneath Bernini's baldacchino." Rising like a sculpted veil of bronze beneath the magnificent dome of St. Peter's Basilica, the *baldacchino* is a towering canopy, over thirty meters high, that covers the high altar directly above what tradition holds to be the tomb of St. Peter.

Hana raised an eyebrow. "The Vatican's heart. The very place where such a secret could cause the greatest harm—or do the greatest good."

Ian folded his arms, face set in deep thought. "That's no small feat. Getting beneath the baldacchino isn't like accessing some forgotten side chapel. That area's monitored constantly—Swiss Guards, surveillance, sensors."

Karl grunted in agreement. "Even Lukas and I can't just stroll down beneath the altar without proper clearance. We'd need approval from Cardinal Severino himself, and that's no simple request."

"Unless," Teri interjected quietly, "we can engineer a reason for authorized entry. Something urgent enough to justify the exception."

Hana's gaze sharpened. "A credible threat. Something that demands inspection immediately—perhaps a potential structural vulnerability or an artifact in danger of deterioration."

Ian nodded thoughtfully. "We could suggest a restoration urgency—carefully coordinated through official channels."

Michael hesitated, troubled by the risks involved. "If we're caught manipulating this, the consequences will be dire."

Hana met his eyes evenly, her voice firm. "But if we

don't act now, Alessandro moves first. Clement's warning couldn't be clearer. This is the pivotal moment."

Michael finally nodded, acknowledging the grim necessity. "Then we proceed carefully. Ian, Teri—prepare the restoration request. It must look entirely legitimate. Karl, Lukas—coordinate quietly with the guards. They must expect our arrival without knowing our true intent."

The team dispersed swiftly, each to their respective tasks. Michael remained at the central table, eyes fixed on Clement's letter.

Hana stepped beside him, her voice soft yet resolute. "Michael, Clement entrusted this secret to the future—to us. He believed, despite everything, that truth had value greater than safety."

He looked at her, drawing quiet strength from her certainty. "I know. And yet I fear the cost Clement himself foresaw. He saw something terrible in this gospel, something that frightened even him."

"Perhaps," she conceded gently. "But remember his own words: *'Bearer of light.'* He trusted that someday, someone would have the courage he didn't have."

Michael exhaled deeply. "Then let's ensure his trust wasn't misplaced."

Within the hour, Ian and Teri had carefully crafted the urgent restoration authorization, routing it through internal systems in a manner designed to withstand scrutiny. Karl and Lukas made subtle inquiries, ensuring their appearance beneath the basilica would arouse no immediate suspicion.

Just before midnight, the group approached St. Peter's Basilica, its immense façade looming majestically beneath the moonlit sky. The great bronze doors, usually thrown wide in welcome, stood closed, an imposing barrier.

Inside, under Karl's guidance, they moved through shadowed aisles toward the baldacchino, the immense bronze canopy beneath Michelangelo's soaring dome. Michael felt the weight of history and faith pressing down, more tangible now than ever.

Karl nodded toward a discreet stairwell near the altar, ordinarily used only by clergy or restoration specialists. Lukas produced the approved access documents for a waiting Swiss Guard, who inspected them briefly before stepping aside. The descent felt interminable, each step echoing softly, carrying them deeper into the Vatican's concealed foundations.

Finally, beneath the central altar, they entered a crypt-like chamber, its air cool and heavy with antiquity. Dim lights illuminated the ancient masonry walls, lined with the tombs of past popes and martyrs. The quiet here was dense, palpable, charged with the silent weight of centuries.

Michael's eyes scanned carefully, recalling Clement's words. "Look beyond mere words."

Hana moved deliberately, flashlight in hand, illuminating small inscriptions and carvings as she methodically traced every detail etched into the ancient walls. The symbols here were subtle, many nearly erased by the slow erosion of time. Minutes stretched on, tension coiling tightly with each passing second.

"There's nothing obvious," she murmured in frustration, her voice echoing softly off the stone.

Michael joined her, examining each carving intently, his mind racing through Clement's coded guidance. The carvings depicted faded biblical scenes, allegorical symbols—keys, chalices, olive branches—each examined and dismissed.

Lukas spoke from behind, his voice tense. "We shouldn't linger. If anyone's been tracking us, they'll know we're here."

Karl stood rigidly at the crypt's entrance, vigilant, a quiet sentinel aware of the vulnerabilities surrounding them. "Keep searching," he urged softly. "We've come too far to turn back now."

Michael's fingers brushed gently over worn masonry until they rested on a particular niche, almost completely hidden behind a row of eroded inscriptions. The stone felt subtly different here—smoother, almost polished, suggesting recent intervention in a place otherwise untouched by modern hands.

"Hana, bring the light here," he whispered urgently.

She directed her beam carefully, revealing a small carved panel almost invisible beneath layers of accumulated grime. Michael carefully scraped away centuries of dust and residue, gradually revealing a familiar shape—the delicate outline of a sunburst, Pope Urban's unmistakable seal.

"Urban's seal," Hana breathed, excitement tempered by caution. "But it's too deep. It looks recessed, deliberately hidden."

Karl moved swiftly to their side, assessing the carving with professional precision. "This isn't just carved stone," he mumbled. "It's a separate panel, fitted tightly—likely a concealed compartment. Stand back."

He produced a small, precise pry tool from his gear and began carefully working around the edges, his movements methodical, patient, aware of the fragility of the ancient stonework. The sound of metal gently scraping stone felt amplified in the oppressive silence.

Sweat beaded on Karl's brow as the minutes ticked

slowly past. The panel refused to yield easily, firmly resisting their efforts.

"It won't budge," Lukas murmured tensely, glancing nervously toward the crypt entrance. Karl reached over and brushed dust from Lukas's sleeve, a quick, unconscious gesture. Lukas gave him a look—half reprimand, half gratitude—and gave his partner a knowing smile.

Hana stepped forward, studying the panel closely. "Wait," she said thoughtfully. "Clement was meticulous. Perhaps there's another step, something we've missed."

Michael's mind flashed rapidly through Clement's previous letters, the cryptic phrases he had committed to memory. His pulse quickened as an idea took hold. *"'Beyond mere words.'"*

"Words," he murmured, darting back to the faded Latin inscriptions nearby. "The key might be in the inscriptions."

Hana directed her flashlight beam again, illuminating the worn text. They read swiftly, urgently searching for anything significant. One phrase stood apart, less faded: *"Lux in tenebris lucet"*—"Light shines in the darkness."

Instinctively, Michael pressed gently against these words, feeling the stone shift ever so slightly beneath his touch. Encouraged, he applied firmer pressure. With a soft grinding sound, the stone moved slightly inward, releasing a hidden mechanism.

At the exact moment, Karl again pried at the panel bearing Urban's seal. This time, it yielded slowly, opening just enough to reveal a narrow hollow inside.

Michael reached cautiously into the dark recess, fingers brushing against something smooth and cold—a reliquary of cedar and silver, precisely as Clement had described. But even now, its extraction was delicate, each movement painstakingly precise to avoid damaging either the artifact or the fragile masonry around it.

After long, tense minutes of careful maneuvering, Michael finally lifted the reliquary free, placing it reverently upon the stone surface before them.

Hana's eyes reflected awe and quiet triumph as he slowly lifted the lid.

Inside, wrapped meticulously in crimson silk, rested an ancient manuscript—the *Gospel of the Beloved*.

Silence filled the chamber, profound and reverent. Michael's voice broke the hush softly. "We've found it. Clement's fear and hope, hidden in shadows for centuries."

Hana gently touched the ancient silk. "Now, we must decide what comes next. Because whatever we choose, history will remember."

Above them, Rome lay unaware of the profound revelation unfolding in its silent heart. Yet somewhere in the darkened city, Alessandro de' Medici felt a subtle shift, an instinctual understanding that the game had changed irrevocably—and not in his favor.

CHAPTER

TWENTY-TWO

VATICAN CITY

Michael's breath felt trapped in his chest as he stared down at the ancient manuscript, illuminated softly by the golden glow of the flashlight Hana held steady. Beneath the massive bronze baldacchino of St. Peter's Basilica, the air was thick and silent, heavy with history and secrets.

"The *Gospel of the Beloved*," Michael murmured, the name a whispered reverence. He reached out with a gloved hand and gently peeled back the crimson silk, revealing delicate, meticulous script in Greek and Coptic, written with a precision and elegance that defied the centuries.

Hana leaned in, eyes wide with awe. "It's breathtaking," she whispered. "It looks untouched by time."

Karl and Lukas stood close, their stance protective, their eyes alert to any sound from above. Lukas shifted slightly, glancing toward the stairwell. "We shouldn't linger. This place isn't secure."

Michael nodded reluctantly, carefully closing the reliquary and wrapping it again in the silk. He felt the weight of responsibility as tangible as the manuscript itself. "We must get this to the Archives immediately. Securely. And quietly."

Karl stepped forward. "Then we move now."

Ascending the narrow stairway felt even more arduous than their descent. Each creak of ancient stone beneath their feet seemed to echo loudly through the hallowed basilica. At the top, the Swiss Guard posted near the altar merely nodded respectfully, oblivious to the magnitude of what they carried past him.

Outside, beneath the cool Roman night sky, their steps quickened. Michael kept the reliquary close, his fingers curled protectively around it. His heartbeat was steady but fast, an underlying rhythm of urgency propelling him forward.

Ian and Sister Teri met them at the entrance of the Archives. Their faces showed immediate relief upon seeing the team return safely.

"Thank God," Ian breathed, stepping forward quickly. "Did you find it?"

Michael held the reliquary toward him, expression grave. "It's here, Ian. It's real."

Ian's breath caught audibly. "Let's get it inside. Teri has secured the digital trails, but Alessandro's people are relentless."

Once deep within the vaults of the Archives, behind layers of encrypted security protocols, Michael finally allowed himself a moment to breathe. Under the sterile white light of their private examination room, he once more opened the reliquary. Together, the small group stood silently, their eyes tracing lines written nearly two millennia ago.

Michael spoke first. "Clement wasn't exaggerating. If authentic, this gospel would completely transform our understanding of the early Church."

Hana's voice was firm. "Then we need to verify it, thoroughly and beyond question."

Michael nodded. "We start with non-invasive analysis. Ink composition, parchment dating, stylistic comparisons. Ian, get the infrared and multispectral imaging set up. Teri, I need a secure database comparison against known apocrypha—quickly and discreetly."

Ian and Teri moved efficiently, each familiar with the protocol of examining sensitive materials. The examination room became a quiet hive of activity, meticulous and reverent.

Michael stepped aside briefly, motioning Hana to join him.

"Hana," he began softly, "this is beyond us. If this gospel proves genuine, the implications reach far beyond our control. We might be facing the very schism Clement feared."

She studied him carefully. "But this isn't just about doctrine, Michael. It's about truth. Clement knew that— even when he hid it."

Michael exhaled deeply, the weight of centuries pressing down upon him. "We must inform Cardinal Severino. I trust his wisdom—even in this."

Hana hesitated. "And if he orders it sealed away again?"

Michael's gaze was steady. "Then we face that decision together."

A quiet knock interrupted them. Karl stood in the doorway, his expression serious. "A woman named Valentina Ruspoli was permitted entry to Vatican City twenty minutes ago, acting as a representative of Alessandro de' Medici. She's making direct inquiries about your movements tonight."

Michael's jaw tightened. "He moves fast. Well, we just need to be faster."

Karl nodded grimly. "We'll delay her. But whatever you're going to do—do it quickly."

Back at the manuscript, Ian straightened abruptly. "Michael, look at this."

The infrared scans revealed hidden annotations in the margins—notes invisible to the naked eye, written in faint, precise Latin.

"It's Clement's hand," Michael said, recognizing the writing instantly. He read aloud slowly, translating: "'*Here lies truth that Rome is not prepared to bear. Preserve it, for when the soul of the Church is ready.'*"

Hana's voice was solemn. "He intended this for the future—knowing it would one day be found."

Michael stepped back, looking around the quiet circle of faces. "Then we honor his intention. We protect and preserve this gospel until it can be safely revealed to the world. We document every aspect meticulously. And above all, we keep it hidden from those who would destroy it."

Teri raised an eyebrow. "And Alessandro?"

Michael's voice dropped to a careful whisper. "We give him what he expects—decoys, false leads. Let him chase shadows while we secure the truth."

Karl and Lukas exchanged approving glances. Ian nodded gravely.

Hana stepped close beside Michael, her eyes determined. "Then let's get started. Authenticate first."

And deep beneath the Vatican, shielded by secrecy and shadows, they began their careful, sacred work—knowing that the truth they now protected was powerful enough to either redeem or rupture the very foundations of their faith.

CHAPTER

TWENTY-THREE

SANTA CECILIA MONASTERY, ROME

In the soft half-light of the Vatican Archives' inner sanctum, Michael stood motionless, his gaze transfixed on the ancient manuscript. The *Gospel of the Beloved* lay gently illuminated beneath the specialized lamps, each ink stroke clear and vibrant, defying the erosion of time.

Ian approached quietly, his tablet glowing softly. "Initial scans confirm everything, Michael," he whispered. "The parchment and inks date accurately to the first century. No evident signs of forgery or later alterations."

Michael nodded slowly, exhaling a long-held breath. "Then it's authentic. This truly could be a gospel contemporary to Christ himself."

Hana glanced up, eyes wide with barely contained excitement and caution. "We must confirm beyond doubt.

We need independent scholars, experts who won't bend to the Church or the Medici."

Michael considered this carefully. "Yet how do we reveal it without inciting the chaos Clement feared?"

"Controlled exposure," Ian suggested gently. "One scholar at a time, trusted but independent, each unaware of the others. If we're careful, we can validate without risk of leaks or manipulation."

Michael nodded. "Then we proceed quietly. Hana, reach out to our contacts at Cambridge and Heidelberg. Ian, arrange secure transfers of anonymized scans—no physical exposure yet."

Karl appeared in the doorway, expression tense but resolute. "Valentina Ruspoli has been spotted again, now closer to the Archives. We need to move."

Michael's jaw tightened slightly. "Secure the manuscript in the deep vault. Triple-layered encryption. No access without my personal biometric clearance."

Ian moved quickly, carefully sealing the manuscript within its protective casing, each action meticulous, methodical, and respectful of its immense value.

Minutes later, Michael, Hana, Karl, and Lukas emerged into the cool Roman night. Their steps quickened as they traversed the familiar, shadowed pathways of the Vatican. As they passed beneath the bronze gates, Michael felt the weight of unseen eyes following them, the prickling sensation of Alessandro's extensive network.

Lukas spoke quietly, urgently. "A black sedan, second street, fifty meters behind."

Karl nodded subtly. "I noticed it earlier. They've been tracking us since we left the Archives."

Michael's pulse quickened. "We need to throw them off."

Hana motioned toward the narrow side streets near Castel Sant'Angelo. "Through there. It's a maze they won't navigate easily."

Moving swiftly, they entered the winding Roman alleyways, footsteps echoing off ancient brick and stone. The sedan slowed behind them, its headlights casting long shadows ahead.

Karl led decisively, guiding them through alleys barely wider than their shoulders, under arches scarred by centuries, until the vehicle's lights vanished completely. They emerged cautiously near the Tiber, breathing heavily, senses heightened.

Michael turned, his voice low but determined. "Alessandro won't give up. We're only buying moments."

"Then let's use them wisely," Hana urged. "We must secure a safe location outside the Vatican where we can breathe. Someplace neutral."

"Trastevere," Michael suggested quickly. "There's a monastery—Santa Cecilia. The abbess owes me a favor. It's secluded, quiet, and most importantly, beyond Alessandro's immediate reach."

They crossed the Ponte Sisto at a brisk pace and vanished into Trastevere's maze of narrow streets. The district's late-night stir—voices behind closed shutters, clinking glasses, scooters echoing down side alleys—was perfect camouflage. Skirting the last of the tavernas, they approached the monastery as its soft lantern glow came into view.

A young nun answered the door, her sandals whispering against the stone as she stepped into the lantern glow. She was no more than twenty, with clear, earnest eyes and the quiet composure of someone still learning the rhythm of monastic life.

"Buona sera," she said softly. "You are expected?"

Michael inclined his head. "Sister Maria Francesca will know why we've come."

The young nun nodded, then motioned for them to follow her through the cloister walkway. Their footsteps echoed beneath the arches, the scent of damp stone and rosemary trailing with them as they crossed the dim courtyard. She led them through a side corridor lit only by a pair of wall lamps, then paused outside a modest chamber door.

"I will tell the abbess you've arrived," she whispered, disappearing inside.

A moment later, Sister Maria Francesca emerged, her expression warm with recognition and framed with just a trace of concern.

"Father Dominic," she said, her voice calm and steady, "what troubles bring you here tonight?"

Michael spoke plainly, voice quiet yet firm. "We need sanctuary, Sister. The Vatican is no longer safe for what we carry."

Her gaze softened with understanding. "Come, quickly."

Within minutes, the group settled in a modest yet secure room deep within the monastery walls. Michael carefully laid out the digital scans, the virtual evidence of their astonishing discovery.

Hana took a deep breath, steadying herself. "We must consider every step from here carefully."

Karl and Lukas stood guard outside the room, their vigilant eyes alert to every movement, every shadow. Inside, Michael faced Sister Maria Francesca solemnly.

"We hold a gospel that challenges every cornerstone the Church rests upon," he admitted quietly. "We need your help to protect it until we're ready to present it to the world."

The abbess nodded slowly, thoughtfully. "Then it shall be so. The walls of Santa Cecilia have guarded secrets before, Father Dominic. They will do so again."

Michael's gratitude was clear, but so too was the gravity of his task. "Hana, Ian, you know our next moves. We must work swiftly and carefully."

Ian began setting up secure communication lines, discreetly routing signals through multiple encrypted channels. Hana meticulously organized data packets for anonymous dissemination to selected scholars.

Outside the monastery, across Rome's dark rooftops, Valentina Ruspoli stood silently, watching. Her posture was one of patient determination. Her phone vibrated softly.

"Report," Alessandro's voice commanded quietly.

"They've secured temporary refuge at Santa Cecilia," she responded evenly. "Dominic thinks he's bought time."

Alessandro's voice was calm yet icy. "Then let him think so. Watch closely. The moment they reveal their contacts, intercept swiftly. Ensure the manuscript never reaches the public."

Valentina acknowledged this briefly, her eyes never leaving the monastery. The night stretched silently around her, a chessboard on which the final moves were slowly, inexorably being set into motion.

Within Santa Cecilia's secure walls, Michael sat with quiet resolve, eyes fixed on the digital screen, watching the encrypted messages travel to their first recipients. The truth Clement had hidden, entrusted to them across the gulf of centuries, now rested heavily upon his shoulders.

Hana placed a reassuring hand on his arm, her voice gentle but unwavering. "Whatever happens, Michael, we'll face it together."

He met her eyes, finding strength and certainty in her steadfast gaze. "Together," he echoed softly.

Outside, Rome lay still, unaware of the quiet revolution beginning beneath the stars.

CHAPTER

TWENTY-FOUR

SANTA CECILIA MONASTERY, ROME

Within the quiet sanctuary of Santa Cecilia, Michael Dominic had barely slept, his mind endlessly churning through the labyrinth of revelations and threats now converging upon him.

He stood at the small window of his guest cell, gazing pensively at the waking streets beyond the monastery walls as dawn crept softly over Rome. Amber light stretched across terracotta rooftops and marble domes, gently nudging the Eternal City awake. Each passerby below seemed suspect now—a potential watcher sent by Alessandro or a shadowed emissary of a Curia unwilling to confront the truths stirring beneath its foundations.

A soft knock sounded, followed by Hana's voice from the adjacent cell. "Michael? Are you awake?"

He opened the door that connected their two small

rooms. Hana stepped into the threshold, wrapped in a simple wool shawl the sisters had provided. The rustle of fabric was the only sign of her fitful sleep.

"Any news?" she asked, rubbing a hand through her hair.

"Nothing yet," Michael said quietly. "Ian's analysis should come through soon. We'll know definitively if the independent scholars support the authenticity of the gospel."

She moved closer to the window, careful not to cross fully into his room, and looked out at the peaceful streets below—a deceptive tranquility masking deeper currents of danger. "Even if they do, Alessandro won't stop. He'll escalate."

Michael nodded, brow tightening. "We need to anticipate his next move. He's been cautious, careful to avoid direct confrontation. But patience has limits, even his."

Another knock—firmer this time—cut through the quiet. Michael opened the outer door to find Karl waiting in the corridor, his expression grave.

"You need to see this."

Michael and Hana exchanged a brief, tense glance, then followed Karl quickly to the small library where Ian and Teri sat hunched over a laptop. Ian's normally composed demeanor was visibly shaken.

"What is it?" Michael asked.

"Cambridge and Heidelberg scholars confirmed the manuscript's authenticity," Ian said, his voice tense but clear. "And somehow, Alessandro's network has intercepted one of the analyses. They now know what we have. Exactly."

Michael's jaw tightened. "How?"

Teri adjusted her glasses, a sheen of anxiety in her eyes. "A digital breach. They accessed our secure channel—briefly, but it was enough. Valentina Ruspoli's signature is all over it."

Hana's voice sharpened, urgency clear. "Then we must move quickly. If Alessandro knows, the Curia might soon as well. We have to safeguard the manuscript—immediately."

Karl stepped forward, his eyes darkly resolute. "There's a secure Swiss Guard facility just outside the city. Discreet, well-protected. Alessandro's reach is extensive, but even he would struggle to penetrate its defenses."

Michael considered this carefully, nodding slowly. "We go immediately. Secure the manuscript and ensure its protection. But first, we need a diversion—something to distract Alessandro, to buy us time."

"I can help," Teri said decisively. "A controlled leak—disinformation fed into their channels. A phantom manuscript being moved to Florence, or even Avignon."

Michael looked at her gratefully. "Do it. Quickly and convincingly."

The group mobilized swiftly, each knowing precisely their role. Ian assisted Teri in crafting the deception, carefully layering enough detail to seem credible yet vague enough to hold Alessandro's attention. Karl and Lukas secured discreet transport, their movements precise, focused.

Within the hour, Michael stood in the monastery courtyard, the ancient cedar and silver reliquary securely encased within a nondescript protective container. He handed it solemnly to Karl, his voice heavy with significance. "Guard it with your lives."

Karl's gaze met Michael's with quiet intensity. "We will, Father Dominic."

The Swiss Guards departed swiftly, their vehicle slipping unnoticed into the morning traffic. Michael watched until it vanished from view, his heart heavy with anxiety yet resolved in purpose.

Hana stood beside him, watching carefully. "Do you think the decoy will work?"

"It must," Michael answered. "Alessandro will chase shadows long enough for us to fortify our position."

Suddenly, his phone vibrated insistently. His eyes widened in alarm as he scanned the message. "We have another problem."

"What now?"

"It's Cardinal Severino. He's demanding my immediate presence at the Apostolic Palace. He says he knows about the manuscript."

Michael felt a cold knot tighten in his stomach. "If Severino knows, it's only a matter of time before the pope himself is involved."

Hana's voice was edged with worry. "Then this confrontation can't be avoided."

Michael steadied himself, exhaling slowly. "I'll go alone. You, Ian, and Teri stay here. Remain hidden until we know more."

"Michael," Hana began softly, concern clear in her gaze, but he raised a gentle hand to silence her.

"It has to be this way, Hana. Severino's summoned me specifically. If he sees a threat, he'll react immediately. We must show strength, not weakness. Protect the truth at all costs."

She met his eyes with deep understanding. "Then be careful. We'll be waiting."

Michael left swiftly, navigating through the bustling morning streets toward the heart of Vatican City. The Apostolic Palace loomed ahead, grand and imposing, its shadow stretching long and deep across the Piazza San Pietro. His footsteps echoed loudly against marble halls as Swiss Guards guided him to Severino's private chambers.

The cardinal stood waiting, his eyes sharp and calculating, his posture rigid with barely suppressed tension. "Father Dominic," he greeted coldly. "I believe you have something that threatens the very foundations of the Church."

Michael held Severino's penetrating gaze without faltering. "The truth, Eminence, is never a threat. Only our fear of it."

Severino's lips thinned into a tense line. "Spare me the philosophy. Do you comprehend what damage this manuscript could unleash? Schism, upheaval, rebellion against centuries of doctrine."

"Or," Michael responded firmly, "it could heal a fracture long hidden beneath layers of secrecy and silence. Faith strong enough to withstand the truth is faith worth protecting."

Severino stepped forward, eyes dark and resolute. "You will surrender the manuscript, Father Dominic. Immediately. This is not a request—it is a command."

Michael stood firm, his resolve unshakable. "I cannot, Eminence. The truth entrusted to me is greater than any single authority."

The cardinal's voice lowered dangerously. "Then you leave me no choice. By defying me, you defy the Church itself."

Michael met Severino's gaze evenly, voice calm but

unyielding. "If it means preserving the integrity of the faith, then so be it."

Severino regarded him silently for a moment, then nodded once sharply. "Then prepare yourself, Father Dominic. You have chosen your path—and its consequences."

Michael turned and walked deliberately from the chamber, feeling the full weight of Severino's threat bearing down upon him. The battle lines were drawn, the stakes unimaginably high, and the storm long brewing was finally upon them.

CHAPTER
TWENTY-FIVE

ROME

Michael moved swiftly back through the Vatican halls, his mind a storm of determination and quiet dread. Severino's warning had been clear—the Church would move against him. Every shadowed archway and corridor felt like it concealed watchers, spies who reported directly to the cardinal or, worse, to Alessandro de' Medici.

He emerged from the Apostolic Palace into daylight so bright it felt like an assault after the oppressive gloom of Severino's chambers. A quick glance around confirmed what he already suspected—two plainclothes figures standing discreetly near the colonnade, observing his every movement.

Heart racing, Michael made an immediate decision. He took out his phone, swiftly dialing Ian. "They're watching me," he said quietly into the phone, not waiting for a greeting. "Clear everything sensitive from Santa Cecilia. Now."

Ian's voice was clipped, professional. "Understood. We'll move immediately. Stay visible, keep their attention away from us."

Michael ended the call and deliberately slowed his pace, allowing the observers ample opportunity to follow as he walked openly across St. Peter's Square toward the bridge leading to Castel Sant'Angelo. Each step felt loaded with consequence, his pulse quickening as his followers subtly moved closer.

Across town, Ian, Teri, and Hana worked urgently within the quiet sanctuary of Santa Cecilia, swiftly dismantling their makeshift analysis station. Ian secured the digital data onto encrypted drives, passing them carefully to Hana.

"We'll move in pairs," Ian instructed calmly. "Separate routes, separate safe locations. We regroup only when we know it's clear."

Hana nodded, her expression tight but resolute. "Teri, you're with me. Ian, meet us at the agreed-upon location tonight. Do not engage anyone."

Within minutes, they dispersed, each slipping silently out of the monastery into the bustling anonymity of Rome's streets.

Michael continued across Ponte Sant'Angelo, the statues of angels lining the bridge silent sentinels to his perilous journey. Midway across, he paused, feigning contemplation of the Tiber flowing beneath. From the corner of his eye, he confirmed his pursuers' presence—closer now, closing in subtly.

"Father Dominic," came a voice behind him—smooth, cultured, yet laced with menace.

Michael turned slowly, confronting Valentina's cool gaze directly. Her composure was unsettlingly calm. "Signora Ruspoli, I presume," he greeted, maintaining his outward calm.

"We both know what you possess," Valentina said evenly, getting to the point. "You cannot possibly believe you'll win this. Alessandro is not a man who tolerates threats."

Michael's expression hardened. "Truth is not a threat, Signora. It's a revelation. Your employer's resistance only proves its necessity."

A slight, cold smile touched her lips. "Idealism won't save you or your friends, Father Dominic. Give us the manuscript, and you might walk away from this unharmed."

Michael met her gaze steadily, unwavering. "'*Might?*' How reassuring. Even if I had it, I would never yield it to those who seek its destruction."

Valentina's eyes narrowed dangerously. "Then understand this clearly—you've left us no choice. Alessandro will move decisively, and you will regret your defiance."

With that, she turned and walked swiftly away, vanishing into the crowd.

Michael's heart pounded painfully in his chest. He knew precisely what her words meant—immediate, ruthless action. He urgently dialed Hana's number.

She answered instantly. "Michael?"

"They're accelerating," he warned quickly. "Get off the street. Get to safety immediately."

"Understood." Hana's voice was steady, focused. "We'll find cover. Stay safe, Michael."

Michael pocketed his phone and moved swiftly off the

bridge, weaving through the crowded Roman streets, each face a potential threat. He navigated instinctively toward the Swiss Guard facility where Karl and Lukas had secured the manuscript. The city blurred around him, urgency propelling him forward.

At the secure facility, Karl met Michael with grave eyes. "We received word about your encounter. We're preparing for possible intrusion."

Michael nodded tightly. "They'll come quickly, Karl. Alessandro won't risk waiting."

Karl led Michael inside, through corridors buzzing with tense, disciplined activity. In a secure chamber, Lukas stood vigilantly beside the sealed reliquary. He nodded curtly as they entered. "All is quiet for now."

Michael approached the reliquary reverently, placing a protective hand upon it. "Ensure this is guarded at all costs. No matter what happens to me, this manuscript must survive."

Karl's eyes blazed with determined loyalty. "We will protect it with our lives, Father Dominic."

Michael felt a brief, profound gratitude before the sound of raised voices echoed urgently through the facility corridors.

A young guard appeared breathlessly at the doorway. "Intruders approaching the perimeter, heavily armed. Confirmed hostile intent."

Karl and Lukas exchanged immediate glances of tactical understanding, their training taking over instantly. "Secure the reliquary," Karl commanded. "Seal the chamber."

Lukas quickly moved to secure the artifact within a reinforced vault.

Michael felt helplessness twist sharply within him, knowing he could do little now but wait.

Outside, the sudden sound of gunfire shattered the afternoon peace, sharp and unmistakable. Karl moved swiftly, weapon drawn, positioning himself protectively between Michael and the entrance. "Stay here," he ordered firmly.

Chaos erupted rapidly outside—shouts, gunfire, alarms blaring urgently. Michael's pulse hammered in his ears, each second stretching painfully. The facility shook as an explosion echoed through the halls, followed by silence, chilling and absolute.

The chamber door shuddered violently under sudden assault, blows raining down with relentless force. Karl braced, weapon aimed, eyes steeled with resolution. Michael stood behind him, heart pounding, prepared to face whatever came next.

The door burst violently inward, smoke and debris clouding the entrance. Armed figures surged through the breach, their intentions unmistakable.

Karl fired immediately, precise and disciplined, yet vastly outnumbered.

Amid the chaos, Michael glimpsed Valentina entering calmly, her expression unchanged despite the violence surrounding her. Her eyes met his across the chamber, cold, unwavering, utterly resolved with her gun aimed at him.

"Father Dominic," she said coolly over the gunfire, "it's over. Surrender the gospel, or watch everyone you care about fall."

Michael's gaze flickered briefly to Karl's determined defense, then returned to Valentina's ruthless stare. His voice was firm, resolute. "The truth will survive, even if we do not."

She calmly raised a weapon, its barrel fixed unwaveringly upon him. "Then you've sealed your fate."

TWENTY-SIX

ROME

Gunfire echoed in Michael's ears, the acrid tang of smoke sharp in his nostrils. He stared unwaveringly at Valentina Ruspoli, the cold barrel of her weapon fixed steadily upon him. Behind her, the chaos momentarily paused, suspended in a fragile silence filled only with harsh breathing and the muted hum of distant alarms.

"You won't shoot," Michael said quietly, his voice oddly calm despite the tremor of adrenaline in his veins.

Valentina's lip curled slightly, her eyes calculating. "You underestimate my resolve, Father Dominic."

"I understand your orders," Michael countered evenly. "You're here to retrieve the manuscript, not destroy it. Shooting me risks losing the gospel. I'm the only one who knows precisely how and where it's secured."

Her eyes narrowed, suspicion and intrigue battling openly. Michael took the momentary hesitation to speak clearly, raising his voice so all could hear. "This manuscript is worthless to Alessandro if destroyed or damaged. We both know he won't tolerate failure."

A flicker of doubt passed over Valentina's composed expression. In that instant, Michael saw the opening he had hoped for.

Behind him, Karl subtly shifted his stance, silently signaling to Lukas. The Swiss Guards had trained extensively for precisely this scenario—rapid improvisation under extreme duress. Michael needed only to buy them seconds.

"We can negotiate," Michael offered deliberately, stepping forward slightly to hold her gaze firmly. "A solution exists without bloodshed."

Valentina hesitated further, glancing swiftly toward her team. The brief distraction provided the moment Karl required. He moved instantly, triggering a small device hidden beneath his uniform belt.

"Now!" Karl shouted on a prearranged signal. As he and the rest of the team shut their eyes and covered their ears, a sudden, blinding flash erupted through the chamber, accompanied by a disorienting sonic burst. The attackers staggered, momentarily incapacitated. Valentina stumbled, dropping her weapon as she clutched at her ears and eyes, completely overwhelmed.

"Move quickly!" Karl prodded, grasping Michael's arm urgently.

Michael surged forward, still blinded, Karl leading him as he and Lukas rushed through the haze of smoke and confusion. They darted into a narrow, reinforced passage, which had been secured earlier as an emergency escape route. Karl sealed the heavy steel door swiftly behind them, locking out the chaotic scene of their narrow escape.

"We only have moments," Lukas urged, activating the small comm device at his wrist. "Ian, Hana—status?"

Ian's voice crackled immediately over the channel, tense yet clear. "Secure at rendezvous. What's your situation?"

"Compromised but temporarily contained," Michael replied breathlessly. "We need immediate extraction. Do you have contingency ready?"

"Prepared as planned," Ian responded confidently. "Exiting north perimeter. Five minutes."

Karl nodded sharply, leading them urgently through dim corridors beneath the facility, the hum of distant alarms still echoing faintly above. Each step resonated with urgency, their breaths quick and controlled.

They emerged abruptly into a hidden garage, where a sleek black van idled quietly—Teri at the wheel, her expression intensely focused. The doors slid open smoothly.

"In, quickly!" Teri commanded urgently. "We don't have long."

Michael and the Swiss Guards piled swiftly into the vehicle. The doors sealed shut, and Teri accelerated sharply, merging into Rome's bustling traffic with practiced ease. Behind them, the facility receded rapidly, lost in the blur of buildings and crowded streets.

Hana exhaled sharply from the front passenger seat, her relief palpable. "Are you all right, Michael?"

He nodded, allowing a brief, tight smile. "Thanks to Karl's ingenuity. I hadn't anticipated such a dramatic escape."

Karl offered a rare, quiet grin. "Standard contingency planning. Alessandro's agents rely heavily on predictable scenarios. The flash-bang device was a risk, but one calculated precisely for situations like this."

Hana turned, eyes sharp with renewed determination. "But Alessandro won't rest now. We need a more permanent solution—something he won't anticipate."

Michael considered this carefully, his mind swiftly assembling scattered threads. "We control the narrative now. Alessandro believes we're cornered. But what if we expose a part of the truth ourselves—publicly and in a way he cannot easily suppress?"

Ian raised an intrigued eyebrow. "You mean preempt his next move? Announce the discovery in a controlled release?"

Michael nodded decisively. "Exactly. Alessandro's power relies on secrecy and control. Expose just enough, and he loses both."

Hana's eyes brightened with understanding. "If we engage respected scholars, international media, and neutral third parties simultaneously, Alessandro's threats become impotent. He won't dare risk open exposure."

Michael nodded, his resolve crystallizing rapidly. "Then we prepare carefully. Ian, arrange a secure and discreet conference. Invite reputable scholars and press contacts we trust implicitly."

Teri glanced quickly in the rearview mirror, her voice steady despite the stakes. "We'll need to move swiftly. Alessandro will regroup rapidly."

"Then let's act decisively," Michael affirmed. "We meet Alessandro not with secrecy, but with openness. A controlled revelation—the truth, protected by transparency."

They drove rapidly toward their secure location, the air thick with tense resolve. Michael felt a renewed sense of purpose, understanding fully the dangerous path ahead but also knowing it represented their best chance at defeating Alessandro's shadowy reach.

While checking his equipment, Karl lifted the leather pouch containing Clement's letters, turning it over in his hands. "Something feels off," he murmured. There's a lump or something here."

Lukas took a small scanner from his pack and passed it over the seam. The device emitted a soft chirp. "There," he said, prying open the lining with a pocket blade. Inside, a coin-sized disc glinted under the lamplight.

"Tracker," Karl said flatly. "They've been tailing us since Florence."

Michael exhaled, shoulders tightening. "Destroy it."

Lukas set the device on the car floor, stomped on it with his boot until it cracked open, then rolled down a window and threw it out into a weed-filled field. "Consider it done," he said.

As Rome's streets flowed swiftly past, each face resolute, Michael allowed himself a moment of quiet conviction. The battle lines were clearly drawn now, the stakes higher than ever. Yet, amid the danger and uncertainty, a path toward victory emerged clearly before them—bold, daring, and rooted firmly in the truth Clement had entrusted them to protect.

CHAPTER
TWENTY-SEVEN

A VILLA OUTSIDE ROME

The safe house was an unassuming villa tucked discreetly amid the rolling hills outside Rome, hidden from casual view by groves of ancient olive trees and sprawling vineyards. It was a temporary sanctuary, chosen precisely for its isolation and simplicity. As Michael stepped inside, he felt an immediate sense of relief tempered by a persistent unease that came with knowing Alessandro was still out there, regrouping.

Hana was already at work, carefully laying out documents and secure communication devices across the long dining table. Ian had connected laptops, ensuring their data remained encrypted and virtually invisible. Michael glanced at the tightly organized display, feeling a brief moment of pride at the efficiency of their small, dedicated group.

"We have less than twenty-four hours," Ian began, addressing them all with characteristic calm. "Our media and scholarly contacts have responded positively. They'll attend the briefing virtually, under encrypted conditions. Our challenge is to prove credibility without physical access to the manuscript."

Hana interjected thoughtfully, "We must provide comprehensive scans and precise authentication data. The scholars already confirmed preliminary validation—this next phase must be flawless, beyond reproach."

Michael nodded in agreement. "We'll present a cohesive narrative, one that underscores the historic, theological significance without sensationalizing. Facts, transparency, and careful moderation."

Karl approached quietly, his expression still tense from their narrow escape. "Security remains critical. Alessandro will undoubtedly attempt interference. We need robust contingency plans."

Lukas moved beside him, voice firm. "We have surveillance drones and defensive perimeters established around this villa. We'll know immediately if anyone approaches."

Michael felt his confidence solidify, buoyed by the quiet strength and competence surrounding him. "Then let's finalize our presentation and secure every detail. Tomorrow, we shift the balance decisively."

The hours passed in intense, focused preparation, each team member diligently executing their roles. Hana's attention to historical accuracy and clarity was meticulous, while Ian managed technical details with assured precision. Teri monitored digital channels closely, watching for any sign of Alessandro's attempts at intrusion.

As evening settled softly over the villa, Michael stepped outside for a brief moment of air. The sun dipped slowly behind distant hills, bathing the landscape in warm, golden hues. It seemed inconceivable that amid such peaceful beauty lurked so much danger.

"You should rest," Hana said gently from behind him. She stepped beside Michael, her presence comforting as she hugged him.

"I will," he replied quietly. "It feels like we're on the verge of something immense, Hana—transformational, yet also terrifying."

She nodded, eyes reflecting quiet resolve. "History often hinges on courage, Michael. Clement knew that. Now it's our turn."

A soft sound disrupted their quiet moment—the low buzz of Karl's communicator. Karl appeared swiftly, his expression immediately alert. "We have movement at the perimeter. Two vehicles approaching from the south, cautious but persistent."

Michael and Hana exchanged an urgent glance, swiftly returning inside. "How long?" Michael asked tersely.

"Ten minutes, maybe less," Karl replied. "Drones indicate armed personnel, likely Alessandro's team."

Michael's mind raced, evaluating their options. "We cannot risk a confrontation here. Initiate protocol Alpha. Evacuate immediately through the northern tunnel. Ian, secure all data. Teri, initiate digital diversion protocols."

The group moved seamlessly into action, their preparations flawless from previous drills. Documents were rapidly packed, devices secured, and within minutes, they hurried toward the hidden exit beneath the villa. The northern tunnel led discreetly to a concealed garage equipped with another inconspicuous vehicle—part of their carefully orchestrated contingency.

As Michael settled into the passenger seat beside Karl, he glanced at the rearview monitor. Alessandro's agents had breached the villa grounds, moving swiftly, systematically. Michael's pulse quickened, grateful for their preparation and rapid response.

Karl accelerated onto a quiet rural road, disappearing swiftly into the deepening twilight.

Ian checked their secure network remotely, voice calm but tense. "All data safely routed to secure offshore servers. The villa's hard drives are wiped clean. Alessandro gains nothing."

Michael exhaled sharply, feeling a measure of relief. "Tomorrow's revelation must be flawless. Any misstep, and Alessandro regains the advantage."

Hana leaned forward from the back seat, determination clear in her voice. "We control the narrative. Tomorrow's announcement will eliminate secrecy. Alessandro's power dissolves when he can no longer operate from shadows."

"Agreed," Michael affirmed, his voice strong. "Let's ensure everything is ready. We have one chance—no mistakes, no second attempts."

They sped toward their final location, the quiet night shielding their movements. Michael gazed into the darkness, acutely aware of the stakes—truth balanced precariously against powerful forces desperate to silence it.

THE GROUP ARRIVED at another secluded estate, further concealed and heavily fortified. Before settling in, they ran their final checks. Teri confirmed no digital interference anywhere along their encrypted systems. "Quiet as a monastery," she said, eyes scanning the last of her diagnostics.

Karl and Lukas completed a perimeter sweep, returning with matching nods. "No movement, no tail,"

Karl said. "If they were tracking us before, they've lost the scent."

For the first time in days, a thin breath of relief moved through the room.

The next few hours passed swiftly, each team member reviewing their role with precise clarity. Just before dawn, they gathered around the secure terminal. Michael keyed in his authentication sequence; Hana verified the layered encryption; Ian activated the final relay. A soft chime, followed by a cascading series of green indicators, signaled that the protected network was live. With a last glance around the room, Michael pressed the command to start the conference.

One by one, scholars and trusted media professionals appeared on the screen, joining from dimly lit studies and university offices around the world. The secure channels hummed to life, each connection sealed behind layers of anonymity.

Michael began confidently, clearly articulating the manuscript's historical context and profound theological significance. Hana followed with a detailed account of the validation process, outlining every test performed without embellishment or hesitation.

When the session concluded, reactions rippled swiftly through the encrypted feeds. Affirmations appeared in steady succession, expertise aligning across borders. It wasn't merely agreement but conviction. Within minutes, a quiet consensus solidified: the gospel's credibility was no longer in question.

Moments after the virtual meeting ended, Ian's alert flashed urgently. "Incoming call, unidentified number, encrypted."

Michael took the call cautiously, prepared for anything.

"Father Dominic…" Alessandro Medici's voice was chillingly calm. "Impressive strategy, but you underestimate the depth of my resolve."

Michael's reply was steady, defiant. "Your threats no longer matter, Signor Medici. The truth is known, secure beyond your reach."

Alessandro's voice lowered dangerously. "You've made a formidable enemy, Father Dominic. Enjoy your brief victory."

The call ended abruptly. Michael felt a surge of both relief and heightened apprehension.

With a firm hand, Hana reached out and placed it on his arm to steady him. "We've shaken him. Now we must hold firm."

Michael nodded. "Agreed. Today, we've changed history. But the battle isn't over yet."

CHAPTER

TWENTY-EIGHT

VATICAN CITY

Cardinal Giovanni Severino's private study within the Apostolic Palace was thick with incense, though no Mass had been said there. The scent masked the musty tang of old stone and the faint metallic trace of dust stirred from centuries of bound books. Heavy velvet drapes shut out the Roman morning, muting the golden light of dawn into a murky glow. It was a place designed not for prayer, but for power.

Severino stood before his tall, arched window, hands clasped behind his back. He wore his red silk cassock loosely, his posture taut, as if the fabric itself carried a burden. His eyes fixed not on the view of St. Peter's dome, but on the reflection of his own figure in the glass, measuring the weight of his choices.

The discreet knock on the door drew him from his thoughts. A secretary entered, head bowed. "Eminence, Signor de' Medici has arrived."

Severino's jaw tightened. "Bring him."

Moments later, Alessandro de' Medici entered the chamber, his presence as commanding as Severino's was austere. He wore a tailored suit of dark linen, his expression one of cool precision. Valentina Ruspoli shadowed him silently, a figure of composed menace.

Severino gestured toward the carved walnut chairs. "Sit. We have little time."

Alessandro declined with a subtle shake of his head. "Time is exactly what we control, Cardinal. Dominic and Sinclair believe themselves ahead, but their game is fragile."

Severino's eyes narrowed. "They have unveiled too much already. Letters, manuscripts, whispers of a gospel. The Holy Father cannot be shielded much longer. Clement XV demands clarity."

Alessandro smiled faintly. "Clarity is malleable, Eminence. What matters is not the truth itself, but who shapes it. That is why we're allies."

Valentina stepped forward, producing a slim folder. She laid it on Severino's desk with deliberate care. "Their controlled revelation reached sympathetic scholars last night. Encrypted, yes, but intercepted, nonetheless. We know the extent of what they claim. They hold the manuscript. And they are preparing to broaden their circle."

Severino opened the folder, scanning the intercepted screenshots—images of parchment, faint ink in Greek and Coptic, Clement's unmistakable marginalia. His lips pressed into a thin line. "Unacceptable."

Alessandro's voice remained smooth. "Then let us act. We no longer aim to intercept. We destroy. Their credibility, their networks, their sanctuaries. Dominic will learn the cost of defiance."

The cardinal hesitated. "And if the gospel is real?"

"Then it dies with them," Alessandro replied simply. His words carried no hesitation, no burden. Only resolve.

Silence hung thick in the room, broken only by the faint crackle of a fire in the hearth. Severino lowered himself into the high-backed chair, steepling his fingers. "The Church cannot be seen as complicit. Yet if the pope is forced to choose between the prefect and the stability of the Curia..." His eyes flicked to Alessandro. "He will choose stability."

Alessandro inclined his head, satisfied. "Then the matter is settled. We will provide you with deniability. Our agents move quietly. Dominic will be discredited. Sinclair will be silenced. The manuscript will vanish, blamed on thieves or extremists. The Vatican emerges untouched."

Severino's throat tightened, but he didn't speak of the unease pressing at him. He had served too long to confuse morality with survival.

Valentina broke the silence. "We've already planted a false lead in Avignon. Another will emerge in Florence. Dominic will chase ghosts until he's worn down. Meanwhile, his enemies will close the circle."

Severino rose, turning back to the window, his reflection staring back at him with hollow eyes. "Do what you must, Signor de' Medici. But ensure that when the ashes settle, the Church's garments are clean."

Alessandro gave a thin smile. "Of course, Eminence. History has always remembered the Medici not for what we destroyed, but for what we preserved. Let us keep it that way."

A VILLA OUTSIDE ROME

Across the city, the safe villa hummed with tension. Ian sat hunched over his laptop, firewalls spiking red as he countered fresh digital intrusions. Teri paced behind him, her brows drawn tight. "They're probing harder. Whoever's running this knows our patterns. I can keep them out for now, but not forever."

Michael stood at the long table with Hana, the relic scans spread before them. He rubbed his temple, fatigue etching into his features. "Severino will not stay silent. If he's aligned with Alessandro, then the Holy Father will be pressured to act."

Hana looked up, her voice steady. "Then we stay ahead. Clement left us more than letters. He left a design— a puzzle meant for the one who dared to follow. We've only begun to understand it."

Michael's eyes softened, meeting hers. "You think the letters themselves hide more?"

"They do," Hana replied firmly. "The phrasing, the imagery. Clement wrote with layered intent. He wanted to guide without exposing himself. And in those layers lies the path to the final truths."

Karl entered from the villa's veranda, his expression alert. "Perimeter sweep clear, but there's movement on the road. Could be nothing. Could be eyes."

Michael straightened. "It's only a matter of time before they press harder. Alessandro has already tried force. His next move will be more subtle, more devastating."

Hana tapped a line from Letter VI she had been studying. "Then we beat him at his own game. If Clement trusted the future with riddles, it's time we start solving them."

The room fell into focused silence, each member of the team aware of the tightening noose. Outside, dawn spread over Rome like a warning: the hours of secrecy were dwindling, and the age of confrontation was at hand.

CHAPTER

TWENTY-NINE

A VILLA OUTSIDE ROME

The afternoon light slanted across the villa's study, catching the edges of the parchment scans spread before Hana. She leaned close to her laptop screen, brow furrowed, as though sheer will might force Clement's words to yield more than they already had. The others had drifted into their own tasks—Michael in quiet prayer near the balcony, Ian muttering at his code, Karl and Lukas trading watch shifts outside—but Hana was fixed to the letters, convinced that Clement's voice hadn't yet finished speaking.

Her conviction proved correct.

A secure notification pinged faintly across her encrypted channel. The sender was anonymous, the address untraceable. Hana hesitated, her pulse quickening. She glanced toward Michael, then clicked it open.

What appeared on the screen wasn't an ordinary message, but a short Latin verse:

181

Lux abscondita sub stella septima, ubi scriptura et caelum conveniunt. Quaere ibi, et invenies quod etiam Petrus timuit.

She read it twice, softly translating aloud: "'*A hidden light beneath the seventh star, where scripture and heaven meet. Seek there, and you will find what even Peter feared.*'"

Michael crossed quickly to her side. "Who sent this?"

"No signature. No trace," Hana said, still staring at the lines. "But it echoes Clement's style. Layered. Cryptic. It could be authentic."

Ian looked up from his laptop, his voice sharp with suspicion. "Or it's bait. Alessandro has the resources to forge this easily."

Karl stepped in from the veranda, having caught the last words. "So, either Clement left us one more clue... or Alessandro wants to lure us into a trap."

Michael studied the verse, his brow furrowed. "The seventh star. That could reference the Pleiades, or an astronomical marker. Scripture and heaven meeting— possibly a church with celestial frescoes, or an observatory chapel."

Hana tapped the edge of the screen thoughtfully. "And the line about what Peter feared—that's no random flourish. Clement was obsessed with the fragility of apostolic succession. He meant something specific."

Teri's voice carried from the comms console. "If this is genuine, it's more than just poetry. It's pointing you somewhere tangible."

Hana nodded, determination sharpening her features. "Then it's a puzzle. And if Clement left it, it could lead us to the seventh letter."

Michael exhaled slowly, the weight of choice pressing on him. "We can't dismiss it. If it's real, it could bring us closer to Clement's final intent. But if it's false, following it could expose us."

Ian folded his arms. "So, what's the plan? Test it here, or chase it out there?"

Hana's eyes gleamed with a familiar spark. "We chase it. But carefully. First, I'll cross-reference every church, convent, and archive in Rome and Florence tied to astronomy or Marian symbolism—the seventh star, the scarlet veil. Somewhere in that overlap lies our answer."

Karl exchanged a look with Lukas, then back at Michael. "If she's right, then Alessandro won't be far behind."

Michael gave a grim nod. "Then we move faster. Hana, work the riddle. The rest of us will prepare to move at a moment's notice."

The room grew tense with quiet purpose. Hana bent once more over the verse, her pen scratching lines of translation and possibility. For her, the world outside faded. There was only Clement's riddle and the path it promised.

Somewhere beyond the villa walls, Alessandro's agents were tightening their net. But Hana was already one step into Clement's game, and for the first time since discovering the gospel, she felt the weight shift—not away from them, but toward her.

CHAPTER

THIRTY

A VILLA OUTSIDE ROME

The morning after the cryptic verse appeared, the villa stirred with unease. Hana remained glued to her notes, eyes red from a sleepless night, her pages crowded with Latin translations, astronomical charts, and cross-references. Michael hovered nearby, torn between his admiration of her tenacity and worry for her well-being. The riddle's imagery—the seventh star, where scripture and heaven meet—echoed relentlessly in his mind, yet its meaning remained maddeningly elusive.

Meanwhile, Ian paced the living room with his laptop under one arm, muttering about corrupted feeds. "Something's wrong with the Vatican press circuits. Every channel I monitor is spiking. Severino or Alessandro has planted something."

Karl entered from outside, pulling off his gloves, his face tight. "Locals are restless too. I overheard rumors at the café down the road, people whispering that Father

Dominic and a journalist are at the center of a Vatican scandal."

Michael stiffened. "What scandal?"

Karl shrugged. "Details were vague. But the words blasphemy and forgery came up."

Ian set his laptop on the table, fingers racing across keys. "Give me two minutes."

The villa fell silent except for the rhythmic tap of his typing. Then Ian swore under his breath and turned the screen toward them. The headline of *La Repubblica* blazed across the page:

Vatican Archivist and Foreign Reporter Fabricate Ancient Gospel: Investigation Underway.

Hana's stomach sank. "Fabricate?"

Ian clicked to expand the article. "Listen: '*Sources within the Curia allege that Father Michael Dominic, Prefect of the Vatican Secret Archives, conspired with foreign journalist Hana Sinclair to forge an apocryphal gospel attributed to Mary Magdalene. The pair are accused of manipulating fragile manuscripts and misleading international scholars in a scheme to profit from sensational revelations.*'"

Michael felt his chest tighten as he read the accusations aloud. "They're saying we tampered with manuscripts, sold access for money, and falsified Clement's letters!" His voice hardened. "This reeks of Severino."

Teri's voice buzzed over the comm line from her monitoring post. "Not just Severino. This has Alessandro's fingerprints. The timing, the precision—it's a coordinated strike. And it's spreading fast. I'm tracking reposts on international wires already."

Hana's hands clenched the table's edge. "If the public

believes this, every step we've taken loses legitimacy. Clement's letters, the gospel—they'll dismiss it all as fraud."

Lukas entered from the kitchen, his normally steady demeanor shadowed with anger. "And if the Vatican launches a formal inquiry, they'll confiscate everything. The gospel won't be protected in a vault—it will disappear."

Michael pressed his palms against the table, grounding himself. "We cannot allow that. Truth doesn't vanish because of lies."

Hana's eyes sharpened with resolve. "Then we fight back—with clarity, with evidence. We prove the gospel authentic in ways no smear campaign can deny."

Ian grimaced. "That's easier said than done. Alessandro's got half the Italian press on his payroll, and Severino controls internal Vatican channels. We can counter, but it has to be smarter, faster, and louder."

Michael turned to Hana. "How far along with the riddle?"

She sighed, rubbing her temples. "It's incomplete. But the line about the seventh star keeps circling back to one thing: Santa Maria Sopra Minerva. Its vault's frescoes depict a celestial map, including the Pleiades."

Michael nodded slowly. "Then that's our next step. While Alessandro wages war in the press, we follow Clement's trail."

Karl frowned. "But if the story goes viral, the moment we set foot near Minerva, we'll be swarmed. Cameras, police, maybe even Curia officials."

"Which is why," Michael said firmly, "we go covertly."

• • •

By MIDDAY, the smear campaign had spread like wildfire. International outlets repeated the claims. Headlines varied but carried the same sting:

Vatican Scandal Rocks Archives
Archivist and Journalist Under Fire
Forged Gospel?

Hana scrolled through her phone in disbelief, seeing her name plastered across feeds worldwide. Her career, once defined by unearthing truths, now dangled precariously under accusation.

In Paris, her editor left a terse voicemail: "Hana, call me. The board is furious. They want answers, and they're considering suspension."

She slammed her phone onto the table. "They're trying to erase me."

Michael gently touched her shoulder. "They're trying to erase us both. But remember—truth stands even in darkness."

Karl's communicator buzzed sharply. He answered, his expression darkening. "Our safe villa has been compromised. Locals spotted surveillance vans nearby."

Lukas was already packing their gear. "We move. Now."

THAT EVENING, the team regrouped in a cramped rented apartment near Piazza Navona, stripped-down and temporary, their supplies condensed into backpacks and locked cases. Ian hunched over a folding table, his screen glowing faint blue. "I'm crafting a counteroffensive. If

Alessandro wants a media war, we'll give him one. But it'll be unconventional."

Michael raised an eyebrow. "Explain."

Ian's grin was tight, fierce. "We leak Clement's handwriting samples, ink analysis, and multispectral imaging data anonymously to academic networks. No names attached. Just raw, verifiable evidence. If scholars debate authenticity in real time, Alessandro loses control of the narrative."

Teri chimed in over comms, "I'll plant the data across multiple servers worldwide. By the time anyone tries to suppress it, it'll already be mirrored in dozens of research hubs."

Hana's eyes lit with renewed determination. "And I'll draft an open letter—not to the press, but to independent scholars. I'll frame this as an appeal for truth, not profit. If Alessandro paints me as a fraud, I'll stand as a witness instead."

Michael nodded approvingly. "Good. We strike with evidence and integrity. Let the scholars carry the debate where propaganda cannot reach."

THAT NIGHT, Hana sat at the small desk by the apartment's lone window, pen poised over paper. She wrote carefully, her words measured yet passionate:

"To the community of scholars and seekers of truth: A document has surfaced that challenges assumptions long buried in history. While accusations swirl, the evidence must speak for itself. We invite your scrutiny—not to prove us right, but to prove the past wrong or true. Let history be examined, not silenced."

When she finished, she handed the draft to Michael. He read it silently, then looked at her with quiet pride. "This is stronger than any denial. It's an invitation. And it's unassailable."

Ian tapped away at his keys. "It goes live at dawn. By then, Alessandro's smear will have competition."

Karl and Lukas checked their weapons and supplies. "And in the meantime," Karl said, "we prepare for Minerva."

THE NEXT MORNING, Rome awoke to headlines divided. Some still trumpeted the scandal; others now buzzed with debate over newly leaked imaging data of Clement's letters. The hashtag **#MediciHeresy** trended globally. Scholars on social media posted magnified handwriting comparisons, arguing passionately about the authenticity of the documents. The smear campaign had fractured.

Alessandro de' Medici read the feeds in his villa outside Rome, his jaw tight. He hurled his glass of wine against the wall, crimson streaking down ancient plaster. "They're turning the scholars into their shield," he spat. "Valentina, escalate. Make them bleed credibility."

Valentina's cool eyes narrowed. "And if we fail?"

Alessandro's gaze turned steely. "Then Dominic dies. And the gospel dies with him."

BACK AT THE APARTMENT, Michael gathered the team. "The smear has slowed but not stopped. We've bought time. Now we use it. Tonight, we enter Santa Maria Sopra Minerva. Hana believes Clement left the next clue there."

Hana's pen traced a constellation she had drawn

hastily in her notebook. "The seventh star, the meeting of scripture and heaven—it fits the fresco. And if I'm right, the seventh letter waits for us there."

Michael nodded solemnly. "Then tonight, we test Clement's riddle. And we prove that no smear, no lie, no threat can erase the truth he entrusted to the future."

CHAPTER

THIRTY-ONE

ROME

Night had settled over Rome, cloaking the city in muted tones of amber and shadow. The bells of Santa Maria Sopra Minerva tolled faintly in the distance as Michael and his companions moved silently through the narrow backstreets. The smear campaign still crackled through headlines, but here in the dark heart of the city, their battle wasn't fought in words—it was fought in whispers, puzzles, and faith.

Hana clutched her satchel tightly, her notes on Clement's verse carefully tucked inside. The Latin lines had burned in her mind all day:

Lux abscondita sub stella septima, ubi scriptura et caelum conveniunt.

A hidden light beneath the seventh star, where scripture and heaven meet.

She had circled and underlined phrases, cross-referenced maps and diagrams, and every trail pointed to Minerva—the Dominican basilica whose frescoes carried a celestial motif, where theology and astronomy once collided.

Karl and Lukas walked ahead, dressed in plain clothes but carrying concealed weapons, their eyes scanning every corner. Ian trailed just behind, muttering softly into a comm line with Teri, who monitored digital channels from their temporary apartment near Piazza Navona.

They turned a final corner, and the church loomed before them. Its façade was simple compared to the grandeur of St. Peter's—unassuming, with a Gothic rose window and a modest portico—but its significance was vast. Within these walls, nearly a century after Clement VII, Galileo Galilei had stood trial for heresy, and within its crypts rested popes, cardinals, and saints. Tonight, Hana believed, it held Clement's seventh letter.

INSIDE, the basilica was hushed, lit only by scattered votive candles. The high vaults absorbed sound, amplifying even the softest footsteps.

Karl kept watch at the rear of the chapel while Lukas checked the side aisles. "No one's following. We're clear for now."

Michael moved toward the altar with reverence, bowing his head slightly. "Lord, grant us wisdom in what we seek," he whispered.

Hana drew out her notebook, turning to a sketch she had made of the vaulted ceiling. "There," she said, pointing upward. The fresco depicted a night sky, constellations painted in muted blues and golds, a symbolic representation of Creation's order. "The Pleiades. Seven stars. Clement must have chosen this deliberately."

Michael tilted his head back, following her finger. "But where does scripture meet heaven?"

Hana scanned the nave, then moved quickly to the left side chapel. Its fresco depicted Mary Magdalene at the empty tomb, her hands raised toward the risen Christ, and above her head the faint outline of a star cluster.

Her pulse quickened. "Here. Magdalene beneath the stars. Scripture and heaven meeting in one image."

Hana kneeled before the fresco, her fingers tracing the faded lines of paint. "Look for a hidden light. There must be a marker." She shifted her flashlight to a low angle, letting the beam graze across the plaster. Faint ridges and indentations appeared—subtle, almost invisible from above.

Michael crouched beside her. "A star carved into the plaster itself."

She nodded. "The seventh star. The faintest one. Clement's clue."

They examined the fresco more closely, finding a small cavity beneath the star. It had been plastered over, the seam nearly indistinguishable. Hana's hands trembled slightly as she worked a thin tool along the edge, carefully prying it open. A puff of ancient dust spilled forth, followed by the faint glint of something metallic.

Inside the cavity lay a small bronze tube, tarnished with age, sealed at both ends with wax impressed with Clement's papal insignia.

Michael exhaled slowly, reverently lifting it free. "The seventh letter."

But the triumph was short-lived. A sudden creak echoed through the nave.

Karl stiffened instantly, hand going to his weapon. "We're not alone."

Footsteps approached from the main aisle, deliberate and steady. Valentina Ruspoli's silhouette emerged from the shadows, flanked by two men in dark suits. Her expression was calm, her eyes sharp. "You really are predictable, Father Dominic. Clement leads, and you follow. But you never notice who else is following you."

Hana rose slowly, clutching the notebook to her chest. "You intercepted the verse."

Valentina's lips curved faintly. "Of course. Did you truly think Alessandro would let you solve these puzzles without supervision?" She stepped closer, her heels echoing against the stone floor. "Hand me the letter, Dominic. Don't make this more painful than it needs to be."

Michael held the bronze tube tightly, his voice steady. "Clement entrusted these truths to the future, not to those who would destroy them."

Valentina's eyes narrowed. "You mistake destruction for preservation," she murmured. "A truth like this doesn't survive without casualties. Give it to me."

Karl and Lukas moved subtly, positioning themselves between Michael and Valentina's men. The standoff crackled with tension.

Then Hana spoke, her voice clear and unwavering. "You want the letter? Then prove you understand it. The verse wasn't just a clue. It was a test. If you believe Clement feared the truth, tell me—what is the seventh star?"

Valentina's gaze flickered, just briefly. "A celestial symbol."

Hana shook her head. "Not enough. Clement chose the faintest star of the Pleiades. The hidden one, often overlooked. He was saying that the faintest voice holds the greatest truth. That's why he tied it to Magdalene. That's why the letter is hers to reveal—not yours."

The moment of Valentina's hesitation was all Karl needed. He lunged forward, squarely striking one of Valentina's men, disarming him in a fluid motion. Lukas followed nearly simultaneously, forcing the second back against the pillar. Valentina cursed sharply, stepping back toward the shadows.

Michael secured the tube beneath his coat. "Go!" he shouted.

They sprinted toward the sacristy, the sound of scuffling as the men righted themselves and Valentina's shouts reverberating behind them. Hana clutched her notebook, heart pounding, as they pushed through a narrow side door into the cloister. Moonlight spilled across the courtyard, their breath rising in sharp clouds.

Ian's voice crackled in their earpieces. "Teri's picked up police chatter. You have two minutes before local units converge on Minerva. Move now!"

Karl led them through the cloister to a hidden service door. They spilled into a narrow alley, boots slapping against wet cobblestones. Behind them, Valentina's voice shouted orders in Italian, her operatives giving chase.

Michael gritted his teeth, clutching the tube close. "We have the letter. Now we just have to survive long enough to read it."

•　•　•

BACK IN THE rented apartment near Piazza Navona, the team regrouped breathlessly. Hana leaned against the wall, her chest heaving, while Karl and Lukas secured the doors.

Michael placed the bronze tube carefully on the table. For a moment, silence filled the room. Then he broke the wax seal, his hands trembling.

Inside was a parchment, Clement's handwriting unmistakable, though the ink had faded to a fragile sepia. Michael read aloud:

> **To the one who has followed thus far:**
>
> *Know that you stand upon the threshold of what I could not bear to reveal. The gospel was not my only burden. There is a codex, older still, which bears witness to voices Rome silenced long before mine. I placed its secret in the hands of the stars, that one day a seeker with courage might find it. Seek the place where the fishermen sleep, where dawn sends its narrow blade of light beneath the stones. There the stars reach farther than the living ever could. Seek also the oldest foundation of all, where Rome buried its first witness, and where the heavens mark each passing season upon the crypt.*
>
> ✝ *Clemens PP. VII*
> *Pontifex Maximus*

He lowered the parchment slowly, his voice hushed. "The codex. Clement knew of something beyond the gospel. Something even before it."

Hana's eyes burned with determination. "Then the puzzle isn't over. The eighth letter holds the final key."

Ian leaned back, running a hand through his hair. "And Alessandro won't stop until he gets there first."

The room fell silent, each of them feeling the weight of Clement's words. They had the seventh letter, but with it came not closure, only the widening of the chasm they had already risked everything to cross.

Outside, the bells of Minerva tolled midnight, their echo lingering across the city like a summons none of them could refuse.

CHAPTER

THIRTY-TWO

ROME

The next morning, the rented apartment near Piazza Navona hummed with unease. Michael sat at the small kitchen table, Clement's seventh letter spread carefully before him, its faded lines still carrying the sting of revelation. The words were clear: there was something more than the gospel. A codex older still, hidden beyond Clement's lifetime, waiting for discovery. The eighth letter would point the way. But where was it hidden?

Hana paced nearby, her notebook filled with transcriptions, marginalia, and speculative diagrams. She spoke without looking up. "The codex Clement describes —it's not just commentary. It's something foundational, something Rome wanted obliterated. If it survived, it might reinforce—or change—everything we thought the gospel alone might do."

Michael rubbed his forehead, weary but resolute. "And

198

Alessandro knows it now. Valentina saw us recover the seventh letter. They'll assume we've read it. The chase just escalated."

At the far side of the room, Ian frowned over his laptop. "Speaking of escalations, I've found something troubling. Remember the forged metadata trails? The false entries planted in the Archive logs?"

"Yes," Michael said, looking up sharply. "What about them?"

Ian turned the screen toward him. "I backtracked server pings from last night. While we were inside Minerva, someone in the Vatican Archives accessed your private credentials—your *actual* credentials. They tried to mask it, but the trail ends at one terminal: Donato Scarella's."

Hana stopped pacing. "The liaison from the restoration division?"

"Exactly," Ian confirmed. "He's not just complicit. He's the mole. Every breadcrumb, every misdirection—it came through his terminal. He's funneling intel straight to Valentina."

Michael leaned back, his jaw tight. "And if Scarella has access to my credentials, then Alessandro knows every movement I log. Every file I touch. No wonder they appear everywhere we go."

Karl entered from the hallway, tucking his sidearm beneath his jacket. "So we cut him off. Expose him."

"Not so simple," Ian countered. "If we act too openly, Scarella burns whatever evidence ties him to Alessandro de' Medici. We need him watched. Pressured. Make him lead us to his handler."

Teri's voice carried through the comm line from her secure hub. "I can ghost his system. Feed him false confirmation codes. If he thinks he's reporting real intel, we can track his outputs directly to Alessandro's network."

Hana nodded, a spark of determination lighting her eyes. "Turn his treachery into our advantage. If Clement left a puzzle to guide us, let's use Scarella to misguide them."

Michael exhaled slowly. "Do it. But quietly. No alarms. Alessandro must believe we're still vulnerable."

By late afternoon, the team relocated to a discreet safe house within Trastevere—a cramped apartment tucked above a bookbinder's shop, its windows obscured by ivy and its walls thick with centuries of plaster. Ian worked quickly, plugging into secure lines while Teri orchestrated from her hub.

"Scarella just logged in," Ian announced. "He's pulling Clement-related metadata again, feeding it straight to an external channel flagged with Medici markers."

Michael leaned over his shoulder. "Can you see what he's sending?"

Ian smirked grimly. "Better. I'm editing it. He thinks he's found a reference to Avignon's tribunal records— specifically a phantom sub-archive labeled *Numéro Trois*. He'll pass it to Valentina within the hour."

Hana's brows lifted. "That phrase appeared in the slip we found in the Index of Prohibited Books. Clement anticipated this. He used repetition as confirmation."

Karl crossed his arms. "So, we're sending Alessandro after smoke while we pursue the real trail."

"Exactly," Ian said. "Scarella becomes our unwitting courier of disinformation."

. . .

THAT NIGHT, in the Vatican, Donato Scarella sat hunched in his dim alcove, sweat beading on his balding head as he nervously keyed in data. The false references scrolled before him, so seamlessly woven he never suspected fabrication. With trembling hands, he routed the data to the channel Valentina had provided, whispering under his breath like a penitent reciting confession. He never noticed the ghost protocols wrapping around his transmission, tagging every packet with traceable markers.

BACK IN TRASTEVERE, Hana sat with Michael, her notes spread across the small wooden table. "The seventh letter pointed us forward, but it also warned us. Clement said the eighth would reveal the codex. He tied it to the stars. One reference in that letter that hints of a new location is, '*I placed its secret in the hands of the stars.*' Astronomy again. I think the key is an alignment—something that points not just to a place, but to a time."

Michael leaned closer, listening as her pen traced patterns across constellations. "You think Clement used the heavens as a cipher?"

"Yes," Hana said firmly. "Astronomical events were the one thing no inquisitor could erase. They leave imprints across calendars, sermons, even art. Clement embedded his trail in the skies themselves. And the letter's references aren't random," she went on, tracing her finger under the lines. "Dawn light beneath the stones, the oldest Christian foundation, the fishermen asleep. No other place in Rome fits all three except the necropolis under St. Peter's."

Ian interrupted from across the room. "Heads up. Our

mole just sent the Avignon lead. Valentina's people are already responding. We've got at least twelve hours before they realize it's false."

"Then that's our window," Michael said. "We follow Clement's stars while Alessandro chases ghosts. We use every shadow, every ally, every fragment Clement left us. The puzzle isn't complete, but the pieces are aligning."

Hana closed her notebook, her eyes bright despite the fatigue etched into her face. "Clement knew the cost of silence. Now it's up to us to finish what he began."

The room fell quiet, each of them absorbing the weight of what lay ahead. Beyond the ivy-clad windows, Rome's night hummed with unseen watchers and whispered plots. But here, amid paper, ink, and faith, the path of the puzzle stretched forward—toward the eighth letter, the codex, and the ultimate truth Clement had guarded with his life.

CHAPTER

THIRTY-THREE

PROVENCE, FRANCE

The flight from Rome was shrouded in secrecy. Hana sat near the window of the Dassault Falcon 900, her pen scribbling furiously across her notebook as the dark sweep of the Mediterranean passed beneath them. Every few minutes, she would pause, glance at Michael across the aisle, and murmur a line of Clement's seventh letter. Each word seemed to widen the riddle rather than solve it.

Michael leaned back in his seat, fingers steepled, eyes closed but mind restless. The gospel was secured for now, hidden beyond Alessandro's reach. But the seventh letter had opened a deeper wound—a codex Clement hinted at, older and perhaps even more dangerous. To find it, they would need the eighth letter.

Karl and Lukas, seated at the rear of the cabin, whispered in German as they checked their weapons and gear. The tension between vigilance and weariness weighed heavily on them both. Ian sat nearby, tapping at his laptop, monitoring digital chatter.

Hana looked up, her eyes alight with quiet determination. "The slip Clement left in the Index, the reference to *Numéro Trois*—it wasn't just misdirection. It points to Avignon, yes, but also to the Palais des Papes tribunal chamber. That's where silence was imposed on prophets. Clement used history itself as part of the puzzle."

Michael nodded slowly. "And if Alessandro thinks Avignon holds the eighth letter, he'll chase it—which gives us time in Provence to follow the real trail."

THE FALCON 900 touched down at Marseille Provence Airport just before dawn. A discreet black Mercedes van awaited them at a private hangar, arranged through one of Hana's contacts. They drove swiftly through the countryside, past rows of sleeping vineyards and lavender fields silvered by morning mist. The horizon blushed faintly with light, casting long shadows across the rugged landscape.

Their destination lay in the hills outside a small Provençal village, a place rarely marked on maps. Hana had found the reference in an obscure Dominican register: a hermitage once tied to Clement's papacy, long abandoned after a fire in the late sixteenth century. Local rumor held it was cursed ground, for the blaze that consumed it was said to have begun during a midnight Mass when the altar suddenly erupted in flame. Some whispered it was lightning, others that heretics had set it as vengeance. But villagers told darker tales—that the monks had guarded forbidden texts, and the fire was heaven's judgment upon them. Generations avoided the ruins thereafter, claiming to hear phantom chanting in the hills and see ghostly lights flicker where the chapel once stood.

As the van wound upward along narrow roads, Karl scanned the surroundings. "No tails yet. But Alessandro's people won't be far behind."

Lukas adjusted the rifle case at his feet. "We'll make sure they don't get a clean shot if they follow."

Michael glanced at Hana, who sat with her notebook open on her lap. "You're certain of this site?"

"As certain as Clement allows us to be," she said softly. "He never left straight lines—only constellations of hints. The hermitage is linked to both stars and silence. That's his pattern."

THE VAN PULLED up near the crumbling ruins of the hermitage. A solitary stone arch marked the entrance, its keystone etched with a half-eroded sunburst. Weeds and ivy clung to the fractured walls, and the roof had long since collapsed. Birds scattered as the group approached, their cries sharp against the morning stillness.

Michael paused before the arch, tracing the worn stone with his hand. "Pope Urban's seal again," he murmured. "Clement used repetition to confirm authenticity."

Hana's eyes darted across the ruin. "The chapel stood on an east-west axis, aligned with the solstice. Astronomy again. He wanted us to look not just down, but up."

Inside, the floor was littered with debris—charred beams, broken tiles, fragments of fresco clinging stubbornly to the walls. Ian set up a portable scanner, sweeping for anomalies. "I've got density shifts beneath the apse. A chamber maybe a meter deep."

Karl and Lukas moved to clear debris while Michael and Hana studied the remnants of the fresco above the apse. Faded but still discernible, it depicted a cluster of stars—seven prominent, one faint, painted just above the figure of Mary Magdalene.

Hana whispered, "The hidden star again. The faintest voice." She pointed to a fragment of Latin text painted beneath, reading and translating it: "'*Non vox clamat, sed lumen scribit.*' '*It is not the voice that cries, but the light that writes.*'"

Michael felt his pulse quicken. "Clement's code. He hid the letter where the fresco aligns with the rising sun."

They waited in silence as dawn fully broke. The first rays of sunlight pierced through the ruined arch, striking the fresco at an angle. The light traced the faint star and fell directly onto a crack in the apse floor.

"Here," Hana said sharply.

Karl knelt and pried at the crack with a crowbar. Stones shifted reluctantly, revealing a small cavity lined with ash. Inside lay a scorched wooden box, its iron hinges rusted, its lid nearly fused shut.

Michael's hands trembled as he lifted it carefully, brushing away centuries of dust.

When he pried it open, the interior revealed a bundle of parchment wrapped in linen, blackened at the edges by fire yet preserved within. Atop the bundle rested a slip of vellum, Clement's handwriting clear despite the fading ink.

Michael read aloud:

"This diary I leave not as proof, but as confession. Within are the thoughts I could not seal in letters. If you seek the eighth, follow the heavens from Rome to where the Tiber bends, wherein silence reigns and the heavens mark the hour. There, beneath the weight of silence, you will find what I could not burn."

Silence hung over the group as the words sank in. A diary. Clement's personal reflections, hidden for centuries, preserved against fire and time. And within it, the path to the eighth letter.

Hana's fingers traced the vellum slip reverently. "Clement left us not only letters, but his own witness. And now we know—the eighth is in Rome. Beneath silence. Likely within the Vatican itself."

Michael glanced at Clement's faded script. The words leaped at him like living fire. His eyes burned with conviction. "We have to reach Rome. The eighth letter is there."

Karl scanned the tree line, his voice low. "Then we leave quickly. We're not alone."

Even as he spoke, the crunch of tires echoed down the hill. Black SUVs wound their way up the narrow road, their windows dark, their engines predatory in the stillness of morning.

Lukas slung his rifle and muttered grimly, "Alessandro's agents."

Michael clutched the diary tightly. "We have what we came for. Now we fight our way out."

THIRTY-FOUR

PROVENCE, FRANCE

The morning air in Provence was brittle with tension. Michael crouched behind the fractured wall of the hermitage, Clement's diary clutched tightly against his chest. The distant rumble of engines grew louder, bouncing off the rocky hillsides. Black SUVs crawled up the winding road like predators circling prey.

Karl scanned the ridge through a pair of compact binoculars. "Three vehicles, maybe eight men, all armed. They're moving in formation."

Lukas adjusted the strap of his rifle, his eyes narrowing. "Alessandro doesn't send amateurs. They'll box us in if we don't move now."

Crouched near the archway with her notebook still in hand, Hana glanced at Michael. "We can't leave without the diary. Clement's words are irreplaceable."

Michael met her eyes, voice firm. "We won't. But

survival comes first. If they take us, the diary is lost anyway."

Ian tapped urgently at his laptop, the glow of the screen pale against the ruin's shadows. "I've got a temporary signal uplink. Teri's feeding satellite views—there's a goat path east, leading into the ravine. It's narrow, but it bypasses the main road."

Karl didn't hesitate. "Then that's our exit. Let's move, now."

THEY SLIPPED through the crumbling apse and down the rough path, stones shifting beneath their boots. The air smelled of char and damp earth, a haunting reminder of the centuries-old fire that had gutted the hermitage. Hana clutched her satchel tightly, heart hammering in rhythm with their hurried steps.

Gunfire cracked suddenly, echoing through the valley. Bullets splintered stone near the arch they had just left. Alessandro's men had sighted them.

"Down!" Karl barked, shoving Hana low as Lukas returned fire, controlled and precise. Dust and shards exploded around them.

Michael's grip on the diary tightened as he ducked behind an outcrop. He whispered a prayer, not for himself but for the fragile vellum within the scorched box. Clement's voice had survived fire once; it must not be silenced now.

Ian shouted from behind a cluster of rocks, "We can't hold this position! We have to draw them into the ravine!"

Karl nodded sharply. "Cover fire. Lukas, on my mark."

The Swiss Guards coordinated with seamless precision. Lukas unleashed a quick volley, forcing the advancing operatives into cover. Karl signaled the retreat, and the group sprinted along the goat path, boots pounding against loose gravel. The ravine yawned below, steep and jagged, its depths filled with scrub and shadow.

They slid into the ravine's cover, lungs burning. The sound of pursuit grew louder, legs crashing through the underbrush above.

Hana pressed against the rocky wall, whispering hoarsely, "They're not letting up."

Michael steadied her shoulder. "Then we turn the ground to our advantage."

Karl scanned the terrain quickly. "There's a choke point ahead, a narrow passage. We can funnel them there."

They pushed forward until the ravine constricted into a natural bottleneck, walls closing in tight. Karl and Lukas positioned themselves with practiced calm, setting cross angles while Michael, Hana, and Ian pressed into a recess.

The first operative appeared at the bend, weapon raised. Lukas dropped him cleanly with a precise shot. Shouts erupted behind him, the rest rushing forward blindly.

Karl's voice was cold steel. "Now."

The Swiss Guards opened fire in tandem, forcing Alessandro's men to scatter. Bullets ricocheted off stone, the confined space amplifying every shot into a deafening roar. Hana covered her ears, pressing herself tighter against Michael, who shielded both her and the diary with his body.

Ian ducked low, pulling a compact flash device from his pack. "Fire in the hole, eyes shut!" he warned.

A burst of searing light flooded the ravine, followed by stunned cries from their pursuers. Karl and Lukas seized the moment, unleashing precise volleys that sent the attackers scrambling back up the slope.

For a moment, silence fell, broken only by the ragged breathing of the team.

Karl exhaled slowly. "That bought us minutes, no more."

Lukas scanned the ridge. "They'll regroup. Alessandro won't accept failure."

Hana's gaze locked with his, determination blazing. "Then we waste no time. Clement's puzzle is nearly complete. And Alessandro is closer than ever."

Ian shut down his laptop, slinging it over his shoulder. "I'll arrange extraction. We can't risk roads—too exposed. Teri's working a contact in Marseille who can get us airborne within the hour."

Karl tightened his grip on his weapon, nodding. "We'll carve a path if we have to."

As they climbed out of the ravine, the Provençal sun broke fully over the horizon, bathing the ruined hermitage in gold. To the villagers below, it remained cursed ground, haunted by fire and whispers. But to Michael and his companions, it had yielded something far greater: Clement's hidden diary, the voice of a pope who had feared too much and revealed too little.

Now that voice pointed them home—to Rome, to the Vatican, to the final letter and whatever it held that Alessandro would kill to erase.

The pursuit had only just begun

CHAPTER
THIRTY-FIVE

The train from Marseille carved a silver line through evening fields, pushing toward Italy as if the rails themselves had urgency. In a quiet compartment, Father Michael watched the landscape blur and tried not to count the choices that had brought them here. On the small table between Hana and him, Clement's diary lay wrapped in linen like a wound bound against infection. Every so often, Hana untied the cloth, read a line, and tied it again—as if exposure might damage the words or heal them.

Karl sat nearest the door, posture easy but eyes relentless. Lukas watched the corridor behind Michael's shoulder, the reflection in the compartment glass giving him a second field of view. Ian typed softly, green glyphs sluicing down his screen as he mapped Medici network chatter across half a dozen anonymized relays.

"They know we left Provence," Ian murmured without looking up. "Valentina has two hypotheses—Rome or

Paris. She's splitting resources. It buys us time, but not much."

Hana kept reading. Her finger followed the lines, lips moving silently until she found the passage she had marked before. "Listen to this again." She angled the diary so Michael could see the fragile script.

"In the silence beneath Peter's crown, I hid the voice I could not burn. Not in gold, not in relic, but in the shadows where prayers fade into echoes. There lies the eighth, my last confession. The heavens will mark the hour."

Michael's gaze softened at the phrase *"voice I could not burn."* He imagined a tired pope standing alone with a candle, making choices that would outlive him and wound him for all of time. "We need to be precise," he said. "'*Beneath Peter's crown*' can't mean the high altar chamber, where we found the gospel itself. Clement wouldn't reuse the same space. He means the necropolis more broadly—the Scavi, the burial grotto beneath St. Peter's—but a different gallery. Somewhere silent enough that prayer becomes an echo."

Hana nodded. "Yes, a side corridor. A sealed loculus. And it's not just *where*—it's *when*. 'The heavens will mark the hour' implies an alignment. We'll be searching in the dark unless we understand the timing."

Lukas leaned forward. "Astronomical? Solar angle into a vent shaft? Moonlight through a grate? Old basilicas used alignments sometimes."

"Renaissance chapels too," Hana said. "And Clement lived through both worlds—medieval devotion and humanist precision. He could have embedded a temporal key."

Karl's mouth quirked. "So, we need a sky map to open a tomb."

Michael smiled faintly despite himself. "Something like that, yes."

THEY ARRIVED in Rome under a sky the color of pewter. The city's familiar dome-lines rose out of twilight like signatures—St. Peter's against the fading west, Sant'Agnese over Piazza Navona, the lantern of the Pantheon.

Back in the apartment, they ate simply—bread, pecorino cheese, olives, a bottle of Chianti opened as quietly as a confession. Then Hana covered the small table with paper: Clement's diary excerpts, the text of Letter VII, an old plan of the Scavi Michael had memorized and redrew from memory, and star charts Ian pulled from an offline database.

"Constraints," Hana said, tapping her pen. "One: not the high-altar reliquary chamber—already used. Two: *'Silence beneath Peter's crown'*—so within the Petrine footprint, below the basilica, where sound dies. Three: *'The heavens mark the hour'*—so an illumination or alignment occurs at a particular moment."

Ian rotated a star map. "If it's solar, we can predict shafts of light. If lunar, timing gets trickier—but also less policed. No one schedules liturgies by moonlight."

Michael said, "If a window or shaft aligns with the sun or moon at a specific time—"

"—then a beam hits a mark," Hana finished, her eyes brightening. *"'The heavens mark the hour.'"*

❧

ELSEWHERE, in the Palazzo del Sant'Uffizio, Cardinal Severino urged the Curia to authorize an inquiry into "archival misconduct," giving the appearance of propriety while clearing the way to confiscate evidence.

Across town, Alessandro de' Medici instructed Valentina to widen surveillance. "He cannot resist the Vatican. The eighth letter is a magnet. When he moves, we close in."

CHAPTER

THIRTY-SIX

ROME

Rain swept across Rome in uneven sheets, blurring the dome of St. Peter's into a gray silhouette against the storm. Inside the apartment, the fire snapped and hissed, filling the dim library with the scent of pine and old paper. Maps, parchment reproductions, and pages of Clement's letters covered the table between them—an organized chaos that only Michael seemed to understand.

Tracing the translation with her fingertip, Hana read, *"'In cedar shall it rest, bound with brass, where light from heaven may still descend.'* He's describing more than craftsmanship—he's describing a place."

Michael nodded, leaning closer to the text. "Clement's words aren't metaphor. Light from heaven could mean a literal shaft of sunlight. A site open to the sky."

Karl folded his arms. "That narrows it down to half the churches in Rome."

216

"Not quite," Lukas said, pulling up a satellite image on his phone. "Think like an architect. Sunlight reaching belowground means an aperture or a skylight—something designed to illuminate a crypt."

Hana looked up from the letter. "Beneath St. Peter's, there's the necropolis—the grotto where the early popes and martyrs were buried. It's one of the few places in Rome where sunlight filters through openings from above, all the way down to the tombs."

Michael's gaze shifted toward the rain-darkened window, where the faint outline of the basilica's dome loomed through mist. "Clement would have known those catacombs. He would have chosen them precisely because no one would dare look there."

Ian turned his laptop toward them, his red hair catching the lamplight. "The papal excavation records from the 1940s mention an uncharted alcove sealed by masonry—'unidentifiable Renaissance workmanship,' according to the notes. It was never reopened."

Karl raised a brow. "So, a Medici-era crypt beneath the basilica, sealed for five hundred years? That's no coincidence."

Michael rubbed a hand over his jaw. "Clement's reliquary—the cedar and brass box—could still be there."

Hana leaned back, eyes distant. "Light from heaven may still descend." She said it softly, the phrase taking on a new gravity. "A reliquary buried beneath St. Peter's— waiting for the light to find it again."

For a moment, the storm seemed to pause outside. The thunder that had been pacing the city's edges rolled off into the distance.

Ian broke the silence. "I can arrange access to the necropolis through Sister Teri. Maintenance window's coming up—they shut down public tours for cleaning twice a month. We could slip in with a small team, after hours."

Karl's tone was pragmatic. "Security will be tight. Swiss Guard rotation every two hours, plus motion sensors in the grotto corridors."

Lukas gave him a faint grin. "Then it's a good thing we know the guards."

Michael smiled slightly, but his voice was solemn. "This isn't a heist. It's a pilgrimage. What Clement buried, he did out of fear. If we find it, we answer that fear with truth."

Hana nodded. "Then let's make sure truth has a key."

The fire cracked behind them, scattering embers like stars. Outside, rainwater ran down the apartment's old glass, blurring the reflection of the basilica's dome into shifting gold and shadow.

Michael looked at it and said quietly, almost to himself, "Beneath heaven's light—where the condemned are remembered. That's where he hid it."

Ian tapped his screen, pulling up astronomical simulation software he had quietly pirated years ago. "I've overlaid the Scavi orientation with lunar, solar, and planetary data. Three candidate alignments within the next two weeks. One is a solar shaft at noon on the Feast of the Chair of St. Peter. Another is a Venus-Moon conjunction visible just before dawn in a few days, projected through a grotto grate. And the third is a midsummer alignment— too far off."

Karl's brows furrowed. "Which is most likely?"

Hana chewed her lip, considering. "The Venus-Moon conjunction. Clement loved symbolic resonance. Venus as morning star, Magdalene as witness, moonlight as hidden light. He wove poetry into geometry. That's the one."

Michael nodded slowly. "Then that's when we move."

Karl rubbed his eyes. "We'll need uniforms and a reason to be there."

Michael nodded. "The basilica's night staff rotates predictably. There's a maintenance window after closing when the Scavi's security camera loops sync for firmware checks. The system is modern—but not perfect."

Ian's grin was fox-like. "I'll just borrow that imperfection for an hour or so."

Michael nodded. "But until then, we secure ourselves. Alessandro will tighten the noose. Severino will push the Curia. We need allies."

ACROSS THE RIVER, Cardinal Severino sat with two monsignors in the Apostolic Palace. He spoke with the authority of a man who had weathered storms for decades. "Dominic has crossed lines. His association with Sinclair compromises Vatican integrity. He has fabricated manuscripts. He misuses the Archives." He let each accusation drip like acid.

One monsignor asked hesitantly, "And the Holy Father?"

Severino's lips thinned. "Clement XV values stability. He does not want scandal. If Dominic forces our hand, the pope will side with order. Alessandro has assured me that contingencies are in place."

MEANWHILE, in the Villa Aurelia Medici, Alessandro stood

on his terrace as dusk wrapped the cypress trees in long shadows.

Valentina reported crisply, "Dominic has returned to Rome. He's hidden in Trastevere. Surveillance nets are tightening. Shall I move to extract?"

Alessandro sipped his brandy, eyes never leaving the horizon. "No. Patience. Let him burrow deeper. The eighth letter is near, and he cannot resist it. When he reaches for it, we close the trap."

Valentina inclined her head. "And if he stalls?"

"Then we force him," Alessandro replied, his voice cold. "A whisper in the press. A forged leak. Sinclair's credibility will burn faster than any gospel."

BACK IN TRASTEVERE, the team's debate continued through the night. Hana filled the margins of her notes with star paths, Latin phrases, and architectural sketches. Ian mapped Alessandro's digital probes, feeding him false data through Scarella's compromised terminal. Karl and Lukas alternated watch shifts, their movements disciplined, their silences heavy with foreboding.

Finally, Michael placed his hand gently over Hana's notebook. "Enough for tonight. You've carried Clement's riddles long enough without pause. Rest."

She met his gaze, fatigue softening into trust. "One more line," she whispered, "then I'll sleep."

She wrote it at the bottom of the page: *'When Venus greets the moon, Magdalene speaks.'* Then she closed the notebook, her hand brushing Michael's for a moment that lingered longer than either would admit.

Michael rose and stood by the shuttered window, looking out over the sleeping quarter of Trastevere. He whispered a prayer for strength, for Hana, for his friends, and for a Church that might not survive the truth entrusted to him.

By the time the rain eased, the storm had left the city rinsed and luminous. The streets below glistened in the reflected light of the basilica's dome, and thunder rumbled distantly toward the sea.

Hana closed her notebook and glanced at the stack of Clement's letters spread across the table. "These need to be stabilized before we go below. The parchment's brittle enough to crumble if we breathe on it."

Michael nodded, considering. "Sister Maria Francesca has a preservation chamber at Santa Cecilia—the kind used for illuminated manuscripts. She can safeguard the letters until we return."

Karl looked up from the map he was folding. "And you want her blessing, don't you?"

Michael smiled faintly. "Her clarity. There are times faith needs another voice to steady it."

Lukas fastened his holster and adjusted his coat. "Then we go to the abbess before we go underground."

The others nodded.

Michael gathered the letters into the cedar tube, sealing it gently with the care of a man entrusting the past to the future. "Tomorrow," he said, "we carry light into the dark."

Outside, the last of the rain fell like incense, and the city seemed to breathe again. By morning, they would make their way to the monastery on the Tiber's quiet edge —to place Clement's relics in safe hands and seek wisdom from a woman who had long understood the cost of silence.

CHAPTER

THIRTY-SEVEN

SANTA CECILIA MONASTERY, ROME

The monastery of Santa Cecilia was unusually still that morning. Outside, the rain had passed, leaving the courtyard glistening with dew. The scent of rosemary and wet stone filled the air. Hana and Father Michael sat with Sister Maria Francesca in the cloister garden, a simple table between them covered with the cedar reliquary tube, their notes, and the remaining letters of Clement VII.

The abbess poured tea into small earthen cups. "It's strange," she said, "how the past refuses to stay buried. You think you've laid it to rest, and then it knocks on your door with another secret."

Michael hesitated. "I noticed the fit of this case—it's deeper than it should be. It feels… incomplete."

Hana looked at him sharply. "You think there's more inside?"

He nodded, turning the tube gently in his hands. "Clement was deliberate in everything he did. He could have nested the letters—one inside another. The seal at the bottom hasn't been disturbed."

The abbess folded her hands, watching quietly as Michael set the case on the table. "Careful," she said softly. "If he meant for it to stay hidden, he'll have hidden it well."

Michael took a slim restoration probe from his satchel and ran it carefully along the inner wall. There was resistance halfway down—a faint, dull sound, like parchment sliding against wood. He twisted gently, and something shifted. When he withdrew the tool, a narrow roll of brittle vellum clung to its tip.

Hana drew in a breath. "Five hundred years sitting in plain sight."

Michael unrolled the fragile sheet slowly, revealing a faint papal seal pressed into cracked wax. The handwriting, though shaky, was unmistakably Clement's. At the top, beneath a smudge of age-darkened ink, was a line of Latin:

Epistola VIII – Benedictio Pulveris.
   The Benediction of Dust.

Sister Maria Francesca made the sign of the cross. "The pope's final words."

Michael nodded. "It seems so. The handwriting suggests it was written in his last days."

He spread the parchment flat on the table, smoothing its wrinkles with gloved fingers. "Let's see what was so important that he buried it twice."

The abbess bowed her head. "Then may we read with reverence."

Michael took a breath and began to translate aloud.

To the one who follows the trail I began:

The Gospel was not my only burden. There is another record —a codex of those whose voices Rome chose to forget. I could not destroy it, yet I feared its light. So I sealed the Codex of Voices beneath Peter's resting place, where silence guards what faith could not bear.

When Venus greets the Moon and the dawn is still unborn, a lamp will draw its shadow to the wound I left in stone. There you will find my last confession.

Forgive me for doubting the courage of those who would come after me.

✞ Clemens PP. VII
Pontifex Maximus

When he finished, the silence in the garden deepened until only the fountain's trickle could be heard.

Hana stared at the page. "*Beneath Peter's resting place.* That's not metaphor."

Michael nodded. "No—it's precise. Clement left a location, and even the time of day. 'When Venus greets the Moon, and the dawn is still unborn.' He's describing a celestial alignment—light entering through an opening before sunrise."

Karl's voice came from the cloister archway; he and Lukas had just entered. "You mean the shafts beneath the basilica? The necropolis?"

"Exactly," Michael said. "Clement hid it under St. Peter's itself—the *Codex of Voices.*"

Sister Maria Francesca's expression softened into quiet wonder. "You'll go down there, then."

"Yes," Michael said. "It's what he wanted—for someone to find it, to face what he couldn't."

The abbess stood, adjusting her habit in the light breeze. "Then may the saints guide you, and the truth keep you humble."

Michael folded the letter gently and placed it back inside the cedar tube. As he did, sunlight slipped through the cloister arch and struck the reliquary's brass trim, a sudden glint of gold against the shadows.

The abbess stopped them at the door and pressed a folded piece of linen into Michael's hand. Inside was a crimson ribbon. "If you must hide something holy, wrap it with care," she said. "It reminds the soul that secrets are temporary."

The bell for midday prayers began to ring, its echo threading through the courtyard as the team gathered their things. They would return to the Vatican before nightfall, and then—guided by a dead pope's final confession—descend into the heart of the earth.

CHAPTER

THIRTY-EIGHT

VATICAN CITY

Two days later, the morning sun washed St. Peter's Square in pale gold, pooling between the great colonnades like spilled light. Pilgrims and tourists crossed the cobblestones in slow tides, their voices a mingled prayer and chatter that echoed softly against Bernini's marble arms.

Michael moved through them unnoticed, collar turned up, a small messenger bag slung over his shoulder. He paused at the base of the basilica's steps, watching two *sampietrini* sweep dust from the stairway with ancient straw brooms. Everything here, even cleaning, had the gravity of ritual.

Hana waited by the south transept entrance, camera bag slung across her shoulder. Her dark hair caught the morning light. When Michael reached her, she held up her phone, displaying a star chart. "I recalculated the alignment. The conjunction will be visible just before dawn. Venus and the Moon rise together—right over the Scavi ventilation shafts."

"So, the light will enter the corridor then," Michael said. "Clement's timing was exact."

"He must have known the masons who built those shafts," Hana said, almost admiring. "He thought like an engineer."

They quietly entered the basilica and joined a small guided tour descending into the necropolis. The air below was cool and close, the smell of damp stone and candle wax replacing the jasmine sweetness of the square above. The custodian's voice echoed in the narrow passage, rehearsing his script about the pagan tombs and Christian burials that shared the same ground.

Michael tuned it out, noting instead the faint draft that brushed his cheek, the thin slit of a vent high in the wall, and the uneven tone of the bricks near the south corridor's bend. Hana caught his glance and raised her camera, pretending to photograph the mosaics while she noted the angle of the slit and the direction of the light.

When they returned to the surface, the heat of midmorning hit like a physical thing. They crossed the piazza and ducked into the shade of a service archway, where Karl and Lukas waited beside a black van. Ian sat on the hood, his laptop balanced on his knees.

"Firmware update for the Scavi cameras tonight at twenty-three hundred," Ian said, looking up with a grin. "I can use it to loop the feed for when you infiltrate, same as last time. This time, I'll add a heartbeat signal, making it look alive to the system."

Michael's breath went out in a sound that was almost a laugh. "One day, we'll confess these things properly."

Ian shrugged. "I'm Irish. We confess recreationally."

Even Karl cracked a smile at that. Lukas, ever serious, unfolded a printed map of the necropolis and laid it across the van's hood. His pencil marks were meticulous—angles, distances, timing windows. "We enter through the maintenance stair," he said, tracing the route. "From the grotto, down to the south corridor. Ninety-eight paces to the sealed patch. Two-minute patrol gap. We're invisible if we move like clockwork."

Hana leaned over the map. "The conjunction peaks at 04:13. The light will strike the wall about two minutes before and last three minutes after. That's all the time we get."

Karl nodded. "Five minutes, start to finish. Anything more and the guards will wonder why the dead have company."

Michael looked up from the diagram. "No improvising. If something feels wrong, we leave it. We reseal the wall exactly as we found it."

"I've prepared for that," Ian said, producing a small metal case from his backpack. Inside, neatly arranged tools glinted under the weak light: a chisel no larger than a pen, a fine brush, linen tape, and a pouch of mortar dust. "We work like archaeologists, not thieves."

The humor was gone now; even Ian's grin had settled into focus. Hana studied the tools, then looked at Michael. "If this fails, we still have the letter. We can walk away."

He shook his head. "Clement didn't write for us to stop halfway."

Just then, Michael's phone vibrated with a text message: **To the Reverend Father Michael Dominic: The Secretariat requests your presence tomorrow, at the ninth hour, regarding matters of inquiry.**

Teri's message followed seconds later: **Not a subpoena. Yet. If you attend, we gain time. If you refuse, they'll act**.

Michael put the phone in his pocket. "I'll go. I can answer questions without lying. That alone will confuse them."

Hana frowned. "It's still a trap."

"Maybe. But every day we buy brings us closer to finishing what Clement started."

THAT EVENING, the team gathered in the small logistics office beneath the museum wing, a windowless space smelling of paper and coffee. Lukas had laid out their disguises: plain overalls, staff badges, clipboards, and lanyards. They looked like ordinary *sampietrini*, the maintenance workers of the Vatican.

Karl handed Michael a simple cloth bag with the basilica's insignia. "For the object," he said. "No markings, no words. Just weight."

"Good," Michael said. "We're not stealing anything. We're returning a voice, Clement's *Codex of Voices*, to daylight."

They went over the plan again—routes, signals, and escape options. Ian would monitor the security feed remotely; Karl and Lukas would handle timing and cover. Hana would work the tools. Michael would oversee and reseal the wall.

When they finished, the clock read just past midnight. Michael walked outside for air. The Vatican Gardens shimmered in moonlight, the smell of pine needles and stone fountains hanging in the warm night. He thought of Clement's plea—*Forgive me for doubting the courage of those who would come after me*. He looked up at the dome and whispered, "You can rest now, Your Holiness. We're coming."

CHAPTER

THIRTY-NINE

ROME

Rain drifted over Rome like ash the next morning, turning the cobblestones of Borgo Santo Spirito into slick ribbons of gray. The Vatican's walls loomed ahead, their ocher plaster glistening in the thin light. Michael moved through the mist with a calm born more from resignation than confidence. His summons had come at half past eight, escorted by a plainclothes gendarme whose politeness was more chilling than a threat.

He crossed the cobbled courtyard of the Apostolic Palace under an umbrella that did little to keep him dry. The Swiss Guard at the entrance recognized him and let his gaze drift past—an act of kindness to spare Michael the humiliation, now that word had clearly spread that he had been called to account. Inside, marble floors gleamed like polished bone. The smell of beeswax and history pressed in on him.

A young monsignor in black clerical dress waited at the foot of the grand staircase. "Father Dominic," he said with mechanical courtesy. "If you'll follow me."

They walked in silence through corridors lined with oil portraits—popes and cardinals whose eyes seemed to track them as they passed. The building was a labyrinth of power: stone polished by centuries of ambition, echoing decisions that had altered continents. Michael knew its pulse all too well.

The monsignor opened a set of heavy double doors and gestured for him to enter. "His Eminence is expecting you."

The room was part library, part tribunal chamber. A crucifix hung above a long mahogany table. Shelves of canon law and encyclicals lined the walls. The single window behind the desk framed the dome of St. Peter's, blurred by rain.

Cardinal Giovanni Severino stood at the window, hands clasped behind his back. He was tall and impeccably groomed, his scarlet zucchetto perfectly centered on his silver hair. When he turned, his smile was thin and precise.

"Father Dominic," Severino said. "Punctual as ever. Sit, please."

Michael took the chair opposite the cardinal. The monsignor closed the doors and withdrew, leaving them alone. The room felt heavier for the silence that followed.

Severino began without preamble. "You've placed the Church in a difficult position."

"I've done my duty," Michael replied evenly. "My duty is to truth."

"Truth," Severino repeated, almost wistful. "A beautiful word. But so easily confused with pride."

Michael said nothing. The cardinal slowly circled the table, his robes whispering against the marble floor.

"Do you realize what your discovery has done?" Severino continued. "The press speaks of a 'lost gospel,' an affront to doctrine. Scholars speculate about heresy before authentication is complete. And now the Curia is divided between those who see you as a visionary and those who see you as a liability. Tell me, Father—what are you?"

Michael looked up. "A priest who believes God is not threatened by His own words."

Severino's smile faded. "Spare me the rhetoric. You've allowed a journalist—an outsider—to meddle in Church matters. You've smuggled artifacts without proper authority. And now you hide behind the Holy Father's generosity as though it were absolution. He is at present hesitant to take a stand on the matter. But that is likely to change, with influence."

Michael met his gaze calmly. "If authority had protected Clement's letters, we wouldn't be having this conversation."

That drew the faintest flicker of anger from Severino's eyes. "Clement VII was a man undone by doubt. His letters were never meant to survive."

"But they *did* survive," Michael said. "Maybe because the truth wanted witnesses."

Severino sighed and sat at the desk, folding his hands. "You speak as if revelation requires rebellion. It does not. Faith thrives on obedience, not defiance."

"Obedience," Michael said quietly, "is virtue only when it doesn't demand blindness."

The cardinal leaned forward. "Be careful, Father. The walls have longer memories than men."

For a moment, the room was still except for the rain

tapping against the window. Michael could feel his pulse slowing, steadying. He had expected threats. He hadn't expected the faint sadness beneath them.

Severino's voice softened. "I admire your scholarship. I always have. You were one of the best we had. But you've become reckless. This… obsession with Clement's legacy—it's dangerous. You're giving our enemies the ammunition they need to destroy the Church from within."

"I'm not the one giving them ammunition," Michael said. "I'm trying to remove the gun."

Severino's eyes narrowed. "You truly believe this codex of yours will save faith?"

"I think it will remind us what faith was before it became fear."

The cardinal stood abruptly, ending the conversation. "You may go. For now. But understand me—if you persist, the consequences will be… thorough."

Michael rose slowly. "Threats from a man of God lose their power once he forgets Whom he serves."

Severino's jaw tightened. "And you? Who do you serve?"

"The same Master you claim to be serving," Michael said. "I'm just not afraid of His truth."

He rested his hand on the doorframe. "You fear what the truth might take from you, Eminence. I fear what silence already has."

He walked out, and Severino, for the first time in years, had nothing left to say.

OUTSIDE, the Vatican corridors hummed with quiet movement, with clerks carrying folders, Swiss Guards changing post, and the occasional bishop gliding past like a ghost in red silk. Michael descended the grand staircase, his thoughts still carrying the cadence of Severino's warning. The Curia had always been a cage disguised as a cathedral. He wondered whether Clement VII had sensed its bars tightening around him in the turmoil of the Renaissance, a scholar pope who wrestled with conscience and power in equal measure. By contrast, Clement XV governed in an age of scrutiny rather than swords, yet the same ancient walls pressed on him as fiercely as on his predecessor. Michael couldn't tell whether this modern Clement would choose to unbolt the cage at his side or keep the key hidden in his own pocket.

In the courtyard, the rain had eased to a fine drizzle. He stepped beneath the colonnade and spotted a familiar figure waiting beside one of the pillars—Hana, hood pulled up, raindrops glinting on her coat. She had ignored his order to stay clear.

"You shouldn't be here," he said, though he felt a quiet relief at the sight of her.

"Neither should you," she replied. "How bad?"

"Bad enough," he said. "They'll move to seize anything connected to the letters."

Hana fell into step beside him as they crossed toward the Porta Sant'Anna gate. "Then we need to finish before they do."

They passed beneath the archway and out into Borgo Pio, where the smell of coffee mixed with the exhaust of early traffic. The ordinary life of Rome carried on, oblivious to the storm building within the Vatican walls.

At a café on the corner, Ian sat at a table under the awning, laptop open, a small espresso steaming beside it. He looked up as they approached.

"Good news or bad?" he asked.

"Both," Michael said, taking a seat. "Severino threatened to bury me, but he also confirmed what we suspected—he's losing control. The pope's hesitation must be driving him mad."

Ian grinned. "Mad cardinals make mistakes. That's good."

Hana poured sugar into her coffee, stirring absently. "We can't rely on mistakes. We have to stay ahead."

"I'm working on that," Ian said, turning the laptop around. The screen showed a map of Vatican network nodes, dots glowing like constellations. "I piggybacked on the firmware loop we used last night. Found a trace ping coming from inside Severino's office—someone's sending regular updates to an encrypted address registered to a Medici subsidiary."

Michael frowned. "Who?"

"Has to be Donato Scarella," Ian said. "He's feeding her information about our movements."

"Then we use them," Hana said. "Feed them what we want Alessandro to believe."

Ian smiled. "Now you're thinking like a hacker."

Michael managed a faint smile. "Let's think like honest thieves, then. What do you need?"

"Time," Ian said. "And a clean signal. I'll write a false data stream that points them toward an empty corridor in the Scavi—the old maintenance shaft north of the Clementine Chapel."

Michael rubbed his temple, fatigue pressing behind his eyes. "Severino knows I'm still in Rome. He'll double the guards."

"Then we triple our luck," Ian said. "I've been doing that all my life."

CHAPTER
FORTY

ROME

The first sharp edge of morning cut through the blinds of the Trastevere apartment, carving pale bars across the opposite wall. Hana sat at the kitchen table with her laptop open and her coffee going cold, scrolling through headlines that multiplied faster than she could read them.

Vatican Source Disputes Claims Of Lost Gospel. Internal Inquiry Widens.

Archivist Dominic Under Scrutiny For Theft Of Relics.

She shut the laptop before the words could bruise any further.

Michael stood at the window, collar open, sleeves rolled to the elbow. The city outside was waking— shopkeepers rattling up metal shutters, a Vespa coughing to life, the smell of bread from the adjacent bakery downstairs weaving through the damp air. Ordinary Rome, alive and indifferent.

"They're tightening the noose," Hana said.

"They always do," Michael answered, "right before the truth breaks through."

"You sound like Clement."

He half-smiled. "Maybe I'm starting to understand him."

The door opened and Ian stepped in, hair damp from the overnight rain, a paper grocery sack under one arm and his laptop under the other. "Morning, sinners," he said, setting the bag on the counter. "Eggs, bread, and a handful of new enemies."

Karl followed, closing the door with his shoulder. "We were tailed from the bridge," he said quietly. "Two men in an unmarked car. Professional, but sloppy."

"Alessandro?" Michael asked.

"Or Severino's network," Karl said. "They might be sharing eyes."

Ian shrugged out of his jacket and cracked an egg into a pan. "If they're sharing resources, we'll share chaos." He glanced at Hana. "I put a breadcrumb in the Vatican server. If they trace my login, they'll end up chasing a phantom file called *Evangelium Lupae*."

"The *Gospel of the She-Wolf*," Hana said, raising an eyebrow.

"Exactly," Ian said, flipping the egg. "If they want mythology, we'll give them plenty."

Karl leaned against the wall, half amused. "One day, Ian, your cleverness will outpace your luck."

Ian grinned. "Then I'll count on Providence to drive the getaway car."

. . .

By noon, the rain had stopped. Michael stepped into the courtyard to take a call. Sister Maria Francesca's voice came thin but calm over the line.

"The letters are safe," she said. "Two officers came this morning with papers that looked official but smelled of fear. I gave them tea and an empty box labeled 'Liturgical Cloths.' They left with their dignity and nothing else."

"You have a gift for diplomacy, Sister."

"God gives each of us weapons we can use without sin," she said. "Mine happens to be manners. And how goes your war?"

"We've recovered something Clement called the *Codex of Voices*," Michael said. He hesitated. "It's sealed. I intend to bring it to the Holy Father."

"Then hurry," she said. "Storms travel faster than prayers."

Her words lingered long after he ended the call.

By late afternoon, tension had settled into the apartment like fog. Ian sat cross-legged on the floor amid a tangle of cables and open laptops, listening to encrypted comms that Teri piped in from her post inside the Archives. The room smelled of coffee grounds and wet clothes.

"I'm seeing traffic spikes from Severino's office," Teri said over the speaker. "They've isolated the IP you used last night."

"That was the decoy line," Ian said without looking up. "They'll chase it to an abandoned node near Avignon."

"Let's hope," Teri answered. "If they pivot, I won't be able to keep your real channel clean."

Michael paced slowly, the cedar-and-silver case heavy

in his thoughts even while it rested on the table. "Every hour we wait, we bleed ground. We need to move this into the Holy Father's hands before Alessandro or Severino does something we can't undo."

Karl looked doubtful. "If they decide to hold you, there won't be time to react."

"I'll risk it," Michael said. "This doesn't belong to a press release or a police report."

Ian closed his laptop with a soft click. "All right. But I need to go get a signal amplifier from a friend across the river. Without it, I can't blind Valentina's watchers while you move."

"You shouldn't go alone," Karl said.

"I'll blend in," Ian replied, already pulling on his jacket. "Nobody expects an Irish tech nerd to be carrying Vatican secrets."

"Especially not one who confesses recreationally," Hana said dryly.

"See?" Ian winked. "I'm perfectly harmless."

He was out the door before anyone could argue.

EVENING SLID down the buildings like wet slate. Hana took the first watch at the window, chin propped on one hand, eyes moving but not distracted. Karl disassembled and reassembled his weapon on the table. Michael sat on the couch reading Clement's diary one more time, though he could have recited its lines by heart.

The knock came just after eight—three short raps, too light for the police. Karl opened the door and froze.

A stranger stood there, holding Ian's laptop bag. His expression was awkward, his accent French. "This was found on the bank of the Tiber River," he said. "Someone asked me to bring it here."

Hana's blood went cold. "Where is he? Who told you to bring it here?"

"Near Ponte Sisto," the man said. "Black van, shouting. Then nothing." He set the bag on the floor and fled down the stairs without waiting for further questions.

Michael crouched beside the bag. The canvas was damp, the zipper torn. Inside lay Ian's backup phone, still powered on. On the screen was an unsent text to Teri: **They found me. Amateurs. Trying to talk my way out. If not—tell Michael to finish it.**

Karl swore. "He's alive. They won't risk killing him yet."

"Alessandro," Hana said through her teeth. "It has to be."

Michael rose slowly, anger flickering behind his calm. "Then we bring him back—no bargaining, no ceremonies; just us, and whatever it costs."

Inside the Villa Aurelia Medici, the security suite's monitors washed the room in greenish light. Valentina stood with her hands behind her back, watching a grainy live feed streaming from the warehouse on Via Portuense: Ian hunched under a bare bulb, two men pacing, one tapping a baton against his palm.

Alessandro stood beside her, his profile carved out of shadow. "Break him," he said.

Valentina's fingers hovered over the radio, then withdrew. She muted the feed. "He's talking," she said evenly.

Alessandro didn't glance at her. Whether he believed

the lie or didn't care, she couldn't tell. For the first time, she realized she had lied for mercy, not strategy.

VIA PORTUENSE after dark had the feel of a depot at the end of the world—steel doors, broken lamps, and the slow breath of the river beyond. The warehouse glowed faintly through the rain, one window lit above the rest.

They split without debate. Hana and Michael kept the car idling a block away while Karl and Lukas moved in on foot. The radio in Hana's lap hissed with occasional static.

"Two at the front," Lukas whispered. "One at the side door. Inside looks sloppy."

"Get him and get out," Michael said. "No gunfire unless there's no choice."

Inside the warehouse, Ian's voice rose once in defiance, then was drowned by the sound of fists.

IAN HIT THE FLOOR HARD. The air left his lungs in a wet grunt. The two men circling him weren't professionals; their punches lacked rhythm, but their boots spoke fluent violence. One caught him in the ribs, another in the shoulder.

"You don't need to do this," Ian rasped. "I've got nothing you want."

One of the guards laughed. "You've got your mouth."

"Always have," Ian said—and spat blood on the floor.

They hauled him up by his jacket, shoved him into a folding chair under a single swinging light. Crates towered around them, stenciled with Chinese shipping codes. The bulb flickered, throwing jerky shadows across the walls.

Ian coughed, forcing a grin. "If this is an interview, I've had worse."

The first guard raised his fist again—and froze. A faint metallic click echoed behind them, small but deliberate. Karl's signal.

Ian didn't look. He shifted slightly in the chair, angling his body to give Karl a clear shot past his shoulder. The guard to his left hesitated, his eyes following the sound toward the darkened doorway.

Karl moved first. His silenced pistol coughed once; the light bulb shattered, plunging the room into chaos. Darkness swallowed everything, and the men cursed and stumbled, firing blindly.

Ian threw himself sideways, knocking the chair over, rolling toward the closest guard. Pain flared in his ribs, but momentum carried him. The guard went down under his tackle, the pistol clattering away. Ian landed a punch more by luck than aim; the man's head snapped back.

Lukas was through the other door in seconds, his rifle low, firing once into the ceiling to break the panic. Dust rained down. The remaining guard lunged at Karl with a knife, who met him halfway—one blow to the throat, another to the jaw, fast and final. The man dropped like a sack of stones.

"Get up," Karl barked. "Move!"

Ian staggered upright, hand pressed to his side. "Remind me to renegotiate my contract."

Karl checked the pulse of the nearest man. "Alive," he muttered. "Barely."

Lukas scanned the room with his light. "We've got ninety seconds before someone hears and comes."

"Then we're gone," Karl said. He grabbed Ian's arm,

half guiding, half dragging him toward the door. The wind outside smelled of the river—wet iron and diesel.

Lukas yanked the latch, the hinges shrieking. "Go," he said.

The side door burst open. Karl stumbled out first, half-carrying, half-dragging Ian, who looked like he had lost a fight with a stone wall and laughed about it anyway.

"Told you they were amateurs," Ian gasped as they reached the Jeep.

Lukas came out last, firing two quick shots high and wide to discourage pursuit.

Hana slammed the gearshift into drive the instant the men tumbled in. Rounds pinged against the rear panel as they fishtailed through a puddle and took the first corner too fast.

"You all right?" Michael asked, one hand gripping Ian's shoulder, the other pressed to the ceiling to steady himself.

"Perfectly," Ian said, wiping blood from his nose. "They wanted the letter. I gave them theology."

"What theology?" Hana asked, eyes on the road, jaw clenched.

"The part about forgiveness," Ian said, grinning crookedly. "They didn't appreciate the sermon."

Karl barked a short laugh. "Lucky for you they were bad Catholics."

Lukas pressed gauze to a shallow cut on Karl's forearm. "You're bleeding."

Karl smiled. "Only enough to prove I was useful."

Lukas shook his head, but his hand lingered a beat longer than necessary.

· · ·

THE RAIN HAD STOPPED before dawn, leaving Rome washed and bright. Water pooled on the cobblestones outside the apartment, reflecting fragments of the city—the cross atop a distant dome, the yellow gleam of a streetlight, the slow shapes of early risers hurrying toward the market. They didn't stop until they reached a disused grain warehouse in Testaccio—a safe house Karl maintained for nights that refused to stay quiet. The lock turned; the door groaned. Inside, the air smelled faintly of antiseptic and strong coffee.

Ian sat on the couch, a bandage on his temple, his bruised lip split into a crooked grin. Hana crouched in front of him, wrapping his hand with the precision of a field medic. The others hovered close but silent, each one aware that the humor had been beaten out of the night.

"You really should see a doctor," she murmured.

"And ruin your handiwork?" Ian said, wincing as she tightened the bandage. "No, thank you. You've a steadier hand than most surgeons in Dublin."

"Dublin surgeons don't work with duct tape," Karl muttered, leaning against the wall.

"Don't tell the insurance companies," Ian said. "They still owe me for the last exorcism."

He rummaged in his pocket and pulled out a thumb drive sealed in plastic. "Grabbed this in their command room—if you can call a card table and a religious calendar a command room—when they first threw me inside, across said card table. Looks like ledgers. Medici shells, payments through restoration budgets, a list of friendly badge numbers in the Gendarmerie."

Michael took the drive with care, turning it in his fingers. "Enough to expose Alessandro's network."

"And Severino's," Ian said. "Half those transfers were

tagged under cultural preservation grants. Your friend the cardinal launders faith with precision."

"Then we use it," Karl said.

"Not yet," Michael said. "If we move too soon, they'll burn everything before we can prove it. The pope needs to see this first."

Ian gave a weary chuckle. "Straight to the top, then."

"That's where it belongs," Michael said. "Alongside the Codex."

Silence followed. Outside, a train clattered somewhere distant. Hana finished taping Ian's lip and sat back.

"They'll come again," she said. "Angrier."

Michael nodded. "Then we stop hiding. Let's go."

They drove back to Trastevere by a looping route that fooled even Karl's paranoia. By the time they reached the apartment, the rain had started again, soft as thread.

They gathered at the small table under the desk lamp. The Codex rested where Michael had left it, wrapped in linen. The thumb drive gleamed dully on the wood.

"This," Michael said, turning the drive between his fingers, "is our insurance. With it, the Holy Father can see who's been pulling the strings."

"And if he already knows?" Hana asked.

"Then it forces a choice," Michael said.

"And if he won't choose?" Ian said, quieter now.

Michael met his eyes. "Then we show the world."

No one spoke. The lamp hummed.

Michael stood and lowered the lamp's shade, dimming the room. "Soon," he said, "we go to the Holy Father. No more shadows."

The rain answered for them—steady, insistent, washing the city clean for a moment before the noise returned. Somewhere beyond the rooftops, St. Peter's dome glowed faintly in reflected light, and the river kept its counsel, as it always had.

They slept in shifts. Michael sat the last watch, the cross cool in his palm, listening to the city breathe. When the first gray of morning touched the blinds, he rose. The Codex was where it should be. The drive was where he'd left it. In a few hours, he would ask the Pope of Rome to choose what kind of history the Church wanted to live inside.

CHAPTER
FORTY-ONE

ROME

Michael stood near the window, hands clasped behind his back, the first light of morning cutting across his collar. Behind him, the city was waking—vendors rolling up shutters, bells echoing over rooftops, pigeons lifting from the fountain in a burst of gray wings.

Lukas poured two mugs of coffee and handed one to Hana. "Drink," he said. "You haven't slept."

"I'll sleep when this is over," she replied.

Michael turned from the window. "That may not be soon. Alessandro's men won't make the same mistake twice. They know we're closing in."

Ian sipped his coffee. "They know nothing. I fed them enough disinformation to make them chase ghosts for a week. Half of Valentina's people are already on the road to Avignon by now."

"Good," Michael said. "That gives us time to prepare."

He walked to the small table at the center of the room. The cedar-and-silver case lay there, still sealed. Every time he looked at it, it seemed heavier.

"Today we finish planning," he said. "Tomorrow night, we go into the Scavi."

THE VATICAN that morning seemed caught between two centuries—the medieval stone fortress and the modern city-state it pretended to be. Reporters clustered near the gates of the Apostolic Palace, waiting for comment on rumors they didn't understand. Vatican staff moved with nervous precision, aware that someone's career—or faith— might soon be decided.

Inside the Palace, Cardinal Severino sat behind his desk, his reflection staring back at him in the polished mahogany surface. A single folder lay open before him: photographs, reports, intercepted messages. Valentina Ruspoli stood across the room in a charcoal Armani Privé suit—effortless in appearance, yet cut with the same precision that ruled her thoughts: authority tailored in wool, softened only by silk.

"They have the Codex," Severino said. "You let them take it."

"They would have found it whether I was there or not," Valentina said. "Clement left a trail no one could erase. At least this way, we know where it is."

Severino studied her for a long moment. "Do you believe in any of this? This talk of lost gospels and voices the Church silenced?"

"I believe in control," she said. "And right now, you're losing it."

He closed the folder. "And you've become insolent."

"No," she replied. "I've become realistic."

Severino's voice hardened. "You forget who you serve."

Valentina's smile was thin. "You'd be surprised how often I hear that from Alessandro." She turned and left without asking to be dismissed.

The cardinal watched her go, his anger curdling into fear. The machinery he had built was shifting beyond his grasp. Somewhere outside these walls, truth—or something like it—was moving faster than he could stop it.

THAT AFTERNOON, the team met again at the apartment. The air inside hummed with low tension. Hana had pinned blueprints of the basilica to the wall—official ones mixed with older plans drawn by Clement's masons. The contrast was striking: modern lines of engineering overlaid by the imperfect geometry of faith.

"The camera loop gives us fifty-seven minutes," Ian said, pointing to a digital timer on his laptop. "Karl and Lukas will control the outer corridor. Hana and I handle the patch. Michael keeps watch at the stairwell."

Hana circled the section of the map where the south approach curved under the Clementine Chapel. "Clement's alignment corresponds with a Venus–Moon conjunction. It happens once every twenty-eight months, but the shaft angle narrows it to tonight. After that, the geometry shifts. This is our only window."

Michael studied the map. "What time again?"

"04:13," she said. "We'll be in position by four."

Karl crossed his arms. "And the pope? When do you plan to approach him?"

"After the retrieval," Michael said. "With both artifacts secured, he'll have no choice but to listen."

Ian stretched, cracking his knuckles. "And if Severino tries to intercept us again?"

Michael's eyes hardened. "Then he'll answer to the same truth he's been hiding from."

Evening descended in slow layers over the city. The streets shimmered under streetlamps, and the scent of rain lingered in the air. Hana worked by the window, finalizing her notes. Her hands trembled slightly from fatigue.

Michael joined her, leaning on the sill beside her. "You've barely eaten."

"I'm not hungry."

"You haven't rested either."

She looked at him, faint amusement in her eyes. "You sound like a priest."

He smiled. "It's an occupational hazard."

She turned back to the city. "When I was a student, I used to think faith and knowledge were enemies. One demanded belief; the other demanded proof. Now I'm starting to think they're the same thing. Both require courage."

He watched her profile in the dim light. "Courage," he affirmed, "is the one thing Clement never lost."

"And maybe the one thing we can't afford to lose now."

They stood in silence for a while, the city's hum filtering up from below—the clatter of dishes, the distant bells, the faint music from a passing car.

Finally, Hana spoke again. "If something happens to you tomorrow—"

"It won't," he said quickly.

"—if it does," she continued, "I'll finish it. I'll take the Codex to the Holy Father myself."

Michael nodded, his expression unreadable. "You won't have to."

FAR ACROSS THE CITY, at the Villa Aurelia Medici, Alessandro sat in his study, surrounded by portraits of ancestors whose names had been carved into history through blood and patronage. The villa's walls still bore fragments of Renaissance frescoes—angels, lions, and Latin inscriptions fading into cracks.

Valentina entered without knocking. "Dominic has the Codex," she said simply.

"I know," Alessandro replied. "And tonight, he'll try to move it."

Her eyes narrowed. "You plan to stop him?"

"No," Alessandro said. "I plan to let him think he's succeeded. Then I'll decide what happens next."

"Severino's losing control," she warned. "He's desperate."

Alessandro smiled faintly. "Desperation makes useful allies. When Dominic presents his prize to the pope, the Curia will collapse under its own hypocrisy. Then we'll rebuild it—cleanly, efficiently, and profitably."

Valentina regarded him for a long moment. "You don't want truth," she said quietly. "You want ownership."

"Truth is useless without ownership," he said. "Ask any pope."

As Valentina stepped out of his study, the echo of his words trailed after her like incense gone sour. In the corridor, one of Alessandro's guards was on his knees, wiping something from the marble—dark, sticky, unmistakably blood. Alessandro's "discipline."

She paused a moment too long, eyes fixed on the stain as it dulled under the cloth. The sharp smell clung to her throat. For the first time, disgust outweighed loyalty. She adjusted her jacket, composed her face, and kept walking, but something within her refused to fall back in line.

BACK IN TRASTEVERE, the team prepared their gear. Lukas cleaned the tools, laying them out on a cloth like surgical instruments. Karl checked weapons he hoped he wouldn't need. Ian synced his laptop to Teri's encrypted relay.

Hana rechecked the timing of the alignment. "The beam will hit the wall at precisely 04:11. We'll have three minutes before it fades. We need to be done by 04:15."

"Plenty of time," Ian said, though his tone was less confident than usual.

Michael slipped the cross from around his neck and tucked it into his pocket. "This isn't about faith," he said. "It's about honesty."

Hana looked up. "You can't separate the two anymore."

He met her eyes and, for a moment, neither spoke.

Karl cleared his throat. "We should move. Traffic near the Vatican is light this time of night."

THE DRIVE across the city was silent except for the sound of the rain returning. The car passed through empty piazzas and narrow alleys, the streets shining with reflected light. Rome after midnight was another world—its grandeur asleep, its ghosts awake.

When they reached the Vatican perimeter, the gates stood half-lit by sodium lamps. Sergeant Jäger waited at the Bronze Door, his uniform immaculate even at this hour. He glanced at their badges, then at Michael. "Maintenance work again?"

"Just a minor job," Michael said.

Jäger's eyes flicked toward the bag in Karl's hand. "Be quick. The night watch grows curious when certain personnel keep odd hours."

Michael inclined his head. "Understood."

They descended into the grotto. The air was cool and heavy with age. The echo of their footsteps seemed to belong to someone else.

At the southern corridor, Hana set up her instruments —light meter, compass, chisel. Ian's voice came through the comm: "Camera loop engaged. Fifty-seven minutes. You're clear."

They waited. The only sound was the faint whisper of air moving through the ventilation shaft.

At 04:11, the first silver edge of light appeared. It struck the wall in a perfect line, sliding down the bricks until it touched the faint discoloration where Clement's mark lay hidden.

"There," Hana whispered.

She knelt and began to work, her movements steady despite the tremor in her left arm. The mortar flaked away under the chisel. One brick loosened, then another. Behind them, a small cavity waited like an open mouth.

Michael reached in carefully and drew out a scroll wrapped in linen. The air that escaped smelled faintly of earth and incense.

"Got it," Hana said, her voice shaking.

Michael slipped the scroll into the bag and resealed the

wall. The beam of light began to crawl upward as the conjunction shifted.

"Time," Ian said. "You've got one minute before the loop ends."

They retraced their steps through the corridor, up the emergency stairs, and into the grotto. The vacuum cleaner's hum near the Clementine Chapel covered their quiet movements. At the Bronze Door, Jäger looked up, gave a single nod, and waved them through.

Outside, dawn was breaking. The piazza lay nearly empty except for a few early pilgrims kneeling near the fountain. Michael paused at the threshold, breathing the cool morning air. The sky above St. Peter's burned faintly gold, as if Rome itself was waking to something new.

Back in the logistics office, they set the cedar case on the table. Its metal fittings caught the first light spilling through the window. No one spoke. They all knew the weight of what sat before them.

Michael rested his hands on the table. "Tomorrow I answer Severino's questions," he said. "After that, we take this to the Holy Father."

Hana looked at the case. "Do you think he'll listen?"

Michael nodded slowly. "He'll have to. The truth we carry belongs to more than the Church—it belongs to history."

In his study, kilometers away, Alessandro poured himself a glass of Chianti and raised it toward the window. "To Dominic," he murmured, smiling. "And to the chaos he thinks he's mastered."

Valentina watched him from across the room. "Careful, Alessandro. Chaos has a way of choosing its own master."

He laughed quietly. "Then let's see who it chooses."

BACK IN TRASTEVERE, the team gathered around the table as Michael set the scroll beside the sealed Codex. Two relics, two centuries apart, both breathing the same truth.

Ian leaned back, exhaustion in every line of his face. "So what now? You walk into the Apostolic Palace carrying dynamite wrapped in parchment?"

Michael looked at the two artifacts, his eyes steady. "No. We walk in carrying the weight of history—and the hope that this time, it won't be buried again."

Hana closed her notebook, her voice firm. "Then let's make sure it speaks."

The room fell silent. Outside, the city stirred. The sun climbed above the rooftops, gilding the river in light.

For the first time in centuries, Rome was ready to listen.

CHAPTER

FORTY-TWO

ROME

The storm that had threatened all day finally broke after sunset. Lightning flared beyond the rooftops of Trastevere, and rain slashed across the narrow streets, hissing against the cobblestones. Inside the apartment, the team gathered around the table, their faces caught in the flicker of a single desk lamp.

The cedar-and-silver case lay before them like a question that no one yet dared to answer.

Karl had drawn the blinds. Lukas checked the locks a final time, then turned to Michael. "The city's quiet," he said. "Too quiet."

Michael nodded. "They're waiting for us to make the next move."

Ian adjusted the ice pack pressed to his bruised temple. "Then let's not disappoint them."

Hana's eyes stayed on the Codex. "We don't even know what's inside yet."

257

"Maybe we're not meant to," Michael said. "Not until it's safe."

Ian looked up. "And when will that be? Before or after Alessandro rewrites the news cycle?"

"Neither," Michael said quietly. "We take it to the Holy Father tomorrow. No delays, no debates."

Karl frowned. "You really trust him?"

"I trust the office," Michael said. "As for the man holding it… Well, he'll have to decide if he trusts himself."

Outside, thunder rolled across the Tiber like drums from a distant war, slow and sure.

ACROSS THE CITY, the Villa Aurelia Medici loomed behind its high walls, a Renaissance fortress turned modern citadel. Alessandro stood by the tall window of his study, staring out at the rain-slick garden, where statues of long-dead ancestors gleamed in the lightning flashes.

In its day, the Medici line had ruled Florence like merchant princes, building an empire from ledgers and lending. They had financed popes, crowned kings, and turned the very notion of piety into a currency. Cosimo the Elder had bought his city's peace with coin and cunning; Lorenzo the Magnificent had made Florence a kingdom of art, patron to Botticelli, da Vinci, and Michelangelo—men who carved eternity into marble and painted theology into light.

Their wealth had built cathedrals, but their genius had built power. Through art, faith, and banking, the Medici had learned to control the world without ever drawing a sword. Even centuries after their fall, their name still whispered through the Vatican's marble corridors, etched into basilica crests and papal tombs like signatures that refused to fade.

Alessandro had inherited that legacy not as a blessing, but as a burden polished by pride. His ancestors had ruled through patronage and persuasion; he ruled through leverage and information. Where they had shaped faith with frescoes and architecture, he shaped it through markets and data—modern instruments for the same ancient hunger. He had no Florence to govern, no papacy to anoint, only a world still addicted to power. And on nights like this, staring at the storm, he imagined the marble saints outside whispering in judgment that he was merely a Medici without a Renaissance.

Valentina Ruspoli stood a few paces behind him, motionless, a tablet in her hand. "They've done it," she said. "Dominic and his team. He found the Codex."

Alessandro didn't turn. "I know."

"How?"

"Because Severino called an hour ago. He wants to declare Dominic excommunicated for theft and heresy. I told him to wait."

Valentina raised an eyebrow. "That's restraint I didn't expect."

Alessandro smiled faintly. "Dominic believes he's won. But victory is a matter of narrative. Let him deliver his relic to the pope. By the time it reaches the public, I'll decide what it means."

"And if the pope sides with him?"

Alessandro finally turned, his expression as calm as carved marble. "Then I'll remind the world who funds half the Vatican's restorations, and which families built its foundations."

He poured another glass of wine and didn't offer her

one. "Power," he said, "is the only virtue the Church still understands."

Valentina stared at him over the rim of her tablet. "And truth?"

"Truth is useful only when it's obedient."

The words landed harder than he intended. She looked at him—this man she had served without question—and saw, for the first time, not strength but sickness: a fear so old it had learned to call itself wisdom. The realization frightened her more than any enemy could.

Valentina tilted her head. "You've mistaken leverage for loyalty. Rome loves patrons only until it loves scapegoats more."

His smile tightened. "And you? Have you found religion all of a sudden?"

"No," she said. "Just conscience."

He studied her for a moment, something dark flickering in his gaze. "Be careful, Valentina. Conscience is expensive in this house."

She met his stare without flinching. "So is silence."

BACK IN TRASTEVERE, the air inside the apartment had grown thick with fatigue. Hana sat on the edge of the couch, sketching rough diagrams in her notebook: the layout of the Vatican Archives, the timing of patrols, even the route they would need to reach the Apostolic Palace undetected.

Ian watched from the kitchen counter, sipping cold coffee. "You're planning like a thief again," he said.

"Old habits," Hana replied without looking up. "If Severino issues a warrant before we reach the Holy Father, we'll need another way in."

Karl leaned against the wall. "You think the pope doesn't already know?"

"He knows," Michael said. "The question is whether he's ready to face what we've brought him."

Ian opened his laptop. "I've traced communications from Severino's office. He's panicking. He's convened an emergency session with the Secretariat's First Section—General Affairs. That's code for damage control before your audience."

Michael rubbed his temple. "Then we go tonight."

"Tonight?" Hana asked.

"Yes. We won't wait for an invitation. We go in through the north passage, near the Gardens. Jäger will let us through if I ask."

Karl exchanged a glance with Lukas. "If he doesn't, we improvise."

VALENTINA DROVE through the downpour toward the Vatican. The wipers beat a slow rhythm against the windshield, each swipe revealing the blurred glow of amber streetlamps. Her mind was a quiet storm of its own.

In the passenger seat, a small voice recorder blinked red—the one she had used to capture Alessandro's conversation earlier that evening, his cold admission of control, his contempt for faith. It sat now in her coat pocket, heavy as guilt.

The guard at St. Anne's Gate barely looked up. He had seen her face often enough in recent days to mistake habit for clearance. She parked near the Curial offices, killed the engine, and sat in silence. For the first time in years, she wasn't sure whose side she was on.

A flash of lightning illuminated the courtyard. The rain

had stopped. Valentina stepped out of the car, pulled her coat tight, and began walking toward the Apostolic Palace.

IN HIS OFFICE, Cardinal Severino was pacing. The hour was late, but his mind refused rest. The walls of his chamber were lined with shelves of canon law and marble busts of long-dead popes who had stared down heresies greater than this—or thought they had.

A knock at the door made him start. "Enter," he said.

Valentina stepped in, water dripping from her coat. "Eminence."

Severino frowned. "At this hour?"

"We need to talk."

She placed the recorder on his desk and pressed Play. Alessandro's voice filled the room: *"Truth is useless without ownership. Ask any pope."*

Severino listened, his expression shifting from annoyance to unease. "Where did you get this?"

"I was in the room," Valentina said. "He's using you, Eminence. The Medici legacy isn't about faith—it's about power. When Dominic brings the Codex to the pope, Alessandro intends to spin it into a scandal. You'll take the fall for it."

Severino's eyes hardened. "You expect me to believe you're doing this out of charity?"

"No," she said. "I'm doing it because I'm tired of serving men who confuse God with themselves. You don't understand. Alessandro's been listening for months— through cameras, servers, even the Archives' own system. There's nothing he doesn't know."

She turned toward the door. "Do what you want with

the recording. But if Dominic dies, the file goes to the press."

Severino's voice followed her as she left. "You're playing a dangerous game, Signora Ruspoli."

She didn't look back. "Then pray you're better at it than I am."

BACK IN THE APARTMENT, Michael checked his watch. "Time," he said. "Let's go."

The team gathered their gear. The Codex was wrapped in linen and secured in the same nondescript bag Karl had prepared. The air outside was cold and clean. They moved quickly through the side streets, keeping to the shadows.

When they reached the Vatican perimeter, Sergeant Jäger was waiting at the Bronze Door, as promised. His expression gave nothing away.

"Father Dominic," he said. "You bring trouble with you."

Michael smiled faintly. "Only the kind that comes with purpose."

The sergeant sighed, then stepped aside. "Fifteen minutes, no more. After that, the cameras come back online."

They slipped into the corridor leading toward the papal residence. The marble gleamed under low light, their reflections sliding across its surface like ghosts. The only sound was the echo of their footsteps and the soft creak of leather straps.

As they turned a corner, Hana slowed. "Someone's here," she whispered.

Karl raised his weapon, scanning the hallway.

From the shadows ahead, a voice said, "Easy, Sergeant.

You've pointed that thing at me before. Remember how it ended?"

Valentina stepped forward, coat still damp, her expression unreadable.

Karl lowered the weapon, but not entirely. "You picked a bad night for a reunion," he said.

"I came to help," Valentina said.

Michael eyed her cautiously. "Why the sudden change of heart?"

"Let's say I've remembered what conscience feels like," she replied. "Alessandro plans to twist whatever you give the pope into a scandal. He's already set the stage. Severino's finished, but the fire's still burning. If you want this truth to survive, you'll need allies."

"Are you one?" Hana asked.

Valentina's gaze flicked between them. "For tonight. Tomorrow, I start answering for the rest of it."

Michael's expression softened. "Then you're exactly the ally we need."

THEY REACHED the antechamber outside the papal apartments. Two Swiss Guards stood at attention. One recognized Michael and stepped forward.

"Father Dominic," he said quietly. "Sergeant Jäger signaled ahead, but His Holiness was already awake. He said he had a feeling you'd arrive tonight."

The guard opened the door.

Pope Clement XV stood near a small writing desk, a plain white cassock replacing the ceremonial vestments of daylight. His silver hair glinted in the lamplight. He looked tired, but his eyes were alive with alert intelligence.

"Father Dominic," he said, motioning for them to enter. "And your companions."

Michael bowed. "Your Holiness. We bring what Clement VII left for the future."

The pope gestured toward the desk. "Place it there."

Michael set the bag down and unwrapped the linen. The silver fittings gleamed softly under the light. The pope regarded it for a long moment before speaking.

"So, this is the voice that frightened a pope into silence," he said. "And another into courage."

"Yes," Michael said. "Both were men of faith. One hid the truth to protect it. The other tried to free it."

Clement XV rested his hand on the case. "Truth doesn't need guardians. It needs witnesses." He looked at Michael. "Will you stand as one?"

"Yes, Holy Father," Michael said.

The pope nodded. "Then let us see what centuries have kept from us."

OUTSIDE, Valentina stepped into the courtyard, the damp air cool on her face. She drew in a long breath, exhaled slowly, and walked toward the gate. For the first time in years, she felt lighter.

In the papal chamber behind her, history was about to open its mouth and speak.

CHAPTER

FORTY-THREE

VATICAN CITY

The morning after Michael's clandestine audience with Pope Clement XV broke gray and heavy, a ceiling of low clouds pressing Rome into silence. Within the Apostolic Palace, the Curia moved like an old clock wound too tight—secretaries hurrying through corridors, bishops conferring in alcoves, and the hum of rumor rising like a psalm sung off-key.

Cardinal Giovanni Severino, Secretary of State of the Holy See, stood at the window of his office, hands clasped behind his back. The crucifix above his desk reflected faintly in the glass, a pale double over his shoulder. He hadn't slept.

Valentina Ruspoli's visit the previous night had shredded his certainty. He had replayed Alessandro's recorded words again and again—"*Truth is useless without ownership*"—until the phrase had lodged itself like grit in his conscience. He knew it could destroy them all: the

Medici financier, the pope, perhaps even the Church itself if the story reached the world unshaped.

Recalling the echo of her heels on the marble outside told him she was gone for good. He had dismissed her with courtesy, but the damage was done. A career built on control was beginning to slip.

Monsignor Bartoli entered quietly. "Eminence, the First Section is assembled."

"Let them wait," Severino said without turning. "Ten minutes."

He walked to the desk, arranged his papers into perfect symmetry, and faced the crucifix. "If power corrupts, Lord," he murmured, "why did You make obedience so easy?"

When he entered the conference room, a dozen eyes turned to him—priests, economists, diplomats—men who lived by tone and nuance.

"We are losing the narrative," he began. "Father Dominic's discovery has become a spectacle. The Holy Father's decision to open the Gospel and Codex to scholars endangers the Church's unity. We must reassert discipline."

A gray-haired monsignor cautiously raised his hand. "Eminence, the Holy Father's choice was deliberate. Suppressing it now would look like fear."

Severino's voice hardened. "It is fear. The only kind that preserves faith."

No one spoke after that. They knew the meeting was less about consultation than containment. When he finally dismissed them, he felt not triumph but fatigue—the hollow kind that follows a battle one no longer believes in.

.   .   .

BY MID-MORNING, Valentina sat in her car near the Ponte Sant'Angelo, engine idling, eyes fixed on the angels above the bridge. The recorder was gone; she had left it with a trusted journalist in Milan, together with instructions to release it only if she failed to call by sunset.

The city seemed unaware of its own tremors. Pilgrims queued at the basilica gates, umbrellas blooming like flowers in the rain. She envied them their certainty.

Her phone buzzed—an encrypted message from an unlisted number: **He knows you came. Be careful.**

She didn't need to ask who *he* was. Alessandro's network reached everywhere.

She slid the phone into her coat pocket and pulled into traffic, heading south along the Tiber. Whatever came next, she was past the point of hiding.

DEEP BENEATH THE VATICAN LIBRARY, among the server racks humming like a hive, Sister Teri Drinkwater adjusted her headset. Lines of encrypted text streamed down her monitor—financial transactions cross-referenced from Ian's stolen thumb drive. The pattern was unmistakable: restoration accounts funneled through offshore Medici foundations, then washed clean through diocesan endowments.

Her screen flashed: **AUDITOR GENERAL ONLINE.**

Teri: **Confirmed routing through Medici Fund 91 and Gendarmerie auxiliary accounts.**

Auditor: **Understood. Quiet investigation underway. His Holiness notified. Maintain channel.**

Teri sat back, heart thudding. She was one of the few

inside the walls who knew how deep the rot went—and how fragile salvation would be if the story broke before proof hardened. Around her, the servers sustained their patient hymn.

By afternoon, the rain had thinned to mist. In the apartment above the bookbinder's shop, the team gathered around the table.

Ian's face was still bruised, his humor intact. "Well," he said, "Severino's been cornered. The question is whether he'll bite or bolt."

Karl replied, "He'll bite. That's what wounded animals do."

Hana stood at the window, arms crossed. "And the pope?"

Michael exhaled. "He'll announce the commission tomorrow. Independent scholars, a multilingual team, full transparency. It's the only way to protect the Codex from being buried again."

"Or to make sure it burns in daylight," Hana said softly.

Michael looked at her. "Clement's sin was silence. Ours won't be."

Ian tapped a key on his laptop, bringing up a live data feed. "Teri just confirmed movement in the Auditor's office. They're pulling bank records tied to Severino's people. The man's about to find out what sunlight feels like."

Karl glanced at Michael. "And Alessandro?"

Michael's mouth tightened. "He'll fight to the end. But Valentina's recording makes him vulnerable. If the right ears hear it, his empire collapses."

Hana turned from the window. "Do you trust her?"

Michael hesitated. "I trust what she's done, not who she is. That's enough for now."

IN THE LATE AFTERNOON, Severino met with his two closest aides in the Secretariat's private antechamber. The mist outside had turned to drizzle; water ran down the tall windows like veins.

"They're preparing an investigation," one aide whispered. "The Auditor General himself."

"Based on what?" Severino demanded.

"Anonymous sources. Financial irregularities linked to restoration grants."

Severino's knuckles whitened. "Anonymous," he repeated. "Then we will find their names."

He dismissed them with a wave. When the door closed, he allowed himself one unguarded moment of rage—sweeping the papers from his desk so they scattered across the carpet like wounded doves.

In the chaos, a single envelope slid free and landed at his feet. The Vatican crest, embossed in red wax. He tore it open.

By direction of the Holy Father:

Effective immediately, all financial oversight concerning restoration grants is transferred to the Office of the Auditor General pending review.

No accusation, no explanation—only the quiet erasure of authority.

Severino's breath came thin. In fifty years of service, he

had mastered every form of loss except this: the one that arrived without ceremony.

THAT EVENING, thunder growled again above the hills west of the city. The Villa Aurelia Medici glowed with lamplight, its walls catching the flashes like old gold.

Alessandro paced his study, the portraits of his ancestors seeming to watch him as he passed by each one, judgments etched in oil.

"The Medici built empires out of art," he muttered. "And I'll be undone by a priest with a conscience."

His phone vibrated. He answered it on speaker. "Yes?"

A male voice spoke, hesitant. "They've opened a financial review, Signor de' Medici. The Secretariat has frozen several accounts."

"For how long?"

"Indefinitely."

Alessandro set the phone on his desk with surgical precision. "Find the source. And whoever leaked that recording—silence them."

When the call ended, he stood in front of the window until his reflection blurred. The rain outside sounded like applause from ghosts.

AT THE SAME HOUR, Pope Clement XV sat alone in his private library, the Gospel and Codex resting on the desk before him.

He looked toward the window, where lightning flared across the dome of St. Peter's and murmured, "So it begins again."

His secretary entered quietly. "Holy Father, the

Secretariat requests confirmation of tomorrow's announcement."

"Prepare it," the pope said. "And tell them truth is no enemy of faith."

"Yes, Holy Father."

When the secretary withdrew, the pope touched the manuscripts as though testing their temperature. They were cold. "You've waited long enough," he murmured. "Let the world hear you."

THE STORM RETURNED WITH EVENING, thunder marching across the Tiber like legions recalled from forgotten wars.

In the apartment, candlelight flickered across maps and papers. Hana sat cross-legged on the floor, her notebook open. Ian typed quietly, sending one last encrypted packet to Teri. Karl cleaned the sidearm he hoped not to use.

Michael stood at the window, watching lightning dance over the dome. "Tomorrow everything changes," he said.

"Maybe for the Church," Hana replied. "For us, it's just another day of telling the truth."

He turned, with the faintest smile in his eyes. "That's always been the dangerous part."

The thunder came again, closer this time. Rome held its breath.

FORTY-FOUR

VATICAN CITY

Morning broke sharp and colorless over Rome. A pale sun struggled through the mist that hung above the Tiber, turning the water into a sheet of dull pewter. Across the city, the Vatican's bells began to toll—steady, measured, indifferent to the clamor that was about to unfold beneath them.

The announcement had gone out at dawn:

VATICAN TO ESTABLISH COMMISSION TO AUTHENTICATE THE "GOSPEL OF THE BELOVED" AND "CODEX OF VOICES."

By eight o'clock, news crews were setting up cameras in St. Peter's Square. Journalists shouted questions in half a dozen languages; pilgrims prayed beside them. Some knelt on the wet stones, weeping. Others waved signs: **THE**

CHURCH BETRAYS ITSELF! and **TRUTH IS STILL FAITH!** The scene felt less like a religious gathering than a trial convened by history itself.

Michael Dominic watched from the edge of the colonnade, hands in the pockets of his clerical coat. He had given one brief statement to Vatican Radio—simple, cautious, unprovocative—and then stepped back. There was nothing left to say that wouldn't sound like defense or pride.

Hana stood beside him, her eyes sweeping the crowd. "They're afraid," she murmured.

"They should be," Michael replied. "So am I."

The cameras flashed again, blinding for an instant. A reporter shouted his name, asking if the manuscripts contradicted Scripture. Michael didn't answer. The wind off the square carried the smell of precipitation and incense; he tasted both and turned away.

ACROSS THE RIVER, in a modest café near Piazza Navona, Ian Duffy sat hunched over his laptop, a mug of espresso cooling beside him. Teri's voice came through the encrypted line from the Archives.

"They've published the official statement," the young nun said. "The Holy Father's wording was deliberate—'to verify both authenticity and theological context.' That second phrase will drive the Curia mad."

Ian smirked. "It's already working. Social feeds are melting down. Half of Europe thinks Michael's uncovered the Fifth Gospel; the other half thinks he's Judas."

Teri sighed. "Rome's good at that—turning questions into sides."

"Any sign of Severino?" Ian asked.

"He's locked in his office. Vatican accounts are still frozen pending the audit. The man's cornered."

"Cornered men dig down, not out," Ian said. "Keep watching."

He closed the laptop and looked out at the street. A television in the café window played live footage from the Square: Michael's blurred face, the crowd, the captions looping in endless argument. Ian drained his espresso and muttered, "Nothing like a little sunlight to start a fire."

In the Apostolic Palace, Pope Clement XV sat behind his plain oak desk, reading the morning brief. The words blurred after a while. *Commission formed… Curia unrest… media frenzy.* It all felt inevitable, like a prophecy unfolding line by line. He looked up at his secretary.

"Tell them to let the truth breathe," he said.

"Holy Father?"

"If we smother it again, it will come back sharper. I'd rather face it honestly."

"Yes, Your Holiness."

When the secretary left, the pope turned to the window. Beyond the glass, the square seethed with pilgrims and protesters alike. For a moment, he saw himself reflected there—an old man in white, watching history through the same pane of fear that had trapped his namesake five centuries before. But Clement VII didn't have to deal with social media and twenty-four-hour news cycles.

Alessandro de' Medici watched the same scene on a bank of monitors in his villa. He hadn't slept. His empire—built on influence, patronage, and fear—was beginning to crumble in headlines.

He muted the television and poured a glass of wine. "They think they've won," he said.

His advisor, a thin man in a gray suit, shifted uneasily. "The commission could still be steered, Signor de' Medici. Half its members owe you favors."

"Favors expire," Alessandro said. "Fear lasts longer."

The man hesitated. "What would you have us do?"

"Confuse them," Alessandro said. "Leak what we choose. Make the scholars argue about what's real before they even read it. Give the world too many truths to choose from."

He turned toward the window, where the lightning of cameras flashed faintly even from across the city. "And find Valentina Ruspoli. She's the loose thread in this tapestry."

THAT AFTERNOON, the Vatican's press office overflowed. Reporters filled every chair, the air thick with the heat of bodies and the hum of translation headsets.

Michael stood at the podium, flanked by two members of the new commission—a French paleographer and an Argentine theologian. Cameras whirred. Lights glared.

He cleared his throat. "The Codex discovered in the Vatican necropolis will be examined by a team of international scholars. Its purpose is not to challenge faith, but to understand it more completely. The Church has nothing to fear from truth."

A reporter called out, "Father Dominic, does this Magdalene Gospel confirm that women led worship in the early Church?"

Michael hesitated. "The document's content will speak for itself when verified."

Another shouted, "Isn't it heresy to question apostolic authority?"

Michael's eyes met the crowd. "It's not heresy to ask how faith began. It's devotion."

The room murmured. Someone clapped once before remembering where they were.

When it was over, he stepped away from the lights, the sweat cooling on his temples.

Hana caught his arm as they exited. "You just painted a target on your back."

He gave a small smile. "It was already there."

THAT EVENING, Hana returned to the Santa Cecilia monastery. The abbess met her in the cloister garden, pruning a row of basil plants as though nothing in the world had changed.

"They've put your face on television," Sister Maria Francesca said. "You looked tired."

"I am," Hana admitted. "Half the world thinks we're rewriting the Bible. The other half thinks we forged it."

The abbess clipped another leaf and held it to her nose. "Truth is a mirror, child. It doesn't break us—it shows us the cracks we carried already."

Hana smiled faintly. "You sound like Michael."

"He's a good priest," the abbess said. "But this is no longer about priests. Or popes. Or even Rome. It's about whether we remember what we were meant to be."

The bells of evening prayer began to ring, deep and soft.

Hana looked toward the church door. "Do you ever wish we'd left it buried?"

The abbess paused. "Buried things don't stay buried, my dear. They ferment in darkness."

In her hotel room overlooking the Piazza Barberini, Valentina watched the same broadcast replayed on the television. Michael's voice filled the room, calm and measured, but the fury in the world beyond the camera was unmistakable.

She turned the volume down. The voice recorder lay on the desk beside a small glass of whiskey. Her phone buzzed. A message appeared from an unlisted number: **You can't hide behind confession. – A.**

Valentina stared at the screen, then deleted the message. Her hand trembled slightly as she picked up the whiskey. "You taught me that trick too well," she murmured.

Outside, the rain had returned, streaking the city's lights into blurred halos. She closed the curtains and sat on the edge of the bed. For the first time in years, she prayed —not for forgiveness, but for clarity.

At the Trastevere apartment, Ian's laptop chimed. He leaned forward, scanning the code that filled the screen. "We've got a problem."

Michael looked up from the table. "Define 'problem.'"

"Multiple forgeries," Ian said. "Someone just uploaded three different Latin 'fragments' claiming to be pages from the Codex—two in language so bad it would insult a freshman seminar. The third almost looks authentic."

"Alessandro," Hana said. "He's flooding the field."

"Exactly. By tomorrow morning, no one will know which text to believe."

Michael rubbed his temples. "He's trying to make truth indistinguishable from lies."

Karl, seated near the window, said, "That's been Rome's trade since before Christ."

Ian smirked. "And business is booming."

Michael exhaled. "Can you trace the uploads?"

"Working on it." Ian's fingers danced across the keys. "They're using shell servers in Zurich, Geneva, and Tel Aviv. But the encryption signature matches a Medici finance node."

"Then we can prove it's him," Hana said.

"Maybe," Ian replied. "But if we expose it too soon, they'll claim we planted the forgeries ourselves."

Michael thought for a moment. "Not if the pope speaks first."

Late that night, Clement XV addressed the College of Cardinals in a private session. The great hall was dim, its frescoes flickering in candlelight.

"The *Gospel of the Beloved* and the *Codex of Voices*," he said, "are not the enemy. They are a mirror. What it shows us may hurt, but we must not turn away."

Some cardinals nodded. Others exchanged worried glances.

He continued, "The Gospel was never afraid of discovery. Only men are. The Church will examine this text openly, and whatever it reveals—about love, equality, or silence—will not diminish the truth of Christ. It may, perhaps, complete it."

When he finished, the silence in the hall was thicker than incense. He could feel their unease, but also something else—respect, reluctant and fragile. It was enough.

ALESSANDRO WATCHED that speech replayed an hour later from his study. He stood motionless before the screen, glass of wine untouched.

"They think they've won," he whispered.

Behind him, thunder grumbled over the hills. He turned to his aide. "Release the second wave. All of it—the forged fragments, the anonymous essays, the rumors about Dominic's past. I want confusion to become doctrine."

The aide hesitated. "And the pope?"

"Leave him to me," Alessandro said. "Even saints can be broken if you starve them of silence."

He smiled faintly, though it looked more like pain. Outside, lightning illuminated the garden statues—the mouths of the Medici lions open in perpetual roar.

BY MIDNIGHT, the world was already drowning in speculation. Talk shows debated theology like sport. A bishop in New York denounced the Codex as a fabrication; a Jesuit scholar in Paris called the Gospel the most important document since the Dead Sea Scrolls.

In the apartment, the team sat in silence, watching the headlines scroll by.

Michael finally spoke. "The house of glass has cracked. Now everyone's throwing stones."

Hana turned from the screen. "And us?"

"We keep telling the truth," he said. "Until someone hears it."

Outside, thunder rolled again over the Tiber, low and unhurried, like a verdict being written in sound.

CHAPTER
FORTY-FIVE

ROME

Morning came in fragments: a sharp knock at the shutters, the clatter of bells from Trastevere, the subtle echo of rainwater still draining from the roofs. Rome seemed caught between two centuries again—its ancient bones and modern nerves jangling against each other.

Father Michael sat at the kitchen table, half-dressed, reading the first printed papers of the day. Every headline spoke the same language, even if the accents differed.

Vatican Opens Door To Controversy.
New Manuscripts May Change Early Christian History.
Cardinals Divided On Codex Of Voices.

Ian's laptop pinged from the counter. "The news cycle's gone nuclear," he said. "Social media is turning theology into blood sport."

Karl poured coffee into mismatched mugs. "And what's Alessandro doing?"

"Buying time," Ian said. "He's pushing doctored fragments through academic chat forums. Every hour there's a new 'expert' claiming to have the real translation."

"Confusion as strategy," Hana murmured. "It worked for the Borgias."

Michael set the paper aside. "Then we give them clarity. The commission meets at noon. We tell the truth and let it fight for itself."

The Vatican Library hadn't hosted such a gathering in generations.

Rows of scholars filled the long hall beneath its frescoed ceiling—linguists, theologians, historians, and a handful of skeptical journalists granted limited access. Cameras were banned; even pens had to be cleared by security as potential recording devices.

Pope Clement XV had insisted on transparency with restraint, a contradiction only the Vatican could manage.

Michael walked in with Hana at his side. The hum of voices died slowly. At the far end of the table sat Monsignor Giacomo Alberti, chair of the commission, a man whose spectacles seemed to magnify both his eyes and his self-importance.

"Father Dominic," Alberti said, "thank you for joining us. The commission appreciates your cooperation."

"Cooperation," Michael echoed, taking his seat. "That's a good word for it."

Retrieved from the pope earlier, the Codex was placed carefully on the table. The scholars' expressions shifted between reverence and fear, each one aware they were standing at the threshold of history—or heresy.

Dr. Sofia Petrov, the French paleographer, leaned forward. "The binding dates to the fourteenth century. The papyrus leaves, however…" She adjusted her glasses. "Earlier. Much earlier."

"How early?" Alberti asked.

"Possibly first century," she said. "The fibers match those of Judean origin. It could predate most canonical manuscripts."

A ripple of whispers moved through the room.

Michael's heart hammered once against his ribs. Clement's letters had been right: the Codex was no Renaissance forgery.

Dr. Emilio Vargas, a Jesuit historian from Buenos Aires, read aloud from the opening page in Latin and Greek. *"'Blessed are those who bear the light without crown or collar, for the Kingdom knows no steward but Love.'"*

He looked up. "This cannot be Clement's invention. The syntax is pre-Nicene. This is early theology."

"Or blasphemy," another scholar muttered.

Michael spoke before Alberti could. "The danger is not in what it says, but in what we fear it means. Clement VII suppressed this to preserve unity, not to hide truth. We can do better."

Alberti gave him a long, icy stare. "You presume to lecture the Church on unity, Father Dominic?"

"I presume only to ask that we remember why unity matters," Michael said.

The argument flared, scholars breaking into clusters of allegiance and indignation. Hana watched the chaos, taking notes, her expression unreadable.

When the meeting adjourned hours later, nothing had

been resolved except the depth of division. The Codex had been authenticated linguistically, but spiritually, it was tearing the air apart.

OUTSIDE THE LIBRARY, the Cortile del Belvedere swarmed with reporters, their umbrellas forming a field of black domes.

As Michael stepped out, the questions started:

"Father Dominic, does this text prove women were apostles?"

"Is the Vatican preparing to revise doctrine?"

"Will the pope declare it heretical?"

He kept walking.

Hana matched his stride. "They don't want truth," she said. "They want reaction."

He looked over at her. "Then we give them silence."

ACROSS THE CITY, in the Villa Aurelia Medici, Alessandro stood before the portraits of his ancestors. Their painted eyes seemed to glimmer in the candlelight—Cosimo, Lorenzo, Clement VII himself—all men who had mastered the art of control.

"The Medici never feared chaos," he said aloud. "We created it."

His aide, the gray-suited man, waited near the door. "The forged fragments are circulating widely. Several bishops have already questioned the commission's impartiality."

"Good," Alessandro said. "Doubt is currency. Keep spending it."

He turned toward the window. Lightning flashed over

the hills. "Bring me Valentina. One wrong move from her and my world catches fire."

THAT NIGHT, in a small trattoria off Via Giulia, Hana waited in a back booth, a scarf draped loosely around her hair. The doorbell jingled once, and Valentina Ruspoli slipped inside.

She looked exhausted—dark circles under her eyes, rain on her shoulders—but her poise remained intact.

"Thank you for coming," Hana said.

"I almost didn't," Valentina replied. She sat opposite, folding her hands around a coffee she didn't drink.

"Alessandro's forgeries are spreading fast," Hana said. "Can you stop him?"

Valentina shook her head. "No. But I can prove they're his. Every false fragment carries a watermark from one of his archival labs. He was too arrogant to change the code."

Hana's eyes widened. "Can you get me access?"

"I already did." Valentina slid a flash drive across the table. "You'll find server logs and payment trails—enough to trace every forgery to his network."

"Why are you helping us?" Hana asked.

Valentina's smile was brittle. "Because he taught me that truth was a tool. I'd like to see what happens when it becomes a weapon instead."

They parted without another word. As Hana left the café, lightning flickered above the rooftops. She didn't see the man at the corner photographing her departure.

BACK AT THE VATICAN, Cardinal Severino sat in the dark of his private chapel. The walls smelled of candle smoke and damp stone. The crucifix above the altar glimmered faintly in the half-light.

He had spent his life guarding the Church from change, but tonight he no longer knew what he was defending. The pope's commission had stripped him of control; the auditors were still dissecting his finances. His only remaining ally was the one man he despised most: Alessandro de' Medici.

When the phone rang, he already knew the voice.

"Giovanni," Alessandro said smoothly, "we can still salvage this. The commission is divided. One push, and the whole thing falls."

"And you provide the push?" Severino asked.

"I provide survival," Alessandro replied. "You and I both know the Church cannot function without men willing to bear its ugliness. Dominic's idealism will destroy everything we have built."

Severino's silence stretched. "I built faith," he said. "You built debt."

"Debt and faith are the same currency," Alessandro said. "You just spend yours slower."

When the call ended, Severino stared at the phone, realizing he had just spoken to the last person who still believed he mattered.

THE FOLLOWING MORNING, the commission reconvened. The pungent scent of wet eucalyptus drifted in from the courtyard each time the door opened.

Dr. Vargas read another fragment from the Gospel, his voice soft but clear.

"And she said to him, '*Lord, the light you have given does not belong to the priests but to those who carry it.' And he answered, 'Then carry it, and let no man take it from you.'"*

Silence followed.

A woman in the back—a Benedictine scholar—whispered, "That line could have been spoken to Mary Magdalene."

Alberti's fist hit the table. "It was not spoken to anyone! These are forgeries!"

"Then prove it," Hana said. Her voice cut through the room. "Show us the lie in the ink."

Alberti glared at her. "Who are you to challenge the Church?"

"I'm the one who found the shaft of light that led us here," she said. "And if that makes me dangerous, you should ask why."

Michael watched her, pride and worry warring behind his eyes.

The tension snapped when the doors opened. A Vatican messenger entered, pale and breathless. "A fire," he said. "At the outer wall near Porta Sant'Anna. They're calling it a protest."

Everyone rose. From the library windows, they could see the column of smoke rising over the courtyard.

Michael whispered, "The world has begun its reckoning."

OUTSIDE, chaos spread like contagion. Pilgrims fled; cameras swung; the smell of burning gasoline filled the air. A Molotov cocktail had struck the marble wall and scorched a black wound into its surface before the guards contained it.

By evening, news networks called it the Fire Sermon—a

protest turned symbol. Images of flames licking Vatican stone filled every broadcast. The Church had become spectacle again, and Michael Dominic was its reluctant centerpiece.

He returned to the apartment just before midnight. Hana and Ian were waiting, the television muted but flashing red with breaking news.

"They're saying it was an extremist sect," Ian said. "But the manifesto references both the Gospel and the Codex."

Michael sank into the chair. "History repeats itself," he said. "Except this time, we can watch it live."

Hana leaned against the window frame. "What now?"

"We keep going," he said. "The truth doesn't need defending—it needs endurance."

FAR ACROSS THE CITY, in the Villa Aurelia Medici, Alessandro watched the same footage play across three monitors. The flames reflected in his wineglass.

"Perfect," he murmured. "Now they'll fear the truth more than the lie."

His aide hesitated. "And if they trace the forgeries to us?"

"Then we burn the evidence," Alessandro said. "It's a fitting end."

Thunder cracked above the villa, shaking the glass in the frames of his ancestors. Their painted eyes seemed to glare down, accusing.

For a moment, Alessandro felt something like doubt. Then he raised his glass in a toast to the storm. "To the Medici," he said. "Still shaping popes, still shaping history."

. . .

THE NEXT MORNING, smoke still hung over the city. Michael stood with Hana in the square before the basilica. The marble showed a faint scar from the night's fire, a line no amount of scrubbing could erase.

"Scars remind us where we've healed," Hana said.

"And where we haven't," Michael replied.

The bells of St. Peter's began to toll. The sound rolled over them, heavy and deliberate, like a call neither of them could ignore.

"Come on," he said. "The commission reconvenes in an hour. Maybe this time, the world will listen."

They walked toward the bronze doors, the rain beginning again, slow and patient, washing the soot from the stones but not the memory.

FORTY-SIX

VATICAN CITY

Rain washed the dust from Rome overnight, but the morning light brought no clarity. A gray sheen lay over the city, and the streets glistened as if freshly varnished. The Vatican domes rose from it like islands—ancient, patient, and indifferent to whatever storm was gathering below.

Inside the Apostolic Palace, whispers echoed throughout the long marble corridors. Staff walked faster, voices lowered. It was the day the commission reconvened after the so-called Fire Sermon. The Codex's words had burned as fiercely as the Molotov on the wall.

Michael arrived early, Hana at his side. The air in the library was cool and still, the light diffuse. The dependable scent of eucalyptus again drifted through the room— brought in on damp coats and the occasional gust when the heavy doors opened. The guards had stationed two men at the entrance now; even scholarship needed protection.

The commission members sat in uneasy silence. Dr. Sofia Petrov examined the parchments under magnification. Dr. Vargas murmured translations to himself. Monsignor Alberti scribbled notes with the energy of a man trying to reclaim control by ink alone.

Michael spoke softly to Hana. "They're all waiting for someone to declare certainty, and none of them want to be the first."

She nodded. "That's how history always begins—reluctantly."

At the head of the table, Alberti cleared his throat. "Before we proceed," he said, "we must address the violence of yesterday. The Holy See condemns the attack on the Vatican walls. We do not, however, attribute it to theological debate." He paused, letting the irony settle. "We shall continue our work."

He motioned to Dr. Vargas. "The next passage, if you please."

Vargas adjusted his spectacles and read: *"'And they asked him, "Who may speak of the Kingdom?" He answered, "Those who have listened longer than they have spoken." And a woman replied, "Then it will be the women who speak first."'"*

The room seemed to exhale. Petrov murmured, "It's consistent with early Coptic syntax. Authentic."

Alberti snapped, "Or fabricated to flatter modern sensibilities."

"Language doesn't flatter," Petrov said quietly. "It only survives."

Michael looked from one to the other. "If it's genuine, it changes nothing fundamental about faith. It only changes how we've told it."

Alberti glared. "You presume to know the will of God?"

"No," Michael said. "Just His handwriting."

By midday, the argument had knotted itself into exhaustion. When Alberti finally called recess, Hana slipped outside with her notes. She walked the covered colonnade that overlooked the Vatican Gardens. The rain had stopped, but droplets clung to the leaves, small mirrors catching fragments of sky. Somewhere below, gardeners were sweeping puddles toward drains.

She stopped at the balustrade and closed her eyes. The scent of damp cobbles and rosemary mixed with something older—the faint musk of paper and time that seemed to follow her from the library. She thought of Clement VII sealing the Codex away, convinced that he was saving the Church from collapse. She wondered if she and Michael were saving it or breaking it again.

A voice startled her. "You shouldn't wander alone, Signora Sinclair."

She turned. Cardinal Severino stood at the far end of the walkway, his red cassock darkened by moisture. He looked thinner than she remembered, paler, the polished certainty gone from his eyes.

"Eminence," she said. "I didn't realize I needed an escort."

"I'm not here as your escort," he replied. "Or as your enemy."

Hana studied him warily. "Then what are you?"

He walked closer, hands clasped. "A man who has discovered that defending God often means defying Him. I came to speak with Father Dominic."

"About what, if I may ask?"

"About ending this before it destroys what little faith people have left."

"He's inside," she said, gesturing toward the library. "But you'll find he's not so easily convinced."

"I'm not asking to convince him," Severino said. "I'm asking to understand him."

INSIDE, Michael was reviewing images of the Codex under ultraviolet light when he heard footsteps. Severino entered, water beading on his shoulders. For a moment, neither spoke. The cardinal's presence still carried authority but no longer command.

"Father Dominic," Severino said. "You and I have been fighting the same battle from opposite trenches."

Michael straightened. "Some battles have only one side, Eminence—the one facing truth."

Severino approached the table, gaze falling on the Codex. "You believe this… thing can heal the Church?"

"No," Michael said. "I believe it can remind us what healing means."

The cardinal's eyes flicked upward. "You think I'm afraid of the documents. I'm not. I'm afraid of the world that will use them to mock the Church. They will tear it apart for sport, and faith will become another spectacle."

Michael's voice softened. "Then you're not wrong, only tired."

"I am both," Severino admitted. "And I wonder if fatigue and faith aren't the same by another name."

Michael hesitated. "The pope trusts you still. Don't let Alessandro take that from you."

Severino looked away. "It may already be gone."

. . .

AN HOUR LATER, in a high office across the city, Alessandro de' Medici poured two glasses of red wine and gestured for his guest to sit.

"Giovanni," he said smoothly, "you look unwell."

Severino ignored the glass. "You sent for me?"

"I did. You and I, we're relics now—men who understood order before the world discovered chaos. Dominic and his friends think they've liberated truth. What they've really done is open a market."

"I didn't come for philosophy," Severino said. "You wanted something."

Alessandro smiled. "Only partnership. You have access, influence, the pope's ear. I have resources. Together, we could redirect this chaos before it consumes us."

Severino's voice was flat. "And if I refuse?"

"Then you'll share the fate of every reformer the Church ever forgot."

For a long moment, the cardinal said nothing. Finally, he rose. "You mistake endurance for immortality, Alessandro. The Medici have survived every century but this one."

He left without touching the wine.

THAT NIGHT, in the apartment, Ian was bent over his laptop again. Streams of code reflected off his glasses. "We've got a problem," he said. "A serious one."

Michael set down his cup. "Define 'serious.'"

"Someone's inside the Vatican servers. They're cloning the commission's files—Codex scans, translation drafts, all of it."

"Alessandro?" Hana said.

"His network, definitely. They're routing through a London IP, bouncing to Milan. I can block them, but it'll tip our hand."

"Do it," Michael said. "Better a fight than a theft."

Ian cracked his knuckles. "Then let's fight."

Lines of text blurred across the screen as he fired back countermeasures. Somewhere behind the code, invisible hands were clawing for control. He grinned through the tension. "You're good," he muttered, "but I'm Irish."

After several minutes, the connection severed. The screen cleared. Ian leaned back, breathing hard. "They're locked out—for now."

Hana glanced toward the window. "For how long?"

"Long enough," Ian said. "But they'll come another way."

In the Vatican Gardens later that night, Michael found Severino sitting on a bench beneath a cypress. The lamps threw long shadows across the gravel path.

"You came anyway," Michael said.

Severino didn't look up. "You told me not to let Alessandro take my faith. I'm trying not to."

Michael sat beside him. "Then stop carrying his sin."

"Easy words," Severino said. "But I've spent a lifetime building walls. It's difficult to bless the wreckage."

"Walls aren't the problem," Michael said. "It's what we forget to let through."

They sat in silence, the air thick with wet cypress and bay laurel, the faint sweetness of jasmine climbing the walls, and beneath it all the metallic tang of olive leaves crushed underfoot. It smelled of penance and renewal, the scent of a world scrubbed clean but not yet forgiven.

Severino said, "You think this Codex is divine providence."

"I think it's a mirror," Michael said. "The divine part is whether we dare to look."

Severino turned, his expression weary but sincere. "You remind me of men I used to admire. Most of them died misunderstood."

"Then I'm in good company."

The cardinal gave a low, humorless chuckle. "You really believe the Church can survive this?"

"It survived Galileo. It survived silence. It can survive honesty."

Severino rose. "You should pray you're right."

"I already did," Michael said. "Now I'll act like it."

Hours later, a black car slid through the wet streets of Rome toward the Vatican gates. Inside, Alessandro sat alone, reading a dossier illuminated by dashboard light. Photographs, bank statements, names—enough proof to ruin him if it reached the commission. Valentina's betrayal had been surgical.

He closed the file and stared out the window at the basilica's dome, lit like a lantern against the storm. "So it ends where it began," he murmured. "Another Medici brought low by a priest."

He reached into his coat and withdrew a thumb drive identical to the one Ian had stolen days before. "But even priests need ghosts," he said, pocketing it again.

• • •

AT DAWN, the commission gathered for the third time. The storm had passed, leaving the sky brittle and blue. The air held the smell of pine and ozone.

Michael stood before them, the Codex open to a single page under glass. "Before we begin," he said, "I need to show you something."

He placed a separate document beside it—one of Clement VII's sealed letters recovered from the Archives. "This is Clement's private confession, written shortly after he hid the Codex. He writes of another work, a companion commentary written by a Medici cleric who advised him—a document that interprets the gospel through politics, not faith."

Alberti frowned. "You're saying there's another manuscript?"

"Yes," Hana said. "Clement called it The *Second Voice*. It may still exist. If it does, it could explain why he buried the Codex—and what he feared."

The room buzzed with murmurs. Alberti slammed his hand down. "This is conjecture!"

"It's direction," Michael said. "If we find it, we'll know whether Clement was protecting the Church or himself."

The tension hung like static. Then Vargas spoke. "If such a commentary exists, we owe it to history to find it."

Even Alberti hesitated. "And if finding it tears down what's left of faith?"

Vargas looked toward Michael. "Then we build it again."

That night, Michael returned to the apartment. Hana and Ian were waiting, the Codex secured again in its case.

"Well?" Ian asked.

"They believe us," Michael said. "The commission will authorize a search of the Archives. We're to lead it."

Hana smiled faintly. "We're chasing ghosts again."

Michael poured a glass of wine and looked toward the city, where the dome glowed against the dark. "Then let's hope this one finally tells the truth."

Outside, thunder rumbled again, far away but inevitable.

CHAPTER

FORTY-SEVEN

VATICAN CITY

The Vatican dawned clear and cold, the marble of St. Peter's still slick from the night's rain. The air in the gardens smelled of laurel and damp cypress, the kind of scent that seemed older than the city itself—sharp, resinous, purifying.

Michael Dominic walked the path behind the Casina Pio IV, his breath misting. The pope had chosen this morning to announce the commission's next step: a full archival search of the Secret Archives in the Medici Wing, for the rumored *Second Voice*.

The words from Clement's own diary were still burned into Michael's mind. He whispered to himself, "'*The Gospel I sealed, but the Voice I silenced.*'"

He didn't know whether to pray for discovery or mercy.

The announcement went out at eight o'clock. By nine, the halls outside the Archives were a hive of movement—

selected curators, archivists, and security staff in hushed motion. The world beyond the walls hadn't yet been told what they were looking for. For now, it was still a secret search, a Vatican habit older than the printing press.

Hana, Karl, and Ian arrived through the side gate near the Porta di Santa Rosa, passes stamped with the papal seal. Sister Teri met them inside the antechamber, her expression a blend of fatigue and excitement.

"They've opened the Medici Wing," she said. "First time since Pius XII ordered it sealed after the war."

Ian whistled softly. "So, we're walking into seven decades of dust and denial."

"Exactly," Teri said. "And you'll need respirators."

Karl smirked. "Nothing says 'divine revelation' like mold."

The Medici Wing lay two levels below the main archive stacks, accessible through a narrow stairwell of green marble worn smooth by centuries of footsteps. The air grew cooler as they descended. When the last light from above faded, Hana switched on her headlamp.

The corridor opened into a vaulted chamber lined with iron cabinets, each labeled in Latin, many rusted shut. Cobwebs hung like lace over the shelves.

Michael ran a hand along one cabinet door. "**Urban VIII**," he read. "These are papal account ledgers."

"Not what we're looking for," Hana said. "Maybe they would have filed the *Second Voice* under theological correspondence, perhaps under Clement's posthumous papers."

Ian crouched near a set of old power conduits, connecting his portable scanner. "I'll start logging inventory tags. If something was misfiled digitally, I can trace the catalog number."

Teri's voice echoed from the back of the chamber. "I've got something—handwritten labels, Florentine script."

They joined her. She pointed to a narrow drawer labeled *Archivum Clementis—Supplementum Medicorum.*

Michael felt a pulse quicken under his collar. "That's it. Clement's supplemental archive—'*Medici additions.*'"

Hana slipped on gloves and carefully slid the drawer open. Inside were bundles of parchment tied with faded ribbon. The first bore a watermark in the shape of a lion— the Medici crest.

She untied the ribbon and unfolded the first sheet. The ink had browned with time, but the handwriting was elegant and precise. Across the top were the words: *Commentarium de Secunda Voce.*

"*The Commentary of the Second Voice,*" Hana whispered.

They carried the documents to a long table under a suspended lamp. Michael unrolled the top sheet and began to read aloud: "'*When the Word was sealed, another word remained, a whisper among the confessors of Florence. The* Gospel of the Beloved *speaks of equality in spirit; this commentary speaks of order in fear. Clement chose fear.*'"

The words struck like a confession written by history itself.

Hana read further: "'*For the Church cannot serve two masters: love and control. And so one must be crucified to preserve the other.*'"

Ian gave a low whistle. "That's not commentary; that's indictment."

Teri crossed herself. "And the handwriting?"

"Not Clement's," Hana said. "This matches archival samples from Frate Matteo de' Medici, a Dominican scholar, distant cousin of the Medici family. He was Clement's theological advisor during the sack of Rome."

Michael exhaled slowly. "So the *Second Voice* isn't divine. It's political. The Medici wrote their own justification for silence."

Karl leaned over the table. "So what now? Do we publish it?"

"Not yet," Michael said. "We authenticate it first. And then we let the pope decide whether the world's ready for another truth."

UPSTAIRS, word of the find spread faster than permission. By afternoon, half the Secretariat knew something explosive had been uncovered in the Medici Wing. Reporters began to circle like hawks over rumors.

Cardinal Severino received the news in his office with quiet disbelief. He dismissed his aide and sat alone. The paper trembled slightly in his hand. *Commentarium de Secunda Voce.*

He had hoped the legend was apocryphal. A second manuscript would mean the Codex's suppression hadn't just been from fear, but by design.

He looked toward the crucifix above his desk. "Lord," he whispered, "is 'revelation' just another word for ruin?"

AT THE VILLA, Alessandro read the same headline hours later:

**Incriminating Medici Manuscript
Found In Vatican Archive.**

The paper crumpled in his fist.

"Impossible," he hissed. "That chamber was sealed."

His aide kept his eyes down. "They say Dominic found it under papal authorization."

Alessandro's jaw clenched. "Then authorization can be revoked." He threw the paper into the fireplace. "Arrange a meeting with my friends in Milan. If I cannot erase the past, I'll rewrite it louder."

The aide hesitated. "What about Signora Ruspoli?"

"Didn't I tell you to find her?" Alessandro demanded coldly. "If she still breathes, she still threatens me."

THAT EVENING, the Vatican Library's secure reading room glowed under low lamps. The pope himself entered quietly, accompanied by two Swiss Guards.

Michael rose as he approached.

"Father Dominic," Clement XV said, his voice calm but edged with awe. "You've found it?"

Michael nodded. "The *Second Voice*—written by Frate Matteo de' Medici. It's less a commentary than a manifesto."

The pope read the opening lines silently. His expression darkened. "This is how they justified the burial of the gospel—by fear of equality. By confusing order with faith."

"Yes, Holiness."

Clement looked up. "Then the Church must read it as judgment. On itself."

He set the parchment down, hands steady. "Have it authenticated, line by line. But this time, no secrecy. The people will see it as we do."

Michael bowed his head. "And the risks?"

"The same as silence," Clement said. "Only faster."

. . .

LATER THAT NIGHT, Michael and Hana walked the quiet gardens. The lamps glowed in pools of amber along the paths. The air still held the sharp scent of laurel and the sweetness of orange blossom from the Vatican's small grove.

"It's strange," Hana said. "We've spent months chasing ghosts, and every one of them sounds more alive than the men trying to hide them."

Michael smiled faintly. "Ghosts are just truths with good memories."

"Do you think the pope will really make it public?"

"He's the only one who can."

They stopped at the edge of the fountain. The water rippled in reflected light. Hana glanced at him. "You know what this means, don't you? Clement's guilt wasn't just fear. It was deliberate suppression. The Church's silence was a choice."

"I know," he said. "And so was our noise."

She touched his arm lightly. "Then we'd better be sure it's worth the cost."

He looked toward the basilica, its dome glowing against the night. "Every truth is."

AT THE SAME HOUR, in a hotel near Rome's Termini Station, Valentina Ruspoli packed her last bag. Her room was stripped of everything but the hum of rain against the window. On the television, a commentator was reading the first leaked lines of the *Second Voice*:

"The reason Clement was afraid of equality was not due to its perceived lack of validity, but instead because of its undeniable truth."

She smiled sadly. "You finally spoke," she said to the screen.

Her phone vibrated. A single text from an unknown number: **He's coming. Leave Rome**.

She stared at it, then deleted the message. "Too late," she murmured.

She slipped the small pistol from her coat pocket, checked the magazine, and walked to the window. The city shimmered in rain. Somewhere beneath it, truth was waking—and men like Alessandro were running out of shadows to hide in.

By DAWN, the news was global.

Second Vatican Manuscript Reveals Church Fear Of Gender Equality.
Pope Vows Full Transparency.
Medici Legacy Under New Scrutiny.

In Trastevere, the team gathered around Ian's laptop, the glow of headlines washing their faces.

"Well," Ian said, "I'd say we've officially kicked the hornet's nest."

Karl nodded. "And now every hornet in Rome's awake."

Michael watched the sunlight break through the window, touching the Codex where it lay. "Good," he said. "It's about time."

CHAPTER

FORTY-EIGHT

VATICAN CITY

The bells of St. Peter's carried across the river in hollow tones, causing pigeons to burst from the piazza in startled waves. In the Vatican, the echo of those bells bled through the walls of the *Archivum Secretum*, the newly sanctified battlefield of truth.

Michael Dominic was already there when the first members of the commission arrived. The library's vaulted ceiling glowed with the cold light of early morning. The air smelled of wet laurel and dust. A guard's boots clicked on the marble as he opened the outer doors.

The *Codex of Voices* and the *Second Voice* commentary had been placed on twin tables under glass, guarded like relics. To one side, translators hunched over high-resolution scans, their screens pale blue in the dimness.

Hana joined Michael near the display. "They've started the authentication protocols," she said. "Spectrograph analysis, fiber sampling, even pollen residue. Everything short of an exorcism."

"Give them time," he said. "Every minute they're testing it, they're admitting it's real."

By mid-morning, the scholars' debates had spread beyond the library walls. Vatican Radio carried live commentary, while Italian news channels showed stock footage of the basilica over breathless narration. The word heresy was trending on every social media feed.

IN A NEARBY CONFERENCE ROOM, Cardinal Severino faced the storm he had tried to prevent. He had surrendered the accounts to the Auditor General, endured questioning from investigators half his age, and now sat in a chair that felt like Confession.

Across the table, a Jesuit theologian read from his photocopy of the *Second Voice*: "'*Love requires equality; power requires silence. The Church has chosen silence and called it love.*'"

Severino pressed his fingertips together. "It was not silence. It was stewardship. A shepherd keeps wolves from the flock."

The Jesuit looked up. "And if the wolves were never wolves at all?"

Severino said nothing. The argument had become circular—faith chasing fear in endless orbit.

THAT AFTERNOON, Pope Clement XV convened the Curia in a closed session. The air in the Sala Regia shimmered with tension. Every chair was occupied; crimson robes lined the room like a field of poppies.

The pope stood at the lectern without notes. "My brothers," he began, "the Gospel, the Codex, and the Commentary are no longer secrets. They will not be burned, nor will they be hidden again."

A murmur swept the hall. One bishop rose. "Your Holiness, the people are confused. They look to us for certainty."

Clement's gaze was steady. "Certainty is not faith. Faith is trust without proof. Certainty is only pride wearing vestments."

Another bishop stood. "If we endorse this study, we risk dismantling centuries of order."

"Then let us find out whether our order can survive honesty," the pope said.

The words struck like a quiet hammer. Even Severino, sitting near the back, bowed his head.

Across Rome, in a low studio filled with heat and background city noise, Ian Duffy and Sister Teri were fighting their own war. Screens covered the walls, streaming feeds from news outlets and social media. The Medici network had unleashed its counterattack— doctored images, mistranslations, and a forged papal letter claiming the pope planned to "redefine the Gospel."

Teri's fingers flew over the keyboard. "I'm tracing the origin servers. Half of this disinformation is coming from Milan, the rest from Zurich."

"Follow the money," Ian said. "Alessandro always pays in advance."

A new alert flashed red. **UNAUTHORIZED LOGIN – ARCHIVUM DATABASE**.

Ian swore softly. "They're trying to pull the Codex scans."

Teri activated a firewall routine. "Not on my watch."

Within seconds, the connection severed. Ian leaned back, wiping sweat from his forehead. "We just closed the gate. But they'll try again."

Teri glanced at the window, where the dome of St. Peter's shimmered through the haze. "They always do."

In the Vatican Gardens, Michael walked with Hana after the day's sessions ended. The path curved beneath the cypress trees, their resin scent mingling with the sweetness of orange blossom. The noise of the city was far away here, muted to a hum.

"Do you think Clement XV can hold the line?" she asked.

"He doesn't need to," Michael said. "He just needs to stand long enough for the truth to take root."

Hana slowed beside a stone bench. "I keep wondering what Clement VII would think of all this."

"He'd be afraid," Michael said. "That's how you know we're doing it right."

A gust of wind moved through the trees, carrying the faint clang of bells from the basilica.

Hana watched the leaves shift overhead. "You ever think about what happens after? When it's over?"

"It won't be over," he said. "Just quieter."

That night, Valentina Ruspoli returned to Rome. The train from Florence slid into Termini Station under a sky spitting rain. She wore a simple coat and carried only a small leather satchel. On the seat beside her lay a newspaper folded to the front page:

POPE DEFIES CRITICS—CODEX TO REMAIN PUBLIC.

She smiled faintly. *He's bolder than I gave him credit for.*

As she stepped onto the platform, a man in a dark suit detached from the crowd. "Signora Ruspoli," he said softly. "You should have stayed away."

Valentina didn't break stride. "Tell Alessandro he's run out of ghosts."

The man reached for her arm. She moved faster. By the time he caught her sleeve, she had pressed the muzzle of a small pistol under his chin. "Walk away," she said. "Before Rome sees what confession looks like."

He obeyed.

THE NEXT MORNING, the commission reconvened for a joint session with the Pontifical Council for Culture. Scholars from around the world crowded into the Vatican's Paul VI auditorium, their voices rising like surf.

Dr. Sofia Petrov presented the chemical analysis. "The ink and parchment are consistent with first-century composition. The Medici Commentary, by contrast, dates to 1535. Both are authentic. Together they tell a story—not of fabrication, but of fear."

She paused. "The *Gospel of the Beloved* and the *Second Voice* are two halves of one argument: whether love or authority sustains faith."

Michael stood to address the room. "For five centuries,

the Church has chosen authority. Clement VII believed obedience would save souls. But love requires risk. It always has."

A bishop rose from the back. "And what of obedience now, Father Dominic? To the pope? To tradition?"

Michael met his gaze. "Obedience without conscience is not faith. It's surrender."

The hall erupted in murmurs. Some applauded; others hissed under their breath. The Vatican had become a theater again, and history was its playwright.

IN THE VILLA AURELIA MEDICI, Alessandro stood before a wall of screens showing the same debate in real time. His wineglass trembled slightly in his hand.

"They've turned it into a crusade," he said. "Dominic is no longer a priest—he's a symbol."

His aide swallowed. "What should we do?"

"Symbols die like men," Alessandro said. "They just need the right stage."

He turned from the monitors. "Prepare the statement. We'll release it tonight."

"What kind of statement?"

"One that reminds the world that the Medici built this Church. And if we can build it, we can tear it down."

ST. Peter's Square glowed with rain-soaked light. Pilgrims gathered again, candles in hand, singing hymns that rose and fell with the wind. The scent of wet stone and lavender drifted up from the gardens.

Michael looked down at them, thousands of small

flames reflected in his eyes. "They're not waiting for doctrine anymore," he said quietly. "They're waiting for permission to believe again."

"And if the Church doesn't give it?" Hana asked.

He watched the candles shimmer against the night. "Then they'll take it."

IN HIS PALACE, Alessandro finished dictating his statement to the press. His voice was calm, even measured.

"The so-called *Codex of Voices* represents nothing more than the ambitions of a disobedient cleric and the gullibility of those who follow him. The Medici family rejects this heresy and the pope's reckless endorsement of it. Faith built on rebellion is not faith at all—it is vanity."

When he finished, his aide hesitated. "Shall I send it?"

"Yes," Alessandro said. "And then cancel tomorrow's appointments. I may have guests."

"Guests?"

"Dominic. Or someone who speaks for him. They'll come eventually." He looked toward the rain-blurred windows. "Everyone comes to a Medici for absolution."

THAT NIGHT, Michael couldn't sleep. The storm had passed, but his mind hadn't. He stood at the window, watching the lights of the city shimmer on the Tiber. Somewhere below, a church bell tolled midnight.

He thought of Clement VII, sealing the gospel beneath Rome; of Clement XV, unsealing it with trembling hands; of Alessandro, still trying to buy silence with gold.

And he thought of Hana, asleep in the next room, her

notes stacked neatly by the bed. The light from her lamp spilled into the hallway—a small, steady thing, proof that not all fire destroys.

Michael whispered a prayer that had no words, only intent. Then he turned off the light and let the city dream its uneasy dream.

FORTY-NINE

VILLA AURELIA MEDICI

Morning sunlight spilled through a haze of smog and incense over the rooftops of Rome. From the balcony of the Villa Aurelia Medici, Alessandro watched the city breathe. Below him, the gardens glistened from last night's rain—wet marble lions, a fountain whispering under the cypress trees, statues of his ancestors frozen in triumph.

He felt no triumph now.

On the screens in front of him, every network was running the same story:

Vatican To Release Findings On The Codex Of Voices.
Global Commission Confirms Authenticity.

A thousand years of control, he thought, undone by parchment and arrogance.

His aide entered quietly, carrying a stack of newspapers. "They've printed your statement, Signore. But the coverage isn't sympathetic. They're calling you the banker who lost the Church."

Alessandro didn't turn. "Let them. History remembers builders more than critics."

He sipped his coffee, eyes on the dome of St. Peter's glinting beyond the city. "And builders," he added softly, "can always rebuild."

The aide hesitated. "Your accounts in Zurich—some have been frozen."

"Frozen?" Alessandro repeated, taken aback. "But not seized?"

"No, Signore. But the Vatican's auditors have filed requests with Interpol. They've traced the forged Codex fragments to a Milan data server owned by Medici Holdings."

Alessandro's expression didn't change. "Proof means nothing if you own the narrative. Increase our media contracts. Feed them doubt. Fear works faster than truth."

At the Vatican Press Office, reporters spilled out of every hallway. The sound was a constant, overlapping hum—languages colliding, microphones raised like weapons. Michael Dominic walked past them with his collar turned up and his eyes fixed ahead. Hana moved beside him, tablet in hand, her jaw set.

They were ushered into a smaller briefing room adjoining the main hall. Ian Duffy's laptop projected a map of server traces onto the wall.

"Zurich, Milan, and two secondary nodes in London,"

he said, tapping the screen. "All registered under Medici fronts. They've been seeding disinformation for seventy-two hours straight."

"Can we shut them down?" Karl asked.

Ian smirked. "Already did. Twice. They keep rerouting through shell accounts. But we got lucky." He pointed to a highlighted IP address. "They slipped once—an unmasked transmission from the Villa Aurelia. Our friend Alessandro got careless."

Hana exhaled. "So we can trace the entire network."

"Eventually," Ian said. "But the bigger fight is perception. Half the world believes the Codex is fake; the other half thinks the pope's a heretic."

Michael rubbed his forehead. "Alessandro's not trying to win the argument. He's trying to exhaust it. If truth becomes noise, no one listens."

"Then we get louder," Hana said.

He looked at her, surprised by the edge in her tone.

"I mean publicly," she clarified. "A statement from you and the pope—something definitive. No more hiding behind committees."

Michael hesitated. "Clement won't weaponize truth. He'll let it speak for itself."

"Then maybe we do it for him," she said.

Ian raised an eyebrow. "I like her better when she's subversive."

Karl gave him a look. "You like everyone better when they're breaking rules."

"Rules are just suggestions with good PR," Ian said.

WHEN THE MEETING BROKE, Michael and Hana stepped into the courtyard. The morning air carried the scent of wet cypress and distant espresso. A column of sunlight sliced between the buildings, striking the cobblestones where puddles mirrored the dome.

That evening, before the next wave of crises hit, they allowed themselves something rare—a meal outside the walls.

Hana adjusted Michael's collar as they headed out, smoothing the fabric with her fingers. "You always go into battle looking slightly undone," she said.

He smiled. "And you always fix me right before it starts."

She lowered her hand but didn't step back. "Someone has to."

The moment hung between them, gentle as breath. Then Karl's voice echoed from the doorway—"You two coming, or are we staging another miracle?"—and the spell broke. They both laughed, quietly, as they followed him toward the gates.

Trastevere was waking for dinner. Lanterns flickered along the narrow lanes, the air fragrant with garlic, rosemary, and the tang of tomatoes simmering in wine. They ducked into a trattoria where the owner knew Michael by sight, if not by name. He waved them to a corner table under an awning still dripping from rain.

"Chef's choice," Michael said to the waiter. "And something red from the house."

Hana smiled. "You're reckless."

"It's faith," he said. "In pasta."

When the food arrived, it was glorious: pappardelle alla lepre—broad ribbons of pasta tangled with wild hare ragu—and a platter of roasted artichokes glistening in oil and lemon. The wine smelled of cherries and smoke.

For a long time, they didn't talk about the Vatican, or

the Codex, or anything larger than the table between them. The rain tapped softly on the awning above.

"This," Hana said, lifting her glass, "is the first normal thing we've done in months."

Michael touched his glass to hers. "Then let's make it holy."

They ate slowly, tasting each bite as though memorizing it. When the plates were empty, he tore a piece of bread and brushed the last traces of sauce from his plate. "I'd forgotten food could be a prayer," he said.

Hana smiled. "You just remembered."

Outside, the bells of Santa Maria rang the hour. The world felt briefly right again.

BACK ACROSS TOWN, Alessandro's media assault began in earnest.

By nine o'clock, every television in Europe was running his recorded statement:

"For centuries, the Medici family has been guardian to the Church's integrity and heritage. We denounce the so-called *Codex of Voices* as a fabrication and its promotion as a betrayal of faith. Those who spread such heresies endanger the souls of millions."

Hana muted the television in the apartment. "He's not speaking to reason. He's speaking to fear."

Michael paced behind her. "He's building a crusade."

Karl folded his arms. "Then we treat him like a crusader—cut off his supply lines."

Ian looked up from his laptop. "Too late. He's buying airspace. Literally. Broadcast satellites under Medici contracts are running his videos nonstop."

"Then we expose the network," Hana said. "Make the forgeries public, show the proof."

Ian nodded slowly. "Risky. We'd need the pope's permission to release internal audit files."

"Get it," Michael said. "Tonight."

In Sister Teri's control room, deep beneath the Vatican Library, the hum of servers was louder than usual. She watched the data feed scroll by and felt her pulse match its rhythm. A red warning light blinked on her screen.

"Unauthorized upload attempt," she murmured. She typed a command, isolating the intrusion. The source flashed: **AURELIA.MEDICI.NET**.

Her headset crackled. Ian's voice came through. "Teri, talk to me."

"They're trying to overwrite the Codex scans with forged duplicates. If they succeed, the digital archive will be compromised."

"Can you block it?"

"I can isolate it. But I'll need to shut down half the Vatican intranet for ten minutes."

"Do it."

Teri smiled grimly. "Say goodbye to the pope's Wi-Fi."

Within seconds, lights across the data vault dimmed. The system reinitialized. The intrusion froze midstream.

Ian's voice came back, laughing in relief. "You're brilliant, Teri."

"Tell someone who can give me hazard pay," she replied.

When the power stabilized, the Codex files were intact. For now.

. . .

THAT NIGHT, the Vatican Gardens lay under moonlight and rain. Hana stood alone by the fountain, the water rippling silver under the lamps.

Footsteps approached behind her. "You shouldn't be out here," said a familiar voice.

She turned. Valentina Ruspoli emerged from the shadows, trench coat glistening with rain. Her hair was pinned back, her eyes sharp.

"I heard you were gone," Hana said.

"I was," Valentina replied. "But Alessandro never forgets his debts—or his enemies. I'm both."

"What do you need?"

Valentina handed her a small flash drive. "Proof of his last transaction. Offshore payments to the men who attacked you last week."

Hana's stomach tightened. "You're sure?"

"I made the transfer myself," Valentina said. "Under his orders."

"Why give this to me?"

"Because he thinks fear still buys loyalty," Valentina said. "He's wrong."

Hana studied her. "You could still walk away."

Valentina looked toward the basilica rising beyond the trees. "I don't know how anymore."

They stood in silence as thunder rolled in the distance over the hills.

AN HOUR LATER, back in the apartment, the team gathered around Hana's computer. The screen displayed rows of transactions—cryptic notations linking Medici Holdings to Zurich accounts and shell companies in Malta.

Ian whistled. "You realize what this means? We can tie Alessandro to the attacks—and the forgeries."

"Can we prove it publicly?" Michael asked.

"If we leak the data to the international press, yes," Ian said. "It'll ruin him."

Karl leaned forward. "Then do it."

Michael hesitated. "Not yet. Let the pope decide how to handle it."

Ian threw up his hands. "You still think procedure will save us?"

"I think truth should serve justice, not vengeance," Michael said.

Hana looked from one to the other. "The line between them keeps getting thinner."

By DAWN, the Vatican was awakening to chaos. Screens in the press hall blazed with conflicting reports: hacked statements, fake papal decrees, photos of Alessandro attending supposed secret meetings.

At the same time, a real communiqué came from the Holy Father's office: **All Vatican communications temporarily suspended pending audit.**

Clement XV had shut down the world's oldest bureaucracy with one sentence.

At noon, Michael received a summons to the Apostolic Palace. Clement met him alone in the papal study.

"The Codex remains safe," the pope said. "But Alessandro's war is no longer of faith—it's of power. We must end it."

Michael bowed his head. "How?"

"Truth," Clement said simply. "And the courage to stand beside it."

He placed a sealed document on the desk. "The Vatican will hold a press conference tomorrow morning. You will stand beside me when I speak. The world will see that our faith is strong enough for light."

Michael took the envelope, heavy with the papal seal. "And Alessandro?"

Clement's eyes softened. "He will face his own judgment. They all do."

THAT EVENING, in the Villa Aurelia, Alessandro stood before his mirror, adjusting his cufflinks. The reflection staring back looked older than he remembered. The lions on the walls seemed to sneer.

His aide entered, pale. "Sir, Interpol agents are outside. They have warrants."

Alessandro's hand stilled. "For what?"

"Fraud. Conspiracy. International interference."

He smiled faintly. "Faith and fear—the only currencies that never devalue." He slipped on his jacket, walked to the window, and looked out toward the city's distant lights.

"Tell them," he said, "I'll see them after my confession."

ACROSS ROME, thunder cracked again above the rooftops, echoing through the narrow streets. In Trastevere, Hana closed her notebook, Ian shut his laptop, and Michael stood at the window, listening.

"The pope speaks tomorrow," Hana said. "Everything changes."

Michael turned toward her. "For us too," he whispered.

He reached for her hand, their fingers interlacing. "Whatever comes, we'll face it together."

She smiled faintly. "That's the only miracle I believe in."

Outside, lightning flared over the dome of St. Peter's—a flash of white that turned the city into glass, then darkness again.

CHAPTER

FIFTY

TRASTEVERE, ROME

Only a few hours after the storm, the air began to hum again; distant thunder hid behind rooftops, a constant in Rome. The city slept under its wet stones and secret histories, unaware that another reckoning was creeping closer.

Garlic and roasted tomatoes from the night before still faintly perfumed the apartment. Karl and Lukas had cleaned the kitchen with soldierly precision, their quiet domestic ritual leaving the space looking like nothing had ever happened. Yet something had—something small and defiant. For a few hours, they'd been ordinary, and that ordinariness was a rebellion of its own.

Michael rose before dawn. The sky outside was gray marble streaked with violet. He stood by the window, watching mist curl around the cupolas.

Hana came up behind him, her hair still damp from her shower, and wrapped her arms around his waist.

"You didn't sleep," she said.

"I tried."

Her cheek rested against his back. "You're thinking about the pope's address."

He nodded. "And Alessandro. He's desperate. Desperate men make mistakes, but they make them loudly."

She turned him gently to face her. "We've made peace with what we can't control. Remember?"

He smiled faintly. "Remind me again later. Preferably over breakfast."

"Now you sound like Ian," she said, kissing his cheek. "Go shave. You look more prophet than priest."

By MIDMORNING, the streets around the Vatican were crowded again—pilgrims, journalists, locals craning for news. The air smelled of diesel, rain, and the faint citrus that always drifted from the Vatican Gardens after a storm.

Inside the Apostolic Palace, Swiss Guards moved with practiced calm, guiding staff through metal detectors. Every corridor hummed with expectation; even the marble seemed to vibrate under the weight of what the pope might say.

Michael, Hana, and Karl were among the last to arrive at the inner gate. Lukas was already waiting by the door, his uniform pressed, expression unreadable. He nodded to Karl as they passed—no words, just a quiet exchange of breath, the kind of communication built over years of shared danger. And of partnership.

Hana caught the glance between them and smiled. "You two should teach a course in nonverbal theology."

"Better if you don't know the language," Karl whispered.

IN THE PRESS HALL, Pope Clement XV's staff worked in near silence, preparing for the broadcast that would reach every corner of the world. The pontiff himself stood before the window overlooking St. Peter's Square, his profile illuminated by the diffused light.

When he turned to Michael, his eyes were steady but tired. "Are you ready to face the world, Father Dominic?"

Michael bowed his head. "I don't think anyone ever is."

"That's the right answer," the pope said. "Faith isn't certainty—it's consent to risk."

He reached out, resting a hand on Michael's shoulder. "You'll stand beside me when I speak. The world needs to see that the Church is not afraid to share its scars."

OUTSIDE, the morning broke into noise—chanting crowds, camera shutters, the low growl of approaching thunder.

Hana and Ian stood near the barricades, trying to gauge the mood. Some people carried rosaries; others held protest signs. Banners wavered in the wind: **TRUTH WITHOUT FEAR** and **THE CHURCH BETRAYS CHRIST**.

"You have to admire the symmetry," Ian said. "They've both claimed God for their side."

"God's used to it," Hana replied. "He's been claimed by worse."

Karl and Lukas stood a few meters away, their eyes scanning the rooftops. Lukas adjusted his earpiece. "Security's doubled," he said.

Karl nodded. "Then so has temptation."

Lukas gave him a sideways look that only he could read. "You're getting sentimental."

"Only because you'd notice," Karl said.

Lukas smiled—a real one, quick and unguarded. "Later," he said. "Dinner, if we make it that far."

AT PRECISELY ELEVEN, the bells began. The sound rolled through the square, heavy and sure.

The pope stepped onto the balcony, flanked by Michael and two Swiss Guards. His white robes caught the wind; dark clouds were breaking apart above the city, beams of light piercing through like searchlights.

He raised his hands for silence and, against all odds, the crowd obeyed.

"My brothers and sisters," he began, "truth is not a weapon—it is a mirror. For five centuries, we have feared what it might show us. The *Codex of Voices* and the writings of Clement VII remind us that faith was never meant to hide behind authority. It was meant to walk beside love."

His words rippled through the square, translated in dozens of languages over radio and television feeds.

"Love," the pope continued, "is not rebellion. It is the obedience of the heart to something greater than power. The Church will not bury truth again. Let the light fall where it will."

The crowd erupted—some cheering, some shouting in anger. Reporters surged forward.

Michael stood beside the pope, silent, steady, his collar catching the light. Beside him, the Swiss Guards lifted their halberds in salute.

And then, above the noise, came something wrong.

A sound—a single sharp crack.

For an instant, Michael thought it was thunder. Then another crack split the air, and glass shattered above the podium.

"Down!" Karl shouted, pulling the pope backward. Lukas moved at the same moment, his body covering Michael's. Other Swiss Guards quickly followed to protect the pope and the priest. Bullets ricocheted off the marble balustrade, scattering shards into the open square.

Panic surged through the crowd. Sirens wailed.

Hana froze halfway across the plaza, the sound of gunfire ringing in her ears. She saw movement on a rooftop—a figure in black, a rifle glinting.

She shouted into her comm. "Rooftop, north side— fourth building!"

Lukas heard her. "Got it." He sprinted for the stairwell that led to the roof access, Karl right behind him.

They reached the roof in less than two minutes. The shooter was already dismantling the rifle. Rain slicked the tiles underfoot, the smell of cordite sharp in the air.

"Drop it," Karl said, weapon raised.

The man turned slowly. His face was young, uncertain —one of Alessandro's men, a hired zealot. "He s-s-said you'd destroy everything," the man stammered.

Lukas stepped forward, his tone even. "You don't have to die for someone else's fear."

The man hesitated. Then, with a motion too fast to read, he reached for the weapon. Lukas fired once. The man crumpled, the rifle clattering onto the wet stone.

Karl caught Lukas's arm before he could lower the gun. Their eyes met. Nothing needed saying. They stood there for a long moment, the rain cooling on their faces.

Finally, Karl said quietly, "You're shaking."

"Because I'm alive," Lukas said. "And because he isn't."

Karl nodded, resting a hand briefly on his shoulder. "That's what it costs to stay alive."

DOWN BELOW, chaos gave way to order. The pope was unhurt, shielded by the guards. Hana pushed through the crowd, breathless, until she reached the steps. When she saw Michael standing, his cassock streaked with glass, she nearly collapsed.

He caught her as she reached him, arms steady. "I'm fine," he said.

"You're bleeding."

"Just glass."

Her hands were shaking as she touched his face. "You scared me."

He smiled faintly. "It's becoming a habit."

Behind them, sirens wailed louder. Lukas had neutralized the threat; the roof was secure. The pope, unharmed, was being ushered back inside.

Hana looked up at the balcony. "It's not over, is it?"

"No," Michael said. "But it's begun."

Later that evening, the team reconvened at the apartment. The tension hadn't left their bodies, but relief had found a place to sit beside it.

Karl poured whiskey into tumblers while Lukas leaned against the window, his shirt damp, collar open. Ian sat cross-legged on the floor, typing furiously. "Interpol's raiding Medici Holdings," he said. "Alessandro's finished. They found payment transfers to the shooter's account. Proof positive."

Hana sat on the couch beside Michael, her head resting

on his shoulder. "Proof," she murmured. "That word again."

"It's all we ever had," he said.

Karl handed them each a glass. "To surviving."

Lukas raised his own. "To everyone who makes survival worthwhile."

They drank in silence for a moment, the city rumbling faintly outside.

Much later, when the others had gone to sleep, Hana found Michael standing by the window again. The dome of St. Peter's gleamed faintly under the moon, serene and unbothered.

She wrapped her arms around him from behind. "You can stop watching now," she whispered.

"Old habits."

"Maybe start a new one."

He turned, smiling. "Like what?"

"Staying alive," she said and kissed him.

For the first time in months, he didn't think about the Codex, or Alessandro, or the Church's silence. He thought about the simple, saving act of being held—and how, sometimes, that was enough to keep faith alive.

Outside, the city exhaled. Rome had survived another storm.

CHAPTER

FIFTY-ONE

VATICAN CITY

Rain fell again the next morning, soft as static, turning the cobblestones of the Cortile di San Damaso into mirrors. The Vatican was hushed, subdued; the chaos of the previous day had given way to exhaustion. Rome itself seemed to be holding its breath.

Inside the Apostolic Palace, Pope Clement XV prepared for what would be remembered as the most public Curial assembly in modern memory. The Holy Father would address the world another day, but first he would address his own.

Michael Dominic walked through the corridor toward the Sala Regia, the vast ceremonial hall now lined with cameras and crimson-draped benches. He passed Swiss Guards at their stations—still, solemn, their armor glinting beneath chandeliers. The scent of incense lingered faintly in the air, though no Mass was being said.

Hana walked beside him, her notes in hand. "You don't have to speak today," she whispered. "Let him carry it."

Michael shook his head. "It isn't his burden alone. It never was."

They entered the hall. The sound of quiet voices filled the vaulted space—cardinals, bishops, and delegates from across the world. Television crews set up along the periphery, their equipment masked in respectful black cloth. At the front, a dais waited for the pope's arrival.

And at the center of it all sat Cardinal Giovanni Severino, head bowed, hands folded tightly in his lap. His red robes seemed heavier than usual, as though they, too, bore the weight of his guilt.

He looked up as Michael approached. "Father Dominic," he said quietly. "They tell me you'll be testifying."

Michael nodded. "Only to what's true."

Severino smiled without humor. "That word again."

The pope entered to the sound of murmuring that quickly died to silence. Clement XV looked older than he had the day before—his face drawn, his voice quieter—but his gaze carried a clarity that filled the room.

"My brothers," he began, "our Church stands at a threshold between fear and faith. For too long, we have mistaken secrecy for strength. Today, we choose transparency—not as surrender, but as trust."

He paused, letting the words settle. "In recent days, it has become clear that corruption has touched even our highest offices. That knowledge wounds us, but it also heals us, for no wound can close without exposure to light."

The murmurs began again. Cameras whirred softly.

Clement gestured toward Severino. "Cardinal Severino has asked to speak."

A rustle moved through the hall. Severino rose slowly, his hands trembling slightly as he steadied himself on the bench.

"Holy Father," he began, "I have served the Church all my life. I have fought to preserve her dignity, her order, her faith. But somewhere along the way, I confused obedience with love. I believed silence was protection. I see now it was pride."

He looked out at the hall, at the sea of red and white. "I never sought power for myself, but I feared losing it. I feared that if truth prevailed, faith would falter. Instead, it was I who faltered."

The pope inclined his head. "Truth does not destroy faith, Giovanni. It reveals it."

Severino's eyes glistened. "Then may God reveal mercy as well."

OUTSIDE THE VATICAN WALLS, the world was already reacting. News outlets from every continent carried the broadcast live. Crowds filled St. Peter's Square, umbrellas open like flowers in the rain.

In the Trastevere flat, Ian sat cross-legged on the floor, laptop balanced on his knees. Karl and Lukas stood by the window, watching the coverage on a muted television.

"Severino's finished," Ian said. "Interpol confirmed that his accounts were tied to Alessandro's laundering schemes. The auditors just froze his holdings."

Karl nodded slowly. "He was the last pillar keeping Alessandro standing."

Lukas glanced at the screen, where Severino was still

speaking. "Strange. He sounds more like a priest than a politician now."

Karl's hand brushed against his as they watched. A small gesture, natural, unnoticed by anyone else in the room. Lukas turned his palm upward, and their fingers met briefly. The simple act said everything words couldn't—affection as solidarity, quiet as breath.

AT THE SAME HOUR, across the city, Alessandro de' Medici watched the same broadcast from the parlor of his villa. The curtains were drawn tight. His reflection flickered in the darkened screen, caught between images of the pope and Severino.

"They'll come for me next," he said.

His aide, still pale from the night before, hovered near the door. "Interpol has already requested your surrender."

Alessandro laughed softly. "Do you know what power really is, Luca? It isn't wealth or position. It's the illusion of permanence." He poured himself a glass of wine. "And illusions die hard."

"Sir," the aide said nervously, "you should go."

"I've nowhere left to go. But one more meeting to take," Alessandro murmured. He took a slow sip, staring at the screen.

BACK IN THE VATICAN, Severino concluded his statement. His final words hung heavy in the hall.

"If the Church must bleed to be cleansed, then let my name be part of that purification."

He stepped down, and silence followed him—dense, electric.

Clement XV stood again. "The Curia accepts your resignation, Giovanni. You will retire from public service, but not from grace."

A single clap echoed—Hana's. Then another, from Michael. Within seconds, the entire room was on its feet. The applause wasn't celebration; it was absolution.

Severino bowed his head. His eyes met Michael's briefly, and for the first time, there was peace between them.

When it was over, the hall emptied slowly. Michael lingered near the door, watching Severino speak quietly with the pope. The two men stood close, heads bowed. When they parted, Severino pressed Clement's hand to his lips, then turned and walked away down the long corridor, alone.

Hana joined Michael, her umbrella folded under her arm. "You did what you came to do."

He nodded. "So did he."

They stepped out into the courtyard. The rain had stopped, leaving the air damp and cold. A faint scent of bay leaf drifted from the gardens.

"Where to now?" Hana asked.

"Where truth goes when it's finally free," Michael said. "Everywhere."

She smiled faintly. "You sound like a philosopher."

"I'm just tired," he said. "Philosophers get to rest."

Meeting up with the others in the apartment later, the kitchen table was cluttered with wine glasses, newspapers, and the remains of another improvised dinner—bread, cheese, and roasted peppers. The air was thick with smoke and laughter that felt like relief.

Ian raised his glass. "To endings we didn't expect, and beginnings we might actually deserve."

Karl clinked his glass. "To the living."

Lukas added softly, "And to the forgiven."

Hana leaned her head against Michael's shoulder. "Which are we?"

He smiled. "Both."

AT THE VATICAN, Clement XV sat alone in his study, the Codex open before him. Candlelight flickered across the page. The words blurred, not from age, but from tears the old man didn't bother to hide.

He closed the book gently. "Blessed are those who bear the light," he whispered. "For they have already forgiven the darkness."

IN TRASTEVERE, thunder rolled again across the Tiber, softer now, as if Rome itself were finally breathing easier.

Michael lay awake beside Hana, listening to the rain's steady rhythm. Her hand found his beneath the sheets, and the world seemed to steady with it.

He thought of Severino's bowed head, Alessandro's empty villa, the pope's trembling voice. He thought of the Codex—fragile, defiant, eternal.

And before sleep took him, he whispered into the dark, "Let there be light."

FIFTY-TWO

A VILLA OUTSIDE ROME

The drive to the villa wound through Rome's western hills, where mist clung to the olive trees and the last light of evening burned behind a veil of cloud. A sweet, woodsy, earthy scent of stone pines, with fresh overtones of juniper and the ozonic hint of precipitation filled the air. The city fell away behind them, replaced by the hush of cypress groves and the rhythmic pulse of windshield wipers.

Karl was at the wheel, Lukas beside him, their silence the practiced quiet of men who spoke most fluently through trust. In the back seat, Michael and Hana sat shoulder to shoulder, their hands barely touching on the seat between them. Every few minutes, their fingers brushed—not a gesture of affection, but of reassurance. The world was about to tilt again, and they both felt it.

The villa loomed ahead at the crest of the hill, its façade

lit from within by the amber glow of chandeliers. Rain spattered the windshield as they pulled through the open gate. Two black cars sat in the drive, both empty. The marble lions flanking the entrance were slick with water, their faces glinting as lightning flashed far off across the valley.

Karl parked under the portico. "No guards," he said.

Lukas checked the shadows along the colonnade. "He's expecting us."

Michael stepped out first, wearing a dark overcoat, the collar turned up against the rain. Hana joined him, pulling her scarf tight. Together, they crossed the threshold into the house of the last Medici.

Inside, the villa smelled of wax, wine, and dust. The portraits of Medici ancestors lined the corridor—Cosimo, Lorenzo, Clement VII—painted faces that had survived war, plague, and papal intrigue. Their eyes followed Michael as he passed, patient and accusatory.

In the grand salon, Alessandro waited by the fire, a glass of Chianti in one hand. He looked tired but composed, like a general who had lost the war but refused to surrender the parade.

"Father Dominic," he said, voice smooth as the marble floor. "And Miss Sinclair. How fitting that truth itself arrives on a rainy night."

Michael stopped a few paces away. "It's over, Alessandro. The forgeries, the laundering, the manipulation. The Vatican has the proof, and the world knows your name."

Alessandro smiled faintly. "The world always knows my name. It just keeps forgetting why."

Hana's voice was steady. "You tried to erase history. That's not legacy—that's cowardice."

He turned to her. "Ah, the journalist. You mistake preservation for fear. My family built civilization out of faith and commerce. We gave the Church beauty when God gave it chaos."

"Your family bought the Church," Hana said firmly. "That's not beauty."

Alessandro raised his glass. "Ownership is the highest form of art."

Michael stepped closer. "You've confused art with control. They're not the same thing."

"Control built Rome, Father. You of all people should understand that." He took a slow sip of wine. "But let's not pretend this is about history. This is about power. The Codex threatens to unseat the mythology that keeps your collar relevant."

Michael's eyes hardened. "The Codex doesn't need me. It speaks for itself."

Alessandro laughed softly. "So naive. Words never speak for themselves. Someone always gives them voice— or silence."

Lightning flared through the windows. For a moment, the portraits on the wall seemed to glow.

Michael's voice dropped. "You could have used your family's legacy to serve the truth, to lift faith instead of feeding fear. But you chose corruption, and you called it stewardship."

Alessandro set the glass down with care. "I chose survival."

"By destroying everyone else's," Michael said. "Including your own."

The Medici heir studied him for a long moment. "You

sound like a confessor, but you look like a prosecutor. Which are you tonight?"

Michael's reply was quiet. "Neither. I'm a witness."

The silence that followed was broken by the sound of Karl's boots on the marble as he entered, Lukas close behind. "The police are on their way," Karl said. "Interpol, too."

Alessandro's smile didn't falter. "Then they can enjoy the view. It's a good night for a spectacle."

He crossed to his desk and opened a small drawer. Hana tensed, but Alessandro only produced a flash drive —a twin to the one Valentina had given them.

"I imagine you've seen this already," he said. "Every secret transaction, every document. I always keep copies. I learned that from your journalist."

Hana's chin lifted. "Valentina learned more from you— how to survive you."

"Valentina," he mused. "My most gifted betrayal. You see, Father, that's the problem with truth. Once you teach someone to find it, you can't control where they'll point it."

He turned the flash drive in his fingers. "I could end your little miracle right now. Every file in the Vatican Archives, gone. I still have access."

Michael stepped closer, voice even. "You don't."

Alessandro's eyes narrowed. "What?"

"Sister Teri, our network administrator, scrubbed your access last night. Your servers are locked, your data quarantined. Everything you built is a ghost. You're finished."

For the first time, Alessandro's composure faltered. He looked past Michael toward the portraits, as if seeking counsel from men who had outlived every enemy but time.

"You think this ends with me?" he hissed. "You think truth changes anything? The Church will use your discovery as it always does—to feed another lie. You'll see."

Michael met his gaze. "Maybe. But at least this time, it won't be your lie."

A sound echoed from the entrance—sirens outside, tires crunching gravel.

Karl moved toward the door.

Alessandro reached for the wineglass again. "A final toast, then. To the Medici name. To endurance."

Michael shook his head. "To reckoning."

Alessandro smiled. "Same thing."

Then he looked up at Michael, eyes hollow. "Go. Let the law have its theater. I prefer silence."

OUTSIDE, the rain had stopped. Interpol cars lined the drive, lights flashing blue across the wet marble. Agents moved up the steps with practiced precision.

Michael stood beneath the portico, watching them pass. Hana stood beside him, silent. Karl and Lukas waited near the car. The night air smelled of ozone and crushed laurel.

When Alessandro emerged between two agents, he looked smaller, the cut of his suit no longer armor but costume. He glanced once at Michael, and for a heartbeat, they were two men on opposite sides of the same truth— one who had buried it, and one who had set it free.

As the car doors closed, Alessandro's reflection flashed in the rain-streaked glass and was gone.

Karl exhaled slowly. "It's over."

Michael shook his head. "It never is. Not really."

Hana took his hand. "Then at least it's quieter."

He turned to her, eyes softening. "I'll take quiet."

She leaned into him, and for the first time in weeks, he let the weight slide from his shoulders.

They drove back through the sleeping city. Rome at night was a chiaroscuro painting—pools of lamplight spilling over cobblestones, alleys whispering with history. Karl drove, his hand resting on the gearshift until Lukas's fingers found it, settling there, steady. No words passed between them, but their eyes met in the rearview mirror, and that was enough.

In the back seat, Hana slept with her head on Michael's shoulder. He watched the streets unwind beyond the window—the bridges, the fountains, the scattered glow of cafes still open along the river. He thought of Clement VII, of Clement XV, of all the men who had tried to own the story of God. Maybe faith wasn't a story to be owned. Maybe it was a wound that healed only by being seen.

He whispered the thought aloud, not realizing he had spoken until Hana murmured against him, "Then we did what we were meant to do."

He smiled. "Maybe for once."

They reached Trastevere just before midnight. The rain had started again, soft and relentless, washing the streets clean.

Inside the apartment, the air was warm and thick with the smell of wood smoke. Ian was at the table, surrounded by empty espresso cups and open files. "He's in custody," he said without looking up. "Interpol confirmed. Multiple charges. It's a mess, but a poetic one."

"Poetry's rare in justice," Hana said.

Ian grinned. "Then let's eat before it vanishes."

Karl produced a bottle of Barolo from the counter,

Lukas fetched glasses, and the five of them gathered around the safe house table. The food was simple—bread, olives, cheese—but it might as well have been a feast.

When the first round of laughter came, it sounded strange in the small room, like music returning to a place that had forgotten how to hear it.

Michael raised his glass. "To those who still believe."

Hana touched hers to his. "And to those who never stopped trying."

Karl added quietly, "To those who came home." Lukas's hand brushed his beneath the table.

They drank. Outside, thunder rolled distantly over the Tiber—not anger now, but release.

Later, after the others had gone to bed, Michael and Hana stood on the balcony. Across the city, the dome of St. Peter's shone like a pearl above the rooftops.

Hana leaned on the railing. "Do you think they'll remember this? The truth, I mean?"

"Maybe," he said. "But even if they forget, it'll still be there—waiting for the next generation to find it again."

She smiled. "You talk like a priest."

He looked at her. "You talk like a believer."

She laughed softly. "Only because I have reason to."

When he kissed her, it wasn't the fire of triumph but the quiet of absolution—love not as victory, but as rest.

Below them, Rome exhaled, the city of saints and sinners breathing in unison beneath the rain.

CHAPTER

FIFTY-THREE

VATICAN CITY

Morning came muted and slow, the kind of Roman light that seems to filter through centuries before reaching the ground. The rain had passed in the night, leaving the streets gleaming and quiet. A low mist clung to the gardens beyond the Vatican walls, where laurel and cypress exhaled their sharp, clean scent.

For the first time in months, Rome felt still. But it was the stillness that follows an earthquake—the hush before the city decides what remains standing.

Inside the Vatican Library, preparations for the public presentation of the *Codex of Voices* filled every corner. Technicians adjusted lighting and cameras while scholars arranged their notes in nervous order. The ancient manuscripts sat beneath glass at the center of the hall, two relics waiting to speak for themselves.

Michael Dominic stood near the display, watching as

light slid across the glass and spilled over the parchment within. The handwriting seemed almost to breathe in the brightness. Hana moved beside him, her notebook in hand, the morning's tension hiding behind her calm expression.

"You realize this is the first time in five centuries the Church has invited the world to witness its confession," she said.

Michael smiled faintly. "It's about time we practiced what we preach."

POPE CLEMENT XV entered the room quietly, without ceremony, flanked only by two Swiss Guards. His white cassock was immaculate, though the circles beneath his eyes told of another sleepless night. When he saw Michael, his expression softened.

"You've done what I could not, Father Dominic," he said. "You've made the Church remember what honesty sounds like."

Michael bowed his head. "I only opened a door, Holy Father. You're the one walking through it."

The pope's smile was brief, almost wistful. "Doors are easier than destinations."

He turned to the scholars gathered at the front of the room. "You and your colleagues have already tested this text with all the rigor the Church could ask for. You have weighed ink and parchment, language and history, and your judgment is unanimous. This document is authentic."

He looked out at the rest of the assembly. "So today we do not ask whether it is genuine. Today we must begin to ask what it means for us." He faced the scholars again. "Gentlemen and ladies, from this point on, the work belongs to the whole Church. Let every word of this document be read in the light of faith and the discipline of reason. The Church cannot be afraid of what God's people once wrote in love. We can only be afraid of refusing to let that love question us."

Applause followed—not thunderous, but sincere. The sound filled the library's vaulted spaces like a prayer.

When the first presentation began, Hana took a seat near the back. Dr. Sofia Petrov stepped to the podium, her voice steady despite the enormity of the moment. She read the passage that had sparked the greatest debate:

"'Blessed are those who bear the light without crown or collar, for the Kingdom knows no steward but Love.'"

Petrov looked up. "This phrasing predates any canonical gospel by at least two centuries. Its vocabulary suggests the writer viewed spiritual authority as communal, not hierarchical."

Murmurs spread through the room. A few cardinals shifted uncomfortably in their chairs.

Michael felt the eyes of history on his back.

Another scholar spoke—a linguist from Oxford, cautious but intrigued. "This text reshapes our understanding of early Christianity. It doesn't replace the Canon—it reframes it."

Hana scribbled notes, her pen moving faster than her thoughts. Around her, the energy in the room shifted from tension to awe. Even skepticism sounded reverent.

When the panel adjourned for recess, the pope motioned for Michael to follow him into the adjoining chamber.

The private study adjoining the library was small and

filled with the scent of aged paper and candle wax. Sunlight filtered through a stained-glass window, painting the floor in shifting bands of red and gold.

Clement XV poured two cups of coffee from a silver carafe. "Sit, Father. You look as though you've been fasting."

Michael smiled. "Only on sleep, Holiness."

They sat across from each other, the Codex visible through the open doorway, still glowing under the museum lights.

"I meant what I said earlier," the pope began. "You've done what the Church has feared for generations. You've given back a truth it tried to forget."

Michael met his gaze. "Truth has a way of finding its own resurrection."

The pope nodded slowly. "Still, resurrection has a cost. I've spent half my life defending an institution that forgets it was built by fragile men. Now I must ask the world to forgive that fragility."

He looked toward the doorway again, his voice quieter. "Do you believe they will?"

Michael followed his gaze. "Not all of them. But some. And maybe that's enough."

Outside the Vatican walls, the world was anything but quiet.

News agencies were broadcasting live from the square. Commentators argued on air, theologians filled talk shows, and social media feeds boiled with every conceivable opinion. Protesters gathered outside the gates, holding signs both for and against the Codex: **THE TRUTH SETS US FREE** and **HERESY IN WHITE**.

In the apartment across the river, Ian Duffy scrolled through feeds while eating leftover pasta. "It's officially viral," he said. "Every language, every platform, every flavor of outrage."

Teri's voice came through the phone speaker. "And Interpol confirmed it—Alessandro's accounts were real. The Medici network's collapsing faster than the stock exchange in a plague."

Karl, leaning against the window, said quietly, "About time the devils paid their tithe."

Lukas glanced at him. "You mean their due."

Karl smiled faintly. "Same thing, in this city."

By late afternoon, the Vatican Library's main hall had filled again. The second session focused on the *Commentarium de Secunda Voce*—the *Medici Commentary*.

Dr. Emilio Vargas read the translation, his voice deep and deliberate: "*'The Gospel I sealed to protect, but this I write to preserve power. For love makes men equal, and equality makes rulers unnecessary.'*"

The room went utterly silent.

Vargas set down his notes. "This is the clearest confession of intent ever recorded in ecclesiastical history. Clement VII feared what the Gospel would do to authority. He chose control over faith."

Cardinal Serafini, a conservative theologian, rose from the front row. "And yet without that choice, the Church might not have survived at all."

Vargas replied gently, "Perhaps survival and salvation are not the same thing."

The pope's voice broke the silence from his seat at the dais. "Both are miracles when used wisely. Only one is divine when misused."

Even the cameras paused their quiet mechanical whirring, as though reluctant to interrupt the gravity of it.

WHEN THE PRESENTATIONS CONCLUDED, Michael and Hana stepped outside into the waning light. The square beyond the gates shimmered with umbrellas and candle flames. The air carried the mingled scent of incense, wet stone, and citrus from the Vatican's groves.

"Do you think it'll hold?" Hana asked. "The momentum, the hope?"

Michael looked toward the dome. "Hope's stubborn. It outlives institutions."

They walked in silence for a moment, their footsteps echoing on the marble. Hana slipped her hand into his. It wasn't an act of celebration but of anchoring—two souls confirming that the ground beneath them was still solid.

When they reached the bronze doors, Karl and Lukas were waiting. The two Swiss Guards stood together, no longer in uniform but side by side, plainclothes and unmistakably bound. Lukas carried his cap in one hand, his fingers absently brushing Karl's arm.

Hana smiled. "You look like civilians."

Karl shrugged. "We're learning."

Michael raised an eyebrow. "And how's that going?"

Lukas smiled. "We'll let you know after dinner."

LATER THAT NIGHT, Michael and Hana walked back to the apartment through the narrow streets of Trastevere. Rain had returned in a soft drizzle, the kind that polished the stones rather than soaked them. They shared an umbrella, the air between them smelling faintly of night-blooming jasmine.

"You know," Hana said, "for a day that changed history, it felt strangely human."

"It always does," Michael said. "God hides in the ordinary. That's why we miss Him so often."

She looked up at him. "And you still believe in Him? After everything?"

He smiled. "Belief isn't the reward. It's the struggle."

At that, she slipped her hand into his and said, "Then I believe too."

They walked on, the umbrella tilting slightly to one side, the sound of their steps fading into the hum of Rome's eternal rain.

BACK IN THE PAPAL APARTMENTS, Clement XV returned to his desk. The hall outside was dark now; the Vatican slept. On the desk before him lay the Codex, its pages open to the passage the scholars had debated all day.

He traced the words with a trembling finger. The ink seemed to pulse under his touch.

"'Blessed are those who bear the light…'"

He smiled faintly. "Then bless them all," he whispered.

When he extinguished the candle, the last glow of flame reflected briefly in the glass—like the echo of a star that had burned its message across centuries just to be seen tonight.

CHAPTER

FIFTY-FOUR

TRASTEVERE, ROME

Morning sunlight pooled over the cobblestones of Trastevere, pale and forgiving. The rain had finally given up, leaving the air clean and sharp with the scent of stone, citrus, and wood smoke from the cafés opening along the square.

Hana sat at a small wrought iron table outside their favorite café, a cup of espresso cooling beside her notebook. Across the street, market vendors were setting up stalls of flowers and vegetables, calling to one another in melodic Italian that sounded more like singing than speech. She had begun writing again—something she hadn't done in months—and each sentence felt like a wound closing.

Michael arrived carrying two warm *cornetti* wrapped in parchment. He set them down beside her, brushed a kiss against her hair, and took the seat opposite. "You've been working since dawn," he said.

She smiled without looking up. "Old habits. Rome wakes early; I follow."

"Writing?"

"Trying. I don't know if it's a book or a confession."

"Those are often the same thing."

Hana looked up at him. The sunlight touched the line of his jaw, catching the tiredness still buried in his face. "You look older," she said.

"I feel ancient."

He tore a piece of pastry and dipped it into his espresso. "It's quiet this morning," he added.

"Too quiet?"

"Just enough."

For a while, they ate in silence, the world around them beginning its slow, forgiving rhythm. A group of children ran past, chasing a red ball. Bells rang somewhere near the river. The chaos of the last weeks—the gunfire, the debates, the press conferences—seemed to belong to another lifetime.

When Hana finally spoke, her voice was softer. "I thought I'd forgotten how to be still."

Michael smiled. "Stillness remembers you."

Later that morning, they walked through the narrow streets toward Santa Cecilia. The basilica stood hidden behind a simple brick façade, its courtyard glimmering with dew.

Sister Maria Francesca met them in the cloister, her face as serene as ever. "Father Dominic," she said, inclining her head, "and Signora Sinclair. I see the storm has passed."

"For now," Michael said.

The abbess's eyes twinkled. "Storms never end, Father. They simply trade names."

She led them through the cloister to the inner garden.

Sunlight fell across the mosaic tiles, painting their feet in color. The fountain murmured, its water clear as glass.

"I hear you've set the world spinning," the abbess said. "A dangerous hobby for a priest."

"I've learned the world spins whether or not I push it."

"And the Church?"

Michael hesitated. "The Church is learning to stand still long enough to listen."

Sister Maria Francesca regarded him quietly. "You've always been good at listening to ghosts."

"Only the loud ones."

The abbess smiled. "Ah, but the saints are louder than ghosts, and far less polite."

She turned to Hana. "And you, my dear—did you get your story?"

Hana nodded. "I got more than that. I found my ending."

"There are no endings," the abbess said gently. "Only new witnesses."

They prayed briefly in the chapel. The marble statue of Saint Cecilia lay beneath the altar, her face turned away, her hands outstretched as though still catching a final note. Candles flickered in small halos of gold.

Michael knelt in the front pew, eyes closed. For a long moment, he said nothing.

Hana watched him from behind, feeling a kind of reverence she hadn't known she was capable of—faith not in the Church, but in him.

When he rose, he turned to her. "Cecilia heard music where others heard death," he said. "Maybe that's what faith really is—the courage to hear something beautiful in the noise."

Hana reached out and took his hand. "Then we're both listening."

They left the basilica and walked toward the river. The streets were alive again—vendors selling olives and bread, a man playing violin beneath an awning. Rome seemed to pulse with gratitude, as though it, too, had survived the trial of truth.

They stopped at a bakery on Via del Moro, drawn by the scent of sugar and yeast. Inside, an elderly woman was pressing ricotta into *sfogliatelle*, dusting them with powdered sugar.

"For strength," she said in Italian, handing one to Hana. "You both look like you've carried something heavy."

Hana smiled. "We're setting it down now."

Michael bought two more pastries and a loaf of still-warm bread. They ate as they walked, the powdered sugar sticking to their fingers, laughter rising between them like sunlight after rain.

"This," Hana said, "might be the closest thing to heaven I've ever tasted."

"That's because it's Italian," Michael said.

"Do you ever stop preaching?"

"Only for good pastry."

THAT EVENING, the team gathered at the apartment one last time. Ian was cooking—something fragrant and unapologetically rich. The scent of garlic, thyme, and red wine filled the air.

"Whatever that is," Karl said, "it smells like absolution."

"Osso buco," Ian announced, stirring the pot. "And if it turns out half as good as it smells, I expect sainthood."

Lukas poured wine at the table, his movements graceful and unhurried. The light from the window caught the small silver ring on his hand—simple, unadorned, newly placed there a week earlier in quiet defiance of Vatican decorum.

Karl noticed her gaze and smiled faintly. "We don't need approval," he said. "Just patience."

"Patience ages well," Lukas added, setting down the bottle.

Hana raised her glass. "To patience, then. And to endings that feel like beginnings."

They clinked glasses as Ian began to serve. The meat fell from the bone, tender and aromatic. The sauce was thick with tomato and rosemary.

Michael tasted it and closed his eyes. "You've just redeemed an Irishman's soul."

"Just feeding the faithful," Ian said.

Laughter rippled around the table. It was the laughter of survivors—uneven, hesitant, but genuine.

After dinner, they sat in the living room, the city's hum drifting in through the open window. The lamps cast a warm, amber glow over the walls.

"Do you ever wonder what comes next?" Hana asked.

Michael leaned back, his hand finding hers. "Always. That's what keeps us from turning into statues."

Karl looked out at the streetlights below. "For me, next looks like a vacation vineyard in the Rhine Valley. Lukas says he's tired of cleaning other people's messes."

Lukas smiled. "At least in a vineyard, the miracles are predictable."

Ian grinned. "Wine and faith—still competing for who saves more souls."

Hana laughed. "If you ever open a vineyard, I'll write the label copy."

Michael raised his glass in a toast. "Then to vineyards, and to rest, wherever it finds us."

LATER THAT NIGHT, the rain returned—not a storm, but a blessing. It fell softly against the windows, filling the room with its rhythm. Hana and Michael stood on the balcony watching the city shimmer under the streetlights.

"Rome smells different after rain," she said.

"It smells forgiven," Michael said.

She turned to him. "Do you think it is?"

He nodded slowly. "Forgiveness isn't given to the deserving. It's given to the willing."

"Then we're willing."

He smiled and pulled her closer. Somewhere far off, the bells of Santa Maria rang again, low and resonant.

"This city," Hana murmured, "it never stops singing."

"Neither do we," Michael said.

He kissed her, slow and unhurried, the kind of kiss that didn't seek resolution but acknowledgment—a benediction of dust and devotion.

When they finally went inside, the others were asleep. The table still held the remnants of their feast: wine glasses half full, crumbs of bread, a folded napkin beside Lukas's blue velvet ring box.

Michael looked at it and smiled. "Proof of miracles," he said softly.

Hana rested her head against his shoulder. "And of love."

He nodded. "The same thing, really."

They turned off the lights, the room fading into the soft sound of rain. Outside, the city's domes glistened like candles floating on a dark sea.

Somewhere beyond the rooftops, beneath the patient stones of the Vatican, the *Codex of Voices* rested in its glass case—no longer hidden, no longer silent.

And above it all, Rome slept, forgiven and awake at once.

FIFTY-FIVE

VATICAN CITY

Dawn broke clean over St. Peter's Square, the light washing the marble colonnade in gold and shadow. The air smelled faintly of incense and damp stone. Bells rang in long, unhurried tones across the city, their echoes blending into the sound of thousands gathering below the pope's balcony to hear the Holy Father's address.

Father Michael Dominic stood in the portico, hands clasped behind his back, his collar newly starched, his cassock freshly pressed. It felt strange to look out on a Rome at peace—at least for now. For months, the city had lived on adrenaline and argument; now it seemed to breathe again, exhausted but alive.

Hana joined him at the balustrade. "You realize," she said, looking at the sea of faces below, "you've just helped rewrite five hundred years of theology."

Michael smiled faintly. "It was Clement's sermon that did it. I just handed him the pen."

"Still," she said, nudging his arm lightly, "you're the name people are whispering about."

"Then God help them," he murmured. "I'd rather they whisper His."

WHEN THE BELLS STOPPED, Pope Clement XV stepped onto the balcony, accompanied by two aides. The crowd fell into a reverent hush.

"My brothers and sisters," he began, his voice carrying easily through the microphones and the open morning air, "we gather not to divide ourselves, but to remember who we are. The *Codex of Voices* does not rewrite faith—it reminds it. It guides us back to the heart of the Gospel, where love stands before law and compassion outruns fear. For too long we believed that protecting the Church meant protecting silence. But silence has never been the guardian of truth. Truth is what gives the Church breath."

A wave of stillness passed through the square.

Clement continued.

"This moment is not one of triumph, but of honesty. A Church that cannot look at its past with clear eyes is a Church that cannot walk into the future with steady feet. When we name our mistakes, we do not weaken the faith. We strengthen it, because faith thrives only where humility lives. Christ did not build His Church on stone so that we might hide behind it, but so that we might stand upon it and see farther."

He paused, his gaze sweeping the multitude, resting briefly on Michael, then Hana.

"The *Gospel of the Beloved* and the *Codex of Voices* remind us that God has never spoken through hierarchy alone. Throughout history, His voice has risen through the humble, the silenced, the overlooked. The people whom power forgot, but heaven remembered. Their witness, long buried in shadow, belongs to us as surely as Scripture does. And we do not fear it."

Wind stirred the banners lining the colonnade, and sunlight spilled across the square.

"Our past is woven with both glory and sin, brilliance and blindness. Today we admit both. Today we say that love has greater authority than fear, and that the courage to listen is a greater virtue than the comfort of certainty. If we are to be the Church Christ imagined, we must learn again to kneel before truth instead of asking truth to kneel before us."

A murmur spread—part prayer, part collective exhale.

"Let these words be not an ending, but a beginning. A beginning of honesty. A beginning of compassion. A beginning of a Church brave enough to let truth speak in its own voice. May we stand not as judges of the past, but as witnesses to the future. And may those who seek truth never walk alone."

The pope lowered his hands as the crowd stood in a silence that felt like reverence, like reckoning, like the first breath of something new.

Applause swept the square, wave after wave until it became a sound more like wind than noise—faith made audible.

THAT EVENING, the commission, guards, and Vatican staff gathered for a quiet dinner in one of the frescoed halls overlooking the gardens. Long tables were laid with rosemary, candles, and bowls of fresh figs. The kitchen had outdone itself—platters of roast lamb, warm bread drizzled with oil, and carafes of red wine that glowed like rubies under the lights.

Karl and Lukas arrived in full uniform, gleaming and formal, until Lukas caught Hana's grin and gave her a conspiratorial wink.

Ian leaned across the table. "You two look like poster boys for Vatican tourism."

Karl deadpanned, "We're considering it. Guardians of the Gospel, limited edition calendars."

The laughter that followed loosened what tension still lingered. Even the pope's secretary smiled as she refilled glasses.

When the plates were cleared, Clement rose briefly to toast them. "To those who risked faith to defend it," he said. "You have done God's work with mortal hands, and I am grateful."

He looked directly at the four of them—Michael, Hana, Karl, Lukas—and added, "And may you keep your hands ready, for God is not finished yet."

After dinner, they stepped out into the Vatican Gardens. Fireflies drifted among the hedges; the scent of laurel and lemon hung thick in the air.

Karl and Lukas walked a few steps ahead, shoulder to shoulder, their conversation a low rumble of jokes and logistics. Hana watched them with quiet affection. "You'd think after everything, they'd want to rest."

Michael shook his head. "Rest doesn't suit soldiers. Or priests."

She smiled. "Or journalists, apparently."

Behind them, Lukas's voice carried through the garden:

"Karl, if you're cooking tomorrow, I'm filing a complaint with heaven itself!"

Karl laughed—a rare, unguarded sound—and for a moment, Rome seemed lighter for it.

LATER, when Michael and Hana returned to the apartment, the lights of the city spilled across the floor through the open window. The dome of St. Peter's glowed like a beacon beyond the rooftops.

Michael stood by the window, listening to the bells fading into the distance. Hana came up behind him and rested her chin on his shoulder. "It feels like it's ending," she said softly.

"It's never an ending," he said. "Just another chapter waiting to be written."

"And us?"

He smiled. "We're the punctuation. God just keeps changing the sentence."

She laughed, kissed his cheek, and whispered, "Then let's hope it's a long story."

They stood together in the golden light of the city, the hum of Rome rising around them like a promise that hadn't finished keeping itself.

FIFTY-SIX

ROME

Summer warmed the marble of Rome until even the shadows shimmered. Deep beneath the Vatican Museums, far from the crowds and camera flashes, the *Codex of Voices* and the *Gospel of the Beloved* rested side by side within the Riserva—the inner vault of the Apostolic Archives where the Church safeguarded its most sacred and fragile relics.

They weren't on display. No tourists queued, no scholars bent over glass cases. Only a few archivists, sworn to discretion, knew exactly which shelf held them. The climate controls whispered softly; the light never touched parchment directly.

Each document was sealed within its own reliquary, the labels discreet and identical save for a simple inscription beneath both:

RISERVA VATICANA

Preserved under the Pontificate of Clement XV, 2025

"Truth feared is truth half-lost."

No one saw them, yet their presence was felt—the heartbeat of their words now echoed in published texts throughout the world—a reminder that even in silence, truth endures and, in time, is revealed.

KARL AND LUKAS walked their regular patrol path beneath the orange trees of the Vatican Gardens. Lukas carried a small paper bag in one hand; inside were almond biscuits from the kitchen.

Karl reached for one. "You're going to make us soft," he said.

"That's not a complaint," Lukas replied.

They paused near the fountain, watching tourists stroll past. Lukas slipped his arm through Karl's for a moment, casual and unnoticed. The world, for once, seemed content to let them be exactly who they were.

Across the city, Hana and Michael sat at a corner table in their favorite Trastevere café. The air was bright with the scent of espresso and orange zest. Hana's latest article was spread open in *Le Monde,* its headline simple:

The Gospel Of Courage.

She took a sip of cappuccino. "You realize you've become impossible to interview," she said.

"I'm retired from fame," he replied.

"Fame?"

"Infamy, then."

She smiled. "You still think like a priest."

He smiled back. "That's because I still am."

A group of young seminary students passed by the café window, their laughter rising above the traffic. Michael watched them for a moment, the corner of his mouth lifting. "They'll have their own battles soon enough."

"Then they'll need people like us," Hana said.

"People like you," he corrected.

She reached across the table, brushing her fingers against his. "Like us," she said again.

Later that evening, as dusk fell over the city, the bells began their slow chorus. The air filled with the mingled perfume of basil and rain. From their window, they could see the dome of St. Peter's glowing against the violet sky.

Michael opened the window. The sound of the river reached them—the eternal pulse of Rome.

"Listen," Hana whispered.

He nodded. "The same song."

They stood together at the window, the light soft on their faces, the city breathing below them. In the distance, the Vatican lights shimmered over the gardens, where two figures in blue and red still walked their quiet watch beneath the orange trees.

Michael spoke softly, more to himself than to her. "Truth keeps walking, Hana. It never sleeps."

She rested her head against his shoulder. "Then we keep walking with it."

The bells continued their measured toll, each one carrying the sound of promise through the night. And for a moment—fleeting but real—the city seemed to hum in harmony, the voices of saints and sinners, past and present, rising together in the same prayer.

EPILOGUE

Translated from the original Latin by order of Pope Clement XV, 2025.

TRANSLATOR'S NOTE:

The following text is drawn from a Vatican-certified translation of Folio XXII of the *Codex of Voices*, composed during the pontificate of Pope Clement VII (1523–1534). The original Latin manuscript, preserved in the Riserva Vaticana, was translated under papal authorization in 2025. While portions of the Codex are fragmentary, the passage reproduced here is believed to reflect Clement's final reflections on the concealment of the *Gospel of the Beloved*.

EXCERPT FROM THE *CODEX OF VOICES*

(Vatican translation file CV-1530-FOL.XXII — Archival Record: Clement VII, Anno Domini 1530)

I feared love because it made men equal; I feared equality because it made me mortal. The Gospel of the Beloved spoke of light that needed no stewards, yet I built walls to guard it, naming those walls "order." I told myself that silence would save faith, though I knew silence cannot save anything—it only delays the reckoning.

In those days, I summoned the wisest men of Florence and Rome, that they might read this new gospel and counsel me. Some wept when they read its words; others laughed, thinking it folly. Frate Matteo de' Medici called it dangerous, for it spoke of a kingdom without crowns and a Church without hierarchy. He wrote his "Second Voice" to drown the first, believing that fear could restore balance. I let him write because I was weary of having to decide.

I sealed the pages with wax, praying that time would forget them. Yet I wrote still another letter, to whoever might one day find what I had hidden: that the Church would not perish from love, but from the absence of it. For every decree carved in marble becomes a confession of what we most doubt. Mine were many.

The Gospel of the Beloved calls each soul by name. It says that holiness is not bestowed but awakened—that the breath of God moves through woman and man alike, and that authority belongs only to compassion. I could not proclaim this without unmaking the world that fed and crowned me. I called it heresy. I called it preservation. Both were lies of convenience.

Now, as I write these ending lines, the lamps burn low in the Apostolic Palace, and I hear Rome breathing through its wounds. Perhaps God keeps the truth where we cannot reach it, lest we use it as another instrument of pride. But if these words should survive the dust, let them stand as witness: that love was not the enemy of faith, only of fear—and that I, Clement, chose fear, and learned too late that fear is the lesser god.

May those who read what I buried forgive me. May they open the doors I closed. And may they remember that the first voice was never silenced—only waiting for the courage to be heard again.

~

TRANSLATOR'S NOTE:

The manuscript known as the *Gospel of the Beloved* predates all surviving New Testament writings and is believed to have originated within a first-century community of followers centered around Mary of Magdala. The text was rediscovered during the pontificate of Clement VII (1523–1534) and later sealed in the Riserva Vaticana, where it remains preserved beside the *Codex of Voices*. Its language is a fusion of Aramaic and Koine Greek, poetic rather than doctrinal, presenting love as the sole measure of divine authority. The following translation—commissioned under Pope Clement XV in 2025—retains the rhythm of the original without theological interpolation.

EXCERPT FROM THE *GOSPEL OF THE BELOVED*

(Vatican translation file GB-1stC-PAP.FOL.III – provenance: Ephesus, circa A.D. 60–90)

And the Teacher said:

"The Kingdom is not beyond the stars nor behind the veil of death. It is within the breath of those who love without measure. The heart that welcomes another has already entered heaven."

And one asked Him, "Lord, who shall lead us when You are gone?"

He answered, "The one who listens."

And another said, "Shall it be the men who walked beside You?"

He said, "It shall be all who walk in compassion, for no hand is greater than the one that serves."

Then Mary of Magdala rose among them and said, "But the world will not believe the voice of a woman."

And He replied, "Then let the world learn to hear again, for truth has no gender."

And they were silent, for His words undid the chains of their hearts. And He said to them:

"When you speak with love, you speak with My tongue. When you forgive, you carry My cross. Blessed are those who bear the light without crown or collar, for Love alone is the steward of the Kingdom."

SCHOLARS NOTE that the final verse—"*Blessed are those who bear the light without crown or collar...*"—is the same line later cited and suppressed by Pope Clement VII, forming the moral and theological core of what became known as the *Codex of Voices*.

FICTION, FACT, OR FUSION

Many readers have asked me to distinguish fact from fiction in my books. Generally, I like to take factual events and historical figures and build on them in creative ways—but much of what I do write is historically accurate. In this book, I'll review some chapters where questions may arise, with the hope that it will help those wondering where reality meets creative writing.

EPILOGUE:

Both the *Gospel of the Beloved* and the *Codex of Voices* that appear here are entirely fictional creations written for this novel. No such manuscripts exist in the Vatican Archives or anywhere else.

The *Gospel of the Beloved* was conceived as a composite of several early noncanonical texts—the *Gospel of Mary*, the *Gospel of Philip*, and fragments from the Nag Hammadi library—interpreted through the lens of modern theological debate about women's roles in the early

Church. It represents the kind of discovery that could profoundly challenge institutional authority, yet its language and message are my own invention.

The *Codex of Voices* was designed as its historical echo: a Renaissance-era compilation of commentary, council notes, and papal reflections surrounding the suppression of that gospel. Its voice and structure were inspired by authentic Vatican documents of the sixteenth century, particularly the writings and correspondence of Pope Clement VII, but no such codex has ever been found.

Together, these two works serve the story's thematic purpose—to explore how faith, fear, and power have always struggled to share the same altar. They should be read not as theological statements or historical artifacts, but as literary devices: imagined witnesses to an eternal conversation between truth and silence.

GENERAL:

THE GOSPEL OF THE BELOVED

The *Gospel of the Beloved* is the sacred manuscript at the heart of *The Medici Heresy*. Within the story, it is portrayed as a first-century Christian gospel written—or at least inspired—by Mary Magdalene, the disciple often called "the Beloved." Unlike the canonical gospels, it presents a faith founded on spiritual equality rather than hierarchy, and on love as the highest form of authority.

In my fictional world, this gospel was rediscovered during the Renaissance and later buried by Pope Clement VII to prevent its message from fracturing the Church. It is pure revelation... the voice of divine love unfiltered by politics. It represents the kind of discovery that could profoundly challenge institutional authority, yet its language and message are my own invention.

THE CODEX OF VOICES

The *Codex of Voices*, another piece of fiction, was designed as a Renaissance-era compilation of commentary, council notes, and papal reflections surrounding the suppression of that fictional gospel. Its voice and structure were inspired by authentic Vatican documents of the sixteenth century, particularly the writings and correspondence of Pope Clement VII, but no such codex has ever been found. The *Codex of Voices* isn't another gospel but the later collection that preserved—and ultimately concealed—the *Gospel of the Beloved*. As imagined in the novel, it was assembled under Clement VII's direction in the sixteenth century by Medici clerics tasked with analyzing the rediscovered text.

Part historical record, part theological commentary, the Codex contains copies of the Gospel, transcripts of the secret council that condemned it, and writings from Clement himself. It represents the Church's human struggle to contain what it feared: equality, change, and the loss of control over faith's story.

In short, if the *Gospel of the Beloved* is revelation, the *Codex of Voices* is reaction—the echo chamber of faith and fear that followed when truth first spoke too loudly.

Together, these two works serve the story's thematic purpose—to explore how faith, fear, and power have always struggled to share the same altar.

These two documents—one imagined as divine origin, the other as human response—form the central tension of

The Medici Heresy: how far institutions will go to protect belief, and how much courage it takes for belief to protect the truth.

MARY MAGDALENE

Few figures in Christian history have been as misunderstood—or as enduringly fascinating—as Mary Magdalene, about whom I've written extensively in The Magdalene Chronicles series. In the canonical gospels, she appears as one of Jesus' most devoted followers, present at both his Crucifixion and Resurrection, the first to whom he revealed himself after rising from the tomb. Over centuries, however, her identity became entangled with other biblical women—chiefly Mary of Bethany and the unnamed "sinful woman" who anointed Jesus' feet— leading to her mistaken reputation as a repentant prostitute. This conflation persisted until the twentieth century, when modern scholarship and the Catholic Church itself began restoring her original status as *apostola apostolorum*—the "apostle to the apostles." Several early Christian writings discovered in Egypt, such as the *Gospel of Mary* and the *Pistis Sophia*, portray her as a teacher, visionary, and interpreter of divine wisdom. The *Gospel of the Beloved* in *The Medici Heresy* draws inspiration from these texts, imagining her not as a fallen woman redeemed by grace, but as an enlightened disciple entrusted with a truth too dangerous for her age—a voice silenced and, at last, rediscovered.

POPE CLEMENT VII

The historical Pope Clement VII (Giulio de' Medici) reigned from 1523 to 1534 and was, in reality, a cousin of the famous Lorenzo the Magnificent. His pontificate was one of the most turbulent in Church history. He faced the Sack of Rome in 1527, the rise of Protestantism, and the political pressures of both Holy Roman Emperor Charles V and King Henry VIII of England. A cautious intellectual rather than a reformer, Clement's indecision often deepened the crises around him, yet his patronage of famed artists like Michelangelo and Raphael left an enduring cultural legacy. The Clement of *The Medici Heresy* is drawn from that same historical figure but reimagined in his final years—haunted, reflective, and burdened by a secret gospel he believes could both save and destroy the Church he served.

POPE CLEMENT XV

The modern Pope Clement XV—formerly Cardinal Bennett Dreyfus, as longtime readers know—is a fictional pontiff created for *The Medici Heresy* and other novels in the Vatican Secret Archives Thriller series. Though his name evokes historical continuity with the Renaissance-era Clement VII, he represents a new generation of papal leadership: progressive, intellectually courageous, and quietly radical in his pursuit of transparency. Within the story, Clement XV authorizes the rediscovery and translation of the *Gospel of the Beloved* and the *Codex of Voices*, reversing centuries of suppression. His character embodies the kind of reform-minded spiritual authority many readers wish to see in the modern Church—a pope who believes that faith need not fear the truth. There has never been a real Clement XV in history; the title, deliberately chosen, links the novel's moral arc across five centuries, uniting the Medici past with the Church's contemporary struggles to reconcile tradition with revelation.

THE END OF THE MEDICI LINE

Despite centuries of influence that shaped the politics, art, and religion of Europe, the powerful Medici dynasty is long extinct. The family's senior branch, descended from Cosimo "il Vecchio" de' Medici, ended with Gian Gastone de' Medici, who died in 1737 without an heir. His sister, Anna Maria Luisa de' Medici, the last legitimate descendant, ensured the family's legacy by bequeathing its immense art collection—the core of Florence's Uffizi Gallery—to the Tuscan state on the condition that it never be removed from the city. The so-called "Black Medici" line, descended from an illegitimate branch through Alessandro de' Medici, Duke of Florence (1510–1537), also faded from history in the eighteenth century. Though distant families have occasionally claimed Medici blood, no verifiable descendants remain today. The name itself survives only in history, on palazzo doorways, and in the enduring brilliance of the Renaissance the Medici helped create.

The modern Alessandro de' Medici depicted in *The Medici Heresy* is, of course, a fictional creation—an imagined heir to a legacy that ended long ago, embodying the ambition, intellect, and moral peril that once defined the real Medici power.

THE VATICAN APOSTOLIC ARCHIVES

For centuries known as the Vatican Secret Archives, the Vatican Apostolic Archives form one of the largest and most carefully preserved historical collections in the world. The term "secret" (from the Latin *secretum*, meaning "private") never implied mystery or conspiracy—it simply designated the pope's personal archive, distinct from public holdings. The Archives span nearly twelve centuries of history, containing some eighty-five kilometers of shelving and more than thirty-five thousand volumes of catalogued documents. Scholars with advanced academic credentials may request access to specific materials, though only after a rigorous vetting process. While the Archives aren't the warehouse of suppressed gospels and apocalyptic prophecies often imagined by fiction, they do contain priceless original manuscripts—papal correspondence, inquisitorial records, diplomatic letters, and accounts of events that shaped both Church and world. In *The Medici Heresy*, the *Gospel of the Beloved* and the *Codex of Voices* are fictional examples of the sort of treasures that might still lie deep within its restricted vaults, waiting for courage—or providence—to uncover them.

THE VATICAN'S RISERVA

Within the vast network of the Vatican Apostolic Archives lies an inner sanctum known as the Riserva, which I often mention in my books. This restricted area houses the Holy See's most sensitive and irreplaceable documents: original papal bulls, state treaties, trial transcripts, and manuscripts whose provenance or contents require the highest level of protection. Access is limited to the archivist prefect and a handful of scholars under direct papal approval. The Riserva isn't a single hidden chamber but a system of secure vaults scattered throughout the archival complex, some still protected by manual keys and others by modern biometric controls. While conspiracy theories have long surrounded what lies inside, most of its holdings are historical rather than heretical—records of power, diplomacy, and conscience preserved under the Church's quietest seal. In *The Medici Heresy*, the *Gospel of the Beloved* and the *Codex of Voices* are imagined as among the Riserva's most jealously guarded secrets.

THE SACK OF ROME, 1527

The real Sack of Rome, which took place in May 1527, was one of the most devastating events in Renaissance history —and a trauma from which the city, and the papacy, took decades to recover. The attack was carried out not by foreign invaders alone but by Emperor Charles V's own mutinous troops: unpaid German mercenaries, Spanish soldiers, and Italian *condottieri* (leaders) who turned on the Holy City when their wages went unpaid. Over the course of eight brutal months, they looted churches, burned palaces, and slaughtered thousands of citizens. Pope Clement VII, himself a Medici, escaped through a secret passageway to the fortress of Castel Sant'Angelo—that circular fortress you see adjacent to the Vatican—where he remained under siege for nearly a year. Rome's libraries were pillaged, its artists scattered, and the prestige of the papacy shattered. The event marked the symbolic end of the Italian Renaissance and left Clement deeply haunted, his later decisions colored by guilt, fear, and a desire to preserve the Church's authority at any cost. In *The Medici Heresy*, that same fear drives him to suppress the *Gospel of the Beloved*, believing that one more revelation might finally destroy what little remained of faith's fragile order.

AUTHOR'S NOTE

A word before you go.

Stories that touch on faith, scripture, and the hidden corridors of religious history walk a delicate line—and I've always tried to walk it with care. What you've read is fiction, shaped by oral traditions, historical fragments, and the kind of "what if" wondering that keeps writers up at night.

I hold no brief for any particular belief, and I mean that sincerely. Whether you come to these pages as a person of deep faith, quiet skepticism, or something beautifully in between, you are welcome here. The mystery is the point— not the argument.

Thank you for trusting me with your time and your imagination.

~

Writing *The Medici Heresy* was a labor of genuine joy, and if you've made it this far, you have my deepest gratitude. Readers like you are the reason these stories exist.

If Father Michael, Hana, and the secrets buried beneath the Vatican have captured your imagination, I hope you'll continue the journey. The Magdalene Chronicles—*The Magdalene Deception, The Magdalene Reliquary,* and *The Magdalene Veil*—are where it all began, and more adventures are already in the works across both the Vatican Secret Archives and Vatican Archaeology series.

One small favor, if you're willing: a review on Amazon, Goodreads, or wherever you like to share what you're reading makes an enormous difference to an independent author. A sentence or two is plenty—honest words from a real reader carry more weight than anything I could say about my own work.

I'd also love to hear from you directly. Whether you have a question, a thought about the story, or just want to say hello, you're welcome to reach me at **gary@garym cavoy.com**.

And if you'd like to explore the full world behind the books—series details, historical notes, and early word on what's coming next—please visit **www.garymcavoy.com**, where you can also join my private reader list.

Thank you, sincerely, for spending time in this world I love so much.

With kind regards,

GET YOUR CHARACTER BRIEF

YOUR FREE BOOK IS WAITING

Download your free copy now of **CODEX PERSONAE**, containing comprehensive backgrounds and other biographical details of all principal characters in *The Magdalene Chronicles*, *Vatican Secret Archive Thrillers*, and *Vatican Archaeology* series—with my compliments as a loyal reader!

https://garymcavoy.com/character-brief/